GHOST *Walk*

Cassandra Gannon

Published by Star Turtle Publishing
www.starturtlepublishing.com

Visit Cassandra Gannon at starturtlepublishing.com or on the
Star Turtle Publishing Facebook page for news on upcoming
books and promotions!

Email Star Turtle Publishing directly:
starturtlepublishing@gmail.com

We'd love to hear from you!

Other books
The Snow Queen
Travels with a Fairytale Monster
Everyone Hates Fairytale Pirates
Captive of a Fairytale Barbarian
Coming... Eventually_: The Man Who Beat-Up Prince Charming_

For Mom
And vacationing at Williamsburg on the 4th of July.

PROLOGUE

4th of July- One Year Ago

The alleyway was a gory mess.

At this point in her career, Grace Rivera had learned to block out the full horror of it, but she still felt a surge of sadness for the poor woman lying on the pavement. The girl was young, with stringy blonde hair and three piercings in each ear. Given her revealing clothes and the location of her body, it seemed likely she worked as a prostitute and had met up with the wrong man. Still Grace took her death as seriously as she would've the mayor's.

As a crime scene technician it was Grace's job to collect whatever evidence the murderer had left behind. Fibers, fingerprints, blood, and a thousand other small things that even the smartest perpetrators missed. All of it was cataloged and analyzed in hopes of it leading back to those who stole the lives of others. Very often it did. Grace was good at her job and she took it seriously.

Some people said *too* seriously.

They were probably right. But the poor woman on the ground, with the two bullet holes in her head, was counting on her. Just like all the other victims whose cases Grace investigated. She didn't want to let them down… Except, she always felt as if she already had. They were gone and she couldn't help them.

Couldn't *save* them.

To make up for it, Grace did everything she could, every single day, whether she was investigating a dead hooker in an alleyway or a wealthy businessman from Richmond. She studied and worked and did her best to ensure that they received at least some form of justice. She never stopped. Never took a moment to relax. Never *breathed*.

Touching the darkness, with no light to balance it out,

was too much for her. At least, that's what they said later.
Grace had always been a glass-is-half-empty sort of girl. All that
pessimism overwhelmed her. If you stared too long into the
abyss, the damn thing would start to stare back.

Being a savior to the whole world was impossible. It
got harder and harder for Grace to recall that her job was really
about helping people. About stopping killers from striking
again, and bringing comfort to the families left behind. All she
saw were the victims she *didn't* save. The futile, hopeless,
failure of it all. Somewhere along the way, her positivity and
optimism disappeared.

Until one day --inevitably-- the darkness swallowed
her.

She'd pushed herself too hard. Everyone would tsk
about it after her breakdown. It was no wonder she burned
out, really. But who could've predicted that even a Rivera
would snap so completely?

On that 4th of July morning, Grace lost her mind in
front of half the police force.

It started with a torn glove. Just a tiny rip in the latex
that exposed Grace's fingertip. She was so focused on her job
that she didn't notice. Not at first, anyway. She went about her
business, gathering up the shattered bits of evidence. A few
stray hairs... Glass from a broken beer bottle... A cigarette
butt... Maybe it belonged to the killer. More likely it belonged
to any of a dozen people who had frequented the alley in the
last month or two. Still, it all had to be checked. No detail was
too small in forensic work. The key to solving the entire puzzle
could literally be a grain of sand.

Grace meticulously sorted through the dirt and debris
littering the asphalt, finally coming to a flyer for a local band
called "Cornelius and the Monkey-Men." They had apparently
played at the bar next door on July third. The *Planet of the
Apes* inspired font promised an incredible one night only
concert.

Grace wasn't sorry that she missed it.

All she cared about was the single drop of blood on the

blue paper. The speck was so small most people wouldn't even have noticed it. The page must have gotten wet in the storm the night before, because the ink was running. It was crumpled and at least twelve feet from the body. A less experienced technician might have overlooked it entirely. But Grace was *very* good at her job.

That didn't mean she couldn't make a mistake, though.

She snapped some photos and picked up the flyer to put into an evidence bag. When she did, the pad of her thumb inadvertently brushed against the dried blood drop. For the first time in her career, Grace's bare skin touched the blood evidence she was examining.

As soon as she did, it started raining.

It happened so suddenly that she didn't process what was happening for several precious seconds. Water poured down, not like the beginning of a shower, but like it had been storming for hours.

Grace frowned in confusion and looked up at the sky. What the hell...? How did the rain blow in so quickly? It was even blocking out the sun! The alley was abruptly dark, making it seem as if night had fallen in the middle of the day. In fact, was that the *moon?* Why was the moon out at two in the afternoon?

She got to her feet, her mind racing. "Guys, are you seeing this...?" Her voice trailed off in surprise as she realized that the rest of the investigative team was gone. *Gone.* Grace's head whipped around, her heart pounding. She was standing there all by herself.

No. Correction: *Not* by herself.

Despite the rain and rancid smell, two people were using the dark alleyway for a convenient place to have sex. Grace goggled at them for a beat, her hand coming up to slap over her mouth in shock. Jesus, what was *happening?* She quickly turned her back on the grunting duo, trying to think.

She'd always been a cotton-underwear-buying, never-skipping-work, two-coats-of-clear-nail-polish kinda girl. Practical. *Normal.* Saving for retirement and watching the news at six every night. Despite her eccentric family and their endless search for "troll powder," Grace dealt with everything that came her way with a healthy dose of logic. So why was she *completely lost* as to what was going on? Why couldn't she think of one rational explanation for why her colleagues disappeared, or why the moon had risen, or why two strangers were copulating behind her?

And what the *hell* was that noise?

It sounded like someone in the bar next door was shrieking into a microphone to a thrash rock beat. Except this song *had* no beat, so it was just discordant wailing. Even her cousin Halcyon had better taste in music and he mainly listened to the "hidden messages" in TV static. How was she supposed to think of a logical explanation for this craziness when she couldn't hear herself think?

Grace staggered to the entrance of the alleyway, peering up and down the street. Cars whizzed past, but very few would stop in this part of town. Should she try to flag someone down? Should she just drive to the police station and ask where everyone went?

She looked closer. Well, scratch that idea. Her car wasn't there anymore, so she wouldn't be driving anyplace. She'd parked the beige four-door in front of the bar and now a black jeep was in the space. Had someone stolen it? If they did, they must have taken the ambulance and three police cruisers, too. None of the vehicles were in sight. It was as if no one but Grace had arrived at the crime scene.

Grace found she couldn't breathe. It was like oxygen refused to fill her lungs. She bent over at the waist, her hands braced on her knees and tried to calm down. It was alright. She would figure this out. There had to be a reason for all of it. She just needed to focus on something calming and not panic.

Her mind settled on the lush fields of her parents' farm. Before they died, they'd owned two hundred acres of rich Virginia soil. Growing up, she'd spent her days running through the tall stalks of corn. The smell of the earth, and the vivid green of the plants, and the absolute security of her parents' love. Nothing since had ever made her feel so safe.

Think about those peaceful green cornfields.

The music from the bar reached unbearable levels and Grace's frantic brain seized on a target for her terror. The "singer" was screeching about chimpanzees of all things. She couldn't deal with a song about chimpanzees. She couldn't *think* when he was screaming about chimpanzees. God, if their idea of music was chimpanzees and the same two notes on an electric guitar played over and over and *over* again, they all must be drinking more than just...

Wait a second.

Chimpanzees?

Grace looked down at the band flyer which was still clutched in her hand. The words couldn't have been clearer, even in the dim light. "Cornelius and the Monkey-Men. Appearing one night only! July third."

Yesterday.

A slimy, hot/cold ball began to form in her stomach.

Running a hand through her drenched hair, Grace marched over to the entrance of the bar. "Hey!" She stalked up to the bouncer, who happened to be a massive guy in a GNR shirt, reading Dickens. "Is that Cornelius and the Monkey-Men in there?" She gestured to the open door and the grimy interior beyond.

Oliver Twist pointed to the marquee without looking up from his book. "That's what the sign says. Five dollar cover, lady."

"They were supposed to be here *yesterday*, though." She held up the flier, her hands shaking from the cold rain and her strained nerves. "See? One night only. It says so right here."

The bouncer flicked her a bored look. "Yeah and *tonight's* the one night. You wanna see the band or not?"

Grace shook her head. "No, I don't want to see them! I *can't* see them. July *third* was the one night they played!"

"What are you high or something? It *is* July third"

"Today's the *fourth*."

The guy was apparently used to dealing with lunatics. Rolling his eyes, he pulled his cellphone from his pocket and held up the illuminated screen. "See?" He gestured to the date in the corner. "The third. The holiday's tomorrow, but I guess you started celebrating a little early, huh?" He arched a brow. "Now, are you gonna pay to come inside or are ya just going home to sleep it off? 'Cause you can't stand here and listen to the band for free."

Grace stared at the glowing numbers on the screen, not even processing his words. It was impossible. He must have rigged the phone with the wrong date somehow. He was trying to trick her. Trying to make her *think* it was still the night before.

Why would he do that, though?

What could his motivation possibly be? She'd never met this man before. Why would he waste his time on such a useless prank? And where had the sun gone? And her car? And the rest of the crime scene guys, police, and reporters? And there had been a rainstorm last night...

The gunshots interrupted her spiraling thoughts.

Even over the terrible, pulsating music, she heard the unmistakable sound of a weapon firing twice in quick succession. Grace's head snapped around just in time to see a male figure fleeing the alleyway. He was running too fast for her to get a good look at him, but she still knew exactly what had happened.

"Call 911!" Grace screamed to the bouncer and raced back the way she'd come. "*No!*" She saw the woman's body on the ground, precisely the way it had looked when she arrived at the crime scene two hours before. "No, no, no." She dropped to her knees beside the victim and quickly took stock of the situation. There was nowhere to apply pressure and no way to administer aid. Grace tried, but it was hopeless. The girl had been shot twice in the face. She was dead.

Again.

It was the same woman. Grace knew it. Only her body was still warm and the blood pouring out of her was fresh. Grace couldn't explain it, but she knew it was true.

Somehow she'd been zapped back to the time of this

woman's murder.

Not that she'd done her much good. The woman had been killed all over again while Grace stood five yards away. If only she'd known what was about to happen she could've helped the girl. Could've stopped this. Could've…

Just as suddenly as the weirdness started, it was over.

Between one blink and the next, everything went back to normal. The sun was back in the sky, the rain was gone, and Grace was surrounded by her colleagues. It was as if the universe took back its do over and just plopped Grace right back where she'd started. …Or maybe it had never happened at all. Yeah, that was it. It had been some kind of hallucination, brought on by the July heat and fumes from some leaky gas line in the neighborhood.

Except, if it was all in her head, why was she still soaking wet from the storm?

Grace didn't know. *She didn't know.* She had no frigging idea what had just happened, except that her nice, normal life had just imploded. She looked down at the fresh blood covering her palms and did what any nice, normal girl would do in that situation.

She started screaming.

CHAPTER ONE

June 20 1789- The Summer Ball was as dull as I expected. Nothing in this town ever changes, so I'm not sure why I even bothered to attend. The same ordinary people and ordinary conversations...

How I long for something exciting to happen!

JMR provided the only distraction of the evening. He no doubt came to see me, but --of course-- he had to dance with a few other ladies too, else Father and Mother have conniptions. They detest him merely for being alive, when they're dead inside. Still, it was good for a laugh to see him flirting with those foolish girls. I declare, the Pirate charmed even the unlikeliest of targets with his wicked smile. And Anabel Maxwell and Clara Vance could not believe their luck to be singled out by such a handsome and notorious man!

From the Journal of Miss Lucinda Wentworth

"You are --by far-- the worst tour guide I've ever seen." The guy in the souvenir tri-corner hat shook his head in irritation and hoisted himself up onto the top slat of the split rail fence. "The Good Lord knows I've seen *a lot* of them in my time, but you make even the bad ones seem grand. You've just no talent for this job, a *t'all*."

Grace pretended not to hear that, just like she'd been pretending not to hear his complaints for the past half hour.

...But it was pretty darn hard.

"Where's your stage presence, lass?" He waved a hand like a frustrated director, trying to film a hopeless actress in her big scene. "These are supposed to be *ghost* stories. Ya have to give them some *feeling*. Ya won't scare anyone if you sound like you're reciting a dinner menu. Put some *pizzazz* into it, for heaven's sake."

For the entire tour, the heckler had been hovering at the back of the group, making snide comments in a Scottish accent. He didn't even bother to lower his (admittedly beautiful) voice, although the rest of Harrisonburg's Official Ghost Walk had the decency to ignore his bitching. Grace couldn't be so composed. She took this job to avoid stress and this moron was definitely beginning to stress her out. It was all she could do not to kick him right off the tour.

He wasn't even looking her way, so he missed her angry glower. Instead, he was staring up at the night sky, the angles of his striking face reflected in the moonlight. The guy was incredibly, sickeningly handsome, which explained his lousy attitude. Good looking men always thought they were exempt from civilized conduct. He was probably used to acting like a dick and everyone accepting it, because he was so frigging pretty.

Peaceful green cornfields.

Think about peaceful green cornfields.

Dragging her attention away from him, Grace smiled determinedly at the un-irritating portion of the group. There were fifteen other tourists who'd paid to walk around the historic town by lantern light and hear spooky tales for an hour. No wiseass, too handsome, big mouth was going to ruin this for them.

Not that anybody *else* looked thrilled with the Ghost Walk, either.

That was what pissed her off the most. The wiseass, too handsome, big mouth was right. She sucked as a tour guide. Unlike the rest of her family, Grace refused to live her life inside of a *Supernatural* episode. Consequently, she talked about Harrisonburg's significant places and noteworthy citizens, not ghosts and goblins. She tended to go off on academic tangents, which, her boss assured her, bored the tour groups senseless. They wanted to hear about monsters and mayhem. She told them about architecture.

Perhaps it was a different take on the Ghost Walk

script, but --Darn it-- she *wasn't* boring. No matter what her family thought, she could be as exciting and fun as anybody. Besides, why would tourists find some cheap campfire stories more interesting than *actual* history? It didn't make any sense.

History books had gotten Grace through some of the darkest parts of her life. For the past year, she'd lived inside of them. She'd always read about Virginia history for fun and relaxation, but now she felt like it was keeping her alive. Ever since she lost her mind in that alleyway, she'd been struggling to rebuild her life. Without the refuge of her books, she'd be lost. If she could just instill that feeling into others, surely they would understand why they should care about her unflashy tours.

Grace took a calming breath, before she started getting stressed, again. Stress was the enemy, according to her shrink. It was what caused her hallucination. A skeptical little voice (that sounded *a lot* like her aunt Serenity) asked how she could've hallucinated the blood on her hands, when everybody else at the scene had seen it too, but Grace didn't like to listen to that voice. If she did, all the nice normal walls she'd built would come toppling down again.

"You're standing in front of Virginia's oldest tavern, The Raven." She waved a hand at the building behind her. "Built in 1768..."

"176*9*." Mr. Tri-Corner casually interrupted. Who the hell bought those stupid hats at the gift shop and actually looked *good* in them, anyway? It was sooo unfair.

Worse, he was right about the date.

"176*9*." She corrected, refusing to acknowledge him. "The Raven was the site of many clandestine meetings during the Revolution." See? *That* was interesting. She tried to infuse her voice with excitement. "A favorite tavern of luminaries such as Thomas Jefferson, George Wythe, Josiah Oliver, and even Gregory Maxwell, the hero of Yorktown..."

"Hero of Yorktown, my ass. The man was a bloody idiot."

"...it served as the unofficial headquarters for the

patriots in Harrisonburg."

"That's because it had the bawdiest wenches in town. Ach, Mistress Mary..." The jackass in the back gave a dramatic sigh. "Josiah could hardly keep his hands off of her long enough to lead his troops. Almost lost us the war."

Grace's teeth ground together, but she kept going. "The Raven was owned by Edward Hunnicutt, one of the Richmond Hunnicutts."

"Watered down his ale, the cheap bastard. Treated the serving girls quite badly, as well."

"He also had a fascinating history as a cartographer of the region..."

"Maps? Sweet bleeding Christ, you'll really be talking of *maps*, now?"

"...Edward charted portions of the James River," she pointed towards the harbor, "helping to make it navigable to larger ships. He imported goods like tea and cloth from England, opening a shop. It did so well that he doubled his money by selling the store to his sister-in-law, Aggie Northhander, making enough gold to invest it in this tavern."

The tour critic gave an exaggerated groan at that entirely factual account. "Take pity on these poor people, woman! Spin a ghost yarn. Do ya think they want to be hearing of Ned's dull life? The man was a wanker. I've always suspected he was a Tory, at heart."

Grace shot him another glare. "Edward Hunnicutt led a *fascinating* life." She repeated firmly.

For a second, the guy actually shut up, a strange expression flickering over his face. He looked over his shoulder, like he suspected she might be talking to someone else.

Meanwhile, her group didn't look fascinated. A frat kid fiddled with his phone, while his girlfriend examined her vampire-y nails. A man in Bermuda shorts checked his watch for the sixth time in as many minutes. Several of the older customers *looked* like they were listening, but they weren't listening, at all. They were tuning her out the way they would ignore a droning commercial, waiting for some better show to start.

A young teen tugged on her mother's arm. "When are we going to hear about the ghosts, Mom?" She asked in a loud whisper. The group might be politely disregarding the troublemaker, but his comments were infecting all of them.

Drat, what spooky story could she tell?

The tour guide training had given Grace some background on the standard Harrisonburg tales, but panic wiped them from her brain. Everyone was looking at her. What the hell was she supposed to say?

Desperate, she tried to make up some nightmarish tale of horror, but it was less Stephen King and more Mad Libs. Unlike the other Riveras, Grace wasn't the most imaginative person, the occasional hallucination notwithstanding. "Uhhh... Some people say a --um-- skeleton with a... hook? For a hand -- um-- sometimes eats here... sometimes."

Eyes rolled all over the tour.

The gadfly sadly shook his head at that halfhearted campfire story, rallying from his momentary confusion. "Jesus, Mary, and Joseph, I hope you're not depending on this job to keep you fed. If ya are, you'll surely be starving ta death, by the end of the week."

Grace hesitated. He was right. *Again.* Skeletons were just not going to cut it. Somehow she had to do better, before more customers wandered away. She'd already lost three. Crap. She needed this job. What part of local history might interest this group?

She wracked her brain for a minute and then --for no reason at all-- seized on a story that most people in this town wanted to forget. "And it was very near this spot that Harrisonburg's most notorious criminal was hanged for his horrible crimes." She announced. "Captain James Riordan. America's first serial killer."

"Oh *bloody hell*." The guy snapped in disgust, but everyone else perked up at the promise of a grisly tale.

Grace smiled, sensing the story would be a hit. This was going to work! She should've thought of adding good old Jamie to the tour in the first place. "Captain Riordan was the

Jack the Ripper of Harrisonburg. A dashing and devious criminal mastermind. He came from a good family, but he was disowned at a young age for his disreputable behavior. He left Scotland in disgrace and fled to America, where he gambled his way into a ship."

Her detractor scoffed at that. "Horse shit. No one 'gambles their way' into a ship. You have to cheat and not get caught. T'is all *skill*."

"During the war, James Riordan smuggled luxury goods into the Colonies, using Mr. Hunnicutt's maps to evade capture by either side." She tacked that part on just to piss off the heckler. Edward Hunnicutt *was* fascinating, darn it. "After the war, he became an out and out pirate."

"Have you ever *seen* Ned's maps?" The guy demanded, because of *course* he arrogantly assumed he knew more about local history than Grace did. "They mostly led to swamps and dead ends. No one with an ounce of sense used them for anything more than wiping their ass."

Grace tuned out the snarking. "Quite the ladies' man, Captain Riordan wooed all the pretty girls of the colony. He made a good living and he was incredibly handsome. There were few who could resist his charm."

"Incredibly handsome." The jackass repeated with a nod. "*Finally,* you begin to make some sense. ...Although you do make it sound like a disease. Are you a Sunday school teacher, by chance? You sound like a Sunday school teacher to me." It wasn't a compliment.

Grace *had* taught Sunday school back in Richmond, as a matter of fact. "Despite his reputation, Captain Riordan was welcomed into many of Harrisonburg's nicest homes." She continued and then paused dramatically. "But not all of them. Some of the finest young women in Harrisonburg refused his ill-gotten gifts and dishonorable propositions. Furious, he vowed to make them pay for the insult."

"That's *not* what happened."

"Lucinda Wentworth was the first to die." Grace went on, trying to stick to the facts of the case. Now that she was at this part of the tale, she was suddenly remembering *why* she'd never added James Riordan to her tour before. Even discussing a crime that was two and a half centuries old, had her stress level spiking. She pictured peaceful green cornfields and kept going. "Lucinda sneaked out of her bedroom, just a few blocks away," she gestured down the street, "and was never seen again."

Everybody turned to eagerly look in the direction she was pointing.

Well, not *everybody*.

"Why are you telling this story?" The guy hopped off the top rail of the fence, no longer smirking. His eyes stayed fixed on her, glowering in annoyance. "I know you're new here, but I take this tour every night. No one *ever* tells this story on the Ghost Walk."

Grace knew that she was off-script. Harrisonburg's Official Ghost Walk was supposed to be G-rated. The whole village made its profits by appealing to vacationing families wanting to experience a weekend of Revolutionary life. A place where parents could tell themselves their kids were learning something about history and the kids could buy rubber muskets. The residents of Harrisonburg didn't like anything controversial sullying the carefully cultivated, plastic perfection of their town.

Which was why the Riveras had always been a stone in their sensible shoes.

For generations, Grace's relatives had been the fortunetellers in town. Their small shop had been housing tarot card readings and mixing potions since before the Revolution. Way longer than the cutesy antique dealers had been in town.

Regardless of their authentic provenance, though, the rest of Harrisonburg was embarrassed to have their storefront anywhere near their white picket fences. They wanted to forget all the messy aspects of the past and focus on having fife-and-drum parades every day at three o'clock. The Riveras had never fit into that gentrified ideal. From the day her parents died and she moved in with her aunt, until the day she went off to college, Grace had felt out of place. Which is why she'd left this stifling town and never looked back.

Well, until her breakdown had driven her from Richmond and she had nowhere else to go.

Harrisonburg hadn't changed much since Grace left, just like it hadn't changed much in the two-and-a-half centuries before. It was the most complete Colonial town in America, filled with eighteenth century brick houses and cobblestone streets. For generations, it had been forgotten and past by as America grew-up around it. In the 1940s, the Harrisonburg Preservation Association had successfully lobbied to have the entire town set aside as a landmark. Instantly, ruined buildings turned into "historic" buildings and property values doubled. The small town now existed out of time. Entering Harrisonburg was like stepping back to days of John Handcock.

In a completely sanitized way.

The whole place was part history lesson, part Disney World. Unsavory things like slavery, dirt, and James Riordan had no place in their pretty reimagining of history. Friendly actors showed tourists how to make paper or weave blankets in quaint shops. Horses clumped up and down the streets. Musicians serenaded diners with high-spirited fiddle music. ...But there were still three Starbucks within walking distance.

Harrisonburg's modern restaurants and shops fed off happy tourist dollars. It gave the place a sense of artificiality that Grace hated. Harrisonburg should be teaching people what *really* happened, not just what was appealing to the customers. The Founding Fathers had walked these streets and slept in these buildings. Redcoats attacked Patriots not three miles away. The United States had been conceived in the backrooms of these taverns. *That* was what Harrisonburg was really about. *That* was what they should be focused on, even if it meant that the shops on Main Street didn't make a fortune every summer, selling six dollar popcorn in plastic powder horns.

No one else saw things her way, though. Most of the people who actually lived there were retired college professors, small business owners, and paid-by-the-hour employees. All of them liked Harrisonburg just the way it was. They didn't care about historical accuracy. They just wanted to stay the seventh most popular tourist destination in Virginia, even if that meant adding air-conditioning to the historic mansions so no one got too hot while experiencing the "authentic" lifestyle of Colonial America.

Since triple homicides and lynchings didn't exactly blend with the cafes, garden tours, and the annual fireworks display, all the remaining evidence of the murders was locked up in the basement of the Harrisonburg Historical Museum, on permanent non-display. No one would be happy about Grace reminding guests that the town was also the site of America's first serial killing.

Too bad.

She needed the tips.

"Lucinda's family immediately suspected that James Riordan was behind her disappearance. The two of them had been seen around town, in the weeks before the murder. There were whispers and speculation. Her sister Eugenia nearly fainted whenever she saw him. Men muttered that something should be done. ...But there was no proof."

"Bloody right there wasn't."

"People grew even more suspicious when Anabel Maxwell and Clara Vance went missing in the following days. Like Lucinda, they were never seen again. Anabel disappeared out of the governor's hedge maze at a party and Clara vanished at the 4th of July celebration in town square. All that was ever found of her was a lace shawl, splattered with blood."

The heckler paced around, glowering at her.

Grace almost didn't blame him this time. Even two and a half centuries after the girls' deaths, it seemed tacky to twist the crimes into some macabre form of entertainment. Her rent money was at stake, though, so she kept going. "Since these were the three women who'd rejected Captain Jamie's lecherous advances at the Summer Ball, Harrisonburg grew more convinced of his guilt. The good citizens of the town decided to act."

The tour began to buzz amongst themselves, liking this

tale.

Most of them, anyway.

"Oh bullocks! That isn't true, a'tall!" The loudmouth stalked closer to the lantern, looking even more pissed off. ...And even more stunning in the stronger light. "Whoever told you this was out of his skull." His face was a study in masculine perfection, his auburn hair tied back in the kind of ponytail favored by guys who not-so-secretly longed to be Wesley in *The Princess Bride*.

Who *was* he? He looked familiar. Maybe he was an actor who starred in some pirate TV show that she was too smart to watch.

...Or maybe he worked in Harrisonburg.

Yeah, that actually made sense. Obviously he was a local, since he said he took a Ghost Tour every night. She was surprised none of the other guides had mentioned him. Grace looked him up and down, trying to recall if he worked in one of the local shops. If he did, she was totally going to get his ass fired.

In the light, she noticed that he was dressed in Revolutionary-era style clothes, which backed up her new theory. Many employees wore period costumes, to keep Harrisonburg "authentic," but this guy actually made the leggings and brightly patterned waistcoat seem *not* stupid. That annoyed her nearly as much as his running commentary.

Grace herself was wearing a wide skirt and bonnet that weighed about six thousand pounds. Unlike her unwanted customer, she knew she looked wilted and silly.

Ignoring that depressing fact and the stifling summer heat, she reached the grand finale of her gory tale. "The same night that poor Clara vanished, the angry townspeople vowed not to let Jamie Riordan strike again. They dragged him from his cabin on his ship, the *Sea Serpent*, and carried him down this very street, burning torches and chanting for justice."

"Bloody cowards."

"Then they strung a rope from a tree that stood right there," she pointed to the stump of a giant oak, which had been struck by lightning sometime during the Civil War, "and tied the other end around Captain Riordan's neck. They say he begged forgiveness for his crimes, but Harrisonburg wasn't in a charitable mood. They hanged him, while he pleaded for mercy."

"*That's a fucking lie.*" Long John Idiot bellowed. "You donea know what you're talking about!" His accent was thicker than ever, so it actually took her a beat to translate the snarled "donea" into "do not." "How did you even get this job, woman?"

Grace had had enough. "Would you just shut-up?" She whirled around to face him, jabbing a finger at his chest. "It *is* what happened. James Riordan's crimes are straight from the history books. *Horror in Harrisonburg*, written by Anabel Maxwell's own brother Gregory, outlined the whole story. Feel free to look it up yourself, if you don't believe me."

Several members of the tour jumped back as if she'd surprised them. As if her yelling had come out of nowhere and wasn't *completely* justified given all the crap she'd endured from this jackass. As if *she* was the one acting crazy.

The jackass in question gaped at her like she'd just hit him in the face with a fish. His jaw literally dropped, his mouth opening and closing with no sound coming out. It was almost funny to see someone so cartoon-character astonished.

"Are you talking to *me?*" He blurted out, his patriot blue eyes as wide as Frisbees. "*Holy fuck*, are ya really talking to me?"

"Who else would I be talking to?" Grace retorted. "And would you please watch your language? This is a family program." Unlike most of the Riveras, she wasn't an avid supporter of casual swearing.

The man gave a crazed sounding laugh.

Grace didn't appreciate his attitude. Confrontations made her feel lightheaded and sweaty. Stressful or not, now that she'd started this, she wasn't backing down, though. "I'm serious. You've been harassing me all night and I've had it. If you don't like the tour, *don't take the tour*. I'll give you a refund. But I'm not going to have you yelling at me and calling me a liar, alright?"

"*Who's* she talking to?" The frat guy asked in confusion, looking around.

Grace flashed him a frown. Was he drunk? "I'm talking to *him*, of course." She waved a hand at the costumed idiot who'd been tormenting her for the past forty minutes. "The man in the hat." That should be perfectly obvious to everyone.

Except everyone exchanged sideways glances, like they'd missed something.

Captain Kidd stepped closer to her, his slightly-hysterical laughter fading. His head tilted like he still didn't believe this was actually happening. "Can you see me, woman?" He asked in an intense tone. "Really *see* me?"

Wasn't *that* a typical question? "Yes, I really see you." She rolled her eyes at his conceit. "You're very handsome, alright? Maybe that works with some girls, but not with me. You're being a jerk and I won't tolerate it, I don't care what you look like." She crossed her arms over her chest. "And stop calling me 'woman' or 'lass' or anything aside from my name. It's Grace Rivera."

He let out a shaky breath, bending forward to brace his hands on his knees. "She can see me." He wheezed out. "Holy Mother of God, someone can finally see me. Thank you. Thank you. *Thank you*." He actually crossed himself in prayer. "I'll never be doubting again."

What in the world...? Grace's eyebrows compressed at his theatrics, looking over at the rest of the group for guidance. She could tell from their baffled reactions that she was missing something, but she had no idea what. "What's going on here?" She demanded.

"I don't get it. Is this --like-- part of the tour?" The teenager asked.

"What?"

"Yeah, that's it." Bermuda Shorts smiled at the girl, ignoring Grace's confusion. "Don't you see? She acts like some invisible guy in a hat has been with us this whole time and we all get freaked out thinking a ghost is following us. It's a nice touch. *Finally*, this damn tour is picking up."

Everyone else was nodding, like they understood, but Grace was totally lost. Was this some kind of practical joke? If it was, she didn't understand the punchline. "Invisible? The man in the hat is right *there*."

Everyone smiled humoringly and kept nodded at her. A few of them snapped pictures of some random spot to her left, even though the guy was clearly standing on her *right*.

"They can't see me. No one's been able to see me for nearly two-hundred and fifty years. Except you, Grace Rivera." The guy sounded manically happy, now his words coming out way too fast. "It's a miracle. *You're* a miracle. I thought the Good Lord had forsaken me, but here you are! You have no idea how much I've missed having someone to talk to, lass. Jesus, Mary, and Joseph, I can't believe this is really happening."

Neither could she.

"What?" Grace asked again, fainter this time. No one else was even *looking* at the guy. Wasn't it human nature to look at someone when they were talking? The stress she wasn't supposed to feel began to redline. This wasn't right. This wasn't...

Then, from out of nowhere, she suddenly remembered where she'd seen this man before.

He wasn't on a pirate TV show. His obscenely handsome face was straight off the pages of *Horror in Harrisonburg*. Aunt Serenity owned the large tome on Virginia history and Grace had loved it as a girl. The portrait of Captain James Riordan, painted the year before he died, had always stuck in her mind, because of his eyes. The color of the minutemen's blue coats, they'd sparkled with secrets and mischief. Like he knew some wonderful joke and he was just dying to let you in on the fun.

As a bookish fifteen year old, she'd spent countless hours daydreaming about James Riordan. Knife-wielding lunatic or not, he'd fascinated her. It helped that Jamie didn't look like a murderer. He looked like the kind of guy who sailed through life on his extraordinary charm and staggering good looks. A scoundrel, who, after two drinks at a bar, could somehow convince a nice woman to quit her steady job and travel around the world with him. A pirate, who evaded capture by being just a little bit more daring than all the stodgy people he robbed. A free spirit, who stood at the helm of his ship, the wind in his amazing hair, and just *loved* being Jamie Riordan.

Even a normal girl like Grace had been taken in by the charisma of the man. His eyes in that picture had glinted with adventure and charm. They promised that he was Robin Hood. Jack Sparrow. Dean Moriarty.

…And those same eyes were staring at her right now. *Oh God.*

This wasn't happening again. She wasn't going to lose her mind *again*. No way. If she just told herself that he wasn't real and willed him away, he'd disappear.

Except the guy didn't disappear.

Grace's vision waivered in panic and she began to hyperventilate. Was she going crazy? She had to be. For the past year, she'd been terrified of this and now it was finally happening. Insanity. She took a step backwards, her mind racing. The stress had finally fried her circuits and now she was hallucinating infamous historical figures.

"I see ya are becoming vexed, but you must listen to me." The guy who looked *waaay* too much like Jamie Riordan stepped closer to her, quickly closing the distance she'd created. His gaze was frantic now, like he was afraid to even blink for fear she'd disappear. "You're the one I've been waiting for. You can't be leaving me, lass. I need your help."

She gave her head a frenzied shake. "You aren't real." She whispered, her eyes locked on his way-too-real-seeming face. "This isn't happening. I just need to think about peaceful green cornfields and you'll go away." Her parents' farm was still the place she returned to in her mind when she was stressed. Her therapist had told her it was all about "centering" herself, but mostly it was about Grace wanting to recapture an elusive feeling of safety.

"*Cornfields?* Are ya mad?"

"Apparently, *yes!* I am! I'm seeing you and you're not really here!"

Blackbeard waved that aside. "Of course I'm here. Donea be daft. We must *talk*. Well, *I* must talk and you must listen. I have been *screaming* for someone to listen to me for centuries."

"Peaceful green cornfields. Peaceful green cornfields. Peaceful green... *Why aren't you going away!?*"

"I'm not going *anywhere!*" He loomed over Grace, like he was instinctively trying to get as close to her as he could. "Two hundred years I've waited in this dismal place. I need *help* and you're here to provide it. I'm not leaving your side, woman."

Grace squeezed her eyes shut and tried harder to find her calm place. The pressure of *not* finding it just added to her growing anxiety and made it all the more impossible to find. "Peacefulgreencornfields, peacefulgreencornfields, peacefulgreencornfields."

"Would you bloody *stop* that?!"

"Are we sure this is part of the tour?" The frat guy's girlfriend asked no one in particular. "The guide lady is acting kinda wiggy."

The rest of the group clearly agreed with that diagnoses, edging away from Grace like she might be contagious. Their wary looks weren't helping her feel frigging peaceful!

"I'm not insane." She snapped at them, mostly trying to convince herself. "I just can't be around stress. *That's* what this is about. I'm under too much stress and it's manifesting in some kind of Colonial-era delusion."

"*You're* feeling stressed? Try being dead, woman!"

"You're not even real! I told you, you're just a *delusion*. And don't call me 'woman!'"

The tour group exchanged nervous looks, wondering if they should make a run for it.

"Listen to me." The delusion laid a hand against his

chest, obviously trying to appear sincere. "This is really happening. It is. I'll explain it to you, alright?" He nodded like he had some magic words that would suddenly make everything logical and clear. If the real Jamie Riordan had been half so convincingly earnest, the lynch-mob never would have executed him in the first place. "I'm not a delusion. I'm a *ghost*."

Grace gave a high-pitched laugh at that lunacy. "Oh, of course you are!"

"It's true. My name is Captain James MacCleef Riordan. I was hanged in this accursed town on July 4, 1789, for crimes I didn't commit." He gestured towards the oak tree stump. "I was *framed* for killing those girls and I've been stuck here ever since. I swear it. Ya have to assist me in finally clearing my name."

"No, no, no, no, no." Grace kept backing away from him. "I don't have to do anything, except my deep breathing exercises. This is all inside my head. You're a manifestation of my anxiety and my weird fixation with that stupid picture."

She should have known her obsession with that painting would lead to badness. Her first sex dreams had been about a murderer. No wonder she was so screwed up.

Jamie Riordan (No, *not* Jamie Riordan!) moved closer again. "Mistress Rivera, *please*. You were clearly sent to me for a reason. I'm not going to hurt you. I couldn't, even if I wanted to. Regain your equilibrium and everything will begin to… *watch out!*"

Grace was passed the point of even hearing him. She had to get out of there before she had a complete meltdown. As she retreated, the heel of her old time-y shoe wedged between two of the street's cobblestones. Caught off-guard, Grace toppled backwards, her arms pin-wheeling for purchase.

"Shit!" The-delusion-who-maybe-wasn't-a-delusion reached out to try and grab her as she fell. Instead of catching hold of Grace and steadying her, his fingers passed right through her wrist with a strange jolt of energy. She hit the ground, her skull whacking against the pavement. Stars flashed in front of her eyes.

The very last thing she saw before the world went dark was Jamie Riordan's stunning face hovering over hers, his patriot blue eyes bright with concern. "Donea leave me, lass." He said very clearly. "You have no idea how long I've waited for you."

CHAPTER TWO

June 20, 1789- HC snuck in to see me last night, after the Ball. I woke up with my hands tied to the bedposts and his mouth between my thighs. He seemed intent on punishing me for dancing with JMR (He quite detests the Pirate!) and I was begging him for forgiveness by the end. I cannot even write all the wicked things he did to my body while I was helpless. I'm sure Eugenia knows what we did and the gloomy little prude knows that *I* know that she knows, which makes it all the more delicious.

It was quite a marvelous evening!

From the Journal of Miss Lucinda Wentworth

"I wish you'd let the ambulance take you to the hospital, just to check you out." Mrs. Anita Beauregard-Smythe frowned, visions of lawsuits dancing in her head. "You really don't look well and our insurance provider is very clear about getting timely doctors' reports."

As head of Harrisonburg's tour office, Anita was visibly worried about what the guests' comment cards would say if one of her guides had a psychotic break. With lacquered blonde hair fixed in a permanent bubble and a face that never lost its empty smile, Anita had probably been born in her middle-aged pants suit. She couldn't care less about the welfare of her employees, although she tried to cover that bean-counting callousness with Southern manners. Under the phony empathy and flawless make-up, her only real focus was ruling her office fiefdom with an iron fist.

"I don't need to go to the hospital." Grace assured her. "I'm fine." She pointedly refused to look at the delusion of

Jamie Riordan, who was now lounging in the corner of the Harrisonburg Guest Relations Center.

Housed in a two hundred year old building, the inside of the space was a modern mess, filled with computers and overflowing files. At nine o'clock in the evening, Anita and Grace were the only ones left in the office, which was a block from the center of town. The delusion of Jamie Riordan had smugly informed her that it used to be a brothel.

Not that she was listening to him.

Since she'd regained consciousness, Grace had done her best to ignore the big, handsome evidence of her insanity and it was clearly pissing him off. His gorgeous face was set in an irritated expression, as if *she* was the one being unreasonable. The man wanted to talk. He *loved* to talk. Since she seemed to be the only person who could hear his constant talking, he kept up a running commentary to her, whether she responded to him or not.

And she *wasn't* responding to him.

No way.

"How much longer do you plan to tolerate this horrible woman, lass?" He demanded as Anita *subtly* mentioned that she'd had to give refunds to everyone on the Ghost Walk and didn't Grace think it was just a *little* unfair to expect Harrisonburg to pay for Grace's mistakes.

Grace pretended that he wasn't there. If she just ignored him, Thomas Payne-in-the-ass (minus the *Common Sense*) would just go away. He *had* to. Darn it, she *refused* to go crazy, again. "I can reimburse you for the tour admissions, Anita."

"Well, I *do* think that would be the right thing to do. But the guests were also saying that you were talking to yourself." Anita continued in a disapproving tone that she tried to pass off as worry over Grace's wellbeing. "That's very troubling, in light of your history. Were you seeing things, Grace?"

"No. Of course not. I think my electrolytes were just low."

"That's it, lass. Donea tell her anything that will get you locked up. You'll be of no help to me trapped in an asylum."

Grace's lips compressed into a line, but she still didn't acknowledge him.

Anita made an "umm" sound, not convinced by Grace's denials. "Are you *sure* you weren't experiencing anything… odd? You've been under a lot of stress this past year. And then there's your family's… business. No one would blame you if you're having a few… problems."

Faux-Jamie scoffed at all the pointed pauses. "See?" He waved a dismissive (but beautifully shaped) hand at Anita's faux-concern and faux-sympathy. "She thinks you're off your head. Convince her everything's alright so we can be going."

"I'm *fine*, Anita." Grace adjusted her icepack with a bit more force than necessary. Visualizing a safe and happy place was supposed to help with anxiety, but no amount of peaceful green cornfields could stop the throbbing in her skull. "I just need to drink more water."

"I'm sure that's it." Anita obviously *wasn't* sure that was it. "It's shaping up to be a sweltering Independence Day, isn't it?" She patted Grace's arm. "Things will be *so* hectic here over the holiday. Take tomorrow off and recuperate. You can come back for the weekend, rested and ready to go. I think that would be best, don't you?" It wasn't a question.

Grace ground her teeth together at the loss of a day's pay. "Of course."

Her answer was totally unnecessary. Anita was already moving on to her real priorities. "And you have a point. With the temperatures so high, we'll sell record amounts of bottled water this weekend on the tours. I'll just go make a note to order even more." She headed for her private office. "You can get home on your own, can't you, Grace?" She called over her shoulder and then shut the door after her, without waiting for an answer.

Grace sighed.

"Do you truly plan to stay working for that harridan, lass? Jesus, Mary, and Joseph, I'd rather be dead and I *am* dead. You should grow a backbone. Walk out of this place and never come back."

On some level, she agreed with his disapproving analysis. This job wasn't for her. She was terrible at it and very, very bad at confrontations. Everyone knew that. Great-Uncle Devotion once told her she could lose an argument with a stuffed jackalope.

As a crypto-taxidermist, Devotion had a lot of time on his hands to think up witticisms like that. Most of them involved some kind of non-existent animal he was just waiting to discover, hunt down, and pose with on *National Geographic's* cover. Dev's fondest wish was to shoot a unicorn. In this case, though, her crazy uncle was probably right. Grace was stuck in a life that didn't quite fit. Not a single part of it made her happy.

Unfortunately, after Grace's breakdown, Anita had been the only normal person willing to hire her.

She couldn't go back to being a crime scene tech. It had nearly cost Grace her sanity. And she sure couldn't go work with her family. They were a surefire ticket *back* to the crazy house. Not only were her relatives insane, but their potion shop somehow lost money even though they could literally *make money* with their spells. As much as Grace hated to admit it, their magic could actually do --well-- magical things. There was no logical explanation for their powers. So how on God's green earth could they have spent three hundred years dead broke?

It was enough to drive even a really normal person bonkers.

"Why do you let her speak to you so?" The delusion continued, gesturing towards Anita's office door. "You should stand up for yourself!"

Grace looked up at the ugly dropped ceiling and let out a long breath. He was actually right. Was that a bad sign? An even *worse* sign than seeing a delusion in the first place?

Maybe she *should've* gone to the hospital. Grace just couldn't shake the feeling that if she stepped foot into that sterile, cold space, she wouldn't be able to get back out, again. It would be like a year ago, only worse. Just thinking about it triggered claustrophobia and had her doing her deep breathing exercises to calm down.

What she really needed was to just be normal. Normal people didn't see visions of Revolutionary War era criminals. Normal people didn't have relatives who hunted unicorns and spent every free moment trying to recreate the family's long-lost recipe for "troll powder." Normal people didn't visit crime scenes and relive the murders. Normal people were boring and stable and... normal.

Normal was the key to happiness.

She was sure of it, no matter what her family thought. If she could just figure out the secret of normalcy, everything else would fall into place. Her whole life would go back to not sucking. All she had to do was focus on reality and tune out the amazingly attractive invisible man following her around.

Think *normal.*

Speaking of which, she was late for her date. Grace checked her watch. Yes, a nice, normal dinner with nice, normal Robert would make everything fine again. No one was more relentlessly normal than her boyfriend.

Hopefully, he could bore the delusion away.

"Now that we're alone, will you finally listen to me?" The completely *un*-normal Scottish guy demanded. He straightened away from the wall and headed over to her. Aside from some transparency around the edges of his large form, he looked remarkably solid. And really handsome. Amazingly, disgustingly, unbelievably handsome. "We have much to discuss."

He seemed bigger up close, the eighteenth-century clothes molded against the masculine lines of his body. His remarkable muscle-tone made sense. Kind of. If Grace was going to imagine Jamie Riordan, of *course* she'd imagine him as the most attractive man in the world. She'd been obsessed with the pirate from the time she was fifteen and now he was standing there, like that stupid portrait come to life.

Except he wasn't alive.

Refusing to acknowledge him, Grace got to her feet. Instantly, the room spun and she had to catch herself on the edge of the desk. Her head didn't appreciate any sudden movements. She'd diagnose herself with some kind of brain injury, but she'd been seeing things *before* she fell.

Long before if you counted that hallucination in the alleyway.

"Are you, alright?" Make-believe-Jamie loomed over Grace and held out a palm, like he could somehow steady her. His hands really were stunning, his fingers long and perfectly shaped. They should have belonged to an artist, not a pirate. "Maybe you should sit back down, lass. You still look peaked."

Wonderful. The only person who'd shown her any compassion was a John Adams-y-themed figment of her own imagination. God, could she be more pathetic?

Grace waved him away and headed for the door, smoothing her hair down. Hopefully, the long dark curls covered the bruise on her head. She didn't want to have to explain any of this to Robert. It would be too awkward. Anything that even hinted at messiness put him in a sour mood. Robert's inflexibility would have been annoying, except Grace kept reminding herself that it was further proof of his unsurpassed normalness.

Still, he was going to be peeved that she'd missed their standing Friday night, eight-thirty dinner reservation. She was going to have to go straight to his house in her stupid costume, which would also irritate him. Maybe they could skip the restaurant and order in. She didn't feel like going out, anyway. Her head was killing her and her stress level was off the charts.

"Where are you going?" Fake-Jamie followed her out the door and into the stifling heat of the fading Virginia twilight. "Ya cannot ignore me. It *means* something that you're able to see me, when no one else ever has."

Yeah, it meant she was losing her mind. Again.

"We must figure out why this is happening, lass. Denial is no way to deal with life's challenges. Or *death's* challenges, either. We need to face this opportunity head on."

He truly had a magical voice. The accent was like liquid sex drizzled on chocolate cheesecake. ...Even when he was speaking to her like a know-it-all talk show therapist.

Grace put her fingers in her ears and walked faster, trying to block him out. Her car was the most practical four-door in the parking lot. Grace disliked looking at the tan box, but it was *normal* and that was all that mattered. The only slight unique thing about it was the small decal in the back window and even that was sold all over the Chesapeake Bay, so it hardly even registered on the weirdness scale. It was just an innocent little mermaid. Totally within the confines of normalcy.

At least that's what she'd *told* herself... but maybe it was like a gateway drug into the world of strange. Just in case, Grace paused to rip it off the window after she unlocked the car. There was no point in taking chances.

"Oh, I quite liked that sticker." The delusion complained. "Reminded me of my last trip to Jamaica." He gave a contented hum of a sound. "Those were some of the best days of my life. A chest full of gold, a barrel of rum, and mermaids swimming in an azure blue sea."

Grace refused to listen to that beguiling image. The man wasn't even there. She deliberately didn't offer him a ride, but he climbed in anyway. It was hard to keep out a ghost who could just phase though doors.

No. *Not* a ghost.

She was the only Rivera in sixteen generations who didn't believe in ghosts, because she was frigging *normal.* Grace's trembling hands got the key in the ignition and she peeled out onto the street, her hands clenched on the wheel so tight that her knuckles were white.

Very, very normal.

The not-a-ghost beside her kept yammering. "You've been sent to help me. I *know* it." He sat sideways on the upholstery, his patriot blue eyes staring at her profile, willing her to engage in his craziness. God only knew how many poor women the *real* Jamie Riordan had been able to win over with that hypnotic gaze. "Please just listen to me and..."

She reached over and turned the radio dial *allllll* the way up, drowning out his stream of words. Salt-n-Pepa blared out, shaking the windows of the car with the news that he was a mighty good man. Jamie immediately tried to turn the volume down again, but his fingers passed straight through the knob. She could tell he was swearing in frustration, but she couldn't hear it over the thumping music and that was all that mattered.

Paying attention to him would just lead to madness and she'd had enough madness in her life. July 4th was just a few days away. *That* was why this was happening. Grace should have known that the one year anniversary would stir up bad memories and trigger… oddness. As soon as the holiday was over, everything would go back to normal.

And normal was good.

The drive to Robert's house only took five minutes. As curator for the Harrisonburg Historical Museum, he was successful enough to have a large house in the newest section of town. The upscale community was filled with identical homes, all painted in nearly identical neutral colors with names like "summer wheat," "warm toffee" and "fresh cream." Each blade of grass on the identical lawns looked like it had been cut with a ruler. No basketball courts or bicycles marred the identical brick driveways with evidence that children played there. Not even fireflies dared to enter the HOA approved landscape.

Grace felt suffocated every time she visited the manufactured perfection of Robert's neighborhood. The monotonous bland pressed down on her and she just wanted to drive away as fast as she possibly could. But she didn't. Bland was *good*. Bland was *normal*.

She just needed to keep telling herself that.

Grace parked her car, relieved to see that Robert had read her mind and ordered in food. There was already a red delivery truck on the street, out of place among all the luxury leases. Calling for pizza was unexpectedly thoughtful. She'd half-expected him to go to the restaurant by himself, rather than break his precious routine.

"Please donea be telling me you live *here*." Couldn't-be-Jamie took in the rows of cookie-cutter homes and made a face. "Slapped together and hellaciously ugly. This part of town hurts my eyes. I expected better of you, lass."

Because that was *way* too close to what she'd been thinking, Grace shot him a deadly glare. There was nothing worse than agreeing with a jackass. She slammed the car door and started up the curved walkway.

He arched a brow, seeing her annoyance. Like a misbehaving twelve year old, the negative attention just encouraged him. "Oh, so *now* you're pissed." He hurried after her, his boots not making any sound on the pavement. "Why? Because I've pointed out what anyone with working eyeballs already kens? This house is a featureless monstrosity, like everything else built in the last forty years. It should be a crime to fill up beautiful farmland with such dwellings."

James Riordan --serial killer and pirate-- would know all about crimes.

"You may have been sent to help me, but perhaps I'm also supposed to help *you*." He persisted. "So far, your life is smashingly dull, Grace. Surely someone's needing to fix that for you or you'll end up dying in this tomb of beige." He gestured to the house with a disdainful flick of his wrist.

Speaking of dying, if he wasn't already dead and buried, she'd be thinking up ways to kill him.

"How could such a lovely woman surround herself with such a morass of mass-produced...?" He paused his sermon, his eyes falling on the mailbox where "Robert Johnson" was stenciled in an elegant, curving font. "Wait, is this not your home?" He glanced back at her, his stunning face outraged. "Oh bloody hell! Are you here to visit a *man?*"

Grace inhaled a cleansing breath. Stay calm. No negativity could find her in the peaceful green cornfields of her center.

Not that it wasn't trying.

Captain Wouldn't-Shut-Up continued with his rant. "This man should *not* be a part of your life. Not any longer. For whatever reason, you and I have been brought together. You should be focusing on *me*."

Her eyes rolled so hard she nearly blinded herself.

"I'm only trying to look out for you, lass." He tried, switching tactics when she didn't respond to his illogical possessiveness. He made a show of checking her hand for signs of a ring. "It's unseemly for an unmarried lady to call on a man at this hour of the night." He arched a pious brow. "You'll be giving people the wrong impression."

Grace squeezed her eyes shut. Peaceful. Green. Cornfields.

"If a man is courting you, he should be calling upon *your* residence," lectured the moral authority who knew the exact location of the town's former brothel. "In fact, given your injury, a *gentleman* would've come to collect you in his car and driven you safely home. He should be there to assist you through this crisis." He gave a derisive sniff. "I was never a gentleman myself, but I know the breed."

Grace couldn't even imagine Robert coming to "assist her through a crisis."

Maybe her bewilderment showed, because the delusion smirked knowingly. "Of course, ya didn't *call* him for assistance, did you? That says much about your relationship." He watched her, blue eyes seeing far too much. "Do you have no faith in this man? No expectation that he will be of service? Not even a hope that he'll offer you some feeling of safety?" He arched a brow. "Deep down, do you know he's *not* a gentleman?"

Peaceful.
Green.
Cornfields.

Grace was staying *so* frigging calm and envisioning *so* many cornfields that she didn't even bother to knock on the door. She just slammed into the house and headed for the living room. Robert had a bar set up and, possible concussion or not, she seriously needed a drink.

"Holy Mary, the inside is even worse than the out."

The man who wasn't, wasn't, *wasn't* Jaimie Riordan came in behind her and looked around with a disapproving tsk. "Anyone who lives here must be an absolute wanker." Everything in the McMansion had been picked by a decorator to be unobjectionable, but he was apparently not a fan of matching shades of taupe.

How unsurprising.

Braveheart 2.0 was the least subtle man she could imagine. Eighteenth century garb was known for its outrageous use of color. Gentlemen of fashion never wore suits that matched and Not!Jamie was clearly a fashionable guy. Dressed in a vivid yellow waistcoat and a contrasting blue jacket, with shiny gold buttons, no one in the modern world would ever call his outfit "tasteful."

So why did he look ten times better in the gaudy mix of patterns than Robert ever did in his tailored business suits?

"You should have seen *my* home, lass. Your beauty would've glowed in such surroundings."

Grace sent him a surprised look. Was he flirting with her?

He gave her a quick grin, which made her insides dip. Darn it, how was his smile so white, if he was from the 1700s? Didn't everybody have rotten teeth back then? Her subconscious was totally cheating. "Aye, a bonny lass like you would have liked my ship. The boldest shades. The most fashionable furnishings. The best fabrics."

Oh, she had no doubt that he'd built a veritable palace out of his stolen treasures. His personal style was clearly the Playboy Mansion meets Versailles, with a little bit of Elvis-era Vegas tossed in. Grace snorted, already picturing the circular beds and strategically placed mirrors.

The delusion let out a rapturous sigh, ignoring the fact that she was ignoring him. The man kept up a constant, steady stream of conversation. The subject didn't seem to matter as much as the knowledge that *someone* could finally hear him. He'd barely taken his eyes off of her since she'd woken up, like he was terrified to lose their connection.

If this wasn't all happening inside of her head, Grace

would've guessed that he was lonely. Who could blame him? She couldn't even imagine what it would be like to live in total isolation for centuries, with no one to...

No.

She shook her head. No way, no how. She *refused* to feel sorry for someone who didn't even exist. He hadn't been alone for hundreds of years, because he wasn't there at all!

"Sweet Jesus, how I miss the *Sea Serpent*." The pirate-who-wasn't-there continued. "That ship was like one of my own limbs. Sank in the War of 1812, if you can believe it. When I heard of it, I nearly wept in..." He stopped mid-word, muttering a quick Gaelic curse.

Grace turned to see why he'd stopped talking. Even though she was *definitely* ignoring him, she was getting used to his chatter. His sudden silence caught her attention. Looking around, she didn't see anything out of the ordinary with the surroundings. Robert wouldn't have tolerated anything out of the ordinary. Even the fringe on the carpet was combed straight.

"Um..." Maybe-Jamie pushed his tri-corner hat back on his head, his eyes fixed on the French doors leading to Robert's office. He seemed to engage in a quick mental debate and then moved towards her. "Let us be returning *later*, lass." He held out a restraining hand, like he wanted her to stay where she was. "Much later."

What in the world...? Was he hiding something from her? Grace marched forward, determined to see whatever he was trying to prevent her from seeing.

Jamie dodged sideways, attempting to block her. As he did, his elegant palm inadvertently passed through her chest. Passed through her heart. It was like walking into a mist. Cool and tingly against her skin. It wasn't being *touched* exactly, but she felt him and, judging from the astonished look on his face, he felt her, too. For one endless beat of time, blue eyes locked onto hers.

And Grace knew, whatever had just happened, it was real. This man standing in front of her was *real*.

Oh God.

As impossible as it seemed, Jamie was really and truly there. She was kidding herself, pretending that he was some figment of her imagination. She was a Rivera and Riveras weren't normal enough to be crazy.

Jamie's lips parted in astonishment. "Grace..."

"No. *No.*" This couldn't be happening. She *refused* to be some nut who believed in ghosts, like her deranged second cousin Modesty and all her invisible cats. ...Even if Grace sometimes heard their eerie meowing, too. Shaking her head, she quickly looked away from Jamie, desperate to focus on something sane.

Unfortunately, all she saw was her boyfriend's naked ass. Robert was "busy" alright. Really, really busy with his head buried between the thighs of the pizza delivery girl.

Grace couldn't do anything but stare for a long moment, descending into shock for yet another time that evening. The man she'd thought she'd marry was a lying bastard... but that didn't surprise her nearly so much as the *messiness* of the affair.

She wrinkled her nose. Robert was too fastidious to even walk across the carpet in his bare feet and he was having sex on the *floor?* Engaging in oral sex with a girl covered in tattoos? He hadn't even folded his clothes first. They were bunched up on the ground. Maybe Robert was right and she was semi-frigid, after all. Or maybe her therapist was right and she just had "unrealistic expectations" about sex, because all of this just seemed kind of icky to Grace.

Darn it, why did *everyone* have more fun than she did?

Jamie flashed Grace a quick glance, gauging her reaction. "I donea think the man was expecting you." He ventured.

No kidding.

Betrayal roared through her as she watched Robert happily cavorting with the pizza girl. She'd been bored out of her mind for sixth months, because this son of a bitch was supposed to be *normal.* The fact that he'd deceived her about his staid monotony bothered her a lot more than his cheating.

Which really did sort of "say much about her relationship," didn't it?

Crap. This was just what she didn't need today. Her head hurt, she was seeing ghosts, and now she was never going to be able to order pizza again without thinking of this awkward scene. She seriously needed to go home and get drunk.

The woman on the floor finally noticed Grace was there. She gave a panicked yelp, beating on Robert's back and shoving him away. "Your fucking girlfriend's here!" She squealed, trying to cover herself. "I thought you said she wasn't coming over tonight!"

Robert jolted up, looking around with bulging eyes. His dark hair was mussed, his doughy face shiny and red. "Grace!" He groped for his pants. "Jesus! What are you doing here?!"

"It's Friday." She said in a remarkably even voice, all things considered. "We always meet on Friday."

"It's *Thursday!*" Robert sounded like *he* was somehow the injured party.

"Oh." Grace looked over at Jamie, her mind buzzing. "I thought it was Friday."

"Does it bloody matter what day of the week it is?" He shot back. "The man is bedding another wench and that's all you've to say?"

"Yeah. Good point. I should... go." At a loss for what else to do, she turned back towards the door. "I'm going to go now."

"Grace!" Robert shouted, struggling into his Dockers. "Wait!"

"You're just *leaving?* Without even raising your voice?" Jamie frowned like he couldn't understand that decision. "Sweet Jesus, how did a timid little thing like you even get mixed up with such a man? If you can't take care of yourself, someone should be watching out for your interests. Perhaps that's why you've been given to me."

Timid? Grace shot him a glare. "I'm not timid and I wasn't *given* to you."

"Oh, it's bloody clear you're mine now." He argued as if she was being totally unreasonable. "Why else can you see me? How else could you even begin to explain it? You belong to me as surely as I'm standing here."

"Except you're *not* standing there." Grace retorted, ignoring his territorial words. "...And I'm taking care of myself just fine." She tacked on a little belatedly.

"Well, prove it, then. Go over there and punch the son of a bitch."

"What good would that do?"

"T'would make him bleed! Which the wanker fucking *deserves*."

He probably did, but Grace never wanted to see blood again. Shaking her head, she headed outside with Jamie hot on her tail. "I just want to *go*." She insisted quietly.

Jamie made a frustrated sound. "Lass, confrontation is good for the soul. It's unhealthy to repress your feelings. Just beat him about the head and you'll be shocked at how much better you feel."

"Grace!" Robert fastened his belt, dashing across the lawn after her. "Darling, this was *nothing*. I swear. The woman means *nothing* to me. A passing diversion." He made a frustrated sound when she kept walking and reached out to seize her arm. "Listen to me, damn it!" He gave her an impatient shake.

Jamie's expression grew even darker. "That wanker is putting his hands on you!"

Grace tried to pry herself free, but Robert wasn't letting go.

"I wouldn't have even looked twice at her, if you weren't semi-frigid." Robert continued, his fingers digging into her flesh. "I have needs, you know. Sometimes I have to fulfil them with a cheap slut, but that pizza-tramp has nothing to do with us."

There was evidently no in-between for Robert: Women were either semi-frigid or pizza-tramps. And in that sexist dichotomy, it seemed like Grace was cast as the boring, icy, un-fun one.

He really was a wanker.

"Son of a *bitch*." Jamie was still seething about Robert manhandling her. If he could've touched anything, there would've been a whole lot of bloodshed on the professionally lawn-serviced lawn. "Grace, leave him *now*."

Like she wasn't trying. Grace finally jerked herself free of Robert's painful grip and kept heading for her car.

"But my heart belongs to *you*." Robert went passionately, still not taking the hint. He made another grab for her and Jamie all but snarled at him. Grace evaded his grasp, walking faster. "You know that. We're alike, you and I. Made for each other. All my friends say so. Don't spoil everything with some juvenile fit of jealousy."

"Donea listen to a *word* he says." Jamie warned, slanting Robert a deadly look. "If you even *think* of forgiving such a man, I will bloody well lose my mind."

Grace tuned them both out and dug her keys from her purse. Until that moment she didn't realize how little Robert mattered to her. Her family had tried to warn her that he wasn't her true Partner, but she hadn't listened.

Except, on some level, she *had*.

She'd never given Robert everything inside of her, because she'd never felt safe with him. Grace had never felt safe with *anyone*. Some part of her always held back.

Now she was angry and hurt, but her heart wasn't breaking. She wouldn't forgive him, so she didn't see the need to yell or cry. There was simply no reason to. He cheated on her and now it was over. Like flipping a light switch, her tepid feelings for him snapped off forever. Part of his appeal had always been how little he affected her. Grace could see that now.

She *had* known that he wasn't a gentleman.

Jamie's disapproval was making her feel inadequate, though. He clearly wanted her to have a huge, dramatic scene. Given the fact that he had no problem saying every thought in his invisible head, it was no wonder he couldn't understand her reticence. But the last time she'd shared all her thoughts, she'd been locked in a padded cell for a week. Grace never, *ever* wanted to go back into that hospital. Losing control, again... *No*. Just the idea panicked her.

Peaceful green cornfields.

Peaceful green cornfields.

Peaceful green cornfields.

Robert smoothed down his dark hair, casting a furtive look around. It looked like the pizza girl had used clumps of it as handles, so it stuck out in wild spikes. God only knew what the neighbors would think. "And really this wouldn't have even happened if you hadn't mixed up the dates, Grace. Honestly, how could you not know it was Thursday?"

"You're lucky I'm a ghost, ya wanker. *She* might not want to punch you, but I sure as hell would." Jamie glowered down at her. "Are you *really* going to let him get away with this?"

Grace *refused* to care about his obvious disappointment in her. Absolutely refused. "I don't like confrontations." She muttered.

"You donea like confrontations?" He echoed incredulously. "How can you not like confrontations?"

"I just *don't*, okay?"

No, it clearly wasn't okay with him. "Where's your spirit, lass?" He asked in a confused and troubled voice. Someone so extroverted would never know how scary it was for her to feel the chaos of heightened emotions. To fear that saying too much would unravel everything in her life again.

Grace unlocked the driver's side door. "I lost my spirit last year, along with everything else." She muttered. "I burned out."

"You burned out? What does that...?" Jamie stopped short. "Wait." His patriot blue eyes flashed over to hers, suddenly realizing she was acknowledging his existence. "You're speaking to me!" His handsome face lit with hope. "You're believing I'm real then?"

"No. But, I know I'm not crazy and that's enough for the moment. If I was crazy, this would all make more sense."

"What?" Robert frowned, thinking she was talking to

him. "Are you feeling alright, Grace?" He didn't bother to wait for a response, because he didn't care. "Look, I'll need to get dressed, if we're going somewhere. Since you're determined to be so childish about this, I'm willing to spend all evening making amends, but I can't be seen in public without a shirt and tie."

"Relax, Robert. *You're* staying here with Miss Pepperoni. *I'm* the one leaving and I'm not coming back."

"Thank bleeding Christ." Jamie crossed himself in relief. "*Finally* she sees reason. Maybe there's some hope for the woman, yet."

Robert wasn't nearly so thrilled by the news of their break up. "But, darling…"

Grace cut him off. "I don't think we're made for each other, Robert. In fact, I think I've been kidding myself for the past year. You see, I've just realized something very important." She climbed into the car and started the ignition, leaning forward to glower at him out the passenger's window. "I suck at being normal."

CHAPTER THREE

June 21, 1789- JMR is quite the handsomest man in town. He's also charming, energetic in his love-making, and willing to spend his gold on pretty things. Such a shame he isn't in some respectable trade or I'd convince him to marry me, regardless of what Mother and Father had to say.

But no respectable girl can have her good name linked to a pirate!

From the Journal of Miss Lucinda Wentworth

For the first time since he died, things were looking up.

Jamie smiled at Grace, hoping he appeared as nonthreatening as a specter could *possibly* appear. The girl was a jumpy little thing. He didn't want to scare her into ignoring him again. "Feeling better?"

"Well, I'm still seeing ghosts, so I'm certainly not doing great." Grace sat across from him in an overstuffed floral arm chair, drinking wine straight from the bottle, and eating ice cream for dinner. (Low fat vanilla, of course. The girl truly needed to expand her horizons.) A patchwork mountain of pillows was piled around her. They matched the rest of her mismatched furnishings. "God, this is just the worst night of my life." She muttered and drank some more wine. "Which is *really* frigging saying something."

"You're well rid of such a man, lass." Jamie detested her ex-boyfriend with a passion he'd once reserved for Red Coats. The bastard had tried to steal what was rightfully Jamie's and had not even treated her well. He wouldn't soon forget the sight of the man shaking Grace, his hand leaving angry red marks on her arm. Back in his day, Jamie would have run the wanker through with a sword. "That Robert is a waste…"

"Oh who cares about him?" She interrupted. "Jesus, Robert's the least of my problems. I watched *Grey's Anatomy*. Seeing ghosts? It usually means a brain tumor." Grace's dark curls were drawn up in a messy topknot and a few more tendrils fell around her shoulders as she shook her head. "I can't deal with a brain tumor. I don't even have health insurance anymore." She reached up to rub her forehead. "Darn it, I cried through that whole season."

"You donea have a brain tumor."

"That's probably *just* what a brain tumor would say." Grace flashed him an impatient glare. "Look, I need some time to think, alright? Why don't you go warn someone the British are coming or something? Either that or just shut up for once."

At least she was looking at him now. Jamie counted that as progress. "Of course." He agreed. He would have agreed to whatever she asked, at this point. Getting the woman to like him was of paramount importance.

"Good. Because if you're not a brain tumor, then you're real. I think that might even be worse."

"There was a time in my life when I'd take a pretty girl home and she'd like *everything* I had to say." He told her in his most charming tone.

Grace didn't look charmed. "She must've been even drunker than I am to fall for your crap." She muttered and ate a spoonful of her ordinary-flavored ice cream. "And you're *still* talking to me. I *told* you, it freaks me out when you talk to me. At least wait until I finish the whole bottle."

"I apologize. I'll wait for you to become inebriated."

"Good." Grace nodded firmly and washed down her ice cream with some more wine. Then she hesitated. "I don't normally approve of excessive drinking, you know." She tacked on in a prissy tone. "Don't think I do this kind of thing all the time. I'm a very moral person."

Jamie nearly grinned. "Oh, I donea doubt that."

"Uptight" was the modern word for her condition, if he wasn't mistaken. He'd yet to hear her mummer so much as a mild oath and she drank wine with her pinkie extended. The woman might as well wear a sign declaring herself a Sunday school teacher. She'd also changed into the most unappealing, matronly bathrobe ever sewn, so it was a real mystery to him how she managed to be so alluring.

Perhaps, it was the magic in her blood.

Even before he became a ghost, Jamie had always believed in the supernatural. He'd experienced it himself, growing up in Scotland. Fairies and spirits flited through the green hills of his homeland. They would glow in the dark night, enchanting him. As a boy, he used to point them out to his parents.

…Until he'd realized that not everyone had a kinship with the unseen world

He learned quickly that it was better to hide his gifts. To lie about what he saw. He even tried to block it out entirely, but it was impossible. He'd always felt the magic around him. Always known things that others didn't. His mother said he was kissed by the fay. His father said he was cursed by demons. Whatever you wanted to call it, Jamie had a twinkle of *knowing* about him.

And so did Grace.

There was a smidgen of the otherworldly about her. Something that hinted of feminine mysteries and untapped enchantments. Something that drew his eye and held it like no one else ever had.

She was the woman he'd waited several lifetimes for. The deepest part of him recognized her. Grace was the one. He knew it with a deep and unshakable belief that was growing stronger all the time. If she had been born in his time, he would have been certain she was his bride.

She *belonged* to Jamie.

The girl wasn't beautiful in the glittery, bawdy way that he'd been attracted to in life. She was far too thin, and scrubbed free of makeup, and her nails had been chewed to the quick. With her upturned nose and petite frame, she looked a bit like a fay herself. A repressed, timid little fay. The woman would probably faint if a man tried to kiss her. And she clearly didn't have much of a backbone, if her dealings with her harridan boss and dickhead boyfriend were any indication. Jamie had always liked strong, flashy women, who knew exactly what they wanted.

But he'd been captivated by Grace from the first moment he'd laid eyes on her.

Almost like he recognized her.

It was why he'd switched tour guides and joined Grace's Ghost Walk instead of following Nadine like he usually did. Time stretched on and on and *on* when you had an eternity to fill. Jamie spent every night wandering around Harrisonburg, listening to costumed idiots get history all wrong. Nadine did better than most. She was an elderly lady, who knew how to spin a yarn. For nine years, he'd been taking her tours. It gave him something to do. When Jamie saw Grace, though, his standard evening plans with Nadine had been abruptly cancelled.

That twinkle of knowing had told him to follow Grace.

That she was special.

She was also a bloody *horrible* tour guide. Grace missed the romance of the ghost stories, delivering the information like she was lecturing to bored twelfth graders. She was uncomfortable under all the attention, uncomfortable with the Colonial dress, uncomfortable in her own skin. Jamie had been offering her advice, because talking to himself was the only way to break the unrelenting solitude. He had absolutely no idea that she'd even know he was there.

No one else ever had. Not since 1789.

When Grace lost her temper and snapped at him, it had been the most wonderful moment of his life. And death. She *saw* him. For the first time in over two hundred years somebody *saw* him. If that didn't prove this neurotic girl had magic in her blood, he wasn't sure what did.

"Overall, I think you're taking this quite well." He assured her. "Many people would be having vapors if they saw a specter."

"Last time I had 'vapors,' they put me in a straightjacket." She muttered dourly.

Jamie had no idea what that meant. "A what?"

"Never mind." Grace ate another spoonful of ice cream, apparently forgetting that he wasn't supposed to talk to her. "I come from a family that's used to weirdness. My cousin Faith once tattooed her face because a hibiscus told her to. This is probably a lot less freaky than it should be."

"Fortunate for me."

She grunted. "So, what's it like being a ghost? Is it terrible? I bet it's terrible."

"It's terrible."

Grace nodded as if she'd expected as much. "What's the worst part? Never being able to change out of that outfit?"

Jamie frowned and glanced down at his ensemble. It had been the height of fashion when he died. "What's wrong with my outfit?"

Chocolate-brown eyes widened. "Oh... Nothing." Grace said quickly. "Nothing, at all. It's very... *bold*. Colorful." She took another gulp of wine and licked a drop from her lower lip.

The woman had bloody *perfect* lips. Lush and pink and delicately shaped. She clearly had no damn idea what to do with them, given she was forever chewing on them and twisting them into frowns, but Jamie could think of at least a dozen places he wanted to feel that soft, unpainted flesh. Sadly, there was no way that would ever happen.

Dying played hell with a man's sex life.

Not being able to touch women was so fucking unsatisfying that he'd given up voyeurism back in the 19th century. It was too depressing to watch what he couldn't have. Grace Rivera was making him reconsider that stance.

The pirate in him wanted to seize every piece of her that he could get. Jamie had always been a possessive man. What he'd stolen, he didn't give back. Grace was *his* now. Every instinct in his ghostly body wanted to claim her before some other Robert showed up and tried to steal her away. His eyes slipped down to the collar of her robe, already picturing what was underneath.

"Right. Um. So," she cleared her throat, not even noticing that he was mentally undressing her, "why are you still here? Like *on Earth,* I mean. You're not --like-- a vengeful spirit or something, right? Out to destroy the living, like in *Poltergeist?*"

"Of course not. I couldn't hurt anyone, even if I wanted to. I'm not corporeal." He waved a hand through the arm of the hideous chair to prove his point.

Grace appeared relieved. "Did you not walk into the light or something? Like in *Ghost?*" She paused. "That's a movie. You know that, right?"

"I know. I've seen it." For a man born before electricity was harnessed, Jamie had a fairly good knowledge of films and television. Over the years, the flickering images had kept him sane. "And I also saw plenty of lights when I died. ...But, only because the mob that killed me carried torches. Otherwise things stayed dim and quiet that night."

And had remained that way ever since.

If there was a Heaven, Jamie clearly hadn't been invited to the party. No angelic guides setting him on his new path. No glowing beams drawing him upward. Nothing but Jamie, all alone in an endless pit of time. He'd been a selfish, irresponsible bastard in life, so, for several decades, he'd been sure that he was in purgatory. That this was all a test or a penance. As the years passed, he began to see that it was so much more horrible than that, though. He wasn't being punished.

He'd simply been forgotten.

Jamie was forsaken in a misty realm between one plane of existence and the next. No one could see him or feel him or hear him. He didn't exist.

...Except he *did*.

He was *there*, goddamn it. Trapped and invisible, but *there*. No matter how loud he yelled or how hard he tried, he couldn't get anyone to notice that he was still a part of this world. The solitude had been never ending. Suffocating. A thousand times worse than dying. He'd given up hope of ever escaping his endless loop of days.

But now he had Grace. God had finally remembered Jamie Riordan and sent him someone who could *listen*. Sure, she lacked spirit and seemed irrational as hell, but that was a small matter considering she was also his savior.

Grace's dark brows tugged together. "It must've been terrible for you. Dying, I mean."

"Nah, t'was over in a flash. One minute, I was hanging by my neck and wishing I could breathe. The next, I was standing outside of my own body. I never felt a thing."

That was a lie. Ghosts didn't sleep, but sometimes Jamie still dreamed of murderous faces and twisting flames. In life, Jamie drank a bit, and stole a bit, and tupped more than a few willing women, but he'd never been a *truly* bad sort. At least he didn't think so, no matter what his father had claimed. Not even spending his childhood under that asshole's thumb had prepared him to witness the mindless savagery of Harrisonburg's lynch mob, though. The hatred and evil and fear. Even in death, he couldn't escape the nightmarish memories.

Grace stared at him, as if she understood the shadows passing over his face. As if she'd seen the darkness, too.

Jamie cleared his throat and glanced away from her. It was a crying shame that he couldn't have some of that merlot. …Even if it was a shockingly inferior vintage. "The hardest part of being a ghost is not being able to touch anything." He said abruptly. "You're powerless to change or interact with a single bloody thing around you."

"Well, you're sitting on that sofa."

Jamie looked down at the floral cushion. It appeared to be one of the few items in her home that hadn't been rescued from a dumpster or purchased at a yard sale. The woman was clearly on a mission to save everyone else's broken-down, forgotten, and/or homely castoffs.

The soft, flowery upholstery suited her, though. Grace Rivera struck him as a very feminine creature. The kind of lady who would've never consorted with Jamie, back when he was alive. In his day, she would've carried a dainty lace parasol, and poured tea for well-bred gentlemen callers and worn cream-colored pearls.

...And crossed the street to avoid pirates.

In this age, she was stuck in a cramped apartment with no one to challenge that wanker Robert for treating her badly. Sometimes he wondered how people like Grace endured the modern world. The meek were undefended here. Left to flounder alone, as others sped past at impossible speeds. The strong and selfish survived, while weak-spirted girls collected chipped pottery and remained nearly as forsaken as Jamie.

"I'm not sitting on this sofa." He assured her. "I'm just... hovering. Like a mist. I can't actually touch things or interact with anyone."

Although, when Grace had walked through him at Robert's house, Jamie had experienced *something*. Some electrical jolt that zinged through him like nothing else ever had.

He'd *felt* her.

Grace arched a brow, like she was reading his mind. "Then how do you explain what's happening between us?"

"I can't explain it and donea even want to." Jamie wasn't one to look a gift horse in the mouth. He had somebody, now. Another person in this world was talking to him. Seeing him. Calling them an "us." That was enough. "For whatever reason, you're the one, Grace Rivera."

"The one for what? I'm *never* the one. Why is this happening to me?"

"I donea know. There must be something special about you."

"There's not."

"To me, you are the most special person in this world." Jamie assured her. "I need you to help me clear my name."

This uptight woman was his only hope. For over two hundred years, he'd been branded a murderer. More than even dying, he hated that everyone, everywhere thought he was a killer. That, throughout history, he was disparaged and reviled. This was his one shot to prove his innocence.

Grace stared at him for a long moment. "You're out of your invisible mind."

Of course she couldn't make this easy.

Frustrated, Jamie got to his feet and restlessly moved to look at the books on her cluttered shelves. Not one romance or fairytale. Just dry historical tomes, guaranteed to bore the hell out of anyone with an ounce of passion in her soul. "Do you not own a paperback, love?"

"I'm a stable and practical person," she shot back, "except when I'm being haunted by condescending jerks." She shifted on the sofa, so she could glower at him. "Don't try to change the subject. How do you expect me to clear your name?"

"Does that mean you're drunk enough to listen to all I have to say?" Hopefully so, because Jamie was eager to fix his unlife. He had no doubt it would take some convincing to get such a timid lass to lend a hand, so he'd like to get started.

Luckily, there was quite a bit to appreciate about Grace while he waited for her to acquiesce.

His gaze flicked to the long length of her legs. The fuzzy robe had slid up to her knees when she turned, so the view was suddenly spectacular. Of the many things he admired about this century, women's fashions were high on the list. Whoever it was who'd convinced them to do away with long skirts and petticoats was a bloody genius.

"Drunk or not, I'm not sure I *want* to listen to you." Grace muttered, still not noticing his distraction. It was as if the woman didn't even consider her own appeal. "If you're not a brain tumor..."

"I'm not a brain tumor." He was bloody sick of repeating that fact.

"...then you're James MacCleef Riordan."

Finally, she was getting it. "Yes!" He moved to stand in front of her. "I'm Jamie Riordan."

"Captain of the *Sea Serpent*..."

"Yes!"

"...Patriot..."

"Yes!"

"... and notorious serial killer." Grace watched him with a brooding expression. "Did you hurt those girls?"

"*No.*" He crouched down, his eyes locked on hers. "I've never hurt a woman, Grace. I give you my word of honor."

She didn't look convinced. Hell, he didn't blame her. Even when he was alive his word of honor hadn't meant much. The girl was right to be skeptical of a cad like him.

"Gregory Maxwell, the hero of Yorktown, wrote a whole book about your crimes and his poor murdered sister." She said with an obstinate expression on her face. "*Horror in Harrisonburg.* My aunt has an original copy."

"Gregory Maxwell was the biggest moron alive, outside Parliament. I doubt he could write his own name, let alone an actual book. And he *certainly* wasn't a hero at Yorktown. He ran at the first sign of battle. Believe me, I was there."

"I've read that book at least a dozen times." Grace insisted. "It lays out all the evidence against you in a very convincing way."

"If it was even halfway comprehensible, then someone ghostwrote the damn thing for him." Jamie sighed and got to his feet, again. "No pun intended." What could he say to persuade her to help? Nothing brilliant popped to mind, so he went with the truth. "Look, whoever killed those girls put a great deal of effort into the crimes and it netted him nothing but blood. I am not a fellow who puts a great deal of effort into my crimes, unless I'm going to gain a great deal of *coin.*" Jamie arched a brow. "I was a *business man.* I cared about money and all the nice things it bought me."

He cared about having enough that no one would ever hold him prisoner, again. For thirteen years, he'd been a hostage to his father's hatred and the memories of it still shook him to the core. Ian Riordan had been a righteous and God-fearing pastor, with a dark hatred for his only child. Jamie's twinkle of knowing had damned him forever in his father's eyes.

He was an odd-duck, when Ian wanted a swan. Nothing could have convinced him than Jamie wasn't the devil, so "spare the rod" hadn't even been an option. He'd been determined to beat the magic right out of him, the way he had with Jamie's mother.

Fiona Riordan had been a shell of a woman by the time Jamie came along. Once she'd been pretty and lighthearted and saw fairies dancing in the hills, but those parts of her died in Ian's captivity. For so long, Jamie had been angry at his mother. With no way to support herself or her son, she'd squandered her life on that sadistic bastard. She'd stayed with Ian until she finally escaped into death. Maybe his mother was just afraid to leave her comfortable house and servants. Or maybe she'd made the right choice and saved them from dying on the streets. Either way, money had killed her. The lack of it, anyway.

Jamie had left Scotland the day she died, determined that he would somehow acquire enough gold to keep himself free forever. And he *had*... for all the good it did him. Damn treasure was lost, now. Buried with no map to find it, again. Stuck in the darkness.

Just like Jamie.

"You were a pirate." Grace corrected. "Not a businessman."

True enough, but he'd rather she not focus on that part of his biography. It wouldn't help to convince her he wasn't a criminal, if she knew he stole for a living. "I prefer the term 'privateer.'"

"Except you *weren't* a privateer. You were a pirate. Granted, you missed the Golden Age of Piracy by about fifty years, but you made up for that in the sheer amount of stuff you stole. You got rich by robbing merchants up and down the Eastern seaboard. And the rest of Harrisonburg thought you were guilty of far worse."

Lord, she could be a stern little thing. "They also burned a few midwives as witches. Harrisonburg's justice system wasn't exactly foolproof."

One black eyebrow arched. "No one was burned as a

witch in Virginia."

He made a face, because she was technically right. "Well, it wasn't for lack of trying, I assure you. The people of this town would've convicted a melon of a crime, if it came from the wrong family. All they cared about was having a respectable name."

Grace rolled her eyes. "Tell me about it." She muttered. "Still, *Horror in Harrisonburg* points out there was overwhelming evidence against you."

"So you said in that slanderous Ghost Walk you gave. But the evidence was *wrong*."

She kept talking. "You romanced all three of the victims, and you couldn't give an alibi for any of the disappearances, and you had a temper…"

Jamie cut her off. "I'm Scottish. Of *course*, I have a bloody temper! But *I didn't hurt those girls*." He carefully spaced out the words. "Those 'reports' of yours were given by the very fools who hanged me. You think they'd admit that *they* were the actual murderers? I did *nothing* and the wankers killed me in the street!"

"The victims…"

He cut her off. "I danced with them at the Summer Ball, but I had no reason to harm any of them. I danced with quite a few girls that night. Not all of them died!"

"Maybe *these* girls spurned you."

Jamie snorted. "Lucinda Wentworth was the only one I spoke to for more than a few moments. And I assure you, she didn't spurn me at that ball. Or later that night."

Grace blinked owlishly. "You slept with Lucinda Wentworth?"

Despite himself, he smiled at her shocked tone. "My time was not so puritanical as your time would like to believe. Miss Wentworth fancied bold men and wasn't shy about revealing her predilections." He paused, recalling Lucinda with a wry grin. "She wasn't shy about revealing *anything*, actually. Once she even…" He trailed off, because, deep down, he struggled with lamentably honorable impulses. He tried to ignore them, but they were always whispering in his head, telling him *not* to be a jackass. "Well, Lucinda was a lovely girl."

For once, Grace actually looked interested in something he had to say. Her pretty face lit up. "I've seen all the layers women dressed in back then. How did she get in and out of her clothes? Did she take *everything* off when you two met for your dates? It seems like a colossal bother to deal with all the petticoats and stays. How did it work?"

Jamie stared at her for a beat. "Do you really wish to hear what Lucinda wore to our assignations? *That's* what you want to be discussing?"

"No." She reluctantly murmured, even though she clearly wanted to discuss just that. "We can talk about something else." She paused. "I just... I mean... Did you love her?"

His lips curved at that innocent question. Perhaps there was a bit of whimsy in the girl's soul, after all. "No. T'was never a romance between us, just a bit of sport." Lucinda had never been his and he'd never been hers. They were both waiting for other people. "We were friends, though. I liked her and I have no desire to gossip about her undergarments."

Grace's head tilted. "Okay." She said with far less hostility than she'd been showing him thus far. "I respect the fact you're a gentleman."

Jamie frowned. "I'm *not* a gentleman." God, he'd nearly rather be called a serial killer again. "I just never harmed a hair on Lucinda's head. Or Anabel's or Clara's. *That's* what I'm saying."

"You're so touchy. I was giving you a *compliment*." She paused. "And they didn't *have* hair on their heads. That's some kind of evasion thing, right? All of you wore wigs back then. Even the women. Shaved heads and wigs all tallowed into place." She wrinkled her nose in a way that was quite delightful. "The smell must have been God-awful."

The Good Lord save him from this daft woman. "Can you focus on what actually matters here? We need to clear my name."

She made a face. "Except I'm still half-convinced

you're guilty."

Jamie shook his head. "You wouldn't have been sent to me if you weren't the one I was waiting for. I can't rest until I've proven my innocence. Perhaps it's why I'm still here."

"Maybe you're just not trying hard enough to leave." She retorted. "All this happened over two hundred years ago. Maybe you need to just... let it go."

"*I can't let it go*!" He roared. "I was *hanged*, woman! They put a rope around my neck and they *fucking hanged me* on the very street you walk along every day. They left my body strung up for three days, with a sign around my neck calling me a murderer! That's not something I can *let go* of!"

"You're not even trying to..."

He cut her off before she could offer another denial. "You have to help me, Grace." He scraped a hand through his hair, pacing up and down the length of her small parlor. "I need to know who's responsible for killing me. Because whoever murdered those girls? *He* was the one who should've died at the hands of that mob. Not me. *Him*. He killed me too and I want to know the bastard's name."

"That's impossible..." The phone rang, interrupting her protest.

Jamie shot it an annoyed look. Telephones were not a part of modernity that he enjoyed. They were forever making shrill infernal sounds and, more importantly, it was damn hard to eavesdrop on only one side of a conversation. That seriously impacted his social life. With no one to talk to, Jamie spent most of his time listening to *other* people talk. That was much harder to do when one of the parties was only there via a plastic contraption. It was like only seeing half of a movie. Phones, texting, email... They were all a pain in the ass.

He arched a brow when Grace sat there and let the phone ring, again and again. Odd. In his experience the living always jumped at the chance to play with their technology. "Not going to get that?" He prompted.

"Nope." Grace drank some more wine.

"Why not?"

"Because I already know who it is and my night's been lousy enough without anyone reading my mind."

CHAPTER FOUR

June 21, 1789- Eugenia and I had tea with Clara Vance today, as I was too bored to think of a reason to postpone it. Her company only added to my ennui. All she talked of was witches, for God's sake! Like the Puritans of old! Her new fixation seems to be those fortunetellers, the Riveras. Her father, the Reverend Vance, warned her they're devil spawn or some such nonsense. So she's taken to crossing herself when she passes by their shop and now my dreary sister Eugenia vows that she will, too.

I cannot imagine a more tedious Sunday afternoon!

From the Journal of Miss Lucinda Wentworth

"Grace?" The woman's voice was demanding and full of authority. "It's your Auntie Serenity. I *know* you're there, so you might as well pick up the phone. Hiding won't do any good. I'm a *psychic*, in case you've forgotten. I know *everything*."

Grace sank deeper into her collection of pillows, at least half of which were decorated with flowers or mermaids. All of her attention stayed fixed on her carton of vanilla ice cream. "I'm not hearing her say 'I told you so,' right now. No way."

"I told you so about Robert." Serenity said, as if on cue.

Grace sighed, her gaze rising up to the ceiling in a silent bid for patience.

Jamie arched a brow. "Your aunt is a psychic?"

"She's a tarot card reader, if you want to get technical. My family owns a palm reading and herb shop, here in town.

The Crystal Ball." Resigned brown eyes met his. "I'm sure you've heard of it. It's been here since the Revolution, much to Harrisonburg's dismay."

Oh, he'd heard of it alright. "Donea be telling me, you're part of *those* Riveras?" This uptight little creature came from the most eccentric band of fortunetellers this side of Richmond? Well, that explained the magic he sensed in Grace and why she was trying so hard to suppress it. Death hadn't done away with Jamie's sense of humor, so he started laughing. "Bit of the odd-duck in your family, are ya, love?"

Just like he'd been. It was a pleasant surprise to have something in common with this fay girl, even if it was just the fact they both had trouble fitting in with their relatives.

She didn't appreciate his smile. "I'm glad my dysfunctional life is funny to you."

"Oh so am I." He assured her happily. "Would have been a disaster if the only person who could see me was dull."

"Gracie?" Aunt Serenity continued. "There's no sense in sulking. I saw it all happen when I did my nightly reading on you. You're well rid of that asshole Robert. That's all I'm saying. Your cousin had a bad feeling and I *always* trust Charity's feelings, ever since she almost won the lotto that time in Florida."

"She got two numbers." Grace held up her fingers, even though her aunt couldn't very well see them over an answering machine. "Two!"

"I predicted this mess with Robert coming a mile away." Serenity boasted. "It was inevitable. If you'd listened to me, you would have spared yourself six months of tedium. Plus, the man looks as if he kisses like a sucker-fish."

Jamie chortled in delight, both at the woman's obvious hatred of that wanker Robert and at her delightful turn of phrase.

"Oh shut up." Grace snapped at him.

"I'm sure you sensed Robert was an asshole, too, but you never listen to the foolproof Rivera instincts God gave you." Serenity continued with a sigh. "You're so determined to prove you're 'normal.'" She made the word sound like it was a synonym for "scurvy." "Such a waste of talent. Grandpa Truth always said you'd inherited a huge share of the Riveras' gifts and *this* is what you do with them. It breaks my heart."

"Grace, Serenity, Charity, and *Truth?*"

"Shut *up*." Grace bit off, slanting Jamie a glower. "Everyone in my family has a virtue name. It's tradition."

"It's bloody brilliant, that's what t'is."

"Well, fine." Serenity continued blithely. "I'll give you a day or so to lick your wounds. But I expect you over here on Saturday, so you can help get the shop ready for the 4th of July sale. We can't let Madam Topanga's magic shop get the jump on us, like they did on Arbor Day. We need something *big* this time." She sighed. "If only someone had written down the family recipe for troll powder, way back when. *That* would bring in the customers."

"It's no wonder the whole family's broke." Grace told the wine bottle in a sad tone.

"Anyway, the point is, there's no sense in you wallowing in ice cream and cheap wine." Serenity counseled. "Which I don't even *need* my Tarot deck to tell me you're doing."

Grace lifted her Ben and Jerry's carton towards the phone in a silent toast.

Serenity's tone turned singsong-y. "And if it makes you feel any better, the cards tell me that you won't be alone for long. I see a tall, handsome man entering your life soon. And --trust me-- you're going to like this one. He's quite a charmer. That's all I'm saying."

Grace snorted, slanting a meaningful look in Jamie's direction. "*Snake* charmer, maybe."

"I can't wait for you to meet him. He's just *perfect* for you! I can already tell." She paused and then made an inpatient sound. "Oh! I wasn't going to say anything else, but I just can't help it. You know I'm terrible at secrets." Serenity gave a squeal of happiness. "I really think he's going to be your *Partner*. Congratulations! Try to act surprised when you meet him."

Grace froze, the spoon suspended halfway to her lips.

Jamie looked between the phone and Grace, trying to figure out what the hell that meant. The woman looked like she's seen more than just a ghost. "Partner in what?"

"Nothing." She said far too quickly. "It has nothing to do with you. Nothing at all."

His eyebrows slammed together, unaccountably pissed that she sounded so desperate to deny him. "Of course it's ta do with me! What other tall and handsome man has entered your life, recently?"

She snorted as if that indisputable logic was sheer craziness. "Well, I just started watching the *Star Wars* movies, so it's probably Han Solo."

Jamie scoffed at that. "You're being ridiculous. It's clearly *me*." He frowned. "...And you've only *just* seen the *Star Wars* movies? For God's sake, I'm *dead* and I've seen them all twice."

"Plus he wears a hat!" Serenity chirped. "I've always had a weakness for men in hats. It's so *mysterious*, don't you think?"

"I wear a hat." Jamie reminded her, warming to this topic.

"It's not you! God, can't you disappear or something? Leave me in peace."

He could make it so he was invisible to her, but he wasn't about to do such a pointless thing. Possession roared through him, louder than it had ever been. Jamie had had to fight for everything he ever wanted and this was no different. Grace was *his* and he wouldn't share her. *He* was her partner. The thought fixed in his mind and wouldn't let go. His twinkle of knowing was a damn searchlight when it came to this girl.

He pointed to his tricorne. "Han Solo doesna wear a hat."

"Fine. Indiana Jones, then."

He disregarded that foolishness. "I'm also smashingly mysterious. You see how it can be no one but me?"

Grace rolled her eyes. "Please. You talk too much to be mysterious."

"You could use a charming mystery man in your life." Serenity decided. "They're the very best cure for all of life's problems. And they usually look *spectacular* naked. That's all I'm saying."

"That's *never* all you're saying." Grace muttered.

Serenity gave a trilling laugh, as if she'd somehow heard that remark. "Ta for now, darling."

Jamie smiled as she hung up the phone. "And just so you know... I *do* look spectacular naked." He assured Grace without a drop of modesty.

"For the last time, she's *not* talking about you!"

"Of course she is. Who else could she be meaning?"

"Someone who's not dead, maybe?"

Jamie winced a bit, his certainty fading under the unrelenting truth of her words. "Well, that's hardly my fault." He muttered, refusing to be hurt.

The logical part of him knew it was pointless to care about this "partner" absurdity. Whatever it meant to Grace, it was the province of the living and he was no longer one of them. She was the one he'd been waiting for. Alive or dead, Jamie would have known that with all the magic inside of him. He recognized her with a certainty that defied explanation.

...But what good did that do for *Grace?* He was still a ghost. He needed her, but it was no true partnership. It couldn't be.

She *didn't* need him.

In his whole life and afterlife, Jamie wasn't needed by anyone. Growing up, he'd heard that enough times that it had imbedded itself into his psyche. In fact, "No one fucking needs you!" had been the last thing his father shouted after him when Jamie left home forever. It was possibly the only time the old man was completely right. In the two hundred and fifty years since that day, nothing had proven him wrong, that was for damn sure. Nobody had *ever* needed him. No one ever would. Certainly not this fay creature of ice cream and mermaid pillows and clean, shiny hair.

Grace stared up at Jamie for a beat like she could see

into his thoughts. "I'm sorry." She said softly. "I love my aunt, but she drives me nuts sometimes. It's not your fault that I got upset. It's just been a *really* bad day, okay? Let's just get back to the whole 'clearing your name' thing."

If she was willing to discuss finding the truth behind the murders, Jamie didn't have much of a choice but to follow her lead. No doubt she knew that and it was exactly why she was suddenly so eager to tackle the subject. The whole situation still pissed him off, though.

"You just told me clearing my name is impossible." He reminded her sarcastically. "Where else can the conversation go?"

"It *is* impossible. Whoever killed those girls, the evidence against him is probably long gone. You can trust me on this. I used to be a crime scene investigator."

Jamie stopped brooding and gaped at her. "Like on TV?" Sudden joy filled him. With Grace, there was always some new reason for hope. He was beginning to see that. She was forever opening doorways that he'd thought were sealed tight. He could never stay irritated with this small, fay miracle sent to save him. "You know about fingerprints and such?"

"Hang on, ghosts watch TV?"

"What else would I be doing with eternity? I can't exactly hold a book." He demonstrated his insubstantial-ness by passing his hand back and forth through a particularly hideous lamp with a flamingo painted on it. Bleeding Christ, it was like the girl made it her mission to rescue all the hopeless furnishings in Virginia and give them a home. "Movies and television have made my unlife bearable."

Once again, she seemed absurdly fascinated with the wrong thing. "What kind of shows do ghosts like? I mean aside from multiple viewings of *Star Wars*."

"I donea know any other ghosts, so I can't be sure. Personally, I like that show with the magical high school best. The one with the bonnie little cheerleader, who hunts werewolves and loves the Frankenstein boy. They get the facts of ghosts all wrong, but it's quite a nice production."

"*Haunted High*?" Her eyebrows soared. "The teen

soap opera?"

"That's the one." Jamie nodded. "But I watch other shows, too. I can't change the channel, so I have to watch whatever the living do. And about a dozen shows on television are about murders that get solved in an hour, thanks to the computers. *More* than a dozen. Sometimes I think that's the only plot your writers can think of." And it was exactly what he needed. Someone to use the magic of science to clear his name. "You solve murders professionally?"

"I *used* to be a small part of solving murders, but I don't anymore. I told you, I burned out."

So she'd said, except Jamie had no idea what that meant. "Burned out?"

"Yeah, burned out. As in, I used to investigate blood spatter and collect DNA evidence, but now I give ghost tours for minimum wage."

"But you have the skills to..."

She shook her head, cutting him off. "I can't go back to what I was doing. I'll have another breakdown and I can't have another breakdown. Normal people don't have breakdowns."

"Didn't we establish that you're a bit abnormal, lass? I mean --Jesus, Mary, and Joseph-- you're seeing ghosts."

The woman didn't like hearing that opinion. She heaved a pillow at him and only seemed to get angrier when it passed right through his body. "God! You are the most annoying person I've ever met!"

"Nonsense. I met that wanker Robert and he's *far* more annoying than me. Aunt Serenity is right. The man's a complete asshole."

Just *thinking* about him put Jamie in a foul mood, again. His jaw tightened every time he recalled the way Robert grabbed Grace's arm, jerking her to a stop when she tried to walk away from him. It kept playing in his head on a loop, reminding him that he was essentially useless to Grace. The same way he'd been useless when his bastard of a father had manhandled his mother. Robert could have harmed Grace right in front of his eyes and there wasn't a damn thing Jamie could've done about it.

"He's a bad man, Grace. I donea know why you didn't realize it sooner." Jamie paused. "Also his taste is just *abysmal*. Both in furnishings and in women, if he fancied that shrill pizza girl."

Grace hesitated for a beat, realizing there was a compliment buried in there somewhere. Large brown eyes blinked in surprise, just as they had when he'd talked of her beauty back at Robert's. Even a small bit of flirting seemed to befuddle her. "Thank you." She said with a bemused frown. "I think."

Jamie's gaze traced over her amazed face. "You're welcome."

Who would choose another girl over Grace? It made no sense, but he supposed he should thank Robert for his stupidity. Grace had left the wanker and that was all that mattered. Not only was Robert a dangerous man, but Jamie couldn't tolerate the idea of another male having a claim on her. Maybe he *was* just a ghost, but he hated the idea of some living, breathing rival, who could offer her things Jamie couldn't.

The woman was his.

"I'd be happy to haunt the bastard, if you'd like." Jamie offered helpfully. "Least I can do."

Grace drew in a deep breath and muttered something about cornfields again. "I'm *trying* to be normal, alright?" She said. "Maybe it's a work in progress, but I'm not having you paranormally torment my ex and I'm *certainly* not helping you CSI a two hundred year old murder case. Those are not things normal people do."

Jamie wasn't giving up. "Someone *killed* those girls. Two hundred years ago or not, they were *real* people and they *really* died. They deserve to have their murderer brought to justice."

"You *were* brought to justice."

"*Except I didn't bloody do it!*"

The two of them glowered at each other for a long

moment and then Grace looked away, her lips pressed together. "Peaceful green cornfields. Peaceful green cornfields." She rubbed her temples. "Peaceful. Green. Cornfields."

God, but she drove him batty when she did that. Jamie sighed and got himself under control. The last thing he wanted was to antagonize Grace. "I apologize for shouting at you." He held up his palms. "I just want you to believe me."

"Well, I *don't*." She slouched down in her chair, brooding. "And I'm right about the wigs, too."

Jamie threw up his hands at her slightly tipsy stubbornness. "Bleeding Christ..."

"It's true! They have a whole lecture on it at the Harrisonburg wig maker's shop and I've been to it *twice*."

He would never understand why twenty-first century mortals wanted to squander their holidays in Harrisonburg. Back in the 1940s, when the historical society had first proposed the idea of becoming a tourist attraction, he'd laughed his ass off. How could learning about wigs and horseshoes *ever* be entertaining? The eighteenth century hadn't been all that stimulating the first time around. He almost felt sorry for the modern world, if that's how they had fun. He'd had *far* better ways to spend his time, when he was alive.

He wasn't stupid enough to tell Grace any of that, though. For whatever reason, she liked dull things and he was in no position to burn bridges. He backed off, for the moment. "Not everyone wore wigs." He said, going for a safer topic and calmer tone.

"Yes, they did." The woman clearly couldn't hold her liquor worth a damn. It brought out the confrontational side that she claimed not to have. T'was quite adorable. "Is that even your real hair?"

"Aye, every strand."

"Because it's a very beautiful color." She sounded irritated by that, too. "I've never known anyone with hair that was all auburn-y gold like that. I saw a picture of you in a history book and I thought it had to be a wig. *All* of you wore wigs back then."

"I didn't." His mouth curved, liking the fact that she liked his hair.

Grace made a face. "I should have bought more wine at the supermarket. One bottle clearly isn't going to be enough to make you tolerable."

"No one should *ever* buy wine at a supermarket. Life is far too short to settle."

"Oh Lord. Tell me you're a wine snob, too."

"Well, if I could still eat, drink, or taste, I'd surely be more selective than you are." He paused, still irritated by Robert's very existence. "Being a wee bit more discriminating in *all* areas of life would benefit you greatly, if you want my opinion."

"I *am* discriminating." She snapped. "Incredibly, seriously, *amazingly* discriminating, for your information."

Jamie arched a brow.

"Well, how was I supposed to know that Robert was such a louse?" She demanded, correctly interpreting his skepticism. "That doesn't count against me. He seemed pleasant enough and totally safe."

"Pleasant and safe. A rousing endorsement for any man."

Grace glanced away. "All I've ever wanted is to feel safe." The words were barely a whisper.

Jamie's heart hadn't beat in over two hundred years, but he swore it gave a lurch at that soft confession. His lips parted wanting to offer her his protection. ...But that was pointless. What bloody good could a ghost be? He closed his mouth, calling himself a fool. The woman should have someone *alive*. Some solid and respectable gentlemanly partner, who could provide her with security and a happy future. Jamie knew that.

But he needed her too much to care.

He shook his head refusing to even consider the deeper ramifications of claiming Grace for his own. If he thought about the impossibilities of it, he might discover something he didn't want to find. She was *his*. That was all that really mattered.

Grace was rallying again. "Anyway, I was very happy to go out with someone so husband material-y. His behavior is *very* disappointing. Plus, now I'm going to have to take back the birthday gift I bought for him, which will be a real pain, since I didn't keep the receipt. What am I going to do with a beige tie?"

Jamie made a face at her vaguely inconvenienced tone. "You would have been miserable with such a man. You just caught him cheating on you and you're barely caring at all! Obviously it wasn't a love match."

"Maybe not, but after the year I've had, I needed some stability, alright?" She frowned in deep thought. "But the next time I get a boyfriend, I'm going to hold out for a guy who wakes up the pizza-tramp part of me. It seemed like it would be a lot more fun."

Jamie wasn't even going to touch that comment. "What happened last year?" He asked instead.

Her lips compressed into that familiar mutinous line. "Nothing."

"Is that 'nothing' the reason you burned up?"

"Burned *out*." She muttered and ate some more ice cream. "And that's none of your business."

Jamie tried not to notice the way her tongue licked over the spoon. For a fleeting second it occurred to him that he'd been wrong before. The worst aspect of being a ghost was being unable to kiss Grace Rivera's lush mouth. To feel those perfectly shaped lips beneath his, tasting the essence of her and swallowing the gentle sounds she made.

Of course, even if he was still alive, he wouldn't have been allowed to touch her. Ladies like Grace were looking for "husband material." Someone normal and pleasant to keep them safe. Jamie was nothing more than a passing diversion to everyone he met.

God, but that pissed him off.

"You might as well tell me what happened to you."

Jamie flopped down in the seat across from Grace. "I'm going to be here for the next seventy years, so there's no sense in keeping secrets."

She froze, her gaze jumping back to his. "*Seventy years?* Wait, what do you mean seventy years?"

"Well, you're --what-- thirty?"

"Thirty-two, but..."

Jamie cut her off. "Still very young for your century." He assured her. "Now, I donea understand all of the medical advances of this time period, but I've seen that they work wonders. A hundred-and-two will be a perfectly average age, when you're an old woman. I've no doubt that you'll live to see it."

"Even if I do, *you're* certainly not going to be there. You have to *go*, Jamie."

That was the first time in nearly a quarter of a millennium that someone had addressed him by name. The sound of it melted Jamie's insides and hardened his resolve. For whatever reason, this girl had been given to him. Handed into his care. He wasn't sure why or how, but he knew she was a gift from Heaven itself. Without Grace, he was nothing at all. Just a lost voice, screaming into a void.

Prickly or not, he would never, *ever* leave her.

"Oh no, lass." Jamie shook his head. "As long as I'm stuck in this plane, I'm going to be right by your side. And since I sure seem to be stuck here until my name is cleared... and you won't help me clear my name," he shrugged helplessly, "it looks as though we'd best be getting used to each other's company."

He reached over to give her knee a pat and that strange electrical charge zapped through him again. Ghosts didn't need to breathe, but Jamie still released a shuddering breath. He hadn't been imagining it before. He could feel her. Jamie's hand couldn't make contact with her skin, but he could *feel* her.

And she felt better than anything he could imagine.

So many times, over the decades and centuries, he'd tried to recall what it was like to be alive. To be able to touch someone. To have them know he was there. To *feel* them. As hard as he'd tried to cling to the memories, the reality of it was overwhelming. Feeling Grace Rivera was simply… magic.

Maybe she really was part fay.

Grace felt him, too. She jerked back, looking frantic. "No! I mean it, no *way* are you staying here. I have a nice, normal life to live and it can't be infested with spirits." She waved a hand around. "I don't care how sexy your accent is, you're *leaving*."

Jamie decided to focus on the positive aspects of that rant. "I like your accent, too, lass. Southern ladies always have the nicest drawls."

She appeared ready to strangle him. Too bad the lynch-mob had beaten her to it.

"I don't have a…" She stopped and took a deep breath. "No. This isn't going to work. I see what you're doing, but, no matter what you threaten or try, I'm *not* helping you solve those murders." She staggered to her feet, hampered by her bulky bathrobe and the unaccustomed quantities of wine she'd consumed. "I just can't, okay? I'm sorry. I wish you luck, but I'm afraid our association is over. I am going to go in my room and close the door. Come morning, you will be gone and I'll pretend this was all a dream."

"No, I donea think so." Jamie stacked his hands behind his head and leaned back in the chair. "I'm content to stay right here in my new home." He looked around with a sigh. "Granted, it's not the furniture *I* would've chosen, but we're both making compromises in this relationship, so I'll endure."

Emotion put color into her face and made her even lovelier. "We don't *have* a relationship and this *isn't* your home! *I'm* the one who pays the rent and I want you gone!"

"You say that *now*, but I'm a grand fellow to have about. Very witty and *full* of useful advice."

"I don't want your advice!"

"Open your mind, lass! I can help you select your next beau, so you donea end up with another rotter like Robert." Lie. He had no intention of letting any other man near her. "I can follow along on your job each day, so you get all your historical facts straight." Another lie. Grace needed to find other employment, because being a tour guide was clearly crushing her spirit. "Oh and I've got a tremendous singing voice." Damnable lie of there ever was one, but pirates weren't known for their scrupulous honesty. "Why, in a few decades, you'll wonder how you ever got along without me."

Her perfect lips pressed together in frustration. It was a crying shame what she did to that lush mouth. Never letting it smile and forever compressing it into disagreeable lines. "You can't just move into my apartment. I won't allow it."

"How do you plan to stop me?"

Brown eyes narrowed, desperately trying to think of a way to physically boot a ghost out the door. There wasn't one, of course. There was nothing harder to get rid of than a specter intent on staying put.

Jamie waited for her to see it was hopeless.

"I'll give it three days." She finally said in a tight voice. "For three days, I will try my very best to identify your eighteenth-century madman. But you leave on the 4th of July. Got it? When I show you that it's impossible to locate a suspect who's been dead for two hundred years, you *accept* it and vanish out of my life. Agreed?"

Jamie nearly scoffed at that. He was a ghost with a mission and he'd see it fulfilled no matter how long it took. Three days or three decades, it meant nothing to him. And, either way, he *certainly* didn't plan to leave Grace's side. So long as he was trapped on Earth, he would be within five feet of this girl.

No way in hell would he go back to the solitude without her.

"Agreed." Another lie, but she really should know better than to trust his word on the matter. After all, only gentleman had to honor their deals and, dead or alive, Captain James MacCleef Riordan was certainly no gentleman.

CHAPTER FIVE

June 22, 1789- I saw Agatha Northhandler punch a man for stealing twine from her shop today. I think it was quite common. Women need not resort to violence. We can get our own way by using subtler means. The only time a true lady should be around blood is when she's thanking the Good Lord not to be pregnant.

From the Journal of Miss Lucinda Wentworth

"This is a total waste of time." Grace had been repeating that all morning, but a certain jackass ghost wasn't listening. "I'm telling you it won't work."

In an effort to not look like a crazy person when she talked to him in public, Grace wore a Bluetooth earpiece. Hopefully, it would seem like she was really pissed off at someone on the other end of the phone line... rather than being really pissed off at someone invisible to everyone else in the room. So far it seemed to be working, which made her feel kinda smug. Like she was accomplishing something.

Wait... was she actually *proud* of succeeding at craziness? This was seriously getting out of hand.

Jamie shrugged, looking gorgeous and inflexible. Did ghosts sleep? He certainly seemed well-rested, which just irritated her more. "I have nothing *but* time, so it matters not how much of it we waste. It's one of the perks of being dead."

"One of the perks of being *alive* is sleeping in on Saturdays. Or at least it *should* be." She slanted him a glare. "Yet here I am."

"It's Friday, lass."

"Oh shut up."

The two of them stood with a group of twenty tourists in the grand parlor of the Wentworth mansion. It had been meticulously restored to its Colonial era glory, complete with shiny antique furniture, plenty of status-symbol silver on display, and vivid floral-patterned wallpaper. It really was one of the nicest homes in Harrisonburg.

Jamie was quick to point out every inch of fabric and piece of flatware that the restoration got wrong, of course. The man was impossible to please. ...And really, *really* handsome. It was amazing how handsome he was. Even more amazing to her than his ghost-ness.

That didn't mean he was her Partner, though.

"Just in case you need to know for our investigation, the room looked *nothing* like this when the Wentworths were alive." Jamie informed her, not shutting up. He *never* shut up. "The mantle was different, the furniture was different, and the walls weren't this god-awful powder blue." He snorted. "And Lucinda would be shrieking her head off if she knew they'd chosen *that* portrait to hang here for all eternity. She never did like it. Said Eugenia's glower ruined the whole canvas."

Grace glanced at the painting of the Wentworth daughters. Lucinda had a point. Her sister *was* glowering. Probably because poor, plain, pinch-lipped Eugenia was being completely upstaged completely by the beautiful debutant sitting next to her.

Lucinda had blonde hair and an aristocratic nose, her curvy figure cinched into a décolletage revealing period gown. In the modern world, she no doubt would have been president of her sorority, dedicated to keeping the Eugenias and Graces on campus away from all the football players. There was a knowing gleam in Lucinda's blue eyes that told you she was secretly a bitch to all the other girls in town. A smug glint of malice, like she had a dirty little secret she wasn't telling.

That secret was probably what Jamie looked like naked.

Just the idea of that pissed Grace off.

...Not that she would ever seriously consider dating a pirate, of course. Grace was only interested in serious relationships and James Riordan was *not* a serious relationship kinda ghost. Hell, he could star in a PSA about why smart girls should stay far away from *anti*-husband material men. Plus, he was dead. A woman would have to be nuts to get mixed up with him, no matter how gorgeous he was.

And he was really, *really* gorgeous.

Grace glanced up at him, trying not to notice all the star-spangled angles of his American Hero profile. She wasn't sure about Lucinda's picture, but that portrait of Jamie in the history book did him no justice, at all. It missed the golden sheen to his hair and the perfect tan of his skin. Weren't ghosts supposed to be more see-through?

It would be a lot easier to deal with him if he wasn't so darn visible.

Her phone buzzed in the pocket of her sundress, indicating that Robert had sent her yet another text. Grace rolled her eyes. How was he not getting the hint? It was *over*. She was actually relieved to be free of him, so the last thing she needed was the jackass stalking her, now. She had so many more important things to focus on than his whining.

"What was that?" Jamie asked.

"Nothing." No way was she telling him about the twenty-eight unanswered messages on her phone. Jamie would seriously not appreciate Robert begging for another chance. His hatred of her ex was as clear as the Liberty Bell.

He didn't look convinced by her quick denial. "I think your portable telephone is chiming?" It came out sounding like a question. Technology seemed to confuse Jamie. No doubt because the closest his time period had come to a global communications network was "one if by land, two if by sea."

Grace ignored his confusion and went back to his earlier complaint. "And *of course* the house has changed." She told him, wanting to keep the conversation away from Robert. The morning was stressful enough without Jamie's complaints about her lack of spirit and long rants full of Gaelic cursing. "It's been two hundred *years*. That's what I've been trying to get through to you. It's crazy to think we're going to find any evidence of Lucinda's disappearance."

"Nonsense. I have great faith in you." He insisted with the stubborn mindset of someone who had no clue what forensic work really entailed. "TV shows always begin their investigation at the scene of the crime. We must do the same. Now, you promised me three days of investigation, so search for clues, woman." He waved a hand around, like all she needed to do was whip out a Sherlock Holmes-sized magnifying glass and shout, "Elementary, my dear Watson!"

Grace shook her head in frustration. A couple of reruns of *Criminal Minds* and suddenly everyone thought they could do her job. No. Her *ex*-job. "Fine. Whatever. But I'm only doing this to humor you, because we're not going to find anything."

"You've a very negative attitude, Grace. I prefer to live in hope."

"You're not living, *at all*." Grace muttered, but she grudgingly refocused on their goal.

Lucinda Wentworth's former home was owned by the Harrisonburg Historical Society, which gave tours every day at nine, twelve, and two. Since it was the only one of the murder victims' houses opened to the public, it seemed like the best place to start. It was simple enough for Grace to join the group of morning tourists eager to see a Colonial era mansion. A lot of people worked for the town, so no one recognized her as an employee or asked why she was buying a ticket to a historic home on her (forced) day off.

Actually two tickets.

Grace had accidently bought one for Jamie, too, before it occurred to her that he wouldn't need it. It seemed to simultaneously amuse and charm him, which was embarrassing. It was just hard to remember that he was a ghost. Not just because it was frigging *impossible* that he was a ghost, but because Jamie seemed incredibly alive.

He was clever, and charming, and curious about everything. As a conversationalist, he was way better than Grace had ever been and he'd been dead for two-hundred plus years. When she wasn't fascinated by some anecdote he was telling, it kinda pissed her off. She was a social disaster these days, but Jamie could no doubt host his own talk show: *Undead and Awesome.*

"Bloody listen to this nonsense." Jamie shook his head in dismay as the tour guide droned on about the furnishings. "This town must strive to hire the worst storytellers in Virginia."

Grace slanted him a glare.

Jamie didn't seem to notice. "We need to begin our investigation now, because I donea know how much longer I can endure this madness. The man has been talking for ten minutes about floor cloths. And those *aren't* the Wentworths' floor cloths. They look nothing like them! It's like I'm in hell, only it's boring."

Grace felt the need to defend the poor guide from Harrisonburg's biggest tour critic. "We're visiting a historical house. What do you want him to talk about? The Super Bowl?"

Jamie wasn't appeased by that logic. "And --Jesus, Mary, and Joseph-- why are *floor cloths* even on this tour? Why would anyone waste a glorious summer morning looking at some old piece of canvas we used as a rug? Have you all so much time to spare that you can just squander it?" He sighed, like he was the only one in the room with any common sense. "Life is wasted on the mortals of this era."

Grace wasn't in the mood for a "my century is better than your century" debate. Not without even her customary four hours of sleep to bolster her. Grace never slept well. The dreams were too overwhelming. Last night, though, she'd just stayed awake, staring at her ceiling, panicked and full of doubt.

Not over the fact that she'd made a deal with a frigging ghost.

No, she was handling that part with surprising ease, all things considered. Jamie might befuddle her, but she wasn't frightened or freaked out by his presence. Rivera DNA meant she accepted the supernatural far too easily. In fact, it was kind of almost a little bit ...nice having someone around. Even if he was a jackass.

What terrified her was going back to work as a forensic

tech, even if it was just for a few days. The job had nearly broken her last time. She didn't want to give it another chance. But unless she wanted to listen to Jamie whine for the rest of her life, she didn't really have much of a choice. Grace had promised him three days and she kept her promises.

Also, she hated to admit it but a *tiny* part of her believed him when he said he was innocent. Maybe she always had. That picture of him had been drawing her in since she was fifteen, after all. Something in his face convincing her that he hadn't really killed those girls. Clearing his name was the right thing to do, for Jamie and the victims.

But that didn't mean it was going to be easy.

"We need to ditch the rest of the tour and get upstairs." She lowered her voice, hoping none of the tourists overheard her. Luckily, they now seemed enthralled with the original floorboards. "We have to look in Lucinda's bedroom. That's where she disappeared, so we need to start there." She paused meaningfully. "I'm guessing you know where that is."

"You've a prurient mind, Mistress Rivera. I like that in a lass." Jamie glanced towards the stairs, which were through an archway behind them. "They've a velvet rope erected in front of the steps. You'll need to get around it. Then I can lead you to her room."

"*Sneak* around it, you mean." Grace could already feel her blood pressure rising at the idea. "I'm probably going to be arrested and thrown in jail for this. I hope you know that."

"Oh, it's not merely prison for an offense so grave as leaving a tour. T'would be the stocks for sure." He smiled widely at the glower she flashed his way. "Oh, donea be so cantankerous. Just walk up the stairs as if you've every right to do it and all will be fine."

"That's a *terrible* idea."

"No one will stop you if you seem confident. They'll be too afraid of looking a fool if they question you. Always act as if you know *exactly* what you're doing and you can get away with anything. T'is the secret of life."

"Yeah, that probably works great for attractive, pirate-y scoundrels, but --I guarantee-- it won't work for a normal person like me."

His face brightened. "You think me attractive?"

"Oh shut *up*." Grace eased towards the door, hoping to slip out of the room unnoticed. Instantly, it felt as if everybody was staring at her, even though she could see they were all focused on the guide. Grace's grip tightened on her bag, her body barely moving.

"Good Christ, woman. You're stiff as a board and your eyes are darting about like you're expecting the devil himself to be after ya. *Relax*. You could not be looking more suspicious if you were trying."

"You're *really* not helping." She couldn't do this. The longer she stood there, the more she realized it was impossible. She would be caught. She'd go to jail. She'd lose her job. She'd be thrown out of her apartment and have to live on the streets. She'd...

"Grace." Jamie's voice broke through her escalating panic and she automatically looked his way. He caught hold of her eyes and didn't let go. "It will be alright." He said quietly. "I promise you, I'll keep you safe."

Drat.

Grace moved. Without making the conscious decision to take even a single step, she was suddenly halfway across the room. She made it to the doorway and tried to remember how to breathe. So far so good. Now how was she going to do the rest of this? "Go check if anyone is coming down the hall." She got out frantically. "I don't want to get caught."

Jamie rolled his eyes like she was being silly. "I used to make my living sneaking about the seven seas, you know. And a ship is a great deal harder to hide than a wee girl. I think I know how to..."

"Just go do it!"

Jamie held up his hands in surrender. (God, he had beautiful hands.) "Fine." He strolled his invisible self into the hallway and made a production of looking around. "You see? No constables are coming to arrest you. I told you, I will let nothing happen to you."

Peaceful green cornfields.
Peaceful green cornfields.
Peaceful green cornfields.

Grace took a deep breath and skirted into the hall. She ducked under the velvet ropes cordoning off the steps and hurried up the steps two at a time. It only took five seconds, but by the time she reached the upper landing, she was pretty sure she was having a heart attack from panic. No one had seen her. Or at least no alarms and sirens were blaring. That was good news. Right?

God, she was losing her mind.

How in the world had he convinced her to do that? Why had she felt safe enough to try? Grace never felt safe with *anyone*, but now she was willing to trust an adrenaline junkie ghost? Maybe she was sick. She paused in the shadows to take her pulse, already expecting the worse. See? Her heart was going too fast. First she'd keel over of a coronary and *then* she'd get tossed in a prison cell, all because of Jamie.

The oblivious moron wore an encouraging grin. "You've done it! And faster than I ever expected, given your natural pessimism. I knew you had it in ya! It can be quite fun to break the rules, when you give it a go."

Satisfied she wasn't having a heart attack (yet), Grace focused on the idiot ruining her life. "This is not fun, Jamie." She hissed. "I just want to get it over with as quickly as possible, so I can go home and take a Valium."

He made a tsk sound. "You've got to overcome your weak spirit, lass. It's stifling all your potential. There's nothing wrong with being a bit of an odd-duck. Live your truth."

Grace rolled her eyes. He did love his pop-psych crap. She seriously needed to call her cousin Blessing for an anti-ghost spell.

...Or maybe not. The last spell Blessing cast gave Grace green hair for three weeks. Spells *always* went wrong. They were the worst kind of magic, in her opinion. Totally unpredictable. She'd probably just end up with *two* Jamies bitching at her.

"I'm *not* weak spirited or an odd-duck." Grace scowled

at him. "I just like to follow the speed limit, pay my taxes on time, and obey the law. That's being a responsible adult."

"It's being a smashingly dull adult."

"At least no one's lynched me, yet." Grace headed down the upstairs corridor. "Is her room this way?"

"Aye, last one on the left." Jamie followed along behind her, looking irritated. "I wasn't lynched for anything I *did*, ya know. My having a bit of fun with Lucinda and dancing at a ball didn't kill those girls. Hardly fair to blame me for the town being so bloody stupid."

"You were a convenient scapegoat, given your reputation." She glanced up at him. "I don't suppose you have an alibi for any of the disappearances?"

"I was getting drunk at The Raven when Lucinda disappeared. I was there late into the night and then I was passed out in my cabin on the *Sea Serpent*."

"None of your men could verify that."

"Because they were drunk, too! They were bloody sailors!"

Grace rolled her eyes again. "What about when the other girls went missing?"

"How the hell should I know where I was back then? It's damnably hard to recall all the details, when I'm not even sure exactly *when* they vanished."

"Well, the 'details' mean the difference between solving this case or not, so I suggest you try to regain your memory." She arched a brow, just to needle him. "Unless you have a *reason* for your amnesia. The murders stopped after you died, after all. Gregory Maxwell's book tells us that no other girl's disappeared after you were gone. The Hero of Yorktown found that very coincidental."

Jamie's expression darkened. "Gregory Maxwell was *not* the sodding Hero of Yorktown and I did *not* kill anyone, Grace."

"The first serial killings in America all happen within a week of each other." She pointed out, warming to her topic. "That's the behavior of a perpetrator who's gotten a taste for it.

Someone who's going to keep escalating, until he's caught."
She paused. "Then you're hanged and there were no more
killings."

"Except I. Didn't. Bloody. *Do it*." Each word was bit off
like a bullet. "What can I say to make you believe that?"

"I *do* believe it." Really, she did. She'd met killers and
this man wasn't one of them. "It's just hard to separate these
crimes from seeing…" Grace trailed off and shook her head.
"Never mind. Forget it."

Jamie didn't look ready to forget it. "Separate them
from seeing what?"

"Bad things." Anyone with half a brain would've heard
the finality of those words.

Jamie frowned, not pleased with her refusal to confide
in him. Centuries of isolation had obviously left him desperate
for some kind of human connection and she was his only
option. The man wanted to know everything about her. If he
was corporeal, he'd no doubt be reading her diary and
searching through her underwear drawer. "You know, there's
no harm in telling me your secrets. I'm the very best friend you
have."

"You've *got* to be kidding me."

"It's true! You are more important to me than anyone
else, alive or dead. It would be safe to need me back, just a bit.
I wouldn't mind, a'tall." He paused and tacked on with a
suspicious amount of innocence: "I truly could be a grand
partner."

"You're *not* my Partner, Jamie." He couldn't be. "You
don't even understand what it really means." The Riveras were
the ones who gave the word all its capitalized subtext. It was
their family shorthand for the best kind of magic. Even Grace
respected Partners and she worked hard to distance herself
from the supernatural.

"Well, explain it then! What's the point of keeping
things from me? It's not as if I can share your confidences with
anybody else, is it?"

"Not everyone likes to blurt out every thought in their
head."

"Usually, that's only because they're hiding something."

Grace pointedly ignored that, because there was nothing to say. She reached Lucinda's door and pushed it open with a bit more force than necessary.

The bedroom was being used as storage, with piles of cardboard boxes and random furniture. Grace hoped they weren't planning to throw out any of the old knickknacks that were haphazardly arranged on every surface. A little glue and paint and most of them could be saved. She hated to see old things just tossed away, like they'd never meant anything to anyone. Like they had no purpose, just because they'd gotten a few dings.

Everything deserved a second chance at life.

Jamie looked around, an amazed expression on his face. "It looks so different." He whispered.

Grace cleared her throat. "So this is the last place Lucinda Ann Wentworth was seen. Sunday, June 28th, 1789." She began, like it was any other crime scene. "Did you meet with her at all that day?"

"Aye. I saw her in the morning, while the rest of the household was at church. She pleaded a headache and begged off. I stopped by to pay my respects and inquire after her well-being."

Grace sifted through that garbage. "She played sick, so you could sneak in and have sex?"

He shot her a sideways look, amused by her bluntness. "Aye."

"What time did you leave?"

"Just before ten. It was the last I ever saw her."

"You're sure?"

"I was nearly caught pant-less by her sister Eugenia, so I recall it well. The pinched-lipped little thing came back early and I had to hide in the kitchen, with only a flour sack to cover me." He made a face. "Believe me, that part sticks in my mind."

Despite herself, Grace's mouth twitched upward.

"You're completely blowing my image of staid and respectable Olde Harrisonburg, I hope you know that."

Jamie shrugged unrepentant. "Lucinda had a laugh over my predicament, too. She finally tossed me my clothes out the window and I saw her wave goodbye. The next day, I heard she'd disappeared in the night."

"Were you worried?"

"Yes and no. At first, I wondered if she'd left with some man. We all did. Eugenia heard her sneaking out, sometime after midnight. There'd been whispers of Lucinda seeing someone far more important than me."

"Do you have any idea who?"

He shook his head. "No, but she was conscious enough of her place in society that she wouldn't have settled for anything less than marriage. Even eloping would have been out of character for Lucinda. She would have insisted on a large wedding, to show off a bit. When I considered that, I knew she hadn't run away." He paused. "Besides, she never would've left all her frocks and jewelry behind."

"Did she have any enemies?"

"Lucinda had dreams to marry a rich man and move to the biggest house his money could buy. Have fancy balls and exclude half the town." He shrugged. "Maybe she'd pissed off a few other lasses with her flirting ways, but no one would want her dead for it."

"Seems like someone did."

Jamie's jaw ticked. "I've always supposed it was some bastard she'd turned down. Figured he'd just take what she wouldn't give." He looked around as if he was still remembering the cluttered bedroom as it had once been. "She deserved more than being dragged away in the night."

"Lucinda probably never left this room alive."

He frowned as if that idea hadn't occurred to him. "What?"

"According to Eugenia, Lucinda went to bed around nine." Grace set down her oversized bag and took out her makeshift forensic kit. She'd never thought she'd be using any of it again, but she'd kept a lot of her tools. "Her parents were already asleep down the hall. Around midnight she heard a noise that she thought was her sister sneaking out. In reality, it was probably someone sneaking *in*. The next morning Lucinda was gone and so were the bed linens, but nothing else. Add it altogether and it sounds like murder, not kidnapping."

Jamie's head tilted. "What makes ya think so? We all believed someone had taken the girls to defile them."

"Then he wouldn't need the bed linens." Grace pointed out. "No, the linens tell me that there was a clean-up in here." She looked out the small window. "This room is on the second floor."

"Aye."

"And no one heard the front door open. That leaves this window as our probable point of entry." She craned her neck down. "It's a straight drop into the garden. Was it like that back then, too?"

He shrugged. "I suppose. I never climbed through her window, but I donea recall a porch below."

"Was Lucinda sleeping with anyone but you? This mystery man you were talking about maybe?"

"Probably." Jamie said easily. He clearly didn't buy into the "semi-frigid or pizza-tramp" double standard. "She liked to pass a good time."

"Would she sneak out her window to see him?"

"Scale down the side of the house, you mean?" He actually laughed at that idea. "Lord have mercy, *no*. Lucinda wasn't quite so agile."

"So that means someone came in here." Grace looked around. "And it means they left the same way. They must have taken her body with them."

But why?

"Lucinda might not have been dead." Jamie insisted. "He could've just knocked her out and made off with her. Taken her someplace, while she was unconscious."

"*Carrying* a live girl out a window is a lot more difficult than *pushing* a dead one out the window. It would be easier to rape her here, if that was his plan."

Jamie winced a bit at that image.

Grace barely noticed. Her mind was back in the familiar rhythms of collecting evidence. She looped her camera around her neck, documenting everything she saw. As hopeless as this assignment seemed, she wanted to do everything she possibly could to solve Lucinda's murder. Grace was good at her job. (Her *ex*-job.) Maybe there was some scrap of evidence left that she could find.

Only what kind of evidence lasted two centuries?

"DNA and fingerprints won't help us at a scene this old." She mused out loud. "Who could we compare it to? Fibers are going to be useless, for the same reason. That's assuming anything even survived twenty-three decades of cleanings and furniture changes. Window's new, so we can't check the lock." She looked down and blinked. "Hang on." Grace crouched to examine the floorboards. Some of the planks had been replaced, but, like downstairs, most were original. Her brain went "cha-ching!" "Jamie, was there a rug in here?"

"Why are the living in this town so fixated on floor cloths?"

"Just answer the question."

He sighed like a martyr. "I donea know if Lucinda had a bloody rug."

"How can you not know?"

"It was two hundred and thirty years ago!"

Grace made an aggravated sound and moved towards the alcove by the window. It was the natural place to fit a mattress. "Is this about where the bed was?"

"Aye. Right there."

"Of course you remember *that* part." It irrationally annoyed her that he'd had sex with Lucinda in this very room. The floor here looked good, though. It had mostly been protected by various beds, so there had probably never been a rug covering it. "Hand me that screwdriver, will you?"

Jamie didn't move.

It took Grace a second to realize why.

"Crap. I keep forgetting the whole 'you can't touch

anything' thing." She quickly got it from her kit herself. "Sorry about that."

He ran a hand through his hair, looking frustrated. "No, *I'm* sorry. It's my failing, not yours. I'm sorry I can't help you do this. I'm sorry I'm not really here."

She blinked at that phrasing. "You are helping and you *are* here. Trust me, I spent all night trying to convince myself otherwise, but there's no denying that you're standing right in front of me."

"Or I could still be a brain tumor."

"You're way too handsome to be a brain tumor." She said before she thought better of it. Something about Jamie had her blurting out things she'd normally keep to herself. Like she could just say anything and it would be okay.

Like he made her feel... safe.

Jamie slowly smiled at her. "I like it when you call me handsome."

Grace self-consciously swept her hair behind her ears. "Well, we both know it's true." She muttered, feeling her cheeks heat up under his intense stare.

For some reason her blushes always seemed to fascinate him. He studied her for a long moment and then shook his head. "Jesus, Mary, and Joseph, Robert must be daft to want another woman."

Grace appreciated that sentiment, even if outrageous flirting was his default setting. "The compliments are pretty, but not necessary." She knelt by an original section of floor. "And I'm already doing what you want, so there's no need to badmouth Robert to win points."

"I'll badmouth the wanker for fun, then." Jamie decided good-naturedly. "I wish nothing but curses upon his bland and balding head." He paused. "And you're surely not doing *everything* I want, lass. You closed your bedroom door last night."

"Because you would have watched me get undressed."

He didn't even bother to deny that. "I think ya even locked it, which is bloody adorable."

She made a face, because that *had* been kind of brainless. "Yeah, I keep forgetting the 'you can walk right through walls' thing, too."

"I like that you forget." He crouched down so they were at eyelevel. "I like that you see me as a man. I sure as hell see you as a woman."

"Probably because I'm the first one you've talked to in over two hundred years."

"No. That's not the reason a'tall."

Grace cleared her throat and looked away. Since high school she'd been fantasizing about the painting of this pirate and now he was gazing at her like she was the most magical being he'd ever met. It was no wonder she was losing her mind. How was she supposed to think straight when he was so incredibly... Jamie?

"Can we just get back to our crime spree, please?"

Jamie chuckled at the subject change. "You know, I donea think I've ever fancied a shy lass before. 'Tis quite a delightful thing to see you get discomposed."

"I don't even think that's a word anymore." Grace pried up the floorboards, refusing to be taken in by his Scottish-accented appeal. He'd no doubt honed it on every girl in the Revolution, from Betsy Ross on down. "And I'm *not* shy. I'm just cautious around womanizing ghosts."

"No need to be cautious. It's not as if I can do much more than talk to you."

"With you, talking is plenty."

"Kind of you to say so."

Grace shot him an exasperated look. "Would you be quiet and let me do this?"

"Alright, alright." He obediently left her alone, watching her work. "What in Christ's name are you doing?" He asked after about thirty seconds. That was the longest he'd stayed silent since they'd met, so it must have taken some real effort for him.

"This is the same floor Lucinda died on. The surface has been cleaned a thousand times since then, but not the sides. Wood is porous." She finally wrenched a board loose and set it sideways, so she could look at the unfinished edge. "You see?" She pointed at the telltale black stains. "Blood seeps through the cracks and gets absorbed. Two hundred years and it's there." She began yanking up more boards, trying to see how big the pool had been.

Jamie's teasing smile faded. He stared at the growing size of the hole, looking grim. "It might not be blood." He decided a little desperately. "It might be old varnish. Aye, it looks like varnish. There's too much for it to be blood."

Grace didn't take offence. Victim's families and friends often went into denial, at first. Somehow it was easier for Jamie to imagine that Lucinda was alive when she left the bedroom. Maybe because of their time together. His mind kept trying to find a way to escape the truth.

She knew the feeling.

"The human body has more blood in it than you think." Grace kept her voice calm. "Trust me. She bled to death right here."

Jamie squeezed his eyes shut. "Fucking hell."

"I'm sorry." And she was. Lucinda might have been a mean girl, but Jamie had cared for her and she died far too young.

Grace reached over to touch his hand in comfort. Her palm passed through his and she left it there, linking them as best she could. The sizzle of energy sparked, again. She couldn't feel his skin, but she could feel *Jamie*. The little jolts of power ran up and down her arm, growing stronger the longer they stayed linked.

His gaze slashed up to hers. "How do you do that?" He whispered in awe.

"Don't ask me. You're the ghost here."

Jamie shook his head. "I've tried to touch more people than you can imagine over the years and you're the only one I've ever been able to feel. It's *you*, Grace." He curved his long, elegant fingers around hers, like he wanted to hold on. "I was meant to find *you*."

She stared back at him, dazed and a little scared. Holy

cow but the man was trouble. He could make her forget that he was actually dead. Forget that they were at a crime scene. Forget that she was *normal*. Forget everything except the blue of his eyes and the musical sound of his voice.

She swallowed hard. "Do you want me to be sure about the blood?" She blurted out, desperate to get them back on track.

"I do, but..."

"Good." She pulled her hand back from him, refusing to notice the way his fingers made an instinctive move to cling to hers. "I might be able to tell for sure if it's blood or varnish. I don't think it's ever been tested on anything *this* old, but theoretically it should work."

He sighed and gave a jerky nod. "Do whatever you can."

"Alright." Grace got to her feet and pulled down the window shade, so the room got darker. She grabbed her squirt bottle full of luminal and sprayed an even coat across the wood. The chemical reacted with biological materials, making them glow. If someone had bled onto this floor, they were going to be able to tell pretty quickly.

Grace clicked on her UV flashlight and wasn't surprised at all when the wood lit up like Harrisonburg's annual fireworks display. "Blood." She said simply.

Jamie cursed in Gaelic.

The evidence was unmistakable to anyone who'd ever watched *Dateline*. Lucinda had died right there, bleeding onto the floor. The pool of blood had been several feet across, running under the bed and straight back to the wall. The wound that killed her must have been deep and massive. Either that or she'd suffered dozens of smaller wounds, before she'd finally succumbed. Someone had then used the bedclothes to clean up the mess and dumped her body out the window. It was all tragically, terribly, irrefutably clear even to an ex-forensic investigator.

Apparently, Grace been wrong earlier. Even two hundred years later, there *was* still evidence of murder left in this house. She snapped some pictures of the scene, falling into the familiar rhythm of the job.

"It's like magic." Jamie glanced at her. "You can do something like *this* and you choose to give dull tours of this dull town? Why?"

Grace focused on the camera controls. "I told you, I burned out."

That answer didn't satisfy him. Huge surprise. "And I told *you*, I have no idea what that means. Were you injured?"

"No." She hesitated. "Not physically."

Jamie's head tilted, seeing far too much. "So much brutality must have been hard to witness." He finally said. "Hard to forget."

Her lips compressed, refusing to be lulled in by his gentle tone. "The job was important and I was good at it. The stress just got to be too much for me. I started... seeing things."

"Seeing things?" He tried an encouraging smile. "Like ghosts?"

"Kind of." For no reason except she had a hard time guarding what she said around this man, Grace found herself telling him the truth. "I saw a victim before she died. I relived the whole crime scene, just as it was the night of the murder." Her eyes flicked up to his. "I was *there*, Jamie."

His brows compressed like he didn't have an answer for that.

He wasn't the only one floundering for a response. Grace crouched down, her fingers turning the board so she could get a better look at the Luminal-y glow. Her thumb touched the ancient bloodstain and she barely noticed. "For the past year, I've been trying to explain how it happened, but I keep coming up..."

She stopped short as Lucinda's bedroom vanished around her.

Grace was suddenly outside. Like *outside* outside.

It was night, with candle-lit lanterns flickering along cobblestone streets, and no sounds except the quiet chirping of insects.

Grace's lips parted in amazement. It seemed like she

was still in Harrisonburg, but no hybrid cars or signs for WiFi hotspots were in sight. This was Harrisonburg with all the plastic, hipster, tourist-mania burned away.

Harrisonburg when it was new.

The building right in front of her looked exactly like a dirtier, smellier, high-def version of The Raven. In fact, it *was* The Raven. ...Or at least how the tavern must have appeared, just a few years out of the Colonial era. Because she knew in her heart that's where she was:

Smack dab in the middle of 1789, on the night Lucinda Wentworth died.

CHAPTER SIX

June 23 1789- How I wish women could walk into taverns and drink! I was standing outside The Raven today, wondering if I'd ever have the courage to enter right through the front door. Mother and Father would faint dead away. How wonderfully shocked the whole world would be! And I just know all the best gossip happens inside those walls. Alas, I have my reputation to consider and there are some things a lady does not do.

...At least not publically.

From the Journal of Miss Lucinda Wentworth

Grace slowly got to her feet, dread filling her. "Oh crap..."

Just like that night in the alleyway, somehow she was back at a murder scene, reliving everything in IMAX-like reality. This was not normal. This was very, very *not frigging normal*. Grace's breath wheezed in and out as she tried to get her bearings. It didn't feel like a delusion. It felt like it was really happening. Like she was really and truly standing in the middle of another era. What the hell was she...?

"Bloody hell." A familiar voice said very distinctly from behind her. "Either I'm far drunker than I thought or you just appeared out of nowhere, lass."

Grace's head whipped around, her chaotic thoughts screeching to a halt. "Jamie?"

It was really him!

Kind of.

This wasn't *her* Jamie, from the twenty-first century.

This was Jamie, before he became a ghost. A solid, three-dimensional Jamie, wearing an even gaudier outfit than his usual super-colorful mix of fabrics and holding a pewter mug full of ale. She gaped up at him, staggered to see him alive and breathing.

And even more gorgeous.

The flickering light from the oil lamps did great things for the shine of his hair and his already exceptional cheekbones. He tipped his tri-corner hat farther back on his head, looking like the cover shot for some Patriot-themed "Hunk of the Day" calendar. Despite her possible insanity, Grace found herself whispering the word "Wow!" under her breath. God, he looked amazing.

His eyebrows shot up when she called him by name. "Do I know you?"

"I know *you*." She blurted out, staggered by the (maybe) reality of what was happening. Jesus, this was (maybe) *actually happening*. "We met yesterday, right over there." She pointed to the spot where she'd fallen on the tour. In this time period, the curb was made of stone and not cement, but everything around it was eerily the same. "You don't remember?"

"No."

Of course he didn't. It hadn't happened yet.

"Strange, because you would be a difficult lady to forget." Jamie stepped off the porch of the tavern. "I used to see the fay, back in Scotland, and I'm thinking you might be one of them. One minute the street was empty and the next you were *here*. Appearing out of thin air."

"Fay?" It was so hard to think. "You mean fairies?" Oh for God's sake... Grace nearly hit him in general frustration. "I'm not a frigging fairy, Jamie!"

"Well, what other beings just materialize out of the ether? Where do you come from? And what in God's name has happened to your gown?" He gestured to her striped skirt. "You're practically unclothed."

Grace looked down at her sundress. The maxi length and spaghetti straps were perfect for a summer day back in reality, but it seemed like Jamie wasn't sure what to make of her anachronistic outfit. No wonder. In this century, "Old Navy" meant nothing more than a bunch of British war ships.

"I..." She swallowed. "I'm just a regular human, who's a little bit lost, alright?" Really, really lost. As in this-slightly-inebriated-pirate-was-the-only-person-on-the-*planet*-she-knew lost. What if she never got home?

"Lost from where?" Jamie persisted, seeing her distress. "Do you want me to fetch someone to aid you?"

"No." She whispered with a quick shake of her head. There was no one but him. "I need *you*."

"No one needs me." The words were instant and certain, but she'd clearly captured his attention. "I can summon the Watch, if you're..."

Grace cut him off. "I don't want the Watch or the police or the National Guard! *You* have to help me, Jamie! Just stay right there and help me figure this out." She just needed to frigging *think*.

He edged closer to her, at a loss as to how to proceed. "Are you hurt?"

"No. I'm just not sure how I got here. Or why. Or how to get back. Or..." She trailed off, trying to process this madness. "What day is it?"

"Sunday."

"Sunday, the twenty-eighth of June?"

"Aye." He checked the position of the moon. "For another hour or so. Although, if anyone should ask, I'm not one for drinking on the Sabbath." He raised his mug at her with a wicked grin, trying to lighten the mood.

It didn't work.

Holy cow.

Holy *cow*, this was honest-to-God the night Lucinda Wentworth died.

Grace was used to weirdness. Growing up, she'd lived above a store that sold chicken heads and a "magical" number-shaped pasta, which was supposed to somehow reveal winning lotto combinations. But this... This was just totally off the lunacy charts, even for a Rivera.

Grace bent over with her hands on her knees, trying to calm her racing heart. Okay. (Peaceful green cornfields. Peaceful green cornfields.) If this was really real, (peaceful green cornfields) then she didn't have the luxury of panic. She'd panicked the last time and it had gotten her locked up in a padded cell. (Peaceful green cornfields.) This time she had to stay calm and focus on what was important.

Like the fact that Jamie was still alive.

Grace switched her full attention to him, breathing hard. "This isn't a delusion. It wasn't before, either. I *haven't* been going crazy, all this time. I'm... really here." She'd *actually* been traveling through time, to the night of the murders, and reliving it all. There was no "maybe" about it. It was *seriously* happening to her. "And you're here, too."

"None of which explains why a fairy needs my help." Jamie reported, still looking baffled. Who could blame him?

She gave a high-pitched laugh that bordered on hysteria. "Actually, now that I think about it, *you're* the one who needs *my* help."

"Aye, that seems more likely."

Grace ran a hand through her hair, close to hyperventilating. "You're in a hell of a lot of trouble." She paused. "And I'm not a fairy! Jesus, can you focus, please?"

Jamie must be why this had happened. *He* was why she was here. Through the frantic pounding of her heart, she seized on that explanation for her current predicament. She was stuck back in time, because she was supposed to save Jamie.

Not that he deserved it.

The man wasn't paying the slightest bit of attention to the looming disaster. Instead, his gaze was scanning her body as if he liked what he saw. Despite everything, the heat of all that masculine focus had a hot, tight feeling building inside of her. Jamie was alive and feeling her up with his eyes.

"You're going to aid me, then?" Having established she wasn't in dire need of saving, he'd moved onto the business of flirting. "Well, that sounds promising. I've got quite a few ideas on how you can be of service." He winked at her, not at all concerned about his own safety. When he suspected *she* was the one in trouble, he'd been willing to lend a hand. With regard to his *own* life, though, he was mind-blowingly cavalier. "I'll get you a pint and you can regale me with tales of how you plan to rescue me from my dire fate."

Grace waved that aside. "Just tell me… Are you *one hundred percent* certain that it's 1789?"

Jamie paused, his head tilting to one side. "Aye." His tone suggested he now thought she'd had enough pints for the day. His face grew serious, again. "On second thought, we'll forgo the drinks and I'll simply walk you home. You're in no condition to be dealing with the likes of me." He looked her up and down again with genuine regret. "Bloody shame."

"Jamie, this isn't a joke! You need to listen to me."

"Oh, I'm listening to ya." He gave a long-suffering sigh. "Jesus, Mary, and Joseph, the batty woman thinks she's come to save me and looks like a fay creature of moonlight… and I'm just going to walk her home. Why am I forever trying to be a bloody gentleman?"

"I'm *not* crazy." She repeated, ignoring his muttering. "I don't know whether to be relieved or disappointed about that, but it's true."

"This whole evening is becoming a bit strange." He agreed humoringly. "I donea blame ya for being a bit confused. Where is it you live, now? Somewhere here in town?"

"No. Yes. I mean, I live here, but I don't live *here*. You see?"

"Aye, that clears it all up." He smiled like she really was batty. Or drunk. …Or possibly like he was still half-convinced she was from some alternate fairyland dimension. "Just point in the general direction of your home."

"Trust me, we can't walk there."

"Well, I know it's not exactly proper, but it isn't safe for you to be wandering about at this hour." He stopped in front of her and held out an elegant palm. "I'll admit to being a bit of a cad, but I'm not a man who would leave a lady in your condition all alone on the street. There are too many bad sorts in that tavern." He pointed towards The Raven. "This is Ned Hunnicutt's establishment and he's an ass. He attracts *other* asses around him, like flies to a latrine."

That diverted her for a beat. "You seriously *never* like that guy, do you?"

"The maps he sells are bloody awful, he treats the serving girls poorly, and he waters down his ale. I'm sure he was secretly a Tory." Jamie assured her. "Now, I just want to see you home and then I'll be on my way. I give you my word."

"Listen to me: *I can't go home, yet.*" Shock was fading and a new idea was forming in her mind. For the first time in years, the pessimistic voice in her head faded and optimism took its place.

The best way to save Jamie was to prevent the killings.

Maybe she was supposed to rewrite history. Maybe that was why she'd been dropped in this specific moment in time. Maybe she could really do this. Maybe it was all that simple.

Grace took a deep breath. "I have to try and stop him, before it's too late."

"Stop who now?"

There was no way she could answer that. Instead, she grabbed hold of Jamie's beautiful hand, wrapping her fingers around his. "I know it sounds nuts, but you have to get out of Harrisonburg. Tonight." In case she failed, she needed to make sure he wasn't around to hang. If he wasn't here, they couldn't blame him for the murders. "Trust me. You need to get on your ship and sail far, far away. Right now."

Except he didn't seem eager to go.

The sparks when they touched were even stronger when they were both tangible. Jamie gasped, his face growing taunt. Desire throbbed between them. His palm twisted, so he could seize her fingers and press them tight. He seemed more stunned by the sensation of her skin against his than by her agitated words.

Grace knew how he felt. She could actually *touch* him and it made tears burn the back of her eyes. The connection that bound them was real, whether he was alive or dead. And right now he was *alive*. Really, really alive. She intended to keep him that way.

God, he really was her Partner.

What the hell was she going to do about that?

He glanced down at their joined hands, then back up to her eyes. A new awareness lit his face, like he somehow recognized her. "Who are you really?" It was barely a whisper.

Grace smiled, elation filling her despite this newest detour into weirdness. She was sane and Jamie was alive and she (sort of) had her job back. What more could she ask for, really? Positivity roared through her, reminding her of her life before the alleyway.

"I'm the girl who's going to save you, Jamie Riordan."

And then --Because when was she ever going to get the chance again?-- Grace kissed him. Her free hand seized the front of his super-patterny green coat and she dragged his lips down to hers. Not that it took a lot of dragging, which was gratifying. Jamie lowered his head without even a smidgen of hesitation. His lips slanted over hers, drinking deep. The man tasted like magic and oceans and wicked intent. Since she was fifteen years old, she'd been daydreaming about this pirate and he was sooooo worth the wait

Those perfect hands settled on her waist pulling her closer, a low groan rumbling in his throat. She might have started this, but Jamie was in no hurry to see it end. Strong arms lifted her against his chest, like he wanted even more of her. Grace's feet left the ground, clinging to him as she kissed him back. All her therapist's jabber about "unrealistic expectations" and Robert's whining about her semi-frigidity faded to nothing with Jamie. Everything inside of her reached a flashpoint of desire. All she wanted to do was push him to the ground and lick her way down his incredible body.

And Jamie certainly wouldn't have put up much of a fight. The guy was holding her so tight, it was a wonder she could still breathe. "Mine." He got out hoarsely. "*Finally*."

Grace's insides clenched at the hot words. Human or

ghost, he was a pirate who took what he wanted. It turned her on to have all that possessive focus aimed her way. Whenever he looked at her, Grace could feel him claiming her and now that they had the ability to touch, there was no hesitation, at all. Large palms grabbed handfuls of her skirt, clearly wanting to rip it right off of her. He might have no earthly idea who she was, but he sure seemed interested in learning.

...Too bad she didn't have time to explain it all to him.

If there was one person who could help her solve this case, it was Jamie. But what the hell could she say to him now that he would ever believe? Nothing. If she tried to explain it all, he'd have her locked up for her own good and eighteenth-century asylums were an even worse option than modern ones. She needed to do this on her own.

And she needed to do it *now*.

Grace pulled back, breathing hard. "I gotta go."

Jamie reluctantly loosened his grip as she squiggled free. His gentlemanly instincts were warring with his desire to keep her right there in his arms. "Wait..."

"I can't." She backed away from him. "I gotta *go*, Jamie. It might already be too late."

He didn't bother to ask what she was late for. He was too busy following her right down the rabbit hole. "I *do* know you." He said, closing the small distance of her retreat. "God, I would know you anywhere."

Grace hesitated. "You remember me?" How was that possible?

Jamie shook his head. "I never met you a day in my life... but I've still been waiting for you." Dazed blue eyes traced over her face, memorizing it. "I always knew I'd recognize my bride when she finally showed up."

Revolutionary era pick-up lines, now? Unbelievable! "Just stay here and make sure you have an alibi until morning." She took off running, her sandals thudding against the cobblestones. "Then, get out of town!" She called over her shoulder. "I mean it!"

Jamie didn't seem eager to take that advice. "Where the hell are you going?" He shouted after her. "You didn't even tell me your name!"

Grace didn't have the time or oxygen to answer that. She hiked up the length of her dress and jumped over a hedge in her mad dash across town square. Most days, she was embarrassingly unathletic for someone named "Grace" but this wasn't most days. She needed to get to Lucinda's house before Jamie's ex got herself killed.

The Wentworth mansion was three streets over and six blocks up. The quickest way to get there was to cut right through some flower gardens. One of the benefits of living in a place that hadn't changed since George Washington was president was that time travelers didn't need a map. It was simple for her to navigate through the familiar landmarks of Harrisonburg. Sure the houses were painted different colors and the trees were smaller and the stars overhead were a thousand times brighter, but this was still her town. She could've found the Wentworth house blindfolded.

She'd just prefer to find it in a car.

Grace hadn't run full out since high school gym and her lungs really weren't thanking her for the trip down memory lane. It took way too long for her to cover the relatively short distance across town. She was wheezing like a broken accordion by the time she shortcut-ed her way into the Wentworth's backyard.

Instantly, she saw that Ghost-Jamie had left out a very important detail about the back of Lucinda's house. While he'd been right about the lack of a porch under her bedroom, he'd forgotten about the rose trellis. It was attached to the side of the house, providing a perfect improvised ladder for anyone who wanted to climb up to the second story.

"Goddamn it!"

It was the worst language she'd used in years, so of course Jamie was there to hear it.

"You've got a sailor's mouth on ya, lass." He cheerily reported, coming up behind her. "I like that in a woman. Never did care for the timid ones. Much more fun when a girl swears a blue streak and drags you down for a kiss, now and then."

Grace spared him a sideways look, not very surprised that he'd followed her. Dead or alive, the pirate was incapable of following directions. *"You're* going to lecture *me* about cursing?" She scoffed. "Please." He used the word "fuck" a half-dozen times just saying "good morning." She did a quick scan for any footprints in the soft dirt. If she had hairspray and plaster of Paris, she could have made casts of them for comparison. For better or worse, she didn't see any prints, though.

...Also, she doubted hairspray had been invented yet.

"And, FYI, you called *me* timid yesterday." She tacked on distractedly.

"Doena recall knowing you yesterday, so perhaps you're thinking of *another* dashing Scottish captain. One far less perceptive than me. Also, far less handsome, I'm sure."

Grace flashed him an exasperated glance. "Must you flirt with every girl you meet?"

"Just the one I'm going to wed."

"I knew you weren't going to take this seriously. What are you even doing here? I thought I told you to go establish an alibi."

"Aye, ya did. But I've got no bloody clue what that means, so I decided to join you here in the Wentworth's shrubbery instead." He gestured to the bushes, where they were hiding. "Besides, you never told me your name and I'd like to know what to call my future wife."

He really was an incurable scoundrel. "Any future wife of yours could only be called 'crazy.'" She assured him.

"Not true. I distinctly recall you telling me you're *not* crazy and you don't seem one to lie." He leaned a bit closer. "Come on, lass. Just tell me your name. Please?"

God, he was pretty. "Grace." She fumbled in the pocket of her sundress, refusing to be distracted by his charm, and came up with her smartphone. "I'm Grace."

His mouth curved. "Of course you are." He murmured. "No other name would suit you, a'tall."

She didn't even bother to ask what that meant. It was much darker in the past than it was in the modern age of electricity and light pollution. How was she supposed to investigate if she couldn't frigging see? Grace clicked on her flashlight app and shone it up at Lucinda's room. "Goddamn it!"

The window was open, white curtains blowing in the summer breeze.

"What the hell is *that?*" Jamie's tone went from seductive to astonished. He gaped at the glowing smartphone and she realized that she had zero ways to logically explain it. Ben Franklin flying a kite in a lightning storm was a long way from Apple's newest technology.

"Okay, fine." Grace shrugged. "I'm a fairy. Just accept the magic. And, for God's sake, keep your voice down." The last thing she needed was someone spotting him at the crime scene. He'd be hanged ahead of schedule.

Jamie obligingly lowered his voice to a baffled hiss. "What are you *doing* here, pray tell? If you plan to rob the Wentworths, I'd suggest doing it when they aren't all home and abed."

"I'm not robbing them, idiot. I'm trying to *protect* them." Unfortunately, she had the bad feeling she was already too late. How could she be too late? The murder shouldn't happen for hours, according to Gregory Maxwell's book. Why would she be sent back to save Lucinda, if she didn't have time to *actually* save her?!

"Protecting them from what? I've an acquaintance with Miss Lucinda. So if she's in some kind of trouble, I've a vested interest in knowing about it."

"Yeah, I know all about your 'vested interest' in Lucinda." Grace muttered in irritation.

Jamie shot her a quick look. "There's nothing arranged between us, if that's what you're insinuating. I've a fondness for the girl, but it isn't a'tall serious."

"Like I care about that, right now." She *totally* cared about that. Grace sent him a sideways look and Jamie caught hold of her gaze, not letting go.

"Lucinda's not the one I've been waiting for." He said

quietly. "I promise you. The woman does not belong to me, nor me to her."

Grace shook her head, before those sincere blue eyes hypnotized her and she got sidetracked. "You and your love life are your own business. I'm just here to stop a murder."

"You're...?" Jamie's expression went slack. "Wait, a *what!?*"

"Keep your voice down! Look, you have no idea what's going on, so just let me handle this and stay out of sight." She started across the lawn, her attention on that open window.

A feeling of dread settled in her stomach. The same feeling she always got when she arrived at a crime scene. Something moved in Lucinda's bedroom. Some*one*. A silhouette of black against the white curtain.

Goddamn it.

"Stop!" Grace shouted, heading for the house. "Stop right there!"

Behind her, Jamie let out a curse. "Weren't we supposed to be keeping quiet? That surely woke the whole neighborhood."

In the bedroom, the shadowy figure vanished. Grace heard footsteps pounding inside the house as the person fled, but she couldn't tell how big they were or what they looked like. "Jamie, go around to the front!" They needed to cut him off before he fled. "Hurry!"

He was staring up at the window, his snarking silenced by shock. "Was someone inside Lucinda's...?"

"Go!" Praying that the wooden slats held, Grace pulled herself up the trellis. "But whatever you do, don't get caught here yourself. They'll think you did it."

"You can't go up there by yourself, woman!"

"You think this tiny little trellis is going to support you?" Thorns cut her hands and rose pedals cascaded to the ground as she climbed. She seriously needed to get in better shape if she was going to do insane stuff like this. "Hurry!" Her arms burning from strain and her hair full of leaves, she finally managed to heave herself over the window sill and into the room.

Even in the darkness, she saw the blood.

The killer hadn't had time to clean up the crime scene, yet. Lucinda was sprawled there in a white nightgown, already dead and gone. It looked as if her throat had been slashed. *More* than just her throat. Her blood covered the flowered floor cloth, pooling under her body. Thick and sticky, it soaked so deeply into the wooden slats beneath the bed that it would still be there two centuries later.

Grace bit back a scream, her hands shaking so badly she nearly dropped her phone.

Oh God, oh God, oh God.

She couldn't do this. She couldn't deal with this. It was all too much. She *told* Jamie it was too much. She'd failed to save Lucinda, and she was somehow back in time, and she was looking at another dead body, and she was going to lose her mind for real this time. She couldn't breathe. Couldn't *think*.

Peaceful green cornfields. Peaceful green...

Wait.

She swallowed, her brain piecing facts together even through her shock. Wait. Was the blood already cold? The edges of the puddle were beginning to dry. She blinked rapidly, her training kicking in. It was sometime around eleven, according to Jamie, and Lucinda had been dead for over an hour. She was sure of that. That meant she must have died almost as soon as she said goodnight to her sister and went to bed.

Her killer had been waiting for her. Maybe he'd left a clue.

Panic gave way to sudden determination. If she couldn't save Lucinda, at least she could catch who did this. This was a crime scene, after all, and she was the only one capable of investigating it.

Grace's eyes narrowed and she quickly grabbed the camera that was still looped around her neck. Pictures. She needed pictures. Her finger repeatedly slammed down on the shutter button. Photos lit up the cameras LCD screen. The flash revealed much more than her eyes could see in the darkened room. Whoever killed Lucinda had been furious with her. Wrathful. Not only had they cut her throat, they'd stabbed her again and again.

She hadn't been raped, though. Overkilling like this could often be a sign of a sexual predator, but Grace didn't get a feeling of impersonal evil from this scene. This killing was all about rage and punishment. Someone had *hated* Lucinda. Someone who knew her. The camera picked up distinctive smears in the blood, evidence of the killer's frantic movements.

Grace crouched down to examine them closer. Bare feet? Had the killer been naked to avoid getting blood on his clothes? That wasn't unheard of, but it hinted at a high level of criminal sophistication. Who in this town had the smarts to…?

Something under the bed caught her eye. A book was hidden behind the mattress, impossible to see unless you were at floor-level. Maybe it was something the killer touched. Maybe she could get fingerprints. Grace leaned over to grab it, trying to make out the title in the dim light. A diary maybe? It was all handwritten.

As she flipped through the pages, her thumb brushed against an unseen drop of blood that had spattered on the leather cover. Instantly, the disorientating sensation of the world shifting around her struck again.

Just as quickly as she'd left, Grace was back in the twenty-first century.

It was as if nothing had happened, at all. She was kneeling on the floor of Lucinda's former bedroom, surrounded by modern odds-and-ends, and Ghost-Jamie was staring at her. Only something *had* happened. Something that left her scared and shaken and forever *un*normal.

Her gaze went up to Jamie's taunt face. "I saw her." She whispered. There was no denying it. Lucinda's book was still in her hand. "When I touched the blood, I went back to 1789." And the drop that sent her forward again was still wet on her skin. "I saw Lucinda dead. I really *saw* her, Jaimie."

Peaceful green cornfields.

Peaceful green cornfields.

Peaceful green cornfields.

"Jesus, Mary, and Joseph." He knelt down beside her, looking as traumatized as she felt. "Are you alright, Grace?"

"I have no idea." She suddenly wasn't sure of anything. Nothing at all. She stared into Jamie's concerned eyes and swallowed hard. ...Well, maybe *one* thing: I'm going to prove that you didn't kill those girls."

CHAPTER SEVEN

June 23, 1789- HC was quite agitated at our meeting today. Apparently, he's heard rumors in town that connect my name to a "mystery man" and he's worried his wife will discover that it's really him. As if I would ever allow my reputation to suffer like that! The fool probably started the rumors himself, with all his bragging.

I calmed him down, of course. HC can never resist me. ...But then, no man can.

From the Journal of Miss Lucinda Wentworth

"You're going to have to talk about it sooner or later." Jamie called through the bedroom door. "You said you needed time to 'process?' Well, I've given you all afternoon. Now it's time we have a bloody conversation."

Grace had no desire to discuss what happened. It seemed like a one way ticket back to the crazy house. Far better to seal herself away in her favorite fuzzy bathrobe until she could make some sense of what happened.

Her striped sundress was in a heap on the floor, all ready to be bleached and burned. Her sandals were already in the garbage. She'd scrubbed her skin in the tub. But it would still take a long time for her to feel clean again.

There had been so much blood.

Grace pressed her lips together. Once the adrenaline had faded, her old fears and insecurities had come flooding back. Along with all their new friends. Holy cow, she'd really been standing over Lucinda Wentworth's dead body. How was this happening? *Why* was it happening? She was nothing special. Why was *she* the one traveling through time? Why not someone braver or smarter? Had she done something right or wrong or was it all just random? Regardless, what the hell was she going to do about it?

Jamie wasn't giving up. "You can't just go back to ignoring me."

Grace sank farther into the heap of pillows on her bed. Oh yes, she could. At least until she figured out her next step, which was going to take a heck of a lot longer than one afternoon. She'd done her part. She'd calculated the smeared footprint photos and, as far as she could tell, the killer was between 5' and 5'5". Which eliminated basically no one in Revolutionary War era America, where people tended to be smaller than their modern counterparts. ...Except for a certain tall, Scottish pirate, anyway.

She'd also skimmed through the diary, which was mainly just Lucinda complaining about her dull life of privilege, rating her lovers, ridiculing her sister and parents and friends, and using gratuitous exclamation points. Unfortunately, Lucinda had described most of her boyfriends with initials, so the mystery man was still nameless. (The JMR entries got skipped entirely, because it made Grace nauseous to read about Jamie and Lucinda together, but the others revealed nothing useful.) In short, Grace had done all she could with the evidence she'd gathered.

Now she was going to lay in bed and be crazy for a while.

"Damn it, we need to talk, Grace!"

"Go away!" Her voice broke on the last word. "I'm having a nervous breakdown and I need some frigging space!"

There was a long pause and then Jamie won the argument by simply walking through the wall. For a guy who'd been alive when they signed the Declaration of Independence, he sure didn't care much about protecting a person's right to privacy. He stalked into the bedroom and crossed his arms over his wide chest.

"Are you crying?" He demanded, his brows

compressed in concern. "What's wrong? Are you hurt?"

Grace gave a squeak of alarm. "Geez, it freaks me out when you do that!"

Jaimie ignored that. "Why are you crying?" He persisted with a worried look on his face.

Was he kidding? "Maybe because my afternoon has spanned several centuries!"

"Jesus, Mary, and Joseph..." He rolled his eyes looking both exasperated and relieved. "Is *that* all? I thought you were in some kind of trouble."

Grace made an aggravated sound. She'd never liked people in her bedroom. It was her sanctuary. She'd collected the mishmash of knickknacks and yard sale paintings and secondhand furniture, guided by nothing except what caught her fancy. For instance, mermaids had always held a special fascination for her, so, on her dresser, there was a collection of mermaid figurines. Everything in the space was Grace's, but most of it had once belonged to someone else. She'd always been attracted to vintage things. It made her happy to give them a second life. It seemed too revealing to allow others inside such a personal space, though. Like they might see too much of what was going on inside of her.

Still, she wasn't nearly as outraged as she should have been by Jamie's invasion. For whatever reason, he kind of looked *right* standing amid the yellow and green color scheme. Like he belonged there. The word "Partner" whispered in her head.

"I had the door *closed,* you know." She informed him without any real heat.

"Which means little to a specter." Establishing that she wasn't in mortal danger, he switched gears and smiled winningly. Like every other hour of the day, he clearly thought this was the perfect opportunity for some flirting. "Since I'm in here anyway, we might as well have that talk, right? It won't take a moment." His eyes skimmed over her form, obviously enjoying the sight of her cuddled up in her bed. "You just keep doing what you're doing. Donea mind me."

"Jamie, I swear to God, I will have you exorcised."

"Alright. Alright." He didn't get out of the room, but he did get to the point. "No need to get testy."

"Too late."

"I remember you." He announced, as if that was breaking news. "*That's* what I need ta tell ya. I *remember* you, Grace."

"Of course you remember me! I'm sitting right here…" She broke off and blinked. "Wait, you *remember* me? From -- like-- back in 1789?"

"Aye." His gaze drifted back down to the antique coverlet, as if he was picturing her body beneath all the intricate crochet-work. "Are you naked under that robe?"

Grace made a sound of total frustration. "You *knew* I was back there and you're just mentioning it *now!*" If he was tangible, she would have throttled him. "Jackass."

"I could only remember it *after* you went back. Before that, you hadn't done it, yet."

"That makes no sense! If we changed history, then you should only remember the *new* version."

"How the bloody hell should I know how it works?" He ran a hand over his face. "I'm telling you, there's two memories atop each other now. I recall what *really* happened that night. Or what *originally* happened, anyway. And I remember what happened *after* you started mucking about with the past."

"After *we* started mucking about with the past." She corrected. "You're a part of this mess, too. Maybe that's why you're getting both versions."

"Whatever the reason, I remember meeting you outside The Raven, wearing that very same ridiculous dress." He pointed to the rumpled fabric on the ground. "You appeared out of nowhere and you were the most beautiful creature I ever saw. And I knew…" He trailed off and shook his head, like he was trying to get it all straight in his mind. "I knew you were mine."

Grace blinked up at him, unsure what to say to that. "You thought I was a lunatic and/or drunk. Also, I think you proposed."

"I thought you were fay." The corner of his mouth curved. "Maybe I was right."

"Maybe you're an idiot. The rest of my family are the mystics and palm readers. *I'm* the normal one."

"It didn't seem that way a few hours ago." Jamie sat down on the edge of the bed. "...Or two hundred years ago. Depending on how ya want to look at it."

"Oh shut up." Grace glowered over at him. "Whatever's happening, it sure as heck isn't normal and I have no clue how to deal with it. Which means I'm going to have to ask my aunt for some kind of help and that seriously pisses me off." She paused. "And, not for nothing, but you *really* should have gotten out of town when I told you to."

"T'was grand advice, in retrospect."

She snorted. "Since you're still here haunting my bedroom, I'm guessing you didn't catch the killer coming out of the Wentworth house that night?"

"By the time I gave up trying to follow you up that wee trellis and got around front, he was long gone. I barely escaped being arrested myself. All the commotion you made woke the family. They found Lucinda's body and summoned the Watch. I searched the neighborhood, but I never saw anyone suspicious lurking about." He paused. "I searched for you, too. T'was halfway convinced I dreamed you. Thought for a bit I was losing my mind."

"Join the club." She blew out a tired breath. "Lucinda wrote down her lovers' names, but she only used initials. Do you think you could figure out who some of them are? Maybe her mystery man?"

"It's been two hundred years, lass. It would be a guess, at best. Do any of them stand out to you?"

"Well, that HC guy sounds kinky as hell. Her diary entries about him read like *Fifty Shades of Grey*."

Jamie made a thoughtful face. "At least Lucinda had fun before she passed. She enjoyed her short life. That's something, I suppose." He searched his memory for a beat. "Hell if I know anybody with the initials HC, though. Well, Old Howard Carlyle, perhaps, but he was eighty if he was a day.

Doubt Lucinda would fancy him."

"Well, it had to be *someone*. Just give me a couple hours to recover from my panic attack and I'll figure it out."

Jamie hesitated. "Yeah, about that..." He began warily, but Grace cut him off.

"I can already tell you the killer will be in his twenties. Liked to set fires and hurt animals as a kid. Lives in town. Kind of a loner, but not in a way that stands out. He's friendly enough, but no one really knows him. He has secret rooms, secret drawers, all the important parts of him locked away. He doesn't need to show off and display the body. He gets off on knowing secrets. That's why he took her from her room. He wanted the control of being the only one who knows where she is."

"Except, you changed that." Jamie reminded her, looking concerned. "Now Lucinda's body was found right where he left it."

"Exactly!" She agreed enthusiastically. "He's meticulous and we just capsized all his hard work."

"Must you sound so excited about making a killer unhappy? T'is not a *good* thing."

"Right before Lucinda's murder something happened." Grace continued. "Something triggered him to attack her in a personal way. Either she refused to have sex with him or *something*, but he snapped. It's impulsive, but still not disorganized. He's imagined it before. He's shocked, maybe scared, that he actually killed her, but he's also elated by the violence. He leaves... But then he goes *back*. Risky, but not desperate. The behavior of someone who's still in control."

Jamie looked fascinated. "How do you know all this?"

"I took some profiling courses." She said distractedly. "Focus: He went *back* to the scene. He wanted to clean it all up. Make sure he's covered. Make sure it can't be traced to him. And, mostly, just to revel in what he's done. To enjoy all the destruction. He takes off his clothes so they won't get bloody and starts the cleaning in his bare feet."

"Fucking hell."

Her eyes narrowed, barely hearing him. "He's *smart*, Jamie. How did he get out of the house without you seeing him? Lucinda must have been sneaking him in some other way and he used it to escape. He's *thinking*, even in his panic. He's hiding right in plain sight. I just can't figure out the timeline. How long was he there? Why didn't anyone hear him...?" She broke off, rubbing her forehead in frustration. "If I was still on my game, I'd be better at this."

"You've done more than anyone else possibly could." Jamie shook his head. "That's enough for today, Grace. Rest, before you burn yourself up again."

"It's burn *out*."

He ignored the correction, his eyes on her face. "You can't save the whole world, all at once. It's alright to take some time to breathe."

"For a pirate, you say some very self-help-y stuff."

"Before *Haunted High*, my favorite show was *Oprah*. Its cancelation was the greatest trauma since my death, let me tell you."

Grace gave a reluctant smile. "So you think I should lay here by myself and quietly meditate or something?"

"I didn't say '*by yourself.*'" Jamie leaned sideways, so he was lying on the bed. "Technically, I can't feel this mattress, but I can sense it's *smashingly* comfortable." He eased his way up so he was laying on the pillows, his gaze locked on her face. "And it has quite a smashing view, as well." He smoothed an elegant hand over her hair, that amazing electricity tingling through them both. "Granted I can't *breathe*, but there's no reason I can't just meditate here beside you."

Grace swallowed, totally distracted from the horrors of the case. "That's a really bad idea." His beautiful hands couldn't touch her, but with Jamie it didn't seem to matter. She could still feel her body warming and her breasts tightening at his proximity.

"Oh, I think it's the best idea I ever had." He murmured. "And I'm a man with nothing but brilliant thoughts in my handsome head."

"Jamie..."

"Grace..." He repeated in the exact same tone. "What's the harm in letting me lay beside you?"

"Because I can already guarantee you're not going to just 'lay' there."

The man was the picture of wounded innocence. "What else *can* I do?"

"I'm sure you'll think of something."

"You're being paranoid." He scolded, but his eyes gleamed with all kinds of piratical ideas. "Why, it's not as if I'm even *really* here. Being a ghost, I'm not a part of this world anymore. No one can see me, but you. I can't talk to..."

"Of course you're a part of this world!" She interrupted. "You're a part of this world, whether other people see you or not. You're *real*. As real as me and everyone else. You have feelings and thoughts and ideas. *That's* what makes you alive. Don't ever tell yourself otherwise."

Jamie stared at her for a long moment. "If I was not already long gone, you would surely be the death of me, Grace Rivera."

She smiled at that.

He paused for a beat, like he was trying to *not* say something and unable to hold it back. "It was bloody foolish of you to climb that trellis, though."

She frowned at the non sequitur. "At the Wentworth's?"

"What other trellis would I be speaking of?" He'd clearly been brooding about it. "I'm trying to be calm and reasonable and let you breathe, but I remember *all* of it, Grace. There was someone in her room and you went up the damn trellis, anyway. It nearly kills me all over again to recall it. What the hell were you thinking?"

"I thought maybe I could save her. Or at the very least, I could see who the killer was." Grace shook her head, remembering her uncharacteristic flash of optimism. It had been... nice. It left her wanting more. "I just got there too late. The evidence I collected isn't enough, though. If I could have gotten some more..."

"You should not have been there, a'tall!" Jamie interrupted at a very unOprah-ish roar. "And now the killer is pissed off at you, yet you want to continue this investigation."

"Well, how else do you suggest I clear your name?"

"I would not have you endanger yourself for any reason." He shook his head. "Not for *any* reason, Grace. What would have happened if you'd gone into her room and the killer had attacked you? Did you even think of that?"

She frowned. "Not really."

"Not really?" He echoed incredulously. "You're supposed to be a timid lass! Just leaving that bloody boring tour nearly had you in a faint. Why am I having to tell you to stop chasing after murderers alone?"

"I wasn't alone." She turned so she was facing him on the pillow. "*You* were there, Jamie." And maybe that's why she'd climbed up that trellis without hesitation. Because she knew Jamie was going to somehow keep her safe. "You had my back."

He stared at her for a long beat, patriot blue eyes flicking down to her lips. "Do you know what *else* I remember from that night?" He asked in a predatory tone.

"Ummm..." Grace's heartbeat sped up. See? Incorporeal or not, he was *definitely* not going to just lay there. "Whatever it is you remember, I'm sure it's *wrong*. Given the amount of ale you were drinking, I'd say all your memories are fuzzy."

"Not this one." He leaned in closer. "I've got a *real* clear recollection of you kissing me... and that's not a thing I'm likely to forget."

Grace felt herself turning red. She'd always blushed easily and Jamie seemed to delight in triggering it. "I was under a lot of stress at the time. I can't be held responsible for that."

"Well, surely you donea think it was *my* doing?" He splayed a palm on his chest. "Why, I was standing there, innocent as a lamb, when you arrived to lead me astray. I was lured in by your feminine wiles."

"That is *so* not true!"

"Really? Who kissed who again, lass?" His smile

glinted, loving this.

Crap, he had a point. "Like anyone has to work real hard to lead a pirate astray." She muttered. "I supposed all those British merchants 'lured' you into stealing their gold, too."

"Certainly felt that way." He sighed. "I miss my gold."

Grace rolled her eyes at his sad tone. "Just don't tell me you buried it somewhere."

Jamie remained quiet.

"Oh for God's sake…" Her lips parted in astonishment. "You seriously *buried your treasure*, Jamie?"

"Well, I was drunk at the time!" He defended. "It seemed the thing to do. But the map's become slightly misplaced over the years, so I'm the first to admit it was an ill-advised plan."

"You buried a chest of gold and then *lost the map?!*"

"Well, I was dead when it went missing, so I'm hardly to blame. Ned Hunnicutt had it, last I heard. The gigantic jackass was even worse at *following* maps than he was a *drawing* them, though, so he couldn't find my gold." His mouth twitched. "T'was quite amusing to watch him try."

"You *seriously* dislike that guy, don't you?"

"He was a ponce. Treated all the serving girls poorly and water down his ale. Having him get his grubby, probably-a-Tory, hands on my treasure would have been a blasphemy." He frowned. "Having *anyone* else find it would vex me, as a matter of fact. It's *mine*."

The man was nothing if not possessive. "Can't you just *remember* where you buried it?" Grace could go dig it up for him, if it would make Jamie happy.

He hesitated uncomfortably. "Well… As I mentioned, I was a wee bit drunk at the time." He made a face. "I'm nearly positive it's by a tree."

Grace couldn't contain the laughter that bubbled up. "You're the worse pirate I've ever…"

A loud pounding on her bedroom door cut off her teasing comment like the shot heard 'round the world.

"Grace!" Robert bellowed from the hallway. "Open up and talk to me!"

CHAPTER EIGHT

June 24, 1789- Anabel Maxwell's buffoon of a brother Gregory asked to call on me AGAIN!

Obviously I laughed in his face AGAIN! Hero of Yorktown or not, some men just cannot take a hint.

From the Journal of Miss Lucinda Wentworth

Grace sat up in bed, anger flashing across her lovely face. "How did he get in here?" She looked more outraged than scared. "I never gave him a key! Did I forget to lock the front door?" She made a frustrated sound. "Even so, what kind of weirdo just walks into his ex-girlfriend's house, huh?" She belted her robe tighter, preparing to get up. "Is there such a thing as re-dumping, because I think I'm about to have yet *another* awkward conversation with that..."

Jamie cut off her complaints. "Stay quiet, love." He slowly got to his feet, rage and fear filling him. "Just stay right there and donea do anything to draw his attention."

Grace had pointedly bolted her bedroom door earlier, as part of her futile effort to keep Jamie out. The wooden barrier was now all that kept her ex from barging in.

Shit.

Shit.

Shit.

Unlike Grace, he didn't see Robert as some harmless gnat, waiting to be shooed away. The man was twice Grace's size and nursing a bruised ego. Jamie's father had always been at his worst when he was trying to prove his manhood and

Robert was the same sort of bastard.

Jamie had a vivid recollection of the way Robert had grabbed Grace's arm and shook her, when she tried to leave his home. He'd manhandled her like he had every right to force compliance. If Robert had the balls to show up here, demanding her attention, he wasn't going to settle for a firm "no." That fucking wanker was no gentleman. He sounded half-drunk and belligerent... and he clearly planned to reclaim what he'd lost.

Whether she wanted to be reclaimed or not.

Jamie glanced back at Grace, soul-chilling images flashing through his mind.

Grace chewed her lower lip, picking up on his tension. "You think Robert's dangerous?" She guessed, obviously not convinced. "Granted, it seems like he's been drinking, but I don't matter enough to him to risk jail time."

"*He* matters enough to him. Robert's convinced himself that you're his." Jamie heard the possession in the bastard's voice whenever he said her name. "That he has a claim to you."

"I'm not his."

Jamie's gaze cut over to her, again. "No, you're not." He moved so he was standing between the doorway and the mattress. Between Robert and Grace. ...For all the good it would do. Goddamn it, what could he do to protect her when he wasn't even alive? "Keep the door locked, alright? He wouldn't have come here unless he was already spinning out of control."

"I'm not just going to sit in here while..."

"Seeing you will just make him more determined to win." Jamie insisted, cutting her off again. Desperate for her to understand. "I know you think I'm overreacting, but I've met bullies like him before. Liars and arrogant pricks, who think they can take what they want through force and cruelty. I was raised by such a man."

She frowned. "Your father was abusive?"

"He was a fucking asshole, just like Robert."

Robert rattled the knob and it held tight. "Grace!" He

called, not the least bit apologetic over breaking in. His type never saw their own faults, just the imagined flaws and slights of others. "You're being childish. How can we discuss this if you're ignoring me? I just want to talk. You know I won't harm you, for God's sake. This is ridiculous."

"He might go away if I speak with him for a couple minutes." She offered hesitantly. "It's the easiest way to handle this."

"*No.* Donea open that door."

Grace silently stared up at him.

The choice was stark: Put her faith in Jamie or in Robert. For one panicked moment, Jamie worried that Grace would refuse to believe her ex-boyfriend was a threat. That she would ignore Jamie's frantic warnings and let him in.

"Please, love." He whispered. "Trust *me* and not him. Please."

Grace blinked. "Okay." She said simply. ...And just like that, she threw in with a dead pirate over a man who was "husband material."

It was astonishing.

So astonishing that it took Jamie a beat to catch up. "Okay?" He echoed, not fully believing her quick agreement.

"Okay. I'll keep the door locked. But what are we going to do next?"

If Jamie still had a heart it would have flipped in his chest. No one had ever trusted him so quickly and for so little reason. It was humbling. "I donea know. I'm thinking. Just stay right there on the bed."

"I know you're in there, Grace!" Robert shook the door hard enough to rattle the hinges. "Damn it! You at least owe me a conversation, you bitch!" He banged on the wood. "*Let me in!*"

She flinched and her gaze cut back over to Jamie. For the first time, she began to look worried.

In his whole life and death combined, Jamie couldn't recall ever being so furious. She was frightened and there wasn't a goddamn thing he could do about it. If he'd been corporeal, the world would be now down one paunchy museum director. Jamie would have slaughtered Robert without a second thought.

As it was, he was no more effective than a light breeze.

Grace should have a living man here protecting her. Someone worthy and strong and made of pure husband-material. Someone with a fucking heartbeat. The inescapable truth of that did nothing to improve his mood.

"Son of a *bitch*." Jamie took a deep breath, even though ghosts didn't need to breathe. "Where is your portable telephone, Grace?"

"In the kitchen. So's the landline."

"Fuck." He'd never felt so useless. "*Fuck*."

She frowned a bit at his cursing, but he was too agitated to take his usual delight in her uptight-ness.

"Grace?" Robert's tone turned wheedling. "This has gone on long enough, don't you think? I was wrong, too. I'll admit it. But at least *I'm* willing to work this out in a mature fashion. *You're* the one who's trying to throw away everything we have over some cheap pizza-tramp."

"He always says 'pizza-tramp' like it's a bad thing." She muttered. "I'm thinking it's way preferable to being labeled semi-frigid, though."

The door rattled on its hinges. "Jealousy is pointless, darling. I'd rather be screwing *you* that way. You know that. Just open the door and give me a chance to show you what you've been missing."

She made a disgusted face.

Jamie paced back and forth like a caged lion, his eyes on the doorway. "What are you wearing under the robe, Grace?" He asked, already dreading the answer.

"Nothing."

He closed his eyes. "Fuck." He whispered helplessly. The only two things between his woman and that son of a bitch were an old door and a thin bathrobe.

"It was just supposed to be you and me in here, Jamie!" Grace protested, like she thought he was upset with her. "I didn't know *he'd* show up."

Jamie looked over at her, desperation filling him. "I know, love. It's not your fault." It also wasn't her fault she was so fucking *small*. A fay creature hunted by violent, human hands. There was no way she could put up a struggle against Robert. She'd try, but she'd lose. "Truthfully, it's not going to matter what you're wearing. We just need to get you out of here."

Brown eyes blinked up at him, still not fully understanding the seriousness of her predicament. "For real? You want me to flee my own apartment?"

"Yes!" He wanted her someplace --anyplace-- far from here.

Jamie had never been this terrified. Not when he'd heard his father's footsteps coming for him as a boy. Not when his ship nearly went down in a hurricane off the South Carolina coast. Not even when they'd lynched him in the street. Grace was so damn vulnerable and important and special and there was nothing he could do to protect her.

Nothing at all.

"Push the dresser in front of the door." He ordered and strode over to check the window. It was a three story drop onto pavement. "*Fuck!*"

"Cursing is really not going to help." Grace said with another frown in his direction.

"Well it's sure as fuck not going to hurt." Could she break through the wall somehow and get into the next apartment? Doubtful since they were made of solid brick. "Did you have to live in a building that predates the Civil War, lass?" He was actually longing for cheaply thrown together modern construction right now.

"Because things would be so much better if that was a hollow-core door, right?"

She had a point. The antique door was holding. For now. "Would you move that damn thing, please?" He gestured to the painted chest of drawers against the wall, which she still wasn't shoving into position as a barricade. It was ugly as sin, older than even Jamie, and made of solid oak.

Grace made a face. "It's going to knock all my figurines." She muttered, but she reluctantly headed over to push at its massive weight. "Stupid Robert." The heavy dresser slowly inched its way across the floor. On its wide top, chipped and glued statues of mermaids rattled, several of them toppling to the ground. Grace winced as they shattered, but wedged the chest of drawers into place.

Jamie wished that was all it took to solve the problem.

"When are you going to see your own fault in this?" Robert demanded, changing tactics. "I have *needs*, goddamn it. I told you that, but you don't seem to even hear my side of this. It's because you couldn't have an orgasm if three men were fucking you! You told me yourself you've *never* climaxed. How do you think that makes me feel?"

Jamie arched a brow at her, trying to lighten the mood. "Never? Well, that's just a pity."

Grace's face flushed bright pink.

"A man needs someone warm beneath him!" Robert ranted. "He needs to feel *wanted*. You should be *begging* me to take you back. No one else would want you or your lunatic family in his life, you semi-frigid freak!"

Grace looked up at Jamie again, like she was worried he might be falling for that horseshit.

"You know who says women are frigid?" He scoffed. "Assholes who suck in bed. Donea listen to a word that bastard says. I told you he was a liar."

Grace's mouth curved. "You, I imagine, never met a girl you couldn't satisfy."

"It's a point of pride, really. Give me a chance to show you my skills and I'll keep my perfect record intact. I promise you, I can make you *very* happy." He winked at her, hoping to cover his anxiety. "Get back on the bed, now." He didn't want her near the door, in case Robert got through.

The wanker was now trying to kick it in.

Jamie scanned around the room for a weapon she could use. "Do you know how to fight?" It was a longshot, but he was praying she'd reveal that she'd secretly trained with the Navy SEALs for some reason.

Grace shook her head, kneeling on the mattress. "Riveras don't do a lot of hand-to-hand combat. Well, my cousin Destiny tried a ninja spell once, but it resulted in some bad Karate chopping, and smashed up picket fences, and 911 calls." She made a face. "Spells are *always* a bad idea."

Staggering relief flooded through Jamie as he remembered who this tiny girl really was. "You've magic in your blood." How could he have forgotten that? "*You* can stop this, lass. You just need to…"

Grace cut him off, looking scandalized. "I don't use spells! Maybe an occasional potion, but only when I'm *completely* out of normal options."

"We're out of *all* fucking options, Grace!" He stormed over to stand in front of her. "Do something *now* or that fucking little fuck is going to break in here and rape you right in front of me!"

Grace blanched and not at his language. "He wouldn't…"

"He *will*." Jamie interrupted. "I know bad people, lass, and he's a bad person. He *will* hurt you, unless you do something to stop him. Trust me."

The door bulged inward a bit, knocking more of the knickknacks onto the floor.

Tears glittered in Grace's eyes and he knew she believed him. "Jamie, I'm scared."

The tremor in her voice made him want to kill Robert with his bare hands. If it meant taking away her fear, he would have gladly cut a deal with God to return to his wasteland of isolation forever. Jamie would give anything to help her finally feel safe.

To *be* safe.

"I know you're scared." Jamie put his palms on either side of her pale face, the insubstantial edges of his body tingling where they touched her smooth skin. "I know, love." He softened his tone with supreme effort of will. "And I know you want to deny it, but there's power in you. Now's the time to use it."

"No, it's seriously *not!* I only know two spells." She held up two fingers, so he could count for himself. "And one of them is for curing frigging menstrual cramps!"

"Menstrual cramps?" Jamie had always been good at improvised offensives. It was why he'd made such a nice living as a pirate, despite the gentlemanly tendencies that were forever plaguing him. A pain relieving spell could actually work. Anything that dulled pain also dulled senses. "Okay." His mind raced for a beat. "Here's what we'll do, then: I will go out in the hall..."

"No!" She interrupted, horrified. "Don't leave me alone. Please, Jamie." She tried to catch hold of his sleeve, but her fingers passed straight through his arm.

He could've cried. Stepping back from her was the hardest thing he'd ever done. "I'm *never* going to leave you, Grace. I swear it. But we *have* to do this, alright? I'm just going into the hall. When I tell you, you hit the son of a bitch with every fucking ounce of power you have, understand? Dose it up as high as that spell will go and fry him."

"That is absolutely, unequivocally *crazy*. I'm not good at magic. I barely even believe in it. This idea is *never* going to work."

"It'll work. I know it will work." He wasn't sure what they would do if it didn't work. Robert was going to get through the door very, very soon. "We donea have another idea, so this one is what we're going with."

"I can't *do* this." She persisted in an increasingly panicked voice. "You're not listening! I'm a normal person, Jamie! Normal people don't do this kind of crap. And I *hate* spells. They *always* go wrong. I can't *believe* you're asking me to do this!" She began rubbing her temples hard enough to drill right through her skull. "Peacefulgreencornfields, peacefulgreencornfields, peacefulgreencornfields..."

"All I'm asking is for you to try! For me. Just *try* the spell. Please." He would beg if he had to. "I'm scared, too. You have no fucking idea how scared I am, right now."

Grace hesitated. Brown eyes flicked up to his, like those words might have actually gotten through to her.

"I can't touch anything." Jamie continued, seeing he had her attention. The girl had the heart of a savior. If she wouldn't use magic for herself, she might use it to aid him. "You'll have to protect yourself, because I *can't help you*." Admitting that hurt worse than the rope around his neck. Grace deserved so much more than a ghost to aid her. "I'm sorry, my love. I am so fucking sorry. If I could, I would go out there and destroy that rat-bastard for you. I swear it. But it's not possible. So, *please* try this. I'm not sure what else to do to save you."

Grace chewed her lower lip, studying his agonized face. "I guess I could try." She finally said. "It won't work, but I'll try if you want me to."

"I want you to try." He assured her.

Robert hit the door hard enough, to shift the dresser a few centimeters across the hardwood floor. "I'll show you what you've been missing, you icy bitch!"

Jamie stayed focused on Grace. "I want you to try *right now*." He stepped backwards, heading for the hallway. "I'm going out there and we're going to try this, okay?"

She bobbed her head, but she still looked doubtful.

Jamie would take what he could get. "Good." He prepared to phase through the wall. "Just wait for my signal."

"Jamie?"

He turned back to her.

"When this doesn't work, it won't be your fault. Whatever happens, you tried your hardest to help me. Don't blame yourself."

His jaw ticked. "It's *going* to work, Grace. Just this once, try to have a bit of optimism." He ducked through the wall, without giving her a chance to respond.

Robert somehow managed to look hungover and drunk at the same time. Dressed in a suit he'd clearly slept in, his bloodshot eyes glittered in bleary malice as he tried to kick down the door to Grace's bedroom.

Jamie hated the man more than the cowards who hanged him. If he could've wrapped his hands around Robert's throat, he would've popped his skull off like a cork from a bottle.

"Miserable son of a bitch." He instinctively tilted his head, cracking his neck the way he used to before he went into battle. "Ready, love?" He called to Grace.

"This is a bad plan." She shouted through the door, just in case he hadn't understood her reservations the first six times. "Valley-Forge-in-wintertime-with-no-shoes bad."

Robert hesitated, thinking she was talking to him. "What?"

Jamie ignored the idiot. "You are always focusing on the negative, lass. Even a bad plan is better than no plan a'tall."

"I'm pretty sure that isn't true. There are a lot of non-plans that would've been *waaay* better that this idea."

"What are you talking about?" Robert demanded. "Have you lost your goddamn mind?"

"Oh shut up, Robert!" Grace snapped. "Mind your own business!"

Jamie nearly grinned at her incensed tone. How could he have ever thought this girl was weak-spirited? "On the count of three, now." He moved behind Robert, calculating the line-of-sight. "He's standing at about ten o'clock, right in front of that hideous painting of the donkey you apparently commissioned from an untalented kindergartener."

"It's a *horse* and I rescued it from a flea market, actually."

"Not even the fleas would have that thing about, lass." Jamie held up his thumb, beginning the countdown. "One."

"I hate, hate, *hate* this plan, Jamie."

Robert looked behind him and then up at the ceiling, still trying to figure out who she was speaking to. "Who the hell is Jamie?"

"*I'm* Jamie." Jamie snarled at him. "The man she *actually* belongs to." He extended his index finger and prayed like hell. "Two!"

"Jamie, if he gets in here, don't watch." Grace warned. "It'll be harder for you if you have to watch."

She was right. Seeing Grace harmed would be worse

than his own death, but he would still stay with her through all of it. "Three!" He shouted, ignoring her command. "Now, Grace!"

Wham!

Energy slammed out, blasting Robert right in the chest. Jamie's eyebrows soared as the smaller man went flying backwards and careened into the wall. Grace had far more magic in her blood than he'd anticipated. The amped-up menstrual cramp spell hit with the force of a wrecking ball, knocking Robert right off his feet. Lucky for him, the anesthetic quality of the enchantment was increased as well. Old Rob was feeling no pain. He gave a dopey smile and fell forward in an unconscious heap of beige.

Then the hideous mule painting fell right on top of him.

Jamie arched a brow. He'd seen bloody cartoons with more dignity. "Good news, love. You've vanquished the grotesque jackass. ...Also, your rotter of an ex is quite possibly dead."

He heard her pushing the dresser out of the way and opening the door a crack. "He's dead?" She sounded annoyed over that possibility. "Do you have any idea how hard that's going to be to explain to the police?"

"Oh, if he was dead, we wouldn't be troubling the authorities about him. Sadly, the wanker still seems to be breathing, after all." Jamie crouched down next to Robert, wanting nothing more than to pitch him out a window. "Donea suppose I can convince you to finish him off while he's down, can I?" He asked hopefully.

"I'm not killing anyone, Jamie."

"But he's only going to wake up and cause you more distress. If you were to..."

"*No.*"

He made a face at her. "Fine." Problem solving had been a lot more permanent back when he was three-dimensional. Letting Robert live was just asking for trouble. It seemed obvious to Jamie. Still, he could tell that Grace wasn't going to listen to reason. "Call the constables and let's do this the hard way, then." He sighed.

"What am I going to tell the cops? That I used a spell on him? Not even I think that's true and I *frigging know it's true!*"

"The man reeks of bourbon, Grace. You're going to tell them he arrived here drunk, attacked you, and somehow managed to knock himself out."

"You think they'll believe that?"

"What else are they going to believe?" Jamie got to his feet and shot her a triumphant grin. "That you defeated him, using nothing but the ghost of a dead pirate and a magical spell?"

She winced. "Yeah... Good point."

CHAPTER NINE

June 24, 1789- Around town, they say JMR has a treasure buried somewhere nearby. Gold, silver, and gems! All of it hidden away until the Pirate gives it to his bride.

I'm wondering if I can convince him to lend me a few diamonds, while he waits for her to show up.

From the Journal of Miss Lucinda Wentworth

The police did indeed believe Grace's story.

What other explanation was there, really?

They carted Robert off to jail, with a lecture on locking her doors and a yellow pamphlet on restraining orders. Grace figured her ex would be out again by morning... assuming he woke up, at all. That menstrual cramp magic really packed a wallop in large doses. She was a little concerned that Robert would stay unconscious until some handsome prince kissed him awake or something.

Spells always seemed to go wrong.

"We should have made sure he couldn't come after you, again." Jamie repeated for the hundredth time. It clearly drove him crazy that the cops didn't execute Robert right there in her apartment. He paced back and forth in front of the bedroom door, like he was afraid someone might try to break in again. "I donea like that he's still breathing."

"He's in a cell for the night, Jamie. You can relax, for now."

"What about for *later?* Turns out your 'husband material' candidate is a fucking maniac, love. He *will* be back."

Jamie's eyes narrowed thoughtfully. "We need to buy a musket."

"I'll put it on the grocery list."

He didn't appreciate her sarcasm. "You should pay me more attention. I *told* you he wasn't a gentleman, but you didn't listen and now *this* happened."

"Yeah, but you also told me *you* weren't a gentleman, which was a total lie. So, you're still not batting a thousand in that department."

Jamie looked confused. "I'm not a gentleman." He made it sound like she'd accused him of being a sex offender. "I sometimes have half-hearted gentlemanly impulses, which I try to ignore, but…"

"Yes, you absolutely *are* a gentleman." Grace interrupted, climbing up onto her bed again. She'd changed into clothes before the police arrived, but now she was back in her fuzzy robe. "You just saved my life, Jamie."

"You saved your own life. I did what I could to help, because you're mine."

"No." She shook her head. "That's not it, at all. You didn't even know me when I went back in time and you helped me then, too."

Jamie gazed at her for a long beat. "I would always know you, Grace."

Her insides dipped at his quiet words, but she kept going. "I was completely lost and vulnerable and alone… and all you did was offer to walk me home. You tried to protect me. I don't think any other pirate would have done that with a half-dressed, possibly-drunk girl who'd kissed him three minutes after they met."

He pouted a bit at that irrefutable evidence. "Well, maybe I was plotting something nefarious and luring you in." He muttered.

"Maybe you're just a nice guy, under all the come-ons and craziness." She shot him a smile. "It's okay. I won't tell anyone." She clicked on the TV, tuning it to *Haunted High* for him. "I also won't blab about your crappy taste in televisions shows." She settled back to watch the thirty-something "teens" battle supernatural monsters and plan their prom.

Jamie glanced at the screen, his mouth curving when he saw she'd remembered his favorite show. "For you, I wish I *was* a gentleman." He murmured, looking back at her with a soft expression. "I wish I was so many good things for you, Grace."

"I like you just the way you are. And I'm *going* to save you." She made it a vow. The possessiveness he felt towards her was contagious, because she was coming to think of Jamie as *hers.* She'd do her very best to clear his name, no matter what it took. Besides, focusing on solving the murders was a lot more rewarding than talking about her scumbag ex. "The key to proving your innocence is the blood from the crime scenes. I'm sure of it. If we can find evidence from the other murders, I think I can go back and stop them."

Jamie hesitated. "I was thinking just the opposite, really.

"The opposite?"

"Maybe we should stop this investigation, before…"

"Stop it?" She interrupted. "Are you kidding? I just figured out how to clear your name and you want to quit?"

"If it means you're not placing yourself in danger, than *yes*. We should quit." His expression was grave. "I would not have you risk yourself for me, Grace. I would not have you risk yourself for *anything*." He gestured to the bedroom door. "I'm not likely to soon forget that you nearly died right in front of me! Do you think I want to take a chance of that happening, again?"

"I'm doing this." She insisted. "I *have* to, not just for you, but for me. Don't you get it? I thought this… *ability* took everything from me, last year. But really it's giving me a chance to help people. To stop murders *before* they happen. I need to see it through. It's the only way I'm ever going to get my life back. This will get *both* our lives back, Jamie."

He shook his head. "It's not worth the risk."

"You'd rather be *hanged* again?"

"Yes." The word was unequivocal. "I will gladly fade

to nothing before I see you harmed."

Grace stared up at him, processing the intrinsic nobility of the man. He might think a pirate couldn't be a gentleman, but she knew better. "Did you mean it earlier?" She asked abruptly.

Jamie's eyebrows drew together in confusion. "Mean what?"

"Did you mean it when you said you could… um… bring me to… completion, if I gave you a chance."

He stared at her for a long beat, blinking rapidly at the non sequitur. "You're just trying to distract me." He rasped, but his eyes drifted down to the opened V of her bathrobe.

"Kind of maybe a little bit. …But I'd also like to know how you could do such a thing, when no one else has even come close." Unable to withstand the penetrating blue of his eyes, Grace glanced over at the TV, where Liliana-the-banshee-girl was shopping for her prom gown. "Ew, she's not really going to wear that hideous purple one is she? Sebastian will hate that."

Jamie disregarded *Haunted High,* which no doubt showed his high level of concentration. "You truly haven't come *a'tall*." He sounded like he couldn't imagine such a thing. "Not even once in your whole life?"

Grace flushed and shook her head, wondering if this was such a great idea. Her body told her it was the best plan ever, but it was embarrassing to discuss this so openly, even with Jamie. *Especially* with Jamie. He looked more fascinated with her lackluster sex life than he had with the discovery of actual time travel.

"Why?" He pressed, seemingly baffled.

"My therapist concluded I had 'unrealistic expectations about intimacy.'" She muttered, hoping he'd just drop it. "Or, if you want to listen to Robert, I'm just semi-frigid."

"Bullshit. There's nothing wrong with you, Grace. Not a blessed thing."

Grace bit down on her lower lip. "Why has it never happened for me, then?" She asked before she could stop herself. "It happens for everyone else. Why not me?"

"Well, I think that should be obvious." Jamie smiled like he knew the answer to every dirty question ever asked. "You just hadn't met the right man."

She snorted. "Let me guess: *You're* the right man."

"Yes." He sounded certain. "I told you, I can make you happy."

Some heretofore dormant, pizza-tramp-y part of her brain cheered in anticipation. Grace shook her head again, trying to think. "But you can't actually touch me, remember?"

"I donea have to touch you."

She blinked, desperately curious about what he was planning. "...You don't?"

"Nope." He gave a predatory smile and eased onto the bed next to her. "Come on... You know I can do this, Grace. You've been waiting for me. We've been waiting for *each other*. You feel it, too. This connection between us is real."

She did feel it.

"Let me show you what I can do." Jamie shifted so his body was even closer to hers, taking her silence as encouragement. "What do you really have to lose? The worst that can happen is I'm unable to meet all your 'unrealistic expectations.' That would leave you right where you are now. It seems like there's no risk and all reward."

Grace swallowed. "You probably tried that line with every girl in the thirteen colonies."

"Nope. Just the one I would have married."

Corny as it sounded, her heart skipped. "Jamie, you don't have to..."

"Take off your robe."

Yeah... She was totally going to take off her robe. Surprisingly, the commanding tone turned her insides to liquid. Who knew? If anyone could fix her intimacy problem, it was Jamie Riordan. The man had probably invented sex.

Grace's hands went to the knot at her waist, pulling it free before she gave herself time to reconsider. "Okay, but this isn't going to work." She warned, wanting him to be prepared for failure.

"You truly are a pessimistic little thing. It's quite adorable."

"I just don't want you to be too disappointed, if you can't get me... all the way. It's like a mental block or something." It was because she'd never been able to let go with anyone. Deep down, she knew that.

She'd never felt safe enough.

"You should have more faith in me, lass. Even my bad plans have a proven success rate in this room. Besides, bloodthirsty pirates have an inborn talent for corrupting the innocent..." Jamie trailed off and muttered a quiet curse, as the robe slid off her shoulders. His gaze fixed on her bare breasts and stayed there. "Holy God."

Grace had a hard time breathing under the intensity of his stare. "Don't take this the wrong way, but you kinda sucked as a bloodthirsty pirate." She shrugged off the robe and tried to focus on something *other* than her nakedness. The past seemed as good a topic as any, so the words just poured out of her in an anxious torrent. "According to all the textbooks, you just stole from rich British merchants."

His gaze licked over her skin. "They had the most gold." He murmured absently.

"I think it's more than that. You never bothered the helpless or the genuinely innocent. ...Which, I have to admit, always seemed strange to me considering the books also said you were a crazed serial killer." She winced. "Crap. I probably shouldn't have brought up the homicide part, right now."

His lips twitched. "I do love the fact you're a bit of an odd-duck, love. You have the most fascinating pillow talk I've ever encountered."

"Well, you're making me nervous! History helps me when I'm nervous."

"By all means, then. Let's talk about my mediocre piracy." He agreed in the world's most agreeable tone. "*After* you take off your underwear."

Grace swallowed. "This won't work." She reiterated half-heartedly.

"There's that adorable pessimism again. It truly is

becoming a turn on."

"I'm serious. I've been dreaming about you since I was fifteen, but not even you can..."

"Fifteen?" Jamie grinned like she'd just handed him the map to an uncharted isle and --God knew-- he was a man who took maps seriously. "Why that's quite naughty, Mistress Rivera. I'm very impressed."

"...but not even you can do this without touching me." She finished, disregarding his commentary. "It's impossible."

Grace totally believed that. ...But she still found herself slipping her panties down her legs and tossing them aside.

"That's it, my love." His gaze centered on the junction of her thighs and Grace felt it like a physical touch. "That's what I wanted to see." His tone was reverent and territorial and it did wonderful things to her insides. "Let me get a good look at you, now."

She bit back a whimper, her legs obediently parting for him. Jamie liked that she followed instructions and he *really* liked the view. A lot. "Mine." He whispered reverently. "Finally."

They were the same words he'd used back in 1789 and they turned Grace on even more. His possessiveness shouldn't be nearly so hot. Her core was getting wetter by the second and all he was doing was looking at her. "Oh God..." For the first time, she began to believe that he could really do this.

Jamie himself had no doubts, at all. The man's confidence level was as deep as the sea. He leaned in closer to her, his body moving over hers. "So... you read books about me, then?" He asked and she knew that he was trying to distract her from overthinking his newest crazy bad idea.

"Some." Energy licked through her wherever he touched. And he was doing his best to touch her *everywhere*. His beautiful palms couldn't make contact with her skin, but she could still feel them all over her. Her nipples went rock hard as his fingers passed over them, her eyes drifting shut in pleasure.

His mouth curved. "Only *some* books?"

"A lot of books." Her breath was coming in pants. "I took three semesters of Virginia history in college. You were my sophomore term paper."

"I can't imagine you had many flattering things to say about a lackluster pirate hanged for murder."

"Nope."

"And yet here you are with me." His lips hovered over hers and his hand drifted downward, towards her weeping center. "Why is that, do you think?"

"Well," she chewed on her lower lip, "I really wasn't as good a student as you might imagine."

"Oh, I doubt that."

"Really. I needed a magic potion to pass geometry."

Jamie chuckled. "I think fate brought you here." He corrected. "I think you were always supposed to be mine. I think no other man has been able to satisfy you, because none of them were *me*."

She thought he was right.

All the unrealistic expectations that her therapist bitched about were embodied in this one man. They always had been. Only Grace suddenly wasn't sure they were so *un*realistic, after all. Just being close to Jamie was sending her body into complete meltdown. Rockets' red glare and bombs bursting in air had nothing on the fireworks the pirate set off inside of her.

Grace reached for him, needing Jamie more than she'd ever needed anything. Her hand passed through his back and she nearly sobbed in frustration. "Please." Her breathing hitched, her palm moving up to grasp one of the wrought iron bars of her headboard instead. "Jamie, please."

"Christ, you're beautiful." His voice was ragged. "From the first time I saw you --*both* bloody first times-- I wanted you like this. Wanted to hear you say my name, just like that. Needful and dazed. I imagine it every time I look at you."

That shocked her. "You do?"

"Oh yes." It was a purr. "And now I have you."

He'd had her from the time she was fifteen. "First

time I saw you was in a painting." She got out.

"The one with my ship?" He nodded approvingly. "I look damn good in that portrait, if I do say so myself." One of his long, artist's fingers slipped inside her and she gasped. "That's it. Show me just what you like, lass."

"That. I like *that*." Whatever he was doing, she was afraid it would stop working and she was closer than she'd ever been. "Hurry. Jamie, please hurry."

Blue eyes burned hot. "I didn't propose to you when we kissed." He got out, ignoring her pleas. "You said you thought I did, but you clearly weren't listening. A proposal would have meant giving you an option and I'm far too much of a pirate for that. We just *take* the bride we want."

God did she want to be taken.

"If you'd stayed back there, I would have stolen you, Grace. I'd have carried you back to my ship and claimed your pretty body in every way I could think of. And you'd have let me, because you're not such a timid lass, after all, are you? Under that proper exterior, you've got a yearning for a bit of danger in your life."

She had a yearning for *him*. She always had. *That's* why she would have let him have her back in 1789. That's why she was letting him have her now. "You're not dangerous, Jamie. Not to me." She believed that with all her heart. He was the only one who made her feel safe.

"No, not to you. But I would be a fucking monster if someone tried to take you from my arms. I promise you that. Ghost or man, the need I have for you is bigger than anything I can control."

She gulped, her body clenching at his words. "Okay, for real, I think this might actually work." She'd never felt soooo close to something soooo huge. "Can we go faster, now? Please? I don't want this feeling to go away."

"It's not going to go away." He soothed. "I'll give you everything you need. I promise. But this has got to be a team effort. So you just do what I say and this is going to be *beautiful*."

"You're sure?"

"I'm positive. Put your hand where mine is."

Grace was too far gone to even hesitate. Her palm slid down to cover the spot he was touching, pressing deep. "Oh *God*." Her lips parted, her head going back in ecstasy.

"Fuck yes." It was little more than a snarl. "So wet and pink and soft." He watched her hand move with a rapturous expression. "Harder, Grace. Deeper."

"I can't..."

"You *can*." He interrupted. "I want it *all*, Grace. Give it to me. That's it." He let out a groan of pure pleasure as she did what he demanded, her back arching to accept the more powerful thrusts of her fingers. "That's it, my love."

"*Jamie!*"

"I'm here. Christ, I would never want to be anywhere else." He gave a laugh that sounded like he was in pain. "See what having a bit of optimism can do? That's a lesson for both of us."

"I've never gotten this far before. I didn't expect it to be so... tight. I feel really, really *tight*." Her words ended in a whimper that just seemed to enflame him.

He watched her intently, like he was committing every freckle on her skin to memory. "I need you so much, Grace." His voice was unsteady and darker than she'd ever heard it. "I know you donea need me. Not really. I know you deserve more than a dead man in your life and bed. But I'm going to make you come so hard you won't even *think* of another partner, again."

She wanted to respond to that, but she was too far gone. All she could do was gasp as he touched some magical spot with his incorporeal fingers and her body reacted like he'd stroked the very core of her with liquid heat. "*Jamieeee!*"

He dipped his head to her ear. "Come for me, lass. I need to see it. Come now and I'll keep you safe."

That was all it took. Grace screamed as she convulsed against both their hands. The explosion shook her whole body, her knuckles going white around the headboard rail. Her body shattered into a million pieces and Jamie drank in every tremor.

A satisfied smile curved his mouth, like he was the one who'd reached completion. She chanted his name and he whispered endearments in Gaelic and, for a timeless moment, it was all... perfect.

Exactly the way she'd always known it was supposed to be between Partners.

Grace lay there, struggling for breath. "Wow." Unrealistic expectations, be damned. If anything she'd *under*estimated Jamie's abilities. "You really just did that." She panted.

"*We* did that." He settled down next to her, looking smug. "Take your share of the credit, lass. You are bloody amazing at this."

She blinked up at him, owlishly. "Thank you."

"Oh believe me, it was my extreme pleasure." He smoothed a hand over her hair. "I *will* keep you safe." He repeated in a more serious tone and she knew he wasn't just talking about in bed. "I promise you."

"I know." She smiled, more replete than she'd ever been. "I'll keep you safe, too. Which means going back to 1789 and fixing what went wrong." She needed to make sure he knew that, because she wasn't going to change her mind no matter how many orgasms he gave her.

And hopefully it would be a lot.

Jamie gazed at her, patriot blue eyes roaming all over her face. She could see him searching for a way to talk her out of more time travel.

"You can't talk me out of it." She assured him before he ruined the mood. There was no way she was going to let his name be slandered throughout history. Jamie deserved so much more. She couldn't save the whole world, but she could save Jamie Riordan. "You're the one telling me to be more positive. Well, I'm *positive* I can find a way to prove your innocence."

"I donea think it's a good idea to..."

"Help me do this, Jamie. I *need* to do this."

He squeezed his eyes shut at the entreaty. "This

would be far easier if you were a timid lass." He muttered.

"Maybe." She arched a brow, knowing she'd won. "But, then again, a timid lass wouldn't have just taken off her panties for a pirate."

CHAPTER TEN

June 25, 1789- My parents hate me! I should be used to it by now. They see me as an embarrassment and a disgrace to their precious name. All they care about is their standing in the community. To them, I am nothing but a pretty package they can sell off to a suitor of their choosing. They don't care a fig about what I want or think or need! They look at me with cold disapproval and even colder hearts.

I can't even imagine what it would be like to have a loving family.

From the Journal of Miss Lucinda Wentworth

"So you've been time traveling with a ghost." Serenity summed up the next day, after Grace was done explaining everything to her. "Does this mean you *aren't* going to help me get ready for the 4th of July sale?"

Jamie's eyebrows soared at such a blasé response to such unbelievably weird news.

Grace didn't seem surprised, at all. "I knew you were going to start nagging about that stupid sale." She pushed her way through some beaded curtains, shaking her head. "How inconsiderate of me not to focus on what's *really* important, right?"

"My sale *is* important. Do you have any idea how bad business is for us, Gracie?"

"I'm the only Rivera in ten generations to try to organize the accounts around here, so… yeah. I've got a pretty good idea. Have you been looking at the bookkeeping software I set up?"

Serenity sniffed. "I've no time for all that numbers bullshit." She was a tall, curvy woman with red hair and a turban that matched her flowing hippie-ish robes. "I've got to compete with that phony palm reader down the street, who has a fucking *Facebook page*." Her eyes narrowed in determination. "I'm thinking of offering a BOGO on live frogs. Let's see Madam Topanga top *that*."

"Oh for God's sake, would you forget your war with Madam Topanga? I'll help you generate some new business plans later. Not that you'll *listen* to them…"

"Running a magic shop isn't about 'business plans.' It's about helping people find true love, smite their enemies, and occasionally become trolls." Serenity gave a mournful pause. "God, I wish we could find that recipe."

Grace sent her aunt an exasperated look. "I just need you to focus and help me. Please? It's an emergency."

Jamie followed her through the shop, his eyes darting around every dusty nook and cranny. Offhand, he didn't recalled entering The Crystal Ball since the '20s, but it looked pretty much the same. …Just as it had looked pretty much the same for the century before that. The Riveras clearly didn't care much about creating an inviting shopping experience. The dim interior held the same wooden cabinets and shelves, filled with the same morbid knickknacks and bottles of strange liquids. At some point, one of them had added a few strings of skeleton-shaped twinkle lights and a mirror that seemed to somehow be reflecting the wrong image.

Jamie cringed. Even for a ghost, that was a bit creepy. No wonder this family was always broke, if this is how they welcomed their customers.

Grace took it all in stride. "We need some magic, Auntie." She called, heading for a listing bookcase. "A time travel potion. Is there such a thing?"

"Easier if we used a spell."

"I don't like spells. You know that. Potions at least have the façade of chemistry and herbal medicine to hold onto. Spells are messy and they always go wrong."

Serenity rolled her eyes. "Well, a potion could take a while." She warned. "No one in the family has been able to time travel, since your great uncle Recompense went back to the Crusades."

"*Other* Riveras have time traveled and you're just mentioning it *now?!*"

"Like you would have listened before." Serenity scoffed. "You were too busy convincing yourself you were bonkers, until the ghost showed up and talked some sense into you."

No one had ever called Jamie sensible before. He shot Grace a smug look, which she pointedly ignored. She was too busy muttering about cornfields again.

"Point is, time travel is a bit of a recessive talent." Serenity continued. "Not much research on the herbs we'll need. It'll take some real innovation on my part."

"Blue eyes are recessive, too. But could I get *them?* Noooooo." Grace shook her head in adorable vexation.

"I'm quite fond of your eyes just the way they are." Jamie assured her. The chocolatey color was sexy as hell. Especially when they were glazed with passion and Grace was begging him for release.

God, last night had been perfect. Ghosts couldn't come, but Jamie had still been fully satisfied. The way she'd let him touch her, and the sound of his name on her tongue, and her startled joy when she climaxed for the first time... Nothing had ever made him prouder. It made sense to him now why some people thought sex was so important. It had always just been a bit of a lark to him before, but not with Grace. She made it feel like something holy. Every moment of his time with her was imprinted on his memory forever.

Grace looked up at him and gave a reluctant smile. "If you're flirting with me even in this getup, you must *really* want to see me naked again." She whispered.

"Oh lass, you have no idea."

Grace was due back at her tour guide job that afternoon, so she was wearing her Colonial garb. The ridiculous yellow costume was only slightly more authentic than her Keds, but it was still remarkably appealing on her. And Jamie heartily approved of the low neckline. He couldn't wait to see her out of it.

Serenity strolled into the backroom after them, reluctantly interested in a time travel challenge. "I suppose we'll need to update the family Christmas letter, if you're going to start vacationing in the Revolutionary War. Not much in the way of usefulness, but at least you're *finally* using your powers. Grandma Verity will be pleased."

"A dream come true."

Serenity ignored Grace's bad attitude and snapped her fingers in excitement, like an idea suddenly occurred to her. "*Unless* you plan on looking for the lost recipe for troll powder while you're back there!" She pressed her palms together in a quick, silent prayer to some no-doubt scary deity. "The recipe wasn't forgotten until your Great-Aunt Honor died in that sideshow, back in 1899. Rediscovering it could change everything for us."

"For the last time, nobody wants to become a troll!"

"Troll powder?" Jamie repeated looking between them. "Is that really a thing?"

Grace waved a "don't even ask" palm at him. "And this is *not* a vacation." She assured her aunt and grabbed an ancient tome on Harrisonburg history, opening it on an ebony table with carved skulls on the top. "I'm being sent back for an important purpose. I know it."

"Troll powder *is* important. It could help me shut Madam Topanga up, once and for all."

"An important purpose as in *saving someone's life*, Auntie."

Serenity gave a long-suffering sigh. "Well, that *is* usually the reason that this time-traveling power manifests." She admitted in the superior tone of someone who was always eager to impart her wisdom... whether her audience wanted to hear it or not. "Laws of nature aren't usually bent just for the hell of it. Only when something's gone wrong and the Higher Powers want it fixed." She paused. "Well, there was the one time with Cousin Memory's thirtieth reunion and the tornado, but I *still* say that was mostly the leprechaun curse."

"You *always* think it's a leprechaun curse." Grace

muttered under her breath.

Serenity had ears like a vampire bat. "When you're cursed by a leprechaun, it tends to ruin your social life. That's all I'm saying. Cousin Memory should never have taken his gold and bought that jet ski."

"Taking a man's gold is a terrible thing." Jamie put in, although no one had asked his opinion. "I shall never get over the loss of mine."

Grace rolled her eyes.

Serenity kept going. "I told Memory it was a bad idea to follow that damn rainbow, but she didn't listen." She pointed a three inch long red finger nail at Grace. "It's a lesson for you, young lady. Psychics give the best advice. If you don't *listen* to me, one day you'll end up with a shamrock-green cyclone sucking up your high school."

Grace dutifully nodded.

Jesus, Mary, and Joseph. Jamie was beginning to see why she was so keen on being safe and normal. The girl had grown up in a home where every day was Halloween.

"Now then, as I was saying, usually time travelers are chosen to right some wrong." Serenity continued. "Recompense was supposed to save some serfs from a fire, if I remember correctly. Jackass wouldn't stop bragging about it. He always was a bit of a tool."

"I'm supposed to catch this murderer and clear Jamie's name. I know it. To do that, I need to go back to the nights Anabel Maxwell and Clara Vance died and save them."

Serenity pursed her lips, disapprovingly. "Wasn't Clara Vance some Puritanical bitch, who burned witches for fun?"

"There were no witch burnings in Harrisonburg! Why do people keep saying that? I don't think anyone was executed as a witch in this country since --like-- Salem, a hundred years earlier. The Colonial era was the age of Enlightenment, for God's sake."

Serenity frowned, unconvinced. "Some of our ancestors were witches, you know. It's a noble profession. Cousin Mercy used her powers to cure Methyn's Syndrome."

"I've never even *heard* of Methyn's Syndrome."

"That's because Mercy cured it." Serenity explained smugly.

Grace made an irritated sound and ran a hand through her shiny, dark, beautiful hair.

Jamie nearly groaned as the strands slid through her fingers. He wanted to feel the thick curls so badly it was a physical ache. And ghosts didn't *have* physical aches. He'd endured two hundred plus years of not being able to touch anything and came through it all without breaking. ...But not being able to touch *Grace* was going to break him. He could already tell.

Grace didn't notice his torment. "The problem is, we don't have a lot of information on the last two murders. Gregory Maxwell's book skimps on some of the details."

"I cannot believe you think that idiot is an author." Jamie muttered, trying to focus on anything besides his unsatiated need for her. "He was confused by water being wet and trees being green. I promise you, he didn't write *Horror in Harrisonburg* any more than I did."

"Well whoever wrote it, they should've given us more specifics." Grace looked at her aunt. "Anabel Maxwell dies next, but saving her would be a lot easier if I found a way to remind the Jamie-of-the-past about things that haven't happened yet."

Serenity squinted. "Come again?"

"We need to make sure the Jamie-of-the-past knows what *this* Jamie knows. They're the same person, after all. There has to be a way for both of them to remember the same things." Grace waved a hand. "Otherwise he's going to think I'm a raving nut job when I try to explain it to him back there. Can you make a potion?"

"I'll know you, Grace." Jamie assured her quietly. "Donea worry about that. Even without the memories, I'll *always* know you." This woman was his. Alive or dead, every instinct told him so. The old him would be far more interested in bedding her than in having her committed. "Speaking of which, if you *do* go back again, would you do me a great favor?"

She looked up at him and nodded seriously. "Of course."

"Submit to every sordid, twisted, wicked thing I want to do to your body." He endeavored to look grave. "I would dearly *love* those memories, lass."

Grace blinked and then burst out laughing.

Jamie grinned at the happy sound, adoring her.

"I can make a potion for *anything*." Serenity interjected, not liking to be left out of the joke. Her brown eyes unerringly landed on Jamie, even though she couldn't see him. "Even for memory/time travel shit. But are you sure the ghost is worth all this effort, Gracie?"

Jamie glared back at the woman, even though she was probably right.

"I'm sure." Grace flipped through the yellowed pages of the book. "Darn it, I *know* that page is in here somewhere. Isn't there an index to this frigging thing?"

Serenity wasn't giving up. "Because you *really* need to be sure. Your cousin Prudence dated a ghost for a while. ...Until he dumped her for a zombie." She crossed her arms over her chest. "Said Pru couldn't fit in with the 'undead culture' and made himself invisible to her, so she couldn't see him lurking about... probably watching her do God-only-knows what. That's the way it is with all of them. Snobby perverts."

"I've never even *met* a zombie." Jamie put in, just in case Grace was listening to this madness. "And I can make you a solemn promise I've no interest in their drooling, shambling, inarticulate culture. Or in making it so you can't see me." Lord, that would be the *last* thing he'd want.

Serenity snorted, as if she sensed his denials. "These things rarely work out, Gracie. That's all I'm saying. Supernatural beings are just dead-ends, when it comes to relationships." She waved a dismissive hand. "You should just forget about this pirate guy. Especially with your Partner looming on the horizon."

Jamie's teeth ground together. Just the mention of Grace's mysterious "partner" pissed him off. No other man should have a claim on her. Ever. The woman had been given to *him*. She'd slept trustingly beside him all night, and came apart in his hands, and gave his whole unlife meaning. He was never, ever, *ever* going to part with her, no matter what kind of "husband material" jackass thought to steal her away. Dead or not, Jamie would find a way to kill the son of a bitch the minute he showed his normal, pleasant, fucking *alive* face.

Maybe she deserved more than just a ghost, but no pirate parted with his ill-gotten treasure. Not without one hell of a fight.

"You need to be on the lookout for your Partner," Serenity continued, "not wasting your time on…"

Grace cut her off. "Auntie," she met Serenity's eyes. "I'm *sure*." Her voice was full of some deeper meaning that Jamie didn't understand.

Serenity apparently did, though.

"Oh." Her eyebrows soared. She glanced in Jamie's direction again, this time with less hostility. "Well, if you're *sure*, I'll see what I can do to save the boy. He does have a nice, strong energy signature. Usually means a man's hung like a race horse."

Jamie's mouth curved. "Why, your aunt really *is* psychic."

Grace looked towards the cobweb-covered ceiling, like she was praying for patience. "Don't encourage her."

"He's agreeing with me?" Serenity guessed. "Of course he is. I'm always right." She leaned in closer and lowered her voice. "Did she tell you what it means when a Rivera finds their Partner, Ghost?"

"No." Jamie answered, even though she couldn't hear him. He wanted to know *everything* there was to know on the topic, so hopefully Serenity would keep talking.

"Aunt Serenity…" Grace began warningly.

Jamie cut her off, before she stopped her aunt from gossiping with him. "Let the woman speak, lass."

"This has nothing to do with our plan."

"*Your* plan. *I've* been quite clear on wanting you to stay right here in the present. …Not that you're of a mind to listen. All of this madness is you refusing to see reason."

Grace had linked this time travel idea to fixing her "burn out." In her mind, if it worked, she wouldn't be crazy. She could resume her old life and reclaim her job solving crimes. Nothing could derail her now, so he was reluctantly going along with her wishes. At least she was showing a bit of optimism.

"I'm *going* to clear your name, Jamie. Two days ago, that was all that you wanted."

"Two days ago I hadn't seen you naked. Now I want *other* things. Like you alive and well and coming beneath me in bed, again and again and *again*."

She flushed a bright shade of pink and glanced over at Serenity, like her aunt might have somehow heard his suggestive remark.

Jesus, Mary, and Joseph, he loved it when she blushed. And when she *didn't* blush. And every other blasted thing about her. If he'd still had a heart in his chest, this woman would've owned every beat of it.

Jamie cleared his throat. "So *my* only plan at the moment is to listen to what your dear auntie has to say."

"I knew she didn't tell you." Serenity interjected in a smug tone, correctly interpreting Grace's part of the argument. "Gracie's always been a bit shy and Partners can be an... intimate thing for a Rivera."

The thought of Grace becoming *intimate* with some unknown mortal had his jaw clenching. Goddamn it, *he* was the one who'd proved she wasn't "semi-frigid" or whatever the fuck that wanker Robert had claimed. Every intimate thing about her belonged to Jamie, by right of conquest.

"When our family finds a Partner, it's like finding our other half." Serenity explained. "A Partner is the person who helps us. Stands beside us. Completes us. Keeps us safe. We *need* them. Understand?"

Jamie's stomach sank. Every word she said was like a bullet in his gut. Shit, it was worse than he even thought. Grace needed this man. How the hell was he going to compete with that?

Grace looked incredibly uncomfortable with Serenity's speech. "Just make the potion, Auntie. I'll deal with my Partner, alright?"

Serenity made a "humph" sound and went stalking off to gather her ingredients. "How are you going to get the living version of the boy to *swallow* this potion, if he doesn't even know you back then?" She called. "Have you thought about that?"

"I'll figure it out when I get there." Grace's brow puckered and she looked at Jamie. "Maybe I can slip it into your drink or something."

"Just ask me to swallow it. It's far easier."

"*Ask* you? What are you kidding? You think you-of-the-past is going to drink a mystery liquid from some strange girl, just because she *asks*?"

"If the strange girl is you...?" Jamie shrugged. "Probably. Should I hesitate, just offer to let me touch you in dirty ways. I guarantee you, after that, I'll agree to eat very sharp tacks, if you ask."

"You have a one-track mine, Jamie." She pointed to a stool carved to look like a spider. "Sit over there and stay out of trouble."

"Yes, ma'am."

Grace went back to the ancient book, absently fiddling with her necklace. For the first time since Jamie had known her, Grace was wearing a piece of jewelry. A small silver pendant dangled from a chain at her neck. It was a round disc with a mermaid engraved on one side. The whimsy of the piece struck him as a very good sign, considering how she viewed anything that even hinted at individualism as "abnormal." Maybe she was gaining a bit of confidence.

It took about half an hour for Serenity to come back into the room, carrying a vial of green potion. "Okay, this should do the trick. Once he drinks it, the old-him will get all the memories of the ghost-him. For all intents and purposes, they'll be one person."

"For how long?"

"Forever. Can't reverse the potion, once he drinks it. Don't know how long it will take to kick in, though. Like I said, there's not a lot of research into this kind of magic."

"Thank you, Auntie. I'm sure it's perfect." Grace's finger tapped something in the book. "Ah-ha! Here we go." She ripped out the page, disregarding her aunt's exaggerated wince. "Okay, put the potion and the book on my tab." She grabbed the vial from her aunt, kissed her cheek, and headed for the door again. "And I expect the family discount on magic, so don't try to screw me over on the herb costs."

According to Grace, for a family that was always broke, the Riveras loved to overcharge people. Maybe that was why they were always broke.

Serenity didn't look thrilled with the idea of fair pricing. "Where are you going now, Gracie?"

"Wherever this map leads." She held up the faded piece of paper.

"Then you should change out of that outfit, first." Serenity advised. "It might be someplace fancy. And, even for this town, you look ridiculous going out in public dressed like Dolly Madison's fashion-victim of a cousin."

CHAPTER ELEVEN

June 25, 1789- Father likes to say that Eugenia is the brains of our family.

I'm not so sure about that. How could I get away with half of the naughty things I do, unless I was far more intelligent than people give me credit for?

From the Journal of Miss Lucinda Wentworth

Grace slammed the front door of the shop shut behind her, defiantly plopping her costume's straw bonnet on her head. "It's a mystery why I didn't run away, years ago, and join the circus. It would have been so calm and normal in comparison." She dropped the memory potion into the pocket of her apron and rubbed her forehead. "I'm really sorry about earlier, by the way. My aunt takes this whole Partner thing seriously."

"No doubt she should." Jamie said quietly. His eyes scanned the street, just in case Robert showed his wanker face. The damn police had called that morning to say they'd released the man, so he could be anywhere. It made Jamie uneasy. "A Partner is clearly a serious thing."

Grace glanced up at him through her lashes. "You believe her, then?"

"Yes." There wasn't a doubt in his mind that Grace's Partner was coming to claim her. A man would do anything to have such a woman beside him. Kill, bleed, die, beg... And once that bastard finally fought his way to her side, he would take the only thing in the universe that Jamie loved.

Unless Jamie figured out a way to stop him.

It was disconcerting to be on the other side of things. To be the one fighting to keep what he treasured. Everything Jamie ever had in this world, he'd stolen. Even his ship had been won in a damn game of cards. All his valuables were plunder that he'd taken for his own, by being stronger and smarter and luckier than the fellow who'd lost it. Nothing had ever truly been *his*.

Not until Grace, with her incredible hair and Sunday school teacher frowns.

Grace was quiet for a long moment. "So I was thinking..." She fiddled with her portable phone's decoy earpiece, even though nobody noticed that she was apparently talking to herself. Conversing with a ghost didn't cause nearly as many odd looks as you'd fear. Citizens of the modern world were too wrapped up in their own issues to pay much mind to anyone else's. "What do you think will happen when we clear your name? Do you think that you'll --like-- ascend into heaven or something?"

Jamie scoffed at that idea. "I highly doubt heaven will have me."

"But there would be no reason for you to be a restless spirit."

"I'm not a restless spirit." Maybe he *had* been, but finding Grace had eased him. *She* was the reason he'd stayed in this earthly realm for so long. Meeting her brought all of it into focus.

He'd been waiting for Grace.

When she'd traveled to 1789 and he'd seen her with his mortal eyes, he'd experienced the same exact feeling he got when he looked at her now. An overwhelming sense of recognition. Of happiness. Of relief that she'd finally arrived. He'd *always* been waiting for this small, uptight, obstinate woman. Alive or dead, there was no one else for him.

For Jamie, there was just Grace. Now and forever.

Grace took a deep breath, still looking distressed. "Maybe you'll just disappear if we solve these murders. Maybe none of this will have even happened. And, I know that I said I wanted you to vanish out of my life, but... I've kinda changed my mind."

That was gratifying to know. "I am not going to leave you, Grace. Not if I can possibly help it. I told you that yesterday."

Even though a ghost had very little to offer a living woman.

Whoever Grace's Partner was, he could protect her from Robert and give her children and share her future. Jamie's future had been buried for two centuries. She didn't need him here, complicating her life. She didn't need him *at all*. No matter his feelings, was it right to have Grace waste her existence on a dead man? She deserved more. She deserved...

Jamie shook off the idea before it could take deeper root.

He didn't want to think about any of that or he'd eventually reach a conclusion that would kill him all over again. Goddamn it, he couldn't just hand her over to some fucking Partner. He *couldn't*. Maybe she didn't need him, but he needed her desperately.

"You're *sure* you're going to stay?" She persisted.

Jamie's jaw ticked. "I'm sure I *want* to stay." He temporized and that seemed to alleviate her worry.

It didn't do a damn thing to ease Jamie's.

Selfish or not, he had no intention of walking away from his salvation, though. Jamie might not be welcomed through the pearly gates, but he'd still been granted a miracle. As much as he'd tried to ignore his father's religion growing up, his belief in the spiritual world had taken deep root. God would not have brought Grace to him, just to snatch her away again. No. She was the one being in the whole of his life and death that belonged solely to Jamie.

...Or maybe he belonged to her.

However you looked at it, there was a *purpose* in their meeting. A rightness. A grand design. Grace was where Jamie was supposed to be. He *had* to believe that.

"So, we're following a map?" He prompted, wanting

to focus on something he could actually fix. If there was one thing Jamie excelled at, it was maps. He craned his neck to look down at the yellowed page and then swore. "Oh bloody hell. Is that one of Ned Hunnicutt's abominations?"

"I *knew* you were going to say that. You have an unhealthy fixation with that poor man."

"That jackass was the worst cartographer in the Colonies! Plus he watered down his ale and treated his serving girls badly."

"So you've said. Repeatedly."

"Because it's *true*." He gestured to Ned's laughable scribblings with a disdainful sweep of his hand. "Wherever that is leading you, it's no doubt in the polar opposite direction of where you want to go. The man couldn't find east if you pointed him towards the rising sun."

"It's not as if there are a lot of two hundred year old maps around to choose from, Jamie. We're going to have to make do." She held up the poorly-rendered sketch for him to see. "Now, Anabel Maxwell was last seen in the hedge maze behind the governor's mansion. *This* is a diagram Edward Hunnicutt drew of the hedge maze from that same year. It's going to help us retrace her route."

Jamie made a face. "Knowing Ned, it will no doubt zigzag us about for several dizzying hours and then drop us down a well."

"Have a little faith." Grace headed down the cobblestone street, toward the governor's mansion in the center of town. The imposing brick building was impossible to miss. Set back on a wide lawn, it had been designed to awe and intimidate visitors. "The hedge maze is still here, but we can't be sure it's growing in the same pattern. That's why we need the map."

Jamie couldn't imagine ever being desperate enough to "need" one of Ned's lopsided renderings. But Grace clearly wasn't going to listen to him, so he stopped arguing about it. It was a lovely summer morning, Robert was nowhere to be seen, and Jamie was walking beside the love of his life (and death).

There was no sense in ruining the moment.

All around them, Harrisonburg was preparing for the 4th of July celebrations. Workers were erecting a stage for the concert that would accompany the fireworks display. Vendors were already setting up booths around the park to hawk "authentic" baskets and cool lemonade. A lady in a white apron was selling bouquets of sunflowers.

Jamie slowed his steps, his eyes on the bright yellow blossoms. He wished he could buy some for Grace. She *should* have beautiful things. Back in his own time, he could've given her anything her heart desired. He'd had more gold than he could spend and he would have lavished all of it on his bride. It was frustrating that he couldn't do that now.

A new thought occurred to him. Hang on. Maybe he *could*.

"If we're going to be using maps, we should use mine." He said, brightening. "Grace, we should find *my* map."

"Oh Lord…" She rolled her eyes like she thought there was something impractical about a hunt for pirate treasure. "Let it *go*, Jamie. I have enough craziness dealing with the lost recipe for troll powder."

"I'm serious." He insisted, excitement filling him. "My map is real and it's surely still around someplace. No one in this blasted town throws anything away. We just need to locate the spot I buried my fortune and dig it up. That would see you secure for the rest of your life." He arched a brow. "Wouldn't it be nice to have a chest full of gold and gems to spend?"

"Sure. I could build all my unicorn friends a sparkly new castle for our tea parties."

He frowned at the sarcasm. "The treasure isn't a fantasy, Grace. It's somewhere near here, hidden under the ground, and all of it belongs to me. To *you*. All we have to do is find it and you'll be taken care of forever."

She didn't seem enthused by the prospect of being Fuck-'Em-All rich. "Let's just concentrate on solving the murders, okay?" She flashed her Harrisonburg employee ID at a guard and was waved through the massive gates of the governor's house.

The flat-fronted Georgian building was the largest structure in Harrisonburg. It had been called the governor's "palace," back when Virginia was still part of Britain, and the name wasn't far off. The white mansion was huge, with lavish formal gardens and rooms full of gilded furnishings. It was the one building in town Jamie understood people wanting to tour while on vacation. The outrageous opulence of the place suited his personal style to a T. In the waning years of *Oprah* and before *Haunted High* started airing, his favorite show had been *MTV Cribs*.

In his opinion, the governor's home would have made quite a striking state capital. And it *would* have been just that, except Thomas Jefferson had hated living there, when he was governor, and moved the capital to Richmond in 1780.

Tom had always been an ass.

"The hedge maze is this way." Grace headed down a set of shaded steps. "You probably know that. Were you here back in the day or was there a 'no pirates allowed' policy?"

"If you're handsome and rich and notorious, you're welcomed *everywhere*."

She sent him a dry look. "Which means you totally broke in to steal stuff."

"Just small stuff." He winked at her.

"Scoundrel." Grace stopped in front of the maze's entrance, which was blocked off by a chain. A sign dangling from it read: "Do Not Enter Without a Hedge Maze Host."

It was easy to see why. Ahead of them, paths stretched off in three directions. The labyrinth was made of American Holly, to discourage anyone from pushing through the plants Bart Simpson-style, and dense enough that you couldn't see through the walls. Given its massive size, you could easily be wandering around in there for hours.

Especially if you were following Ned's half-assed instructions.

"They used to let school trips in here, but they had to stop a couple years back." Grace said as if reading his mind. "The teachers kept missing their buses, because kids would get lost."

"Perhaps we should take note of that and forget this plan."

"Perhaps *not*." Grace retorted. "If there's any evidence left of Anabel's murder, this is where it will be."

He studied her for a beat, his mind still dwelling on his impossible love for her. "Do you like children?" He asked, unable to stop himself.

"Sure. My family has a ton of them running around. My niece Joy once turned my car into a pink Barbie Corvette, which kinda pissed me off, but they're mostly great to have around."

Jamie sighed. Of course, she liked children. She deserved to have two or three of them underfoot, breaking the already broken knickknacks in her home and filling her life with magical chaos.

...And she would never, ever have that if she was with a dead man.

Grace studied the deplorable excuse of a map for a beat and nodded, missing his growing misery. "So far so good, too. The maze is starting in the same place now as it did back then. Do you remember it?"

Jamie grunted. "A bit."

He'd occasionally snuck into parties at the mansion and the maze had been the most entertaining spot at the stuffy gatherings. The walls were over seven feet high, all full of dark corners and dead ends. Couples could be agreeably alone in the twisty pathways.

"A bit?" She repeated skeptically. "Is that your way of *not* telling me about your sleazy assignations in the garden?"

"Everything that happened before I met you becomes a bit of a blur." He explained piously.

Grace's mouth twitched. "That's a good line." She stepped over the chain barricade and moved down the maze's left corridor. "Let's try this direction. Keep your eyes open."

"For what?"

"Something that was around when Anabel was here. Something that wouldn't have changed." For a woman who'd nearly hyperventilated at the Wentworth's house, she seemed fine with entering the garden without permission to find a blood-soaked crime scene. Probably because she'd forgotten she was trying to fit in with "normal" society.

Grace was kidding herself if she thought she could be anything but brilliant and brave and bursting with enchantment. Her insistence on being "normal" was like a butterfly wanting to cut off its wings and turn back into a caterpillar. You couldn't suppress magic like Grace possessed. The fearless spirit and the love of adventure. Underneath that uptight exterior, the woman had the soul of a pirate. No doubt, her living, breathing, husband-materially Partner was aching to show her how much fun that could be.

Just the idea of it made Jamie crazy.

What the fuck was he going to do?

Grace's camera was looped around her neck. She adjusted the setting to something called "IR" and snapped a picture of a cupid statue. The image that popped up on screen looked... strange. The colors were all wrong. The plants showed up as white and the sky glowed orangey-pink.

"Your camera will show us something?" He asked. Focusing on the past seemed far easier than thinking about the future.

She nodded and kept walking. "Infrared lens can detect blood that's been painted over."

"Like magic."

She shot him a quick look. "It's *not* magic, Jamie. It's science."

"Not much of a difference, if you ask me. They both make impossible things into reality." No wonder she missed her forensic job. Grace's blood cried out for enchantment and investigating crime gave it to her. "Speaking of which, I never did get a chance to ask you... What's the *other* spell you can cast?"

"What?"

"Yesterday, when Robert attacked you, you said you only knew two spells. One was for menstrual cramps. What's the second?"

Grace hesitated. "The Rivera Doomsday Spell." She finally muttered.

"Doomsday Spell? Well, that sounds quite promising. What does it do?"

Grace gave a superior sniff. "I don't ever plan to use it, so it doesn't matter." She took another picture, this time of an arrangement of decorative rocks. "Darn it." She looked back at the map and picked another path, clearly not willing to discuss magic. "Okay, so let's pretend you're Anabel Maxwell. You're at a party, at night, playing in the hedge maze with someone. Is there anything particular you might have done in here?"

He arched a brow at her.

"...*Besides* the obvious."

Jamie chuckled at her prim tone. The woman never failed to delight him. "It doesn't much seem like Anabel to be in the hedge maze, a'tall." He told her. "She wasn't a fun-loving lass, like Lucinda. A man would have to do some fast talking to have her risking her reputation for some frolic in the gardens. She must have known him quite well."

Grace mulled that over. "Was she dating anyone? Or *courting* or whatever you called it in 1789?"

"I have no idea. I barely knew the girl. The whole family were bloody idiots, so I had no desire to socialize with them. Her blockheaded brother nearly lost us the Battle of Yorktown." Two centuries had past and it still annoyed him.

"Gregory Maxwell was the *Hero of Yorktown*. Everyone knows that."

"Bullshit."

"You're just mad he wrote *Horror in Harrisonburg*, detailing all the reasons you were the killer."

Jamie ignored that, because it was patently impossible that that numb-skull wrote any book beyond a "How To" guide on general stupidity. "I was *at* Yorktown, so I vividly recall that jackass nearly..."

"Shh!" Grace suddenly put her finger against her lips to hush him, even though she was the only one who could hear him anyway. "I think someone's coming."

Jamie listened for a moment and --sure enough-- he could hear movement in the hedgerows. "Stay here." He walked through the walls of the maze, scanning up and down the long, green aisles. Near the entrance, he spotted two Harrisonburg employees looking around.

Shit.

"Everything seems okay to me, Morris." One of the guys said. He was college-aged, with a bad goatee and a name badge that read "Emmett."

"I'm telling you, I saw somebody come in here." The boy named Morris was about the same age, with equally atrocious facial hair. His wide hazel eyes were darting around. "It was a pretty woman in an old-fashion dress, just wallllking into the maaaaze." His voice lilted across the words, stretching out the syllables so they had the spooky cadence of a narrator from an old B movie. "She was talking to someone who wasn't there. Like maybe she didn't know she was dead or something."

Jamie squinted at him. "What the bloody hell…?"

"You spend too much time reading those dumb paranormal sites." Emmett opinioned, trying to sound braver than he looked. "We need to check out the pathways and make sure it wasn't some vandal or a lost kid or something." …But he didn't venture any deeper into the labyrinth.

Neither did Morris, who was equal parts excited and scared. "It wasn't a frigging kid, Emmett!" He whispered fiercely. "I think it was really *her*. Anabel Maxwell has come to haunt the spot where she died. Shit like this happens all the time! I *told* you she was real!"

Jamie smiled in delight and ducked back through the hedgerows, returning to the spot where he'd left Grace. Phasing through solid matter was one of the small perks of being incorporeal. It only took him a moment to cheat his way through several hundred feet of maze. "Well, good news and bad news." He told her calmly. "Bad news: Two of your fellow tour guides are poking about in here."

She paled. "Oh no! How am I supposed to find any

blood evidence if I'm locked in a jail cell for trespassing?"

"Which brings us to the good news… They think you're a ghost."

Grace blinked. "Come again?"

"They think you're Anabel, haunting the scene of the crime."

"You've got to be kidding me." She rolled her eyes like the very idea was ludicrous. "Because of the stupid dress? Half the people in Harrisonburg wear costumes! I swear, it's like this town goes out of its way to hire idiots."

Jamie arched a brow at her derision. "Ghosts are such a farfetched notion, then?"

"Oh shut up."

He chuckled. The whole situation had perked him up immensely. "I wouldn't worry much about the boys. They seem a bit terrified of you, lass."

"Wonderful. If they get too close, I'll just yell 'boo!'" She hissed. "For real, what are we going to do?"

"I find that belittling someone's tour-guiding techniques is the best way for a ghost to be noticed."

Grace made a face. "I'm glad you're finding this so funny."

"Aye, I really am."

She deliberately turned on her heel and headed away from him, down another twisty row of vegetation. "Just keep an eye on them and make sure they don't find me. I'm going this way." She consulted the map again. "At least, I *think* I am."

"Following that blasted thing, the only place you're going is 'round and 'round and 'round in circles."

"We're *not* going 'round and 'round and 'round in circles. It just *seems* that way, because everything is all green and leafy."

"And because we've made a loop." He said dryly. "We're standing in the same spot we were ten minutes ago."

She looked around with a perplexed frown. "Are you sure?"

"Very."

Grace kept walking, just to spite him. "Well, the map

says that we need to take this path, so I'm…" She broke off mid-word, realizing that Ned's useless instructions had led them right into a dead end.

Jamie snorted in amusement. "At this rate, you *will* wind up a ghost in here. The teenage tour guides will find your poor skeleton, miles from the entrance and still clutching that so-called 'map' in your wee bony hand."

"You can stop talking now." Grace backtracked, a frustrated expression on her face. "Go check to see where they are. I don't want to be arrested today."

Jamie blew her a kiss and headed off to spy on the other guides again. As funny as the whole thing was, he was *slightly* concerned about the boys being alone in the maze with Grace. They seemed harmless enough, but, after yesterday, he was anxious about the intentions of other men. He was useless in a fight and there were only so many times a menstrual cramp spell would work. It would be better for everyone if they just went away.

When he rejoined the two of them, they were approximately three feet farther down one of the pathways, still bickering about the best course of action.

"We should call Anita down here to deal with it." Morris was arguing. "That fascist bitch is head of the tour guides. Fuck knows, she tells us enough that *she's* the boss. *She* should be the one to deal with emergencies, right?"

Apparently, he was no fan of Grace's employer either. That raised Jamie's opinion of the boy. He wasn't forgetting how unkind Anita had been to Grace when she was wounded. The girl really did need a new job. And Anita needed a good ass-kicking.

"And let her get all the credit?" Emmett shot back, fiddling with the camera app on his phone. "What if this is a real ghost, huh? If we could get a picture of it, do you know how many hits we would get? We'd be internet *royalty!* You just want to hand that kind of fame over to Ms. Beauregard-Smythe?" He scoffed at the very idea. "What the hell would she even *do* with it? "

Morris made a considering face, conceding the point. "She is --like-- *way* old."

"Old? She's probably still on fucking MySpace! Screw that ancient hag." Emmett held up his phone. "If we get a few good shots of something supernatural, we can spend the rest of the summer at the beach, drinking PBR and talking to hot chicks."

Jamie admired the boys' goals, but enough was enough. He didn't want potentially dangerous men alone with Grace, he didn't want her worried about getting caught trespassing in the maze, and he certainly didn't want that harridan Anita showing up to harass her.

"Grace, my love?" He shouted. "Remember when you said you could yell "Boo!" and scare the boys away? That might not be such a terrible idea. They want to see a ghost, so perhaps we should give them one."

She understood what he meant without asking for further details. It was one of the reasons he loved her. Leaves began to rustle in an eerie wave and Grace gave a low moan of ghostly torment that was really quite impressive. Whether she liked it or not, spending her childhood in a haunted house had definitely rubbed off on the girl. It was quite a creepy little show.

Emmett and Morris froze. All thoughts of finding fortune and glory on the internet faded in the face of a possible *actual* ghost. In unison, they edged backwards, towards the exit.

"Did you hear that?" Emmett demanded.

Morris frantically bobbed his head.

"Little more, lass." Jamie called, grinning widely.

She obliged by screaming the most bloodcurdling scream ever screamed. It sounded like she was being attacked by a herd of rapid porcupines... while simultaneously being burned alive with a million blowtorches... at the dentist... in hell. Even Jamie cringed at the god-awful noise. It was bloody brilliant!

Emmett and Morris took off running. They tripped all over each other, dashing out of the maze, never to return. Not even the promise of work/study credits was going to lure them back to their jobs after Grace's performance. No real ghost could have done half as good a job.

Jesus, Mary, and Joseph, how had he lasted two and a half centuries without this beautiful, odd-duck of a woman?

"That did the trick." He was still laughing uproariously as he moved back to her side. She'd found her way into a new row of the maze, which had to have been the work of pure luck. Ned's map really was leading them in circles. "Those lads are quite scarred for life. You should be proud."

"My great-great grandmother had an affair with Bela Lugosi." Grace shrugged uncomfortably and photographed a bench. "It's probably in my DNA." Her picture came up empty again. "Crap." She kept moving. "We need to stay focused on the investigation." Being anything other than white-bread-and-tap-water ordinary still made her uneasy, so it was obvious she'd rather not discuss her acting skills.

But from the sparkle in her eyes, it was also pretty damn clear she'd enjoyed the prank.

He gave her a knowing smile. "You donea have to pretend to be normal with me, you know. You can be just as magical as you truly are."

Grace cleared her throat, ignoring that. "Like I was saying, if Anabel had a connection to Lucinda's mystery man, a boyfriend would give us a place to start investigating. Especially if we could tie him to Clara, too."

Jamie was willing to play along with the subject change. "You're still thinking about that H.C. from Lucinda's diary?"

"He's our best suspect." She gave a pointed paused. "Except for a certain spurned lover with a bad reputation, obviously."

"Anabel was no lover of mine. Setting aside her family's lamentable IQs, her wig was quite off-putting."

"*Everyone* back then wore wigs."

"Just because a book told you that, doesn't make it true. Take, for instance, that libelous tome Gregory Maxwell *allegedly* wrote about me being a killer."

She sent him an amused glance. "For real, it's okay to tell me if that's not your real hair. Even if you were bald, I'd still let you do naughty things to my naked body."

"I'm not wearing a wig, woman. How many times do I have to bloody say it?"

She snickered, clearly wanting to tease him some more. As she turned a corner, though, something caught her attention. She stopped short and consulted Ned's godawful map, again. Using that piece of rubbish, they were probably headed for the Mississippi River by way of the Himalayas, so it was no wonder she seemed confused. They'd have better luck searching for the North West Passage. "Okay, hold on. This part seems different."

"No doubt." It would be a wonder if they could escape the maze before nightfall using all the random lines Ned drew. Jamie fully anticipated having to navigate their course home by the stars.

"No, I mean I think there was once a wall here. See? Right there." Grace pointed to some brickwork lining the edge of the path. "This used to be a little sitting area."

Jamie frowned and actually remembered that feature. He looked around, seeing the old arrangement of hedges in his mind. Plants had died and re-grown over the years, altering the landscape slightly, but it was all familiar to him. "The wall curved this way." He made a sweeping gesture with one hand. "There was a gazebo, too. Couples used to stop here to steal a quick kiss."

...Sometimes more than a kiss.

Grace sent him a suspicious frown and he smiled innocently at her. Not surprisingly, she wasn't fooled. "You were kind of a pizza-tramp back then, weren't you?"

"I just hadn't met the right girl." That would take him another two-hundred and thirty odd years.

She snorted at that and lifted the camera again. Someone had painted the old bricks black, but it did nothing to hide the crime scene from Grace's forensic magic. When she snapped a picture, the dark evidence of blood spatter was visible, even to Jamie's untrained eyes.

"You've found it." He whispered, gazing at the small screen in awe. "This is where Anabel died."

"Dexter Morgan, eat your heart out." Grace beamed up at him, delightfully proud of herself. "For real, how awesome am I at this job?"

CHAPTER TWELVE

June 25, 1789- I should never want to be a man! The power we women hold in our hands is far too intoxicating.

From the Journal of Miss Lucinda Wentworth

The woman was back!

Jamie's body leapt to attention at the sight of her standing in his quarters. A moment before he'd been alone in his cabin on the *Sea Serpent*, taking a bath. The next the woman was standing before him. He wasn't sure how she'd just *appeared* and he really didn't care. All that mattered was she'd returned to him.

Joy filled him, his eyes drinking her in.

Her dress was a great deal more normal this time. A trifle old fashion, but it was no longer a scrap of fabric that barely shielded her soft body. Mores the pity. Her uncovered skin had been the stuff of epic poems and romantic odes. Even all buttoned up, though, he'd never seen a lovelier lass in his whole life.

Maybe she truly was some otherworldly creature sent to tempt him. And it was bloody well working, because he would do anything the woman bid, so long as she stayed. Anything at all. She was the one he'd been searching for. He felt it deep in his bones.

The one blessed thing in the whole universe that belonged just to him.

"This isn't the garden..." She turned to look at him, her eyes wide. "Jamie!" She swallowed. Sunlight shone through the porthole behind her, giving her an angelic halo. "Oh my

God, you're taking a bath." She slapped a hand over her luminous eyes. "I'm sorry!"

"I'm not." Jamie got to his feet, his pulse pounding in his ears.

Grace. That was her name. It had been whispering in his head, ever since she told him. What else would his savior be called? His father would have scoffed at the notion, considering Jamie's list of unpardonable sins. There would be no grace for him in the afterlife. Jamie knew that already. But he had his Grace here before him now and that was enough.

She peeked through her fingers and swallowed hard when he didn't reach for a towel. "For real, I didn't expect to be transported into your cabin, instead of the hedge maze." She blushed a becoming shade of pink, trying to look everywhere but at his growing erection. "Really."

"There's no need for concern. You can come here whenever you wish."

"Um… Thanks?" She licked her lower lip. "I guess. Anyway, have you --uh-- seen Anabel Maxwell recently?"

"Who?"

"*Anabel Maxwell*, Jamie! You danced with her at the ball and now she's missing."

"Oh the Maxwell girl. She's not missing. She's probably at Lucinda's funeral." Which he wasn't welcomed at, since half the town thought he'd killed her for some damn reason.

Morons.

That news distracted her for a beat. "Anabel's not dead?"

"Of course not."

"What day is it?"

"July first." He gave a pointed pause. "And --before you ask-- Yes, it's still 1789."

"Don't be a wiseass." Her swearing was bloody adorable, as was her frown of concentration. "Things are already different." She murmured to herself. "Last time Lucinda didn't *have* a funeral, because there was no body. It's changing. This could actually be a good thing. It's only morning and the killer won't strike again until tonight. I'm ahead of him now."

Jamie tried to piece that together. "You know who killed Lucinda?" It seemed likely, since she'd known the murder was going to happen. If Grace could give him a name, Jamie would gladly run the bastard through himself. Lucinda had been a harmless girl and a good friend. It was the least he could do.

"Not yet, but I'm working on it."

"Donea go looking for a madman, Grace." Just the thought chilled him. Bloody hell, why was no one looking out for this daft woman? Where had she come from? Why did she seem to know him? How had the strange box she'd held outside Lucinda's house glowed without fire? Not a single theory he'd come up with made sense.

Grace ignored that, frowning in deep thought. "Why did I get sent back to *this* spot, though? There had to be a reason."

"Oh, I can give you a reason, lass."

Most of the time, Jamie had no clue what she was talking about and he gave up trying to decipher it. Anabel Maxwell's whereabouts were of no concern at all. Not when he finally had what he wanted standing right in front of him.

For days, his entire focus had been on trying to find Grace. After she entered Lucinda's bedroom, it was like she dissipated into thin air. He'd been afraid the murderer had made off with her, too. No one in the whole bloody town had heard of her, no matter how much gold he offered as a reward. However the hell she'd vanished, it was a sure bet she could do it again.

That made it all the more important that he stake his claim *now*.

"I think we need to find Anabel." Grace decided, chewing on her lip in a way that made all the blood leave his brain and travel southward. "Figure out what she does between now and tonight to incite…" She trailed off with a wary gulp as he left the tub and stepped closer to her. "Jamie?"

"I *know* you." He said quietly, ignoring all her muttering. "And you know me."

She hesitated and then slowly bobbed her head. "How?"

"It's a little crazy. You wouldn't believe me if I told you."

He smirked at that, thinking of fairy lights dancing in the Scottish hills. "Donea be too sure."

"I..." She let out a long breath, her eyes drifting down and then jerking back up. "I'm from the future. You're going to know me in the future. It's how I knew about Lucinda's murder."

Jamie blinked, digesting that story for a long moment. Her claim was preposterous, but so was every other explanation for her presence. He had no idea what kind of magic she possessed, but he knew it flowed in her blood. Hell, it practically glowed through her skin. God only knew what such a creature could truly do. Maybe she was telling the truth.

...Or maybe she was a lunatic.

He shook his head, not wanting to be distracted. Regardless of what else she was, he knew one thing for certain. "You're my wife."

"In the future? No, I'm not."

He frowned in annoyance. "Are you my lover?" If she was telling the truth about any of this, she could only answer yes. Jamie knew himself. If he'd ever met this girl --past, present, or future-- he'd would have recognized her as his and maneuvered her into bed. It was a simple fact.

"Sort of."

The way she spoke confused the hell out of him. "Sort of your lover?"

She bobbed her head.

He moved closer to her, wanting her cornered and knowing it was about to happen. Sure enough, she took a small step back, coming up against the bookshelf. A woman this guileless had no business being in a room with a pirate. She'd already managed to trap herself. Surprise flickered over her beautiful face, but still no genuine fear.

Jamie smirked and put his palm beside her head, caging her in with his body. "What does 'sort of' mean?" He asked casually.

"It's complicated." She got out in a wary voice, looking around and seeing she had nowhere to go.

"Seems simple to me." He untied the string of her bonnet with his free hand, tossing it aside. Thick, black curls tumbled to her shoulders and he nearly purred. "Have I been inside of you?"

Her blush got even deeper, just as he'd hoped it would. He'd never been alone with such a wholesome lass before. It was charming as hell. "No. But you've touched me." Her eyelashes fluttered down and it was all he could do not to rip her clothes off right then.

"*How* did I touch you?" He wrapped a finger around the silver chain at her neck, smiling at the whimsical mermaid pendant she wore.

Her pulse was pounding in her slim throat, but she looked up at him again with absolute faith. It was an intoxicating combination. Most women who sought him out liked the danger of being with a dangerous man. They liked the fact he was frightening. Grace was nervous, but she wasn't scared of him.

In that second, Jamie knew she believed everything she said.

There was no reason for Grace to have any confidence in a man of his illicit notoriety. Not unless she somehow *knew* he wouldn't hurt her. Unless she *knew* she belonged to him. Unless she knew he struggled with gentlemanly impulses, beneath his bad reputation. To her, he wasn't a soon-to-be-forgotten scoundrel she was using to shock her parents. He was...

Husband material.

The strange words flited through his head and, while he wasn't exactly sure what they meant, he knew they were true. Grace didn't see him as just a passing diversion. She trusted him to care for her. To keep her safe. She knew that

Jamie belonged to her, too.

His heart melted.

The woman would have been running for her life with any other man, but she gave the most notorious pirate in Virginia a bashful smile. "You brought me to... um... pleasure." She explained in a rush. "But I couldn't bring you."

"Well, that's a shame."

"I wanted to, but it wasn't really possible, because..." She trailed off and puffed out a breath. "It's *really* complicated."

He shifted close enough that she could feel the hard ridge of his arousal. He nudged her gently, grinning a bit as she jolted in innocent surprise. "This time, I'll simplify it for you, then."

Her wide brown gaze slashed back up to his. "I'm not going to sleep with you, James Riordan!" She protested. "Absolutely not. I'm on a mission here. Jesus, you really do have a one-track mind, no matter the century. And I can't *believe* you haven't even put pants on. You're trying to get me all befuddled!"

But she still didn't try to push past his naked body and flee the room. Instead, her attention drifted downward to the straining evidence of his desire and stayed there. Those small white teeth nibbled at her lower lip again. Whatever she thought they had done in the past (or future) she hadn't seen him naked before. He could tell by her hesitant fascination.

The version of Jamie Riordan she'd met *clearly* needed to learn a few things.

"Is it working?" He asked, letting her look her fill. "Are you feeling befuddled? It only seems fair, since just being around you makes my brain cease functioning."

Her tiny pink tongue touched the corner of her mouth. "Um... Speaking of which..." She seemed to be trying to rally. "Do you think you could drink this for me?" She dug in her pocket and came up with a vial of some unidentified green liquid.

He arched a brow. "Drink it?"

"Yeah. I know it sounds sketchy, but it will help you remember me. Really. Before you say no, just take a few minutes and listen to me explain some of this, okay?" She gave an earnest nod. "And if it helps befuddle you, you can --um-- touch me a little bit while we talk. The other you said to offer that and it seems like a good idea. Honestly, if you're not thinking clearly, it'll probably..."

Jamie snatched the potion out of her hand and belted it back. It tasted like shit, but what the hell? It was still far better than the watered-down ale at The Raven. He tossed the glass container over his shoulder and arched a brow. "No. Still donea recall you, love."

"Oh for God's sake!" She looked exasperated now. "You seriously just drank that, without even asking what it was. I could have been trying to poison you, you idiot! Did you even think of that?"

"You're not here to hurt me."

The confidence in his tone took the wind from her sails. "No." She admitted. "I'm not."

"You've come to save me." He continued, knowing it was true. "Yes?"

"Yes." Her eyes drifted south again. "I came back for you, Jamie."

"And it's about bloody time you got here, too." It was in Jamie's nature to take all he could, regardless of propriety or common sense. It was the only way a pirate got anywhere. He was going to push forward as far as he could until Grace gave him an outright refusal. And so far the lass wasn't refusing. "You have no idea how long I've waited for you to show up."

Reaching over, he grasped her wrist, drawing it forward. That remarkable jolt of power went through him again, just as it had the last time he touched her hand. God, he couldn't wait to feel it on his shaft. Grace's breathing gave a hitch and she instinctively tried to yank back from the hot flesh. Jamie ignored her shy struggle, pressing himself into her hand.

Aw fuck... His eyes closed in pleasure. She truly did feel like heaven.

She looked scandalized. "You want me to...?"

"Aye." He'd never wanted anything more. "You said I could touch you a bit. Instead, let's have *you* touch *me*. I need you, lass. You have no bloody idea how much."

Uncertainty and burgeoning desire flickered across her face. "I've never done that before." She blurted out, forgetting to be modest. "Not with anyone. You're probably going to be disappointed."

Her pessimism was adorable. "I'll bet you this ship that I'm not."

"For real, I'm not very good at embracing my inner pizza-tramp, yet. I'm still kinda semi-frigid." She nodded like that made perfect sense. "You're the only one who's ever been able to give me an orgasm."

Oh, she *really* shouldn't have said that if she planned to talk him out of this. Jamie's whole body reacted to that happy news and he didn't even know what a pizza-tramp was. "All you have to do is touch me." She let him wrap her fingers around him, filling her soft palm. "It's not complicated, a'tall. Touch me just like this. Hard and fast." Jamie guided her up and down for a few beats and then withdrew his hold. "Stroke me. Make me come."

"This is a really bad idea..."

"Now, Grace. Make me come *now* or I'll think of something even more fun for us to do together."

She gave a little gasp at the order and obediently stroked his manhood just as he'd instructed. Apparently, the lady liked to be commanded in bed. That was quite useful to know. He thrust against her, reveling in the pace she set.

"Such a good lass." He leaned in to bury his face in her thick hair. "God, I could drown in the scent of you. You're so pretty and so sweet." Her grip got tighter, emboldened by his praise and he grimaced in pleasure. "*Fuck!* That's it. Just like *that*."

"I could be a lunatic stranger, you know." She informed him in a prim voice that amused him greatly considering what her wee hand was up to. "My story is insane. Even I see that and I know it's true. You should definitely *not* be doing this with me, Jamie."

"You may be a lunatic, but you're no stranger." His lips brushed her temple. "I knew you from the first, Grace. I've waited for you my whole life."

She gave a soft sigh at his words. "You're so hard to argue with when you say things like that."

"Stop arguing then." He nuzzled her temple. "Wouldn't mind knowing your last name, though." Before it became "Riordan" anyway.

"It's Rivera."

His mouth curved. "Like the town fortunetellers?" Well that explained the magic he sensed in her.

"Just focus, okay? I'm trying to help you."

Her nails scratched him lightly and a holy choir of angels sang in his brain. "Oh, believe me, love, you *are* helping."

"You don't understand. I have to *go*. I'm trying to solve…"

He cut her off by trying another command. She seemed to like those and he wanted her to concentrate. "Finish me, Grace." His teeth grazed her ear. "You're not going anywhere until my seed's all over your hand."

Aye, she definitely liked that. Grace stopped objecting, her nipples tightening into points under the fabric of her not-exactly-normal dress.

Jamie's whole body was throbbing with need. Without even thinking about it, he grabbed one of the apron straps on her gown, wanting to pull her even closer. There was a bizarre ripping sound and the damn thing tore right off. Jamie frowned at the strap in momentary confusion. He hadn't tugged her *that* hard. And what was the small fuzzy pad sewn to the end of it?

"It's Velcro." Grace explained, snatching it back from him and somehow reattaching it with a single touch. "It's fine."

"You do wear the most peculiar clothes." He would've been far happier to see her out of them, all together. *Much* happier. Luckily, Jamie was good at figuring out how things worked, so it only took him a moment to tear the "vel-crow" open again. This time, he managed to get the front of her gown gaping.

"The move caught her off guard. "Jamie!"

"Just let me touch you." He pulled her strange undergarment up, releasing the bounty of her breasts. His gaze went to her berry-hard nipples, dismissing everything else from his mind. "Please, Grace. I've waited so long."

She gave a soft moan as he cupped one of her breasts, kneading the soft globe in his palm. "You have the most perfect hands." She breathed, glancing down to watch them shape her supple flash. "They feel so right touching me. I knew they would."

Of course they felt right. Jamie had been born to touch this woman. There wasn't a doubt in his mind. "Mine." He moved his head to kiss her lush mouth. Her lips parted beneath his and he growled at the honeyed taste of her. "Finally."

"The you-of-the-future is a possessive guy, too." She got out breathlessly. "If he gets jealous about this, you can be the one to explain it to him."

"Every version of me is fucking *thrilled* with what we're doing. I promise you."

Grace's mouth curved. "Well, he *did* ask me to submit to every sordid, twisted, wicked demand you made." She whimpered as he switched to caressing her other breast. "I would hate to let him down."

"The future me is a bloody genius."

Except he hadn't claimed this woman yet. If Jamie could've thought straight, that part would have concerned him.

His teeth ground together as her thumb brushed over the crest of him, catching a drop of moisture. "Love, I'm going to come." He wanted to warn her, but it was hard talking through his clenched jaw. "I can't wait."

Of course the woman chose that moment to contrary. "Just another minute." Her mouth curved as she watched him swell in her grasp. "You're so *big*. How big can you get?"

She was about to find out. "*Now,* Grace."

"Not yet." It was her turn to start issuing demands. "Not until I tell you to."

Jamie let out a snarl of lust, about to lose what little control he had. "Grace…"

"Change of plans." She leaned up to nip his lower lip, effectively shutting down his brain. "I don't want you to come in my hand, Jamie."

Oh *shit*. If she asked him to stop, he might just cry. "Please." He wasn't above begging. Not when the situation was so fucking dire. "Love, I *have* to…"

His protest turned into a strangled groan as she dropped to her knees. That perfect mouth opened and she guided him inside, her tongue dancing over his straining flesh. That was all it took. Jamie let out a roar that shook the whole ship. She suckled him dry and it was the best moment of his whole goddamn life.

His hand tangled in her hair, guiding her head, frantically pledging himself to her in Gaelic. It didn't matter who she was, or where she came from, or how crazed her stories were, or what the future held.

This fay creature was his wife.

He truly would have known her anywhere. Grace sat back to smile at him and he touched her face reverently.

"Thank you." It was the only thing Jamie could think to say. "Thank you for finally finding me." His mind whirled with all the ways he could show his gratitude, but Grace didn't give him a chance to suggest some erotic reciprocity.

She bounded to her feet and gave him another quick kiss. "I gotta go." She ducked under his arm, fixing her dress as she headed for the exit. There was a jolly bounce to her step, revealing a pair of bizarre white shoes. "Not that it hasn't been fun, but I have a job to do here." She shot him a stern frown over one shoulder and she grabbed her fallen hat. "And I know you're going to ignore my advice, but you *really* should get out of town."

"Wha…? Wait." Jamie was trying to remember how to breathe and she was already out the door. "Shit! Grace, get back here!" He charged after her, terrified she'd disappear again. "Where the hell are you going?" He thudded up onto the deck, scanning for her dark head.

"I told you, I have to find Anabel Maxwell." She called back, starting down the gangplank and fixing the slightly-wrong looking bonnet on her head. "You probably don't want to follow me until that potion kicks in. You'll only make yourself a suspect, if she winds up murdered tomorrow. Also, you're still stark naked."

Jamie stood in the open air, passersby gawking at his nude body, and swore in frustration.

Bloody hell.

CHAPTER THIRTEEN

June 26 1789- I swear, Anabel Maxwell's wig gets uglier by the day!
Did squirrels sew it together? I've no idea how she manages to show
her face in public with that flea-bitten mop on her head. I'd sooner go
around town bald!

From the Journal of Miss Lucinda Wentworth

The marvelous thing about being a Rivera was you
could introduce yourself to your ancestors as a time traveling
relation and they'd welcome you with open arms.

Lucinda's funeral had been a sad affair. For most
people, anyway. Her Puritanical parents had sat stoically in the
front pew, not shedding a tear. If anything, they looked as if
they disapproved of the spectacle she'd caused with her grisly
murder. It seemed like Lucinda hadn't been exaggerating when
she complained about their contempt for her in that diary,
because Grace had been more broken up over canceled TV
shows than they were over the death of their oldest child.

On the other hand, her sister Eugenia sobbed as if her
heart was breaking. The girl was clearly in mourning. In fact,
most of the town was distraught at Lucinda's passing. It made
Grace more determined than ever to find the killer.

She'd watched everyone who came and went from the
church, but no one seemed intent on harming Anabel Maxwell.
Truthfully, nobody had gone near her at all. The girl had a long
horsey face and a tendency to itch at her head every twenty
seconds or so. Maybe Jamie was right and not *everyone* in this
era wore wigs, but *most* people did. ...And clearly they weren't
very comfortable on an un-air-conditioned July afternoon.

Grace was clueless about who might want the poor wilted Anabel dead. No one in town looked particularly suspicious or evil. She did learn that the governor's ball was still scheduled for that night, so odds seemed good that Anabel remained on course to die in the hedge maze. How was Grace supposed to stop that from happening, when she wasn't even sure who to warn Anabel to avoid? And why would Anabel listen to her anyway?

All in all, it was much easier to solve crimes *after* they happened.

Not exactly sure of her next step, Grace had decided to turn to magic. For someone who spent so long trying to avoid her family's gifts, it was a little disconcerting to now be relying on the supernatural. Sadly, she was running low on "normal" options.

Grace sat in the very same parlor she'd been in with Serenity earlier that day (give or take two hundred years) and smiled at her seventh-ish great-grandfather, Loyal. "So, you see my problem." She summed up. "I need a bit of help catching this killer."

"Seems that way." Loyal took her century-spanning tale in stride. "We get a lot of time travelers around here. The wife and kid love 'em. They're out of town for the solstice or they'd be in here asking you about what's new in Narbotics-Evolution."

"I have no idea what that is."

"Oh." He frowned. "Maybe it hasn't happened in your time, yet. We get visitors from so many centuries, I lose track. Riveras always seem to want to come back and see the shop during its 'golden age.'" He added air quotes to the word. Was the Revolutionary era supposed to have air quotes? "Most of them just want to find the recipe for troll powder... but none of 'em ever give me any useful investment tips in return. Afraid to mess up the future or some shit." He gave her a pointed look. "So, I always tell 'em to forget it."

"Well, I *want* to change the future and I have no interest in troll powder."

Loyal gave a skeptical "humph." "Had a Recompense Rivera visit us from 1979, a few months back. You heard of him?"

"Just today, as a matter of fact." Grace was still pissed that Serenity hadn't mentioned that guy before. "Apparently, he settled in the Crusades and saved some serfs from a fire. It was a whole big thing."

"That a fact?" Loyal chewed on his corncob pipe and made a considering face. "Man could dance one hell of a Virginia reel." He wore a banyan robe, pattered with spooky black cats, and a lopsided negligé cap. It was the eighteen century version of leisure wear. In the modern world, he probably would've been decked out in a t-shirt from some failed truck stop and boxer shorts.

Grace made a vague sound of agreement. "So what kind of potion will stop someone from killing Anabel Maxwell tonight?" She prompted, trying to get the conversation back on track. "There has to be a potion, right?"

When magic was needed, potions were always Grace's first choice.

It was why she was willing to use one to transfer Jamie's memories. In high school, she'd only passed Geometry by drinking Serenity's noxious mixture of rosewater, cabbage leaves, and catfish scales. Hell if she knew how it worked, but she'd somehow gotten a B in that class and she could barely tell a triangle from an oval. Potions were the most kinda-normal type of magic and not even she could argue with their success rate.

"I'm sure I can whip something up." Loyal assured her nonchalantly. He was a pudgy, bespectacled man who bore an uncanny resemblance to a younger Benjamin Franklin. …Except for the fact that his cap was embroidered with the words "Suck it, bitches." "Is Agatha alive or dead? If she's dead, we'll need different ingredients and whatever."

"*Anabel* is alive and I'm trying to keep her that way." Grace had explained that about ten times now. Loyal had a focusing issue. He couldn't even keep Anabel's name straight.

Although if Anabel Maxwell didn't die, Grace would be

a crime scene investigator with no crime scene to investigate. Also, she was pretty sure she'd be stuck in 1789 unless she found a drop of Anabel's blood to touch. That could be awkward, since she had no money and already missed indoor plumbing.

"Alrighty then, let me check the ol' books." Loyal hauled himself to his feet and headed over to the bookcase. "Maybe we can do a protection spell for ya."

It occurred to Grace that his speech patterns had definitely been effected by his time traveling visitors. No one of this era should be using modern slang. With good reason. History would have been so different if Patrick Henry's speech had been something like, "Alrighty then, give me liberty, death or whatever, bitches."

She sighed and hoped for the best. Luckily, half of the ancient tomes on the shelf were the same ones in the shop back home and she *knew* those worked. In fact, everything in the Crystal Ball looked exactly the same. The wood was less worn and the creepy knickknacks were *different* creepy knickknacks, but the essence of the place remained unchanged. There was something kind of awesome about that. As much as her relatives aggravated her sometimes and as God-awful as they were at running their business, Grace was proud of the fact that they had owned their shop longer than America had even been a nation. It said so much about their skills and intelligence.

All evidence to the contrary.

"A spell?" She repeated, thinking over his suggestion. "Isn't there a potion? Spells always seem to go wrong."

Loyal ignored that. "Here we go." He dropped a thick volume onto the table, sending up a wave of dust. "Not a protection spell, but it'll do for ya. This one reveals bad intentions."

"That does sound promising." Grace admitted and hurried over to join him at the table. "It'll show us who the murderer is?"

"No, but it'll ferret out anybody with a grudge against

Agatha."

"Anabel."

"Anabel. Right. Right." He pushed his glasses up his nose. "You can get a bead on who hates the girl."

"Good." Grace would take what she could get. "Cast it. I'm going to spy on her and…" Her words stopped short, as the door to the shop slammed open and a pissed off pirate stalked in.

Jamie.

"*There* you are." He snapped, his eyes settling on her.

Grace's heart leapt happily at the sight of him. "Do you remember me yet?" She asked excitedly.

"I remember that this is your family's shop, so I assumed this is where you would turn up. And I sure as *hell* remember that you left me standing bloody naked on the deck of my bloody ship!"

"Oh." Grace struggled to hide her disappointment. The memory potion hadn't kicked in yet. Or maybe Serenity's magic didn't work in this century. Who knew how time travel crap worked?

Loyal squinted at Jamie over the top of his half-lens. "Friend of yours, Gracie?"

"I'm going to be her husband." Jamie answered, as if that was even remotely true. Apparently he hadn't been kidding about pirates refusing to *ask* for a girl's hand, because his idea of a proposal was more like a command. He ignored the glare Grace sent his way and arched a brow at Loyal. "Are you her kin?"

"Somehow or other." Loyal seesawed his hand back and forth, a serious expression on his face. "It's a bit of a fluid situation, but I'm sure we share *some* DNA."

"Right." Jamie clearly didn't care to hear any details about their family tree or ask what in the world DNA was. The pirate had bigger fish to fry. "Who do I see about permission to marry her, then?"

"We can't get married, Jamie." If she was actually from this century, though, she'd be a lot less certain of that denial. Obviously he'd have to cough up one heck of a diamond, but what other guy could *ever* live up to this one?

He shot her a fuming look. It seemed that leaving him naked on the ship really had hurt his feelings. "Are you promised to another?"

"No, of course not. That's not the point."

"Good. One less man I have to kill." He nodded like it was *exactly* the point and now it was all settled. "I'm trying to be a gentleman and do this properly for you. So stop making it difficult and fetch your father out here."

"Her father's not exactly born yet." Loyal put in with a sigh. "Which isn't to say that he isn't also long dead. Cousin Recompense is presently in the Crusades and I know for a fact he won't be born until 1941." He made a tsk sound. "The Good Lord only knows when her parents might be."

Grace and Jamie ignored him.

"I've seen you being a gentleman, Jamie Riordan." She informed him with a sniff. "This is *not* it."

"This is me *trying* to be a gentleman. It goes against my nature, but I'm not picking you up and carrying you out of here on my shoulder, so I deserve some credit for my restraint." He crossed his arms over his chest. "Since I'm a wee bit perturbed that you left me *again*, though, I donea suggest you push me, lass."

Yep. She'd definitely hurt his feelings. "I'm sorry you're upset, but I didn't really leave you. You need to trust me on this, because I'm doing it for *you*." She gave an earnest nod. "I'm right in the middle of something very important for your future."

"So were we!"

The man was impossible sometimes. "I told you, I'm not sleeping with you today!" Grace threw up her hands. "This mission is life and death, okay? You're just going to have to believe that and let me work."

"Wish the damn future-folks would start staying at an inn." Loyal said to no one in particular. "Every damn time one of them comes to visit, it just gets weirder. And louder."

Grace resisted the urge to punch her sort-of-grandfather. It was a miracle she was holding it together half as well as she was and he was seriously not helping. "You shut up. ...Actually no. You need to keep talking." Every crazy thing that could happen to a person had happened to her recently and Jamie was *not* going to distract her now with his stunning aliveness. She turned back at Loyal, determined to stay focused. "Ignore Jamie and let's get back to business. Do you know anyone with the initials H.C.?"

"No." Loyal paused. "Well, there's Hunnicutt, I suppose."

Her eyes widened. "*Edward* Hunnicutt?"

"Sure." Loyal nodded. "Some of the boys at The Raven call him H.C. Hunni-Cutt."

Grace stared at him for a beat. "Are you kidding me?" Her head whipped around, her gaze narrowing in Jamie's direction. "H.C. is *Edward frigging Hunnicutt* and you never bothered to mention it?!"

"Why the hell would I mention that? I donea even think I *knew* it. Who cares about Ned Hunnicutt enough to recall his blasted nickname?" Jamie shook his head in annoyance. "Jackass makes bloody terrible maps and waters down his ale."

"Well, he was apparently also having an affair with Lucinda!"

Jamie's eyebrows soared. "Ned killed Lucinda?" He actually looked perversely pleased by that news. "You know, I've never liked that wanker. It will give me great fucking pleasure to run him through with a sword."

"Hold on." Grace held up her palms before he went off to challenge Ned to a duel or something. Pirates weren't known for their thoughtful and measured responses. "We don't know he *actually* did it. I told you, I'm still investigating. He's just our new person of interest."

"So I'll stab him, just to be sure, and *then* you can investigate. It'll be far safer for you."

"Stop helping." Grace ordered and turned back to Loyal. "Cast the bad intentions spell for Anabel." She reiterated and headed for the door.

"Are you going to pay for this magic?" He called. "Because it seems like time travelers never pay." There was a pause. "Actually, it seems like *no one* ever pays."

Grace scoffed at that very typical Rivera complaint. Money baffled all of them, which is why they never had any. "I'll give you an investment tip, the next time I visit. Cross my heart."

"The *next* time you visit? What century will that be?"

Grace pretended not to hear that. "Jamie, if you're coming with me, you'd better behave. I mean it."

He made an aggravated sound and fell into step beside her. "No version of me has *ever* mistaken you for timid, love."

She shot him a sideways look as they stepped out onto the (smelly) street. "Remind yourself you said that in about two hundred and thirtyish years. It'll be good for a laugh."

"Two hundred and thirty *years?* How the hell am I still alive two hundred and thirty years from now?"

"You're not."

"Then how am I 'sort of' your lover?" His volume had several people looking their way.

"I told you, it's complicated!" She shouted back. "Just wait until the memory potion kicks in, okay? You're not going to believe me otherwise."

He ran a hand over his face. "You're probably right. In fact, it would be best not to discuss your ideas about time travel, a t'all. They cause my head to pound."

"You'd prefer I lie to you?"

"I'd prefer you say things that make a damn bit of sense."

In Grace's opinion, she was dealing with time travel just about as well as anyone could expect. Being in Harrisonburg, when it was all sparkly and new, still kinda freaked her out. It was the year the frigging Constitution took effect, for God's sake! Everywhere she looked there were horses and buckle shoes. It was darn unsettling. Jamie really could be a little more supportive.

"Maybe you should have thought about all this *before*

you showed up, wanting to ask my father for my loony hand." She told him archly.

"Why?" He didn't seem very concerned over the possibility of wedded bliss with a basket case. "I've seen enough to accept there are many things I've never seen. Much as it annoys me, time travel could well be one of them."

"You've *really* seen magic before?" He'd talked of seeing the "fay" back in Scotland, but, at the time, she'd been half-convinced he was just being his whimsical self.

Or drunk.

"I've seen fairies dance and mermaids swim. I've got a twinkle of knowing in me, lass."

Grace wasn't surprised that he'd believed in the supernatural even before he became a ghost. All iterations of Jamie seemed to accept that abnormal happenings were just a normal part of the world. "You've seen actual mermaids?"

She had always been inexplicably fascinated with mermaids. They were the one type of magical being she wished were real, but not even a Rivera had ever seen one. If they had, her crypto-taxidermist Uncle Devotion would've had it stuffed above the mantle by now.

"Aye. Off the coast of Jamaica, playing in the waves." Jamie shrugged, like it was no big deal. "So I know what it feels like when you're staring at something beyond our mortal understanding. I have that feeling when I look at you. But I donea like entertaining the idea of you slipping back to some time period that I cannot reach."

"Technically, I'm slipping *forward*."

Jamie shot her a sideways glance. "When I look at you, I *know* you're made of pure magic and I *know* you're mine. That's my point. So, maybe you're a mad woman and maybe you're not… But either way, I donea feel the need to explain it. I'm certain we belong together. Now and forever. That's all that matters to me."

Crap.

The man always disarmed her when he said things like that. His words weren't exactly the stuff of Hallmark cards, but it was impossible not to be touched by his faith in their bond.

Grace gave up being irritated and sighed. "We belong together." She agreed quietly. "I know that, too."

No matter what century they were standing in, Jamie Riordan was her Partner.

He flashed her a slant-y smile, his sour mood evaporating. "So, why are we bickering about what we both already ken?" He slipped an arm around her waist, which was no doubt a graphic PDA by post-Colonial standards.

Grace let him, because he was Jamie and she'd let him get away with just about anything. "Because there are problems with our relationship that you don't fully understand." She informed him, ignoring the scandalized looks coming their way. "I'd explain them to you, but I already know you won't listen."

He sure as heck wasn't following her instructions to get out of town. Jamie was going along with most of this, because he could feel their connection. Sure, he'd stab Ned just on general principles, but that was a long way from fully buying her crazy tale of serial killings and time travel. Until the memory potion kicked in, he was just an innocent bystander in this mission.

It was up to her to keep him safe.

"Let us go back to my ship and you can tell me *alllllll* the problems in graphic detail." He suggested with a guileless expression. "I've also quite an interest in learning what a 'pizza-tramp' is. We'll have a good long talk about all of it."

"If we go back to your ship, I'm sure 'talking' will be the last thing on your mind."

"Ah, you really do know me, lass." His eyes traced over the Velcro closure to her tour guide costume, as if he was visualizing her naked breasts. He smirked a bit as her nipples beaded in response. "But I've quite a good brain in my handsome head. We'll compromise. You come with me now and I'll solve everything for you, before our wedding night. You have my word as a gentleman."

No one had ever accused the man of lacking confidence. "You and Rhett Butler, right?"

His brows compressed. "Who?"

"Never mind." Since his life depended on her investigative skills, she needed to focus on finding the killer and not Jamie's good-natured come-ons. Just walking down the street, Grace could see people slanting him suspicious frowns. Half of Harrisonburg was already convinced of his guilt and only Lucinda had died so far. If she didn't save Anabel and Clara, he'd be lynched all over again.

Jamie was still holding her and her free hand came over to grip his fingers protectively.

His mouth curved. "Grace," his tone went soft, "are you trying to guard me from the good citizens of this town? There's no need, love. I did nothing to Lucinda."

"I know, but it's not going to matter. You just need to lay low until I solve everything, alright? I have a plan."

"Which is?"

"To start with, we're going to find out if Edward Hunnicutt has any bad intentions towards Anabel Maxwell." She headed for The Raven, trying to recall the eighteenth century's social mores. "Am I allowed in the tavern or is there some chauvinistic 'boys' club' rule in place?"

"Ladies donea go into drinking establishments."

"Is that like a *law* or just some policy I can choose to ignore?"

"If you ignore it, I'll be put in the stocks for savagely beating the men who haul you out the door."

She rolled her eyes. "Wonderful. You're going to have to get Edward Hunnicutt out here, then. I need to question him."

Jamie wasn't thrilled with that idea. "I donea understand your sudden fascination with that man." He muttered. "He treats his serving girls terribly, you know."

"Oh for God's sake, Jamie. I'm not planning to seduce the guy or..." She paused, a new thought occurring to her. "Hang on. When you say he mistreats his wait staff, what *exactly* are you referring to?"

Jamie hesitated, as if trying to find phrasing that wouldn't offend her. "He makes them do things for their wages that no honorable employer would be making them do."

"Hunnicutt has sex with the girls before he'll pay them?" Grace translated. "Jesus, I'm rethinking the part where you stab him to death. What a total and complete scumbag."

"Indeed. It's why I would prefer you stay far away from him."

Grace shook his head. "No, this is actually a useful clue. Disgusting, but useful. Serial killers are often motivated by power and sexual control. He's definitely our top suspect." She gave Jamie a nudge towards The Raven. "Get him out here and let's see if he has any deviant thoughts about Anabel."

Jamie didn't rush off to do her bidding. "I'm not exactly on friendly terms with the man. How do you suggest I lure him from behind the bar?"

"I don't care. Use your imagination." She made a shooing gesture with her hand. "Go on."

"Grace…"

"Please?"

Jamie swore under his breath. "Are you going to be here when I get back?" He challenged, still not happy. "I donea like letting you out of my sight. You've a tendency to vanish on me."

"I'll be standing right here."

"You promise?"

"I promise." Grace went up on tiptoe to kiss him lightly. "Don't worry. Even when I vanish, I'm only going back to you."

The edges of his lips quirked and his hand touched her cheek. "Maybe so, but I am in no mood to wait two hundred and thirty more years to see you out of that strange dress, lass." He loped off towards The Raven, before she could swat him.

Grace shook her head in exasperation. The man was incorrigible. She leaned against a tree, her eyes on The Raven's door. If Jamie took this a bit more seriously, they'd…

Oh God!

Grace gave a sudden gasp and jerked away from the

oak, realizing where she was. Her eyes went up to the gnarled branches swaying over her head. This is where Jamie died. The spot where they planned to hang him in four short days. The tree was still alive in this time period, ominously looming over the street. She scrambled away from the trunk, her heart pounding. Maybe she should set the blasted thing on fire. Or chop it down. Or do something --*anything*-- to ensure that no one could kill him under its menacing limbs.

His death had never seemed so real to her.

So inescapably, terrifyingly real.

What if she couldn't do this? What if she wasn't smart enough to solve the case? Wasn't fast enough to stop the killer? What if she let Jamie down and never saw him again? She could burn out again at any moment and leave him completely unprotected. She could actually feel it happening.

Peaceful green cornfields. Peaceful green cornfields. Peaceful...

No.

Grace gave her head a clearing shake. No. She wasn't going to give into panic and doubt. No matter what, she *had* to make sure that Jamie survived this. Someone so alive couldn't spend the rest of eternity trapped in limbo. It wasn't fair! She needed to find a way to save him.

She needed *him*. Grace had been crazy in love with that pirate since she was fifteen years old. She wasn't about to lose him now.

The door to The Raven suddenly burst open and a good-looking man with blond hair sailed out like he'd been thrown headfirst. Grace's eyebrows soared as the guy careened into the street, rolling to a stop by her anachronistic, but very comfy, Keds. It appeared that someone had punched him a few times and then tossed him right out of the tavern.

And it didn't take a genius to figure out which Scottish sea captain that "someone" must be.

"Grace, my love, meet Ned." Jamie stepped out of The Raven, dusting his palms together. "He's simply dying to speak with you."

"When I told you to use your imagination to get him

out here, I expected a little more imagination than *this*, Jamie."

"Yes, well, have I mentioned I've no liking for the man?"

Edward Hunnicutt struggled to his feet, an outraged look on his face. "You can't just barge into my goddamn establishment and manhandle me like this, Riordan!"

"Seems that I can." Jamie retorted. "And I'll ask you kindly to be watching your fucking language around my fiancée."

Ned's head swung around to look at Grace. "You agreed to marry this maniac?"

"I didn't exactly *agree*, but I don't think that's going to stop him from planning a wedding." She glanced at Jamie and arched a brow. "A pirate I know recently told me that marriage proposals and kidnappings are kinda the same thing to James MacCleef Riordan."

Jamie's eyes gleamed. "Smart pirate."

"Who is this woman? No *lady* would ever consent to link her name to yours." Edward spat out, glowering at Jamie. "Why even Lucinda knew better than to…"

Grace cut him off. "Oh shut up." She snapped, scowling at the man who she had absolutely no liking for either. Confrontations usually left her sweaty and panicked, but this was one time she felt just fine shouting at somebody.

"As I explained, the lady is my bride." Jamie told Edward darkly. "Be nice or I'll forget I promised her that I wouldn't run you through until after she's conducted her investigation."

"Until after we find out if he's *guilty*." Grace corrected.

"I never promised that."

"What investigation?" Edward demanded. "What the hell do you think you're…?"

"We know you were sleeping with Lucinda Wentworth and now she's dead." Grace interrupted. "I think there are *a lot* of people in this town who'd be interested to know about your affair with her."

Ned's eyes widened. "Who told you that? Riordan? It's all a lie! All of it!"

"*Lucinda* wrote all the juicy details of your encounters in her diary, which I now have. So I suggest you start cooperating."

His face flushed an angry red. "Fine. Say I *was* meeting her on the side." He whispered fiercely. "What would killing her accomplish? You think I *wanted* to lose a woman who looked like that? One who was willing to do the things she was willing to do? Why in the blue hell would I want to get rid of her?"

That was actually a fair point. Grace looked over at Jamie.

He shrugged. "Who's to say why madmen do anything, love?"

"You can't prove I did *anything*." Ned thundered. "Riordan is the one you should be questioning. *He* was the one who was seen around town with her, not me."

"I don't *have* to prove you did anything." Grace retorted. "I'm betting all I have to do is make copies of a few of the more salacious entries and it'll ruin your life." She crossed her arms over her chest. "I especially enjoyed reading about the time you took Lucinda to the stables and used the riding crop and bridle to…"

"What do you want?" Ned interrupted, his eyes frantically casting around.

"I want to know what kind of bad intentions you have towards Anabel Maxwell."

The sidewalks were filling with people, all of them trying to figure out what was going on. Across the street, Clara Vance, Eugenia Wentworth, and Anabel Maxwell were standing in a group, all of them looking appalled.

Anabel gasped, one hand dramatically covering her heart. "Why would you have bad intentions towards me, Mr. Hunnicutt? Why my family's lineage and reputation are above reproach."

"Your idiot brother was the Hero of Yorktown and cost Great Britain the War!"

Jamie's eyes lit up in triumph. "I *told* you Ned was a Tory, Grace!" He couldn't have been more thrilled with the results of their questioning. "I *knew* it!" He paused. "Although, that lack-wit Gregory Maxwell was no more a hero than he is a duck."

"The War is over!" Edward bellowed. "It doesn't matter which nation I fucking supported."

Lucinda's sister fanned herself, looking faint. "Language, gentlemen. There are ladies present."

Jamie instantly tipped his hat at her. "Apologies, Miss Eugenia."

She gave a prudish sniff, but inclined her head in ladylike forgiveness. "I should say so, Captain Riordan." Apparently the rumors of her "fainting when she saw Jamie in the streets" were exaggerated. If Eugenia thought he murdered her sister, she was a master at hiding it under polite censure.

In any case, Grace hoped *she* didn't sound that prissy when she was scolding Jamie about his nonstop cursing. "You never apologize to *me* for swearing." She hissed at him.

"You're not a pinched-lipped Sunday school teacher, as that girl is." He edged away from Eugenia as she crossed the street to get a better (disapproving) look at the chaos. "Never did meet a pinch-lipped Sunday school teacher who wasn't terrifying."

"*I've* taught Sunday school, Jamie."

He grinned at her. "But your soft lips are anything but pinched, lass. I can testify to that, firsthand."

"This is all ridiculous." Ned sputtered. "Aside from disliking her jackass brother, I have no bad intentions towards Miss Maxwell or any other lady of this town." His face darkened with sudden and ill-advised hatred. "Except for my bitch of a sister-in-law."

The residents of Harrisonburg began murmuring amongst themselves.

Jamie's eyebrows shot up. "Aggie?"

"Me?" A redheaded woman blurted out. "How am I involved in this foolishness?"

"You bought my shop for half of what it was worth!" He roared.

"I paid the price *you* asked, Ned! It's not my fault that you're a poor excuse for a businessman."

"My damnably stupid wife might buy your shit, Agatha, but I know better! I still remember how you wouldn't dance with me at my wedding."

"Agatha?" Grace glanced back towards the Crystal Ball a horrible suspicion filling her. Loyal was really, really bad with names... "Oh *no*."

"Because you'd just taken my sister as your wife, but you were trying to feel under my skirts, you pig!" The woman, who had to be his sister-in-law Agatha Northhandler, waved a disgusted hand at him. "I *told* Sarah not to marry you."

"Aggie raises the prices at her shop, every time I need muslin." Someone in the crowd called out. "All she cares about is money!"

"She took my seat in church last Sunday." Another woman cried. "I had to stand and she *knows* that my shoes are too small! She's the one who sold them to me."

Grace squeezed her eyes shut, knowing it was just as she feared. Loyal had cast the spell using the wrong name. Bad intentions towards *Anabel* weren't being revealed. Instead they were about to hear from everyone with a grudge against Miss Agatha Northhander. It was like watching the Boston Massacre begin all around her.

"Aggie Northhander was mean to my dog." A man cried, looking close to tears. "Threw a rock at Old Revere back in '84. She's a violent witch."

"Witch!" Clara Vance screeched, pointing a finger at Agatha like she was auditioning for a community theater production of *The Crucible*. "She's a witch!"

Eugenia staggered against Jamie in a swoon, so maybe there *was* a kernel of truth about her tendency towards genteel vapors. Sadly Grace had no choice but to stay conscious and deal with this mess.

Jamie steadied Eugenia's flailing form and sent Grace a mystified look. "Is this your doing, lass?"

"No!" She paused and made a face. "Well, *sort of*. Mostly, it's Loyal's fault, though. I told him spells never work."

Agatha did not appreciate the whole town turning against her. "I'm not a witch, Clara Vance!" She yelled, seizing on the last complaint. Aggie was a sturdy woman, with a pugnacious face and large hands. She stalked towards the Reverend's daughter with an angry frown, clearly deciding to settle the argument with bloodshed rather than thoughtful discussion. "You take it back!"

Yeah… This wasn't going to end well. Grace moved to intercede, hoping to stop the fight she saw brewing. "Why don't we all calm down?"

Everyone ignored her.

Clara Vance was half Agatha's size, but buoyed by her own sense of moral superiority. She didn't retreat as the larger woman bore down on her. "I *won't* take it back!" She exclaimed righteously.

Crap. Grace tried to get between them. "This isn't going to resolve anything."

"Grace donea interfere with them." Jamie worked to extricate himself from Eugenia's flopping appendages. "It will do no good."

"Only the Lord can cleanse our town." Clara proclaimed, dramatically spreading her arms. She had dark hair, round spectacles, and the kind of voice that was always shouting out answers in class. "Because you *are* a witch, Aggie Northhandler! There are evil forces at work in this town. I've told my father and he's going to pray for…"

Agatha swung at fist at her preachy face. Clara's shrieked and ducked to the side. Instead of pounding Little Miss Inquisition, Aggie struck poor Anabel Maxwell, who was still standing beside Clara, knocking the hideous wig right off her crew-cut head. Anabel's horse-y snout exploded in a red fountain as cartilage cracked.

Blood splattered all over Clara and Grace.

Anabel wailed in pain and panic, clutching her broken nose. Yeah, that was going to leave a mark. Too bad plastic surgery was still a long way off, because her schnoz was seriously *not* going to heal straight without some help.

Clara frantically wiped at the blood on her dress. "Eww!"

Aggie gave a smug nod, not even caring she'd just beat up the wrong girl. "Serves you all right!" She shouted at the bystanders.

Jamie shoved Eugenia aside and ran for Grace.

It was too late. Grace stared down at the gory spatter covering her hands and winced. Anabel's blood had touched her. She had just enough time to look back up at Jamie and see horror cross his face.

He seemed to realize what was about to happen. "Grace, no!" He bellowed. "Donea…"

She vanished before she could hear him beg her not to leave.

CHAPTER FOURTEEN

June 26, 1789- All I can say is that HC can use a riding crop and bridal in ways no stable boy ever dreamed!

From the Journal of Miss Lucinda Wentworth

"And so Jamie Riordan was the biggest jackass to ever show his too-handsome face in our town." Grace concluded with a nod. "Any questions?"

The tourists on the Ghost Walk all stared at her with varying degrees of incomprehension.

Jamie rolled his eyes towards the night sky. He knew he was being a jackass, but he couldn't help it. New memories were crowding his head. The feel of her skin, and the taste of her lips, and the miraculous sensation of her mouth suckling him to completion. Not knowing what he was missing had been *much* easier than actually missing it.

None of that was Grace's fault, of course.

Just as it wasn't her fault that Jamie could recall with crystal clarity the feeling of panic that had swept over him when she vanished right before his eyes. Two centuries did nothing to alleviate the desolation he'd felt when she'd disappeared and left him behind. It was a hell of a way to be convinced time travel existed. If he hadn't died within a few days, he probably would have done himself in out of sheer hopelessness. No way in hell could he have lasted another fifty years, alone and longing for her. The best part of his life had been dying and finally being with Grace.

Except he *wasn't* with her. Not really.

The need he felt for Grace was a tangible thing inside

his ghostly shell. But the divide between the living and the dead was an obstacle not even Jamie could break through. His new memories were making that crystal clear. He could never be with Grace the way she deserved. No matter how he tried to hide from reality, he'd known it from the beginning.

He should let her go.

Grace should have her Partner by her side. Someone to guard her and kiss her and share her world. Not a ghost, with only the memories of life. The miserable truth of it was what had sent him into such a foul mood

He should let her go.

That inescapable fact had been in the back of his mind for days, but spending just a brief time with her as a mortal brought it all to the surface. Given a choice, Grace would stay with him. He knew that. Their connection was too strong and her loyalty went too deep for her to ever send him away. But that would mean that she gave up her chance at a real life.

He should let her go.

Back on the *Sea Serpent*, she'd looked up at him like he was husband material and he *wasn't*. He was just an echo of a man. Jamie couldn't stand by, invisible and selfish, while she wasted her life on a ghost. ...No matter how much he wanted to.

He should let her go.

Grace was *alive*. She was passionate and shy, smart and full of self-doubt, pessimistic and shining with idealism... A mass of perfect paradoxes, with strange taste in furniture and a smile that could drop a man to his knees. Jamie loved her beyond all earthly boundaries. Everything magical about this universe was held inside of her small frame. It had been worth hanging and spending two hundred years in isolation, just to have these few days with her. He would do it all again, without a second's hesitation.

Grace was the very best part of existence and she should have the very best Partner that the world had to offer. Someone far better than a dead pirate.

And so he had to let her go.

And so he was angry and resentful and defeated and

grief-stricken… and being a jackass.

Jamie looked over at his brunette reason for everything. "You can call me as many names as you like, but I'm not changing my mind. Your time traveling adventures are too dangerous, Grace. You need to stop. It's over."

"It's *not* over." She snapped and then remembered her tour group was watching her. Her eyes widened and she glanced back at her confused guests. "The tour, I mean." She told them quickly. "The tour's not over. We're walking this way." She pointed down the street, waving at them to follow her.

Jamie sighed and hopped off the fence rail where he'd been sitting. Grace's Ghost Walk was turning into performance art, mostly because she kept forgetting to ignore him. The tourists were growing more and more baffled, as she repeatedly interrupted the halfhearted ghost yarns to complain at someone they couldn't see. If Jamie been in a better frame of mind, it would have been amusing. As it was, he took it as further proof that he was standing between Grace and the living world.

"Grace." He fell into step beside her. "You've saved Anabel. You've done what you set out to accomplish. There's no more need for you to go back in time. You can return to your crime investigation job, knowing that you're no longer burned up."

With her face swollen up like a bowling ball, Anabel Maxwell had understandably skipped her trip to the governor's party back in 1789. Instead, the girl had traveled down to Jamestown to see her doctor uncle about her broken nose and spent the rest of the summer in hiding. Consequently, she didn't die in the hedge maze. Jamie had recollections of her growing to be a very old woman, with a crooked nose and a successful horse farm. She'd eventually helped with the Underground Railroad. That was all thanks to Grace.

"It's burned *out*. And I plan to help *all* the victims, not just Anabel." Grace hissed back. "Clara Vance still dies. More importantly, *you* still die." She shook her head. "I'll stop when I save you, Jamie. Not before."

Jamie brushed a hand over her hair, wishing he could feel the dark strands. "Maybe you could go back and stop me from hanging," he admitted quietly, "but I'll still be dead, Grace. There's nothing you can do to change that."

She sent him a fuming look. "*I'm* supposed to be the one saying that the plans won't work. You're supposed to be the one who's super-optimistic, remember?"

"I'm the one being *practical*. What will happen, even if you discover the real killer? What good will it do me now?"

"We have no idea what the rest of your life might have been! Clearing your name will change the whole timeline. It'll make things the way they were always *supposed* to be. That's the whole point of this! You won't get lynched by the mob, so you could go on living for decades. You could have a successful life, with a happy marriage and some kids."

"I won't." He told her seriously.

"You don't know that." But her eyebrows tugged together, as if she didn't much like the idea of him living out the Early-American dream without her.

Jamie understood the feeling all too well. Without Grace beside him, he would have nothing. "Saving me from hanging would do me no favors." He knew it with as much certainty as he knew his own name. "I see that now. We're stopping this investigation."

"*We're not stopping, Jamie!*" Grace bellowed. "No matter what it means for us, I'm *not* leaving you back there to die!"

The tour group was staring at her again.

Grace didn't seem to notice. Or perhaps she just didn't care. "There's gotta be a potion or something to fix the rest of it." She insisted. "I can figure it out. I *know* I can. We just need to keep you alive."

"There's no potion to turn a ghost back into a man!"

She winced and looked away from him.

Whatever was left of Jamie's heart cracked in half, but he kept going. If he didn't, he would never be able to finish what had to be said. "Reanimating the dead is beyond even the

Riveras. I'm *gone*, Grace. *You're* the one who's still alive and I mean to keep you that way." Jamie loomed over her, willing her to understand. "There is a *killer* loose in my time."

"No kidding." She snapped, swiping at her eyes. "We've been investigating him for days, so I don't get why you're so upset *now*."

"Um...." A tour guest in tube socks and sandals hesitantly raised his hand. "Excuse me? Were we supposed to get a pamphlet or something to explain this part?"

A blonde woman in a Lakers cap nodded. "Yeah, I'm -- like-- *totally* confused. Is this --like-- a dinner theater thing? Because I'm vegan and I'll need a special menu."

"Damn it, I already ate." Someone else complained. "No one told me there was free food on this tour."

"We're not eating." Grace snapped at them. "What are you guys talking about? Just zip it and let me have a conversation here, alright?" She made a slashing motion across her lips.

Jamie winced a bit. It was at least the fourth time she'd told the guests to shut up since the tour began. The woman had inherited her family's lack-of-talent for customer service.

"That's it. I'm *so* filing a complaint. I skipped the candlelight harpsichord recital for this and it's totally not what *Trip Advisor* promised." The blonde muttered, reaching for her phone.

Several people nodded in agreement.

Jamie ignored the Ghost Walk's outraged (and kinda justified) murmurings. "You weren't one of the killer's targets before now, love. If you return to 1789, you could well become a victim yourself."

"You're being paranoid."

"You're being naive." He shot back. "You said yourself I danced with all the girls he killed. For all we know, that madman selects women I've showed an interest in."

"Except *you* said *your*self that you danced with other girls, who the killer left alone. You're making assumptions."

Jamie ignored her analysis. "There is *no one* I've a greater interest in than you. Not in this time or any other. Half the town heard me saying I planned to marry you, for Christ's sake! He already knows you're mine." How did she not understand the danger? "If I'm right, he'll come after *you* next, Grace."

"If he does, it will be the perfect opportunity to catch him. If it's Edward Hunnicutt, we can…"

Jamie's precarious temper detonated. "*We're not going to use you as bait for a killer!*" He bellowed. "Do you think I'd take such a risk for *anything?* Are you out of your bloody damn mind!?"

"I'll do whatever it takes to solve this case, no matter how loud you shout!" Grace bellowed back. "Now keep quiet and let me work." She pointedly turned back to her baffled tour group, half of whom were busily lodging complaints about her on their phones. "This statue is of Patrick Henry, first Governor of Virginia. His home was built here in town," she pointed towards the mansion, "where lavish parties were…"

"It says on the plaque that the statue is of Gregory Maxwell." Tube socks interjected. "*Ninth* governor of Virginia."

"What?" Grace asked in confusion, surprised out of her rehearsed spiel.

"*Gregory fucking Maxwell* became governor!" Jamie yelled at the same time. If he had a new memory of that, he'd thankfully blocked it out.

Both of them turned to look at the bronze statue of a man on horseback. Sure enough, the plaque beneath it read: "General Gregory Maxwell, Ninth Governor of Virginia. Favorite Son of Harrisonburg, who singlehandedly defeated the British in the Battle of Yorktown and won Americans their freedom."

"'Singlehandedly defeated the British?!'" Jamie threw his hands up in disgust. "He ran off at the first sign of muskets!"

"*General* Gregory Maxwell?" Grace whispered fiercely. "He wasn't a general in the last timeline, was he?"

"Of course not! And he wasn't one in *this* timeline, either. I guarantee it. The man was nothing but an idiot and a liar. Jesus, Mary, and Joseph, I'd just as soon erect a monument to King George himself." Jamie was appalled to the depths of his being. "Who would do such a bloody awful thing?"

"*We* did this." Her amazed eyes stayed on the huge bronze sculpture. "We changed history. We have no idea what kind of chain reaction our actions caused. Something we did must help Gregory Maxwell become governor."

"And still you want to go back and alter *more?*" Jamie scoffed. "Now I have to look at his stupid, deceitful face up there for the rest of eternity. Maxwell's cowardice killed a dozen of our own troops and they're calling him a hero! It's a damn nightmare."

"You heard Aunt Serenity. Whatever we changed was *supposed* to change. That's why I have this ability. To fix what went wrong."

"Gregory Maxwell was never *supposed* to be governor. I promise you that. The man was the biggest simpleton in the Colonies. He couldn't count to three if you spotted him one and two. ...And three!"

Before Grace could respond to that, her harridan boss, Anita, came speeding up in one of Harrisonburg's security golf carts. The ones that were only used for extreme emergencies, like shoplifting from the gift shop, lost children after a parade, and tour guides running amuck.

Jamie groaned. As if the night wasn't bad enough. "Oh here we fucking go..."

"What seems to be the problem?" Anita demanded, all but leaping from the small cart and surveying the unhappy faces of the guests. To get there so quickly, she must have been poised to spring into action. Her shellacked hair didn't move as her head whipped around to face Grace. "I've have complaints about this Ghost Walk." She intoned in a voice that a doctor might use to announce that plague had come to town.

The blonde woman in the Lakers hat nodded smugly.

"Now's not a good time, Anita." Grace told her distractedly, still frowning up at the statue. "Jamie, we're not just saving the murder victims, we're enabling all their descendants to be born and changing the lives of everyone who knew them. Do you have any idea the incredible repercussions it could have to...?"

"Not a good time?" Anita sputtered. "You're ruining this Ghost Walk for our customers. Now is the *only* time!"

"She is --like-- the worst guide *ever*." Lakers Hat announced and half the tour nodded. "Like, her 'ghost stories' are all plagiarized from last season on *Haunted High*."

The woman was technically right, but Jamie still shot her a glower.

"Plus, she keeps talking to herself." Tube Socks chimed in. "It's really distracting, 'cause I don't think we got a pamphlet to explain the show. I know *I* didn't get a pamphlet. Did anyone else get a pamphlet?"

No one had gotten a pamphlet.

"Or a menu." The other guy reminded them. "And I already ate, too, so I'm pissed no one told me there'd be food."

"I'm a vegan." Lakers Hat held up a French manicured hand. "So, I'll probably need to talk to the chef first. Do you have organic flatbreads here? But --like-- authentically Colonial ones? I'm totally serious about honoring the gluten-free parts of history."

Anita's eyes nearly popped out of her head. "Excuse us for a moment, folks." She seized Grace's arm and tugged her far enough away that the tour guests couldn't hear. "What the hell is going on?" She hissed as soon as they were out of earshot. "Are you having another breakdown?"

"No, of course not. I'm just..."

"This is how you repay me for giving you a job?" Anita interrupted, disregarding her denial. "By telling our guests that we're giving them free meals?!"

Grace jerked free of Anita's grip, an angry look on her face. "I didn't tell them..."

Anita talked right over that explanation, too. "Do you have any idea what kind of pressure I'm under here? Two tour guides walked --No, *ran!*-- off the hedge maze assignment today. The irresponsible little slackers took off without notice, screaming about ghosts and probably high as kites." Her lips pursed in disapproval. "We need to take a serious look at what's growing in those gardens, because they no doubt had a whole stash of pot in there."

"Jesus, Mary, and Joseph..." Jamie rolled his eyes skyward.

Grace did, too. "Anita, if you would just..."

Anita kept going. "And now this!" She clasped her palms to her chest, as if Grace had stabbed her through the heart. "No one else would hire the craziest Rivera in town, but *I* gave you a job. And how do you show your appreciation? You go even crazier! How do you think that makes *me* feel? Did you even consider the reputation of the Ghost Walk before you selfishly lost your mind?"

"I'm not crazy and neither is anyone else in my family." Grace announced for possibly the first time ever. "Maybe we're not exactly normal, but we're okay with that. And we're okay that you're *not* okay with that, Anita."

Those three sentences were all it took for Anita to find Grace guilty. It was a shame she'd been born too late for any witch trials, because she would have fit right in with the crazy zealots throwing stones. "I knew it!" She poked a triumphant finger at Grace's chest. "I *knew* I shouldn't have taken a chance on someone with your lunatic reputation! I knew it all along!"

Grace had finally had enough. "You didn't hire me out of the kindness of your heart. You hired me because no one else was willing to work this miserable shift. Not at this miserable salary and in this miserable costume. ...That you made *me* pay for!"

"Well, if you don't pull it together, you crazy bitch, you can find yourself *another* miserable job." Anita snarled between clenched teeth.

"I *quit*." Grace retorted, her eyes bright with satisfaction. "And, FYI, you don't even *need* troll powder to belong under a bridge somewhere, eating little children and bullying everyone who tries to pass."

Jamie's eyebrows soared. For a lass who needed to "peaceful green cornfield" her way through any conversation with raised voices, she was doing a damn good job of holding her own against her dreadful boss. He didn't know whether to be worried or proud. "Grace, are you sure that...?"

"You can't quit!" Anita shrieked, inadvertently cutting him off. "I'm firing you!"

"Either way, you can give your own stupid tours, from now on. I have a real job, trying to *solve* murders, not milk them for tourist bucks." Turning on the heel of her white Ked, Grace headed back towards the tour group. "You morons wouldn't know a ghost if he was standing right next to you in a tri-corner hat. Trust me. I know that for a *fact*."

"I'm *so* leaving her a bad rating on the comment card." Lakers Hat decided with a sniff.

"Love," Jamie hurried after Grace as she marched down the cobblestone road, "mayhaps you should take a moment and consider this."

"Consider what? You've been after me to quit this lousy job since the first night we met."

"But you have no other way of making a living." It wasn't as if Jamie could provide for her. Not with his gold lost and his body moldering in an unmarked grave. The idea of her destitute on the streets did nothing to improve his mood. "Your emotions are high and you're not thinking straight. You're doing something you may regret. Do you have any savings?"

"Nope."

Jamie made an aggravated sound. "You need to go back there and fix this, Grace."

"I *did* just fix it and I've never felt better. I'm getting pretty awesome at confrontations."

It *was* lovely to see her standing up for herself, but it hardly made up for the fact she was now unemployed. "How do you plan to eat with no money coming in?"

She waved that aside as if starvation wasn't a concern. "Which other girls did you dance with?"

He tried to catch up with her non sequitur. "What?"

"At the Summer Ball. Who did you dance with that the killer *didn't* target?"

"I donea know. Some matronly girls, who no one else was paying attention to." Jamie always tried to make sure every lass got to dance at a party. "What does it matter?"

"Maybe there's a clue in his victim selection."

The woman made him want to tear out his hair. "He left the other girls alone because they were Sunday school teachers and old maids. He only had an eye for beautiful victims... like *you*. Which is the whole point of you staying away from 1789."

Grace wasn't convinced. "Yeah, but..."

"Would you stop fixating on the past and think of the present? You're now jobless and broke, because of me."

"Because of you?" She blinked. "It wasn't your fault. *I'm* the one who just walked off the eight o'clock Ghost Tour."

Jamie disregarded those semantics, focusing on the big picture. "Before I entered your life, you had an income. You were in no danger of being the target of a killer. You weren't slipping through time."

"That isn't true. I went back in time last year, before I even met you."

If he'd been solid, he'd have taken her by the shoulders, but it was one more thing ghosts couldn't do. "Knowing me is harming you. Keeping you from living."

She shook her head, refusing to admit the truth. "I'm more alive with you around than I've been in thirty-two years."

"This won't work." Jamie persisted. "I'm dead and you're not. Sooner or later, you'll want someone with a heartbeat."

"No." She sounded very sure. "I've only ever wanted you."

Jamie squeezed his eyes shut. Damn it, she was going to rip him apart. "You should have *more* than me. You should have *everything*."

"Where is this even coming from?" She demanded. "Things have been fine, up until now."

"No, they haven't. We just haven't wanted to see reality. What kind of future can I give you? What will happen when your Partner comes and offers you children and a real life?" Either Jamie would have to stand by and watch her love another man or --even worse-- she would walk away from everything she deserved for a ghost. He scrubbed a hand over his face. "It won't *work*, Grace."

"Let me explain about the Partner thing. Then you'll..." She trailed off and turned to look at him, comprehension dawning on her lovely face. "Wait a second, are you *dumping* me? Is that what this is about?"

He nearly flinched. "I'm trying to save you, as you've saved me." The least he could do was return the favor.

"Except I haven't saved you, yet, idiot!"

She'd saved him, just by being born. "It was wrong of me to ask you to solve these murderers. All that matters now is *your* life. I know you, Grace. So long as I'm here, you will never stop this. Once I go, the investigation is over." He took a deep breath. "And so I'm leaving."

"You're leaving." She repeated quietly, her expression shifting. "And going where?"

"To Heaven."

That was a lie. No pearly gates were opening for Jamie anytime soon. If he'd been a Rivera, no doubt he'd attribute that to the fact he wasn't *supposed* to be dead. Since he was just a Riordan, though, he knew better. God hadn't forsaken him, but He wasn't exactly going to welcome him into the clouds, either. This brief time with Grace was the only paradise he'd ever be granted. This *was* Jamie's eternal reward and it had been a blessing.

"You can go to Heaven?" She asked skeptically. "Since when? You told me you were stuck here."

"Well, now I feel like it's time to move on." He obfuscated, wanting to ease her mind. Ghosts had a few tricks up their sleeves. He could make himself invisible to Grace and she would think he'd found peace. It would be for the best.

...Then he could haunt her for the next seventy years, hating every man who came near her.

Grace's magical brown eyes narrowed slightly. "I know you, too, Jamie. So I know you're not going *anywhere*. Even if you could get up there somehow, you don't *want* to go to Heaven. Not right now. You want to be *here.* It's probably why you're still roaming around. Why are you lying?"

"I'm not." It didn't sound convincing even to his ears. Jamie was an earthly creature and always had been. Heaven was no doubt a very dull place for a pirate. It wasn't as if he'd know anyone up there. Truthfully, anywhere would be dull without Grace. "Look, I just…"

She cut him off. "Is it me? Are you bored with me?"

"Bored?" He actually laughed at that. "Are you fucking crazy? When would I have *time* to be bored? Every ten minutes you're mixed up in some knew lunacy."

"Well, that's not *my* fault." She protested, as if he was complaining. "Most of it, *you've* caused!"

"I know!" He pinched the bridge of his nose. "And I can't keep doing this to you."

"You want to find someone else to help you?" Tears glittered in her eyes, making him feel like a monster. "How? I'm the only one who can see you or hear you or touch…" She paused. "Wait, is it because we touched each other?" She nodded like she'd finally figured it out and wiped at her cheeks. "If that makes you uncomfortable, Jamie, we don't have to do it anymore. I promise."

"Good Lord, *no.*" It was a mystery to him how the woman's mind worked. "I'm dead, but I'm not *that* dead." He scoffed at the very idea. "Have I *ever* shown any discomfort at touching you? In *any* time period? It seems to me, *I've* been the one pushing *you*, not the other way around."

"I don't mind you pushing." She said earnestly. "I'm not nearly so semi-frigid around you."

Jamie's mouth curved and he stepped closer to her. "If I could be with anyone --in any century or world-- it would be *you*, Grace Rivera. You're the only woman for me. Now and forever. I've waited for you for more lifetimes than you can imagine."

"Well, what's the problem then?"

"The problem is I *can't* be with you. Not as a living,

breathing man."

More tears traced down her face, each one burning through his soul. Fairies weren't supposed to weep. "But we can still have *this* and it'll be enough." She whispered.

"It won't." Not for Grace. She deserved so much more.

"So, you'd rather be alone than go on as we are?" She sobbed. "That doesn't make any sense! Being alone again is your worst nightmare. I *know* that."

"No." He laid an insubstantial palm against the curve of her damp cheek and gave her a gentle smile. "My worst nightmare is seeing you harmed, lass. And I'm going to do everything I possibly can to keep that from happening."

Her eyes widened, sensing that this was the end. "Wait!" She tried to grab hold of his wrist, but her fingers passed straight through his hand. "I can figure out a way to fix everything. I know it. Please. Just give me a little time."

"No more of your time is being wasted on the dead." He managed a crooked smile. "It's my last chance to be an actual gentleman, you know. I gave you my word of honor that I'd leave you in peace on the 4th of July."

"Then you owe me three more hours. It's not even nine, yet."

God, he just adored her rule-following, fine-print-reading, scientific precision. "It's close enough. Now it's time for you to live your life. Every minute of it." The backs of his eyes were burning, even though he was fairly sure ghosts couldn't cry. "And stop trying to be normal, because you're *not*. You're so much more magical than that."

"Jamie, don't do this!"

"I love you, Grace."

…And with that he disappeared from her sight.

CHAPTER FIFTEEN

June 27, 1789- Father has hung that dreadful portrait of Eugenia and me over the fireplace, the same way he might hang a picture of his prize horses. Ugh! I shall be embarrassed to look upon it every day. My sister's pinched lips and disagreeable glower will frighten away all the men who come to call. Not that she *cares. No beau will ever seek Eugenia's hand. Although I sometimes get the feeling she's set her eyes on one. I pity the poor fellow, whoever he is! As for me, I cannot wait to find a rich husband of my choosing and leave this horrible place for good.* Nothing *can be worse than living here. I'd truly rather be dead!*

From the Journal of Miss Lucinda Wentworth

On the morning of July 4th, Grace walked into the Harrisonburg Historical Museum with no intention of ever leaving.

This was her last chance to go back and fix the past.

The final day the magic would work.

Somehow she sensed that, the same way she knew she wouldn't be able to use Lucinda and Anabel's blood to travel backwards again. Anabel's blood wasn't even there anymore, since she no longer died in the garden maze. This whole adventure had always been a one-shot deal.

And it always circled back to Independence Day.

Jamie was an idiot if he thought she'd give up this investigation. Grace wasn't going to quit when she was so close. If there was anything left of Clara Vance's blood, it would be housed in the museum. Grace's plan was simply to sneak into the basement and find it. How hard could it be?

Of course it would be a lot easier if Jamie lent a hand.

Grace wasn't thrilled with the idea of breaking into Robert's workplace alone. Her ex was out of jail and she was fairly certain he'd be nursing a grudge. She wasn't about to change her plans for that jackass, though. Hopefully, he'd be able to control himself if their paths crossed. It was a public building, after all, and Robert had a reputation to consider.

Grace warily entered the museum, hating the oppressive place. Even during the town's busiest week of the year, it was deserted. Most tourists had better ways to spend the morning then looking at dusty Revolutionary War muskets and rows of Colonial era coins. Old fashioned cases lined the walls, packed full of antique objects and neatly printed cards explaining why visitors should care.

Only no one did.

It broke Grace's history-loving heart to see a whole building full of awesome stuff being ignored. The museum should give it all a second life! Let the objects be important again. She'd tried telling Robert that people might be interested if he updated the displays and added some interactive exhibits, but he'd been horrified by the very notion of technology creeping into his static time capsule. Like all the Harrisonburg Historical Museum directors before him, he wanted to maintain the status quo. Forever. It was why the place had remained virtually unchanged for sixty years.

It was also why it was always empty.

Well, except for Grace... and one very pissed off ghost.

"What the bloody hell are you doing?" Jamie appeared in front of her for the first time in twelve hours, an outraged expression on his face.

Apparently, he'd been spying on her. Huge surprise. Whether it was some kind of Rivera sixth sense or her connection to Jamie binding them together, she could feel his presence even when he was invisible. Grace might not have seen him since the Ghost Walk, but she'd known he was still around. Heck, she'd known last night that he wouldn't really leave her. Jamie loved her. The two of them were Partners. It was why she'd given him everything inside of her and why she refused to abandon her mission to save him.

But she was still furious at the big, huge jackass.

"What does it look like?" She shot back, shooting him an angry glower. Even whispering, her voice seemed to echo around the deserted interior. "I'm carrying on my investigation alone. You don't want to help? *Fine*. I'll do it myself."

"You were supposed to stop all together! T'is why I left!"

"You haven't left. You're just brooding while invisible and it doesn't suit you. Pirates don't sulk. They solve their problems head-on or they go down with the ship."

"I *did* solve the problem. Being with me will harm you, so I'm being a goddamn gentleman and letting you get on with your life."

"Well, since it's *my life*, I can do what I want with it." She retorted. "And this is *not* you being a gentleman. This is you being scared."

"Bloody right I'm scared. I donea want to see you hurt! How do you not ken the danger you're in?" He followed her through a room full of Colonial era rocking chairs, somehow managing to make himself the aggrieved party in their argument. "You can't *be* here, Grace. Robert could be lurking about, watching you on those damn cameras, for all you know." He gestured to the overhead security system. "Jesus, Mary, and Joseph, where is your head, woman?"

"What business is it of yours what I do? You dumped me, remember?"

"I have never and will never 'dump' you." He snapped. "I told you, I want you to stay alive and to live your life, so I am trying to keep my distance."

"You were invisibly brooding in my apartment all night! How is that keeping your distance?"

"Well, I'm working up to *greater* distances." He defended staunchly. "I did not watch you in the shower this morning, which is some progress, at least."

"Oh, you did so watch me." She'd known he would. In fact, she hadn't even bothered to close the bathroom door, because she'd wanted to torment him at bit.

"Only for the part where you washed your hair. I'm not made of stone. The point is, I'm trying very hard and you're determined to screw up my sacrifice."

"Sacrifice?" She rolled her eyes. "Please. Nobody asked you to be a jackass."

"Nobody ever has to *ask* me to protect you. The desire is a part of my soul."

She glanced up at him, refusing to be taken in by his quiet words. "Well, I'm going downstairs. You can come if you want." She headed for an "employees only" door, thankful that the museum board was too cheap to hire enough guards. "All the evidence from the murders is hidden away in the basement. I helped Robert organize the boxes down there last spring. For free, I might add. Every guy I date is *soooo* unappreciative."

"Donea dare lump me in with that wanker." Jamie followed her down the narrow staircase, a sulky expression on his face. "You're the one who does not appreciate what I am trying to do for you. If you had a bloody clue how much I needed you, you would not be so quick to condemn me."

"Of course I know how much you need me." Grace turned to look at him in surprise. "It's exactly how much I need you. Not that you care, since you *dumped me*."

He scoffed at that. "Why in the hell would you need me? I'm not even here." He passed his fingers back and forth through the railing to prove his point. "You would be safely tucked away in your pastel apartment right now, if it wasn't for me. Parting with you is the *least* selfish thing I have ever attempted and I get no credit for it." He made a face. "Being a gentleman is even less rewarding than I imagined."

"I don't want you to part from me!" She stopped walking and regarded him earnestly, shocked that he didn't see what was so obvious. "Why should I thank you for doing something that hurt me?"

"Hurt you? I would never..."

"You did! Just the idea of being apart makes me miserable, Jamie. You're my Partner! My whole life, I've been waiting for you to show up and save me."

His eyes jumped to hers in astonishment.

"You're my Partner." Grace repeated, when he just gaped at her. "I would have told you that last night if you'd given me a chance. There's no other man, alive or dead, in my future. There's just you. Now and forever."

Jamie's resolve to dump her vanished like it had never been there at all. The great thing about dating a pirate was they sucked at being noble. Gentlemanly impulses or not, Jamie's deepest instinct would always be to grab everything he wanted and claim it for his own. It was part of his scoundrel-y DNA.

"I'm your Partner?" He demanded, sounding desperate to believe it. "You're sure it's truly me?"

"I'm sure. You make me believe in magic. *That's* why I'm doing this and why I'll keep on doing it, no matter how many times you try to leave me. Because I can't bear to go back to my boring, lonely life without you. You're the only one I feel totally safe with." She gave him a smile. "I love you, too, Jamie Riordan."

He moved down onto her step and rested his palm on her cheek. "I love you so much." He whispered in awe. "So much, I donea have words for it."

Grace's heart swelled. "Does the historical version of you love me, too?"

"Aye." He nodded with absolute certainty.

"So if I travel to 1789 and ask you to sail away with me, will you go?"

"Sail away with you?" He echoed. "How the hell could you do that?"

She shrugged. "I'm going to travel to the past and stay there." That was the heart of her new plan. A way to solve all their problems. "I told you I could think of a way to fix things, if you gave me some time. Well, it took me all last night, but I finally figured it out. You want me to have someone alive? Well, I want *you*. ...And you're alive, back in 1789."

Jamie blinked like she was speaking in tongues. Which her Aunt Veneration actually did sometimes and it sounded nothing like her perfectly reasonable plan.

"This will work, Jamie." She insisted when he just stared at her. "So long as I don't touch Clara Vance's blood, I'm not going to travel back to the present. And it'll be real hard to touch her blood if we save her life, catch the killer, and sail off to search for mermaids in Jamaica." Grace was pretty proud of the idea. She was even willing to wear her stupid tour guide costume one last time, in order to see it through. "I've always had a hankering to see mermaids, you know. As an added bonus, you can't hang if you're a thousand nautical miles from Virginia."

Unfortunately, the ghost version of her future (or possibly past) husband wasn't sold on the idea. "It's too dangerous, Grace."

"It's not! We know where the murderer will be tonight. We have the jump on him. And you'll be beside me the whole time. I'll be perfectly safe."

Jamie rubbed his forehead. "Even if everything goes according to your plan... you'd be stuck in 1789."

"So?"

His brows compressed. "So your family is here and I know how much you love them."

"My family is where *you* are, Jamie." Grace did love her nutty relatives, but any Rivera would do the same thing for the man they loved. Her cousin Chastity had moved a mountain for her Partner. Literally. And it had been a big Western-y one. "Now will the other you agree to leave Harrisonburg with me or not?"

Jamie studied her for a long moment. "I'll go anywhere you ask." He said quietly. "Every single version of me belongs to you, Grace. You know that."

Yeah, she kinda did.

"Alright then." She gave a firm nod and headed down the stairs. "That's our new plan. Hopefully the memory potion will kick in and I won't have to explain it all to you again, because it's a little confusing. I'll probably have to make flow charts or something."

"Take your blouse off and I'll believe anything you

say."

She flashed him a grin. "You know former Sunday school teachers very rarely allow pirates to have their wicked way with them. You're lucky I've discovered I'm kind of a pizza-tramp where you're concerned."

"Believe me, I thank my lucky stars each and every day I found you."

Grace reached the bottom of the steps and pushed open the door to the storage room. No one had locked it. Why would they? Everything valuable was upstairs on display. This was where the museum kept the broken, objectionable, and/or oddball bits of the collection. All the stuff that had been donated because its owner died and nobody else in the family wanted it. The junk that wouldn't even sell on eBay. The cluttered room wasn't exactly the warehouse at end of *Raiders of the Lost Ark*, but it was still a hell of a lot of boxes to sort through.

Grace puffed out an irritated breath. This was going to take a while. "I think the Revolutionary era stuff is over by the window." She squeezed through the rows of crates and dusty shelves. The buzzing florescent lights overhead were already giving her a headache. "It's all separated into categories. Look for a box with an X on it. That's the museum's code for 'this item is never, ever going on display.'"

"Why are they holding onto it, then?"

"Because it's a *museum*. You think people are going to will them stuff if it gets out they're tossing away antiques?" She shook her head. "It's easier to just store it all."

"Seems a waste." Jamie paused to frown at a hobby horse that was missing its back half. "They could at least fix some of these objects and put them to use."

That sounded exactly like something she might say. Grace sent him a smile. "They don't have enough money for a lot of repairs. Especially not since Robert authorized a twenty percent raise for himself." What had she ever seen in that idiot? "No one cares about this stuff. It's an appalling attitude for a museum to have, if you ask me."

"Not everybody has your passion for giving old things a second life, lass." He winked at her. "Speaking as one of the old things you're trying to save, we thank you for it."

"You're welcome." She began prying the lids off all the containers that looked promisingly forbidding. "Now focus on our mission and not flirting with me. Anything left from the murders would have ended up down here, hidden away from tourists' eyes."

"Like Clara's shawl." Jamie guessed. "On the tour, you said it was left behind when she was taken."

"You remember that part? I thought you hated my tours."

"I remember everything you've ever said, slanderous or not."

Grace shot him another smile. "I'm really glad you're back, Jamie."

"I never left." His misty lips grazed her temple. "I never could."

"Anyway," she continued, feeling incredibly happy despite their morbid quest, "yeah. The shawl has gotta have her blood on it. All we have to do is find the darned thing."

Which was easier said than done. Three hours later, all Grace had accomplished was tiring herself out and making a huge mess. Stacks of books, moth-eaten clothing, tarnished flatware, and old horseshoes were scattered up and down the aisles as she emptied box after box.

"Crap." She sat back from a container full of tin soldiers and headless dolls, once again finding nothing useful. "This is crazy! Where could they have put the evidence from Clara's death?"

"Perhaps it's all gone. It's been two hundred years, Grace. It could have been destroyed in a thousand different ways." Jamie crouched down to examine a sword with half a blade. "God knows, everything else down here is falling apart."

Grace ran a palm through her hair, unmindful of the dirt covering her hands. She was hot and sweaty, her body ached in a million places, and she was coated in a thick layer of cobwebs and dust.

...But she wasn't giving up.

"No. It has to be here *somewhere*." Her eyes went to the broken saber that had captured his attention. It looked like something Errol Flynn would have swashbuckled with. A new idea popped into her head. "Hang on, they think *you're* the killer, Jamie."

He snorted. "No shit."

"Don't you get it? They think a *pirate* murdered those girls. They wouldn't have stored the evidence in the 'Local Revolutionary History' section of the basement. They'd have put it with all the other boxes full of 'Piracy' stuff." She bounded to her feet, getting her second wind. "That's all stacked over here." She started for a completely different row of shelves. "We just need to..."

Her words ended in a startled gasp as Robert stepped around the corner.

Her ex-boyfriend looked like hell. His normally neatly pressed suit was a rumpled mess, his hair uncombed and greasy. He clearly hadn't showered since he'd been released from jail. From his red-rimmed eyes and unshaven face, she was guessing he'd been too busy drinking.

And getting fired.

There was a cardboard carton in his hands, which seemed to contain the personal contents of his office. Apparently, the museum board hadn't been happy with their director being arrested. What would the donors say?

Jamie bit off a vicious oath in Gaelic. "Grace," his voice was tense, "slowly move away from him, love. Very slowly. Donea set him off."

Yeah, that seemed like a really good idea. Robert was hanging by a thread.

Grace edged backwards, casting a quick glance over her shoulder to gauge the distance to the door. Too far. God, it seemed waaaay too far.

"You've ruined my life." Robert told her in an eerily calm voice. "Do you know that? You've cost me *everything*. I don't even have a job anymore, because of you."

"Um... That's a shame. I lost my job, too." Somehow she didn't think that was going to mitigate his anger, but maybe they could bond over their unemployment checks.

"Your job was *nothing!*" He snapped. "But I was somebody in this town and you took that away!"

"You broke into my house, Robert." Grace retorted, unable to stop herself. "It wasn't my fault you refused to accept it was over between us."

Robert let out a sound of pure rage and heaved the box full of desk supplies at her. "It *was* your fault!" He roared as she dodged to the side to avoid getting hit with a stapler. "All of it was because of *you!*"

"Donea fucking argue with him!" Jamie stepped in front of Grace, like he simply couldn't stop himself. "Stay calm. Three steps back is that sword."

A sword? Was he kidding? Grace wasn't a frigging pirate. What the hell was she going to do with a sword?

Her dumbfounded expression must not have registered with him, because Jamie kept talking. "It's broken, but the blade is still sharp. Donea look at it. Just listen to me and I'll guide you to it."

She nodded, because she didn't have a better plan. No way was it going to work, though. Jamie would probably call it pessimism, but it seemed pretty clear to Grace that she was going to be raped and murdered surrounded by spiders and broken dishes and wearing her stupid tour guide dress. Oh God.

Peaceful green cornfields. Peaceful green cornfields. Peaceful...

Jamie.

The image of him suddenly filled her mind, offering a deeper feeling of security than even the endless rows of corn on her parents' farm. Jamie. She let out a long breath and her eyes flicked up to his stunning profile. He was her safe place.

"I love you." She whispered, because she might not have another chance to say it.

"You *don't* love me." Robert wailed, thinking she was talking to him. "If you loved me, you would have forgiven me for that pizza-tramp! You wouldn't have had me thrown in prison and gotten me fired! *You wouldn't have ruined my life!*"

Jamie ignored his caterwauling. "You're not saying goodbye to me, Grace. I won't lose you. I can't." Patriot blue eyes burned into hers. "Keep moving towards the sword. Two steps. You're going to be *fine*."

She gave her head a frantic nod, wanting to believe him. "Just don't leave me alone."

"Never." It was a solemn promise. "Never again. I was stupid to even try it, Grace. I could *never* leave you. No matter what, I will be right by your side."

"You left *me*, not the other way around." Robert was still sure she was talking to him. "You never considered *my* feelings, at all. Never thought about what *I* wanted and now you show up here to --What?-- try and make things right? Well, it's too late!"

"One more step, Grace." Jamie watched Robert with dark and unfathomable hatred. "Feel for the hilt with your hand."

"I'm not here to see you, Robert." She told him, careful not to look at the weapon as her fingers tried to find it. God only knew what she'd do with it once she held it. Everything she knew about sword fighting she'd learned from watching *Game of Thrones* reruns and she'd had to cancel HBO last year, when her paycheck shrank. "I just want you to leave me alone."

"Then why did you come to the museum?" He demanded, stalking forward to make up the distance she'd created. "Security told me they saw you come down here on the monitors and thought you were looking for me." He glanced around, noticing the dozens of unpacked boxes on the floor. "Wait, are you *stealing* from the museum? From me?!"

"Of course not! I'm…"

He cut her off, a triumphant smile on his bloated face. "You are! You pretend to be so sweet and good, but you're a dirty bitch underneath it all, aren't you?" He reached for her with sick determination. "You're nothing but a thieving whore and that's exactly what I'm going to treat you like."

Jamie's beautiful hand slammed out, trying to shove Robert back from her. If he'd been solid, the smaller man would have been careening into the shelves behind him. Grace's eyes narrowed in sudden consideration. No one noticed. Jamie's ghostly palm passed through Robert's chest and her ex continued his advance. Jamie's cursing could have blistered paint.

But now Grace knew what to do.

Her fingers finally sealed around the broken saber's hilt. She swung it in a wide arc, catching Robert off guard.

He leapt back in surprise, narrowly escaping a long slice across his stomach. "Holy shit!"

Grace arched a brow, holding him a bay. Maybe she had a bit of pirate in her after all, because this was coming pretty naturally to her. "Robert, you're an asshole." She said succinctly.

Jamie gave a chortle of delight that the tables had turned. And also at her cursing. The man really was a scoundrel.

"You think I'm afraid of you, you rotten little slut?" Robert hissed. "I'm going to hold you down and make you *beg* for me."

"There's only one man alive who can do that and he's dead right now." Grace told him seriously. "Nothing is going to stop me from saving him. Certainly not someone as boring and normal as you." She jabbed the jagged sword point at him and Robert went flailing back in panic.

...Right into the shelves behind him.

He floundered against the boxes, trying to keep his balance. It was no use. The shelves tipped like a row of dominos, taking Robert with them. He fell backwards with a frantic scream, buried under cartons of broken pottery and embroidered tablecloths.

"Go!" Jamie bellowed.

Grace went. Rather than run out the door, though, she headed down the aisle of piracy artifacts. Robert would dig himself out in a moment or two. She didn't have much time.

She desperately ripped boxes open, trying to find the shawl. Scrimshaw whales' teeth and model ships tumbled to the floor as she haphazardly dumped the cartons onto the cold cement.

"You have to get out of here!" Jamie tried to grab her arm and drag her to the exit, but his fingers passed right through her skin. *"Fuck!"*

"I can't go yet." She got out breathlessly. "Not yet." If she left now, she'd get no second chance. This was her one and only opportunity to save him. "I have to find it." His name was a frantic chant in her mind as she tried to calm down.

Jamiejamiejamiejamiejamiejamiejamiejamie.

"I am *begging* you, love. Leave *now!* He's not going to give you another opportunity to escape. You've made him too mad. He's going to *hurt* you."

"He won't." Grace tipped a box full of yellowed papers onto the floor. "I'm not going to be here." Once she had the shawl, she'd be safely back in 1789.

"Donea do this." Jamie pleaded, an agonized expression on his face. "It's not worth it. *I'm* not worth it."

"You're worth everything to me." She heard Robert coming for her, trying to find her in the maze of shelves. Oh God. Her Keds skidded on the ancient parchments as she worked her way down the row of boxes. For once, she didn't worry about damaging antiquities. "It *has* to be here."

"Grace!" Robert shouted, his angry voice creating a terrifying echo. "Where are you, you semi-frigid skank?" Seriously, how could someone be semi-frigid *and* a skank? The man was a total moron. "I'm going to teach you who you really belong to."

Jamie was about to lose his mind. "Grace, *please!*"

Robert rounded the corner of the aisle, his bloodshot gaze siting on her. *"There* you are." He snarled, looking nothing like the husband-materially guy he'd pretended to be for so long.

Jamie's eyes widened in horror.

Robert's hands went to his belt buckle as he prowled forward. "Nice try, bitch. But now you'll see who the *man* is around here."

"No, no, no, no, no." Jamie's arm came up, trying to shield her. "Grace, where the fuck is the sword?!"

"Ummm..." She looked around, trying to remember. Had she dropped it in all the historical debris? Everything was happening so fast that...

Robert hit her.

Grace fell to the floor, her ears ringing. Whether that was because she'd just been punched in the jaw or because Jamie's enraged roar was bouncing off the walls at about a million decibels was anyone's guess. Dots flashed in front of her eyes, as she tried to focus. Robert had just hit her! No one had ever hit Grace before. Her mind was lagging a bit, trying to decide on a course of action through the pain.

Robert was on her before something brilliant came to mind. His body pressed hers into the floor, preventing her from getting free. His stubby fingers ripped at her tour guide outfit, tearing open the Velcro fastenings.

Panic hit Grace with the force of a Mack truck, drowning out everything else. "Jamie!" She had no idea what he could do to save her, but calling for him was instinctive.

"Who the hell is this *Jamie?*" Robert demanded, giving her a vicious shake. "Are you cheating on me? Huh?"

"I'm here, lass." Jamie dropped to his knees next to her. "Grace, look at me! Stay calm and look at me!"

She turned her head so she could see him, trying not to sob.

"I'm here." It was amazing he could keep his voice so calm, when she could see the wildness in his eyes. "I'm right here. Can you use that menstrual cramp spell, again?"

She tried to call on either of the spells she knew, but she was too scared to concentrate on the incantations. Robert was trying to get his pants unzipped and she was about to lose it completely. She shook her head, tears spilling down her cheeks. "Jamie, please help me." It wasn't fair to ask him, but she couldn't think straight.

"*Fuck!*" He looked around and she could see him trying to come up with a plan. He might have been a lackluster pirate when it came to bloodshed, but all the history books agreed he was a genius at improvising attacks. "Alright." His face was tortured, but his mind was still in gear. "Alright. I know what to do. Put your hand where mine is." He flattened his palm on the edge of one of the boxes beside them.

Grace instantly did has he asked. She stopped trying to push Robert away and placed her fingers over Jamie's instead.

"Good. Now, when he's above you, pulled it down onto his head."

The container was made of wood, so it weighed a ton. That plan might just work. Grace seized onto it, because what else could she do? She grabbed hold of the box's lip and nodded. "Okay." She swallowed hard. "Okay, I can do this."

"Damn right you can." Robert sneered. He fumbled with her skirts, leaning over her. "You're going to give me everything I..."

Grace yanked at the box with all her might. The heavy wooden crate slammed into his skull, sending him sideways. It didn't knock him out, but it did get him off of her. Mostly. She pulled herself backwards along the floor, trying to escape the rest of his weight.

"Get up!" Jamie yelled. "Get up and run!"

Blood was pouring down Robert's temple. "I'm going to kill you!" He screamed, reaching for her again.

Grace's palm came down on fabric.

Something had come free when the wooden box fell. Something lace. Her gaze went down to it, her lips parting in amazement. The shawl. They'd found it! And just as the rumors said, it was splattered with dark spots that could only be Clara Vance's blood.

"Jesus, Mary, and Joseph..." Jamie whispered, seeing it too and knowing what it was.

Grace smiled at him, knowing they'd just won.

Robert reached for her, intent on causing as much pain as possible. Before he could make contact, though, she slammed her palm down onto one of the blood stains, which looked a heck of a lot like a thumbprint. Her hand fisted around the fabric, holding tight.

And just like that she was free.

It was really kinda awesome and a total victory for the white hats. All around her, the basement disappeared and she was catapulted into the past. There was nothing Robert could do to stop her. Nothing at all. She and Jamie had just swept the field or whatever the hell pirates did when they totally kicked ass.

Grace gave an exultant laugh. Victory was soooo sweet!

Her elated feeling lasted right up until the moment she and the shawl landed in 1789... just in time for the witch trial.

CHAPTER SIXTEEN

June 27, 1789- Clara Vance was jabbering on about those fortunetelling Riveras again and how the Reverend wanted to run them out of town. It was all I could do not to tell her that her sainted father and I have explored the wages of sin behind his pulpit, just to see the look on her face. I only allowed him to touch me, because I knew it would just kill Mother and Father if they ever learned of it, of course. Still, I was surprised at how enjoyable it was! For a man who preaches against wickedness, the good Reverend surely does engage in some deliciously twisted activities.

From the Journal of Miss Lucinda Wentworth

Jamie hated killing people.

Usually, he tried to avoid it at all costs. It seemed that July 4th 1789 was the day he was about to break his own rules, though. He was mad enough to shoot every single citizen of Harrisonburg without a flicker of remorse.

No one touched his woman.

"Am I the *only* one who understands that this is the Age of Enlightenment?" Grace's voice rang out above the angry shouts of the crowd. "You can't *do* this! There's no such thing as witches! You're supposed to know that by now!"

"Quiet, witch!" Clara Vance screeched with all the zealotry in her shriveled soul. "We all saw you vanish into the ether last Wednesday. You disappeared, right from this very spot, and now you returned..."

"Because this stupid tree is bad luck." Grace interrupted and Jamie could tell she was pointing up at the gnarled oak that loomed over the street like a tombstone. For some reason, it had always given him a chill to look at it. "I'm sure of it. I can't wait until that lightning strike burns it down."

Clara kept talking, pretending she didn't hear Grace's complaints. "...And now you've returned to our righteous town to spread your poison. Do you think the good citizens of Harrisonburg will allow that? No! We will *stop* you right now, Devil Woman!"

Dozens of voices shouted their agreement.

"We'll stop you, Devil!" Gregory Maxwell echoed.

Anabel's brother never had an original thought in his head, so he made do with paraphrasing the idiots around him. The man was literally and unequivocally the stupidest man in town. It was no wonder Lucinda had laughed uproariously at all his attempts to call on her. She would have been better off with an orangutan as a suitor. At least their primitive ideas were their own.

"You morons will lynch anyone who stands still long enough!" Grace yelled back at him.

Gregory frowned, puzzled by her words. He was puzzled over a neighborly greeting of "How do you do?" though, so it was no surprise that Grace's bizarre future-isms had him perplexed.

"You won't ruin our Independence Day celebration!" Clara sounded jubilant now. Bolstered by the mob's support, she was basking in the glow of finally being the center of attention. "We will stop you, Satan Spawn!"

The crowd cheered.

Clara beamed out at them from her position on the bed of a hay wagon. She'd climbed up there to be seen and she was getting her wish. For a moment, Jamie thought she might take a little bow.

"You know what? If there *were* witches in this world, they would have totally cured Methyn's Syndrome!" Grace informed the mass of nitwits gathered to kill her. "Which I'm *sure* was a terrible, horrible, skin melting-ish disease. So you guys should be *thanking* them."

"She's threatening to melt our skin!" Clara shrieked. "You all heard her!"

Gregory jammed a fist in the air. "Skin melting!" He bellowed, with no deeper meaning. The man had the attention span of a hyperactive puppy, so it was a wonder he hadn't gone chasing after a leaf in the breeze by now.

Eugenia Wentworth staggered backwards, fanning herself like she was about to faint again. "Oh mercy! Skin melting! Someone do something!"

"We have to burn her!" Clara's frenzy was reaching its crescendo. "We have to burn her *now!*"

"Burn her!" Gregory screamed and --stupid or not-- half the crowd was with him.

"I can't *believe* I'm actually trying to help you, you sanctimonious airhead!" Grace shouted at Clara. "If I wasn't afraid of getting your stupid blood on me, I would have knocked you out by now!"

Jamie could see her now, standing on the wooden sidewalk by the tree. Ned Hunnicutt was holding her arms, preventing her from escaping. Damn it, Jamie should have killed that ass when he'd had the chance.

Grace jerked against his grip, trying to get free. "Look, I am having a real bad afternoon and you nuts are not frigging helping with this revisionist history crap! Nobody burned witches in Virginia!"

Given the number of torches being lit, she was clearly wrong about that.

"Oh God." Grace's eyes went wide at the sight of flames coming towards her. "Jamie. Jamie. Jamie. Jamie. Jamie." She chanted his name like a prayer, ignoring the odd looks Eugenia and Ned sent her.

Jamie's heart turned over in his chest. No one but Grace would ever call on him for help. It was humbling.

He shoved his way through the final throng of people that had gathered outside The Raven. "Clara Vance!" He bellowed, trying to get her attention before she incinerated the love of his life. "You have something of mine and I'll be having her back." And just in case she wasn't inclined to listen to his reasonable request, he leveled a flintlock pistol at her bonneted head. "Immediately."

This time, he'd felt Grace arrive in Harrisonburg.

He'd been on the *Sea Serpent*, contemplating getting rip-roaring drunk to block out the pain of knowing Grace was beyond his reach. Then that twinkle of knowing he'd been born with lit up like that evening's fireworks display. Somehow he'd *known* she was back. When he'd gone looking for her, though, he'd found Grace right in the middle of an execution. It seemed she'd done her magical appearing trick right in front of a meeting of Clara and her fanatics.

No doubt about it, Jamie much preferred it when she popped up in his bath.

Grace's face lit up when she saw him standing in front of her. "Jamie." She breathed. She tried to move towards him, but Ned yanked her back.

Jamie *really* should have killed him.

Clara's beady eyes narrowed, not appreciating the fact that he'd interrupted her moment in the sun. "Not even you would shoot a God-fearing lady, right in the center of town, Captain Riordan." She decided, trying to gauge his resolve. "Your own father was a minister."

"That he was, but I never much liked the man." Jamie arched a brow at her. "Sorry to say, I donea much like you either, Miss Clara."

She gasped like he'd somehow insulted her feelings. "When my father comes back from Richmond, I'm going to tell him you said that!"

"Tell him! Tell him!" Gregory urged.

"Jamie's right." Grace snapped. "No *way* are you smart enough to write *Horror in Harrisonburg*. …Which was an awesome book, even if it was filled with lies."

Jamie and Gregory both squinted at her., wondering what the hell that meant.

Edward Hunnicutt took a threatening step forward, dragging Grace with him. Unlike Clara, he was more offended by the pistol than Jamie's insults. "You good for nothing pirate! You wouldn't dare hurt any of the honorable residents of…"

Jamie switched the muzzle in his direction, cutting off

his bluster. "*You* I can shoot even easier than her, Ned. Trust me. You donea want to test what I'll dare to reclaim my bride. *Let her go*. This is the last time I'm warning ya."

"You can't kill all of us!" Clara pronounced grandly, refusing to give up the stage. "There's only one round in that pistol."

"True, but I can *definitely* kill Ned." Jamie assured her. "I'll bet I can hurry and get off a shot at you, as well. That will be quite satisfying. Possibly enough to make the whole effort worthwhile."

"Goddamn pirate." Ned muttered, but he wasn't looking so confident anymore.

Jamie bit back a smirk. Talking had won him more engagements than arms ever would. ...Which was lucky, since the pistol in his hand wasn't even loaded. He hadn't had time to get fresh powder before wading into the fray. Grace had needed his help and it didn't seem like the pack of assassins was inclined to wait for him to ready his weapon. Of course, none of that was going to slow Jamie down. Not with his whole future at stake.

"I've also got three cannons on my ship, all of them aimed this way." He pointed towards the harbor with his free hand and hoped to hell no one called his bluff. "I can reduce this town to rubble at any moment, with the whole lot of you standing in it." His voice got hard. "And I bloody well *will* unless I have my woman back in my arms *right fucking now!*"

Most of the mob took off, rather than be in the line of fire. Gregory --who'd never been the "Hero of Yorktown," regardless of what he liked to boast in taverns-- ran the fastest of everyone.

Jamie met Grace's amazed eyes and gave her a quick wink. That had been even easier than he thought. It went to show what a grand pirate he was. Reputation took over where reality left off.

Eugenia's lips pressed together in starchy disapproval at his language and crossed her arms over her chest. Unlike so many others, Sunday school teachers didn't scare easy.

Certainly, she looked less frightened than Clara and Ned.

Ned glanced towards the *Sea Serpent*, then at Jamie, and then back again. He believed Jamie's lie. Why wouldn't he? Jamie was the worst pirate in Virginia. He worked damn hard to ensure that everyone knew that and his (slightly exaggerated) infamy was paying off in spades.

With no other option to save his skin, Ned shoved Grace forward. "Take the witch, if you want her so bad. Be my guest, Riordan. As long as she's with you, it's *your* soul she'll be trying to steal."

She already owned his soul.

"Come here, Grace." He held out a hand to her and she hurried over to take it. "Stay behind me, lass." He didn't let out an easy breath until he felt her palm in his and that magical energy of hers playing over his skin.

Jesus, Mary, and Joseph, he couldn't let the woman out of his sight for a second.

"I am really, really glad to see you." She whispered fiercely, gripping his fingers tight. She bent down to grab a soiled shawl with her free hand. "Like *really* glad. You and my Aunt Serenity were totally right about the witch burnings, even though you *shouldn't* have been right." She was talking too fast, riding high on emotions. "Do you think that you were remembering things that hadn't happened yet? Or just --like-- getting a vibe of it? Do you think that's possible?"

Jamie understood approximately three words in that rush of questions. "With you around, I think anything is possible." He said honestly.

Grace smiled. She leaned against him like she needed comfort and, for some reason known only to Grace and the Almighty, she'd chosen Jamie Riordan to give it to her. His eyes closed briefly, his chin resting on the top of her head. The woman was a gift, in every possible way.

"This is the second time today you saved my life." She whispered against his shoulder. "Thank you."

Jamie was fairly certain he'd remember rescuing her at another point that afternoon. "I take it the other rescue was performed by the illustrious future-me?" He guessed quietly, holding her tight with his free arm.

She nodded and pulled back to meet his eyes. "My ex-boyfriend…" She paused, as if trying to find a word he would understand. "Ex-beau? Ex-guy-who-courted-me? Anyway he attacked me and you helped me get away."

Jamie glanced at her sharply, taking in the darkening bruise on her jaw. "Did I kill him?"

"No!"

"Why the hell not?" He truly needed to kill more people when the opportunity presented itself. This business of trying to save the lives of assholes was a bloody nuisance.

"We'll talk about it later, alright? Just give me the gun." Recovering from her distress, she reached for the pistol and he gave it to her. "No offence, but we both know you're not going to shoot Clara. Your gentlemanly impulses are going to get in the way of this plan." She was the first person to ever see through his façade, because she was the only one who'd ever known him. "Don't worry. *I'm* not going to have that issue."

"You plan to murder the girl?" Somehow he doubted it. But maybe he should warn her the gun was empty, just in case.

"Not exactly." Grace turned with the pistol in her hand, aiming it right at Ned. "I might shoot *him*, though. I'm still half-convinced he's a murderer and I'd like to solve this whole thing quickly, so we can be on our way to Jamaica."

The remainder of the crowd took off running, even more scared of an armed witch then an armed pirate. All except Eugenia who just rolled her eyes. She'd always been the brains of the Wentworth family.

"The only murderer here is Riordan!" Ned snapped. "He's the one who killed Lucinda, not me!"

Jamie ignored that and arched a brow at Grace. "We're going to Jamaica? Why are we going to Jamaica?"

"I'm planning a honeymoon cruise."

His lips curved at that happy news. "You're staying this time, then?"

"Yep." She shot him a quick glance. "I've signed on with you for good, Captain."

Jamie couldn't have been more thrilled to hear that. "Well, I'm sure I can find *something* to do with you aboard ship." He assured her lasciviously.

Grace arched a brow at him. "And in the meantime," she glanced back at Ned, who was silently fuming, "I'm going to need some fingerprints from both of you." She yanked the mermaid pendant from her neck and held it out to him. "Press your thumb onto this, please."

Ned and Clara looked at her like she was deranged.

Even Jamie squinted slightly at the odd request. "What is this about now?" He whispered.

"It's about me being amazingly good at my job."

***

"We could just go to Jamaica *now*." Jamie offered. "Whatever it is you're doing with that pendant, I can't imagine it's as important as having rollicking sex on our ship."

"Can you focus, please?"

Grace didn't have her forensics kit in 1789, but she did have her family's collection of potions, powders, and unidentified goo. The Crystal Ball had fully stocked shelves and, after some experimentation, she found that ground up mothswort worked just fine as fingerprint powder. Loyal told her to use as much as she wanted, just so she didn't make too much noise or bother him.

…And just so long as she paid.

Riveras really never changed.

"How about that useful, can't miss investment tip I promised in exchange for the mothwart?" Grace had offered, when he started nagging her about money.

"Something from *this century?*" He'd challenged. "Knowing to buy 'Microsoft stock' in the 1980s does me a shitload of good." He'd added some air quotes around the words. "And that's the only kind of vague financial advice our relatives seem to know."

"Fine." She'd wracked her brain for something useful to tell him and then arched a brow. "I know! The cotton gin's going to be huge in a few years. There. You're welcome."

"What's a cotton gin? Some kinda booze?" He'd looked over at Jamie who'd shrugged.

Grace had disregarded their confusion, because she was on a schedule. "Now go away and let us work." She'd told Loyal and he hadn't argued.

Currently, he was upstairs, reading a Danielle Steele book that some time traveling relation had left behind. It was clearly more important to him than running the shop or Grace's problems. It was no wonder the family was always broke. No Rivera had ever understood the concept of "business hours." In the meantime, she and Jamie had taken over the entire shop, closing it for the day, while she worked on the investigation.

Also, it was a convenient place to hide from the angry citizens who no doubt still wanted her and Jamie dead.

"How can I focus when I donea even know what the bloody hell you're doing?" Jamie hoisted himself up onto a tabletop, absently playing with some futuristic doohickey that looked a little like a glowing Slinky. Whenever that whatsit was from, it sure hadn't been invented in the early twenty-first century. Grace wasn't even going to *ask* who'd given it to Loyal, because it would probably cause some rip in the space-time continuum for her to know. She'd seen *Back to the Future*, so she was taking no chances.

"I told you, I'm comparing fingerprints." She'd tried explaining a sanitized version of everything, but it was still a lot of information for him to process, even omitting the "Hey, by the way, you die today!" spoiler. She glanced at Jamie, trying to get him to understand how vital it was that they catch the killer *now*.

It was July 4th. The day he was hanged. They didn't have much time.

She cleared her throat. "When I came back this afternoon, I still had the shawl in my hand."

"Aye and quite a lovely thing it is." He wrinkled his

nose at the heap of stained lace on the table. "You say it's Clara's?"

"Yes. She's going to wear it when she dies tonight. And you see this?" She pointed to the dried thumbprint on the edge of the cloth. "There's only two people this could belong to: Clara and the guy who killed her. I got Clara and Ned's fingerprints on the pendant for comparison. I've already excluded her as the source of the print, so now I'm trying to figure out if it's Ned's. It's simple fingerprint analysis."

Jamie squinted a bit. "Right. ...And what's fingerprint analysis again?"

Crap. Had that not been invented yet? No wonder he was so confused. "Don't worry about it. I know what I'm doing." She picked up a magnifying glass and went back to comparing the prints. "If I can prove Edward Hunnicutt's the killer we can stop him and be out of here by tonight."

"That does seem a grand idea." Jamie admitted. "What if this 'analysis' proves he's *not* the killer?"

"Then our travel plans will be delayed." And, unfortunately, that was exactly what happened.

Ned's thumbprint didn't match the killer's.

Double crap. Grace got to her feet with a frustrated sigh. There went their best suspect. "Alright." She ran a hand through her hair, trying to think. "It wasn't Ned."

Jamie rolled his eyes. "Can we kill him anyway?"

"*Focus.*" She repeated sternly. "The good news is, we still have the killer's fingerprint. We can identify him, once we find him. The bad news is, we have to --you know-- *find* him."

She checked the grandfather clock in the corner. It was situated in the exact same place two centuries from now. Sort of. In 2001, her cousin Desire accidently sent it into a neighboring dimension, but you could still hear it ticking away, year after year. God only knew how Serenity kept it wound. According to its always-accurate timekeeping, there were just six hours and counting until Jamie was hanged on the street.

Triple crap.

"You could use a spell to find him." Jamie suggested.

"After the debacle with Aggie Northhandler?"

"That was *Loyal's* magic. Use your own, lass. I sense it inside of you. Just tap into it."

Grace shook her head. "I only know two spells and one of them is for menstrual cramps."

Jamie shot her the same fond look he always got when he was amused by her supposed "odd-ducky-ness" "What does the other spell do?"

"I'm not sure." She'd never tested it. Neither had anybody else in her family. ...And if the Riveras resisted using a spell, you knew it had to be bad. They'd been on a century-long quest to reinvent *troll powder*, for God's sake. "It's the Rivera Doomsday Spell. We all learn it. It's the magic you pull out when you have absolutely no other option. Nobody has ever been desperate enough to cast it."

Jamie looked just as intrigued by that as he did the first time she'd explained it. "Sounds quite promising."

"Sounds quite dangerous." Grace corrected, heading over to look at Loyal's shelves for some kind of inspiration. "Concentrate. Who else in this town might have a fixation on Lucinda?"

"Just about every male at The Raven, for starters." He'd clearly rather be discussing the Doomsday Spell.

"Who specifically, though? It's probably someone who knows her and maybe had a grudge against her." Grace plucked a vial from Loyal's shelf of potions and dropped it into her pocket. Anti-magic leanings aside, it didn't hurt to be prepared for Plan B. "Maybe some guy who..." She stopped, a new idea popping into her head. "Wait! Remember when you said you'd always thought Lucinda had been killed by a man who she'd turned down?"

"No."

"Well, that's because you haven't said it yet." When was that memory potion going to kick in, anyway? "Point is, she didn't turn down *that* many men." Grace held up her palms. "Now, I'm not slut-shaming the girl. I'm just saying she was into sexual liberation *way* before most people."

"She liked to pass a good time." Jamie agreed with a

shrug.

"Right. In my time, she'd have her own reality show and a teen makeup line. In this century, though, she was a bit unusual. So, maybe you were right, all along."

"I so often am."

Grace ignored that, her mind racing for another likely suspect. "Maybe Lucinda turned down someone who took it personally that she'd sleep with *other* men, but not him. That would give us a new place to start looking for suspects. Who did Lucinda rebuff? Did she tell you anything about that?"

Jamie made a considering face. "Well, she turned down Gregory Maxwell's advances about twice a week. Thought it was quite a joke."

Grace recalled something about that from the diary. "The dumb looking guy at my witch trial? Anabel's brother."

"That would be him."

"But he's all set to be Governor of Virginia, now."

"Oh bloody hell! Gregory as governor?! I'd sooner campaign for Cornwallis."

Grace disregarded his elaborate shudder. "Besides, that would mean Gregory had killed his sister in the original timeline." She frowned. It was always hard for her to imagine someone killing their own family. As much as the Riveras annoyed her, she loved them all. "How likely is Gregory to hurt Anabel? Are they close?"

"Anabel never refers to him a'tall, without adding 'my idiot brother' in front of his name, so I'd say not." Jamie said dryly. "But the man's not smart enough to be a killer. He once lost a checkers game to a sleeping pig."

"You don't have to be a genius to wield a knife."

Jamie made a considering face. "True enough, I suppose."

"And it would explain why Anabel went into the hedge maze with someone, when you told me she was worried about her reputation. What other man would she trust in the darkness?"

He paused, thinking it over for a long moment. "Gregory's a liar and a braggart, so I'd put nothing past him.

Alright," he nodded like it was all settled, "let's shoot Gregory *and* Ned and be off to Jamaica, then."

"I have a better idea." Grace gave her magnifying glass a Wyatt Earp-y twirl and dropped it into her pocket. "Let's go get his fingerprints and fix the future, once and for all."

CHAPTER SEVENTEEN

June 28, 1789- I find that I quite enjoy being watched in the throes of passion. It's why I don't cover up that peephole. There is a voyeuristic pleasure in having another know you're being well-pleased by a man.

From the Journal of Miss Lucinda Wentworth

"The fireworks go off in an hour." Grace looked around the town square, frowning at the crowd of people who'd already gathered. "We know that Clara vanishes sometime around then. We have to find Gregory Maxwell quickly and get his thumbprint for comparison." Unfortunately, she didn't see him anywhere.

"Never thought I'd ever be *trying* to find Gregory Maxwell." Jamie mused with the lazy unconcern of a man who didn't know he was scheduled to hang in a few hours.

Grace still didn't see the point in telling Jamie that this was the day he died, but she couldn't get it out of her head. Sometime before midnight, Jamie would be lynched, unless she could figure out a way to save him. She took a deep breath and glanced up at his stunning profile. "Maybe we should split up, so we can find him faster."

"Not bloody likely." He shook his head with a dismissive scoff. The setting sun reflected off his hair, turning it an even more amazing shade of auburn-gold. "If you're right and a murderer is about to strike, you're staying right where I can see you."

"This is *important*, Jamie. You have no idea what's at stake."

"Nothing is more important than your life." He retorted stubbornly. "Gregory isn't here, yet. When he *is* here, I'll hold him down and you can cut off his whole hand if you like. Satisfied?"

She debated arguing with him, but Jamie didn't look like he was going to budge and she didn't have time to make him. "Fine. Let's find someplace out of sight to keep watch until then. I don't love the idea of being tried as a witch again today."

They headed up a small hill, towards a secluded area at the edge of the park. The town munitions were stored there, in an octagonal stone building that was "guarded" by men who'd snuck off to the celebration. If they somehow survived into the twenty-first century, the guys would make wonderful additions to the Harrisonburg Historical Museum's crack security team.

"Of course, if he doesn't show up, Plan B is just to kidnap Clara ourselves." Grace mused. "She can't be murdered by a serial killer, if we have her tied up on your ship all night. We'll just grab her and get the hell out of town."

He chortled, delighted with both the idea and the swearing. "You've got a pirate's soul, Grace Rivera." He slung an arm around her shoulders. "T'is one of the many reasons I love you."

It was the first time *this* version of Jamie had said those words and Grace beamed up at him. "I love you, too."

"I know." He winked at her.

She snorted at his Han Solo-y confidence. "You know, huh?"

"Aye. There's no other explanation for why a lovely woman like you would want a jackass like me."

"Well, I'm not exactly normal."

His mouth curved in amusement, love shining from his eyes. "All versions of me are yours, Grace Rivera. Now and forever."

"I know." She leaned up to kiss his jawline. "You're my whole future, Jamie. And I'm going to save you tonight. So, I'm serious about kidnapping Clara. Plan B won't catch the killer, but we'd at least save her life." (And Jamie's.) "If something goes wrong, she has to be our first priority."

"*You* are my first priority. Always." He frowned a bit. "Wait, how are you saving me tonight? I accept that you're my savior. I've always felt that. But what is going to happen that...?"

Grace winced and cut him off. "Just make sure Clara doesn't die. Trust me. It would be bad for us."

The armory was partially surrounded by a brick wall for security. Embrasures in the masonry had been built so guns could be fired from the square openings, but they also provided a clear vantage point of most of the park below.

"Okay." Grace nodded, pleased with their hiding spot. "Now if we can just continue to avoid the guards who are supposed to be watching the munitions, we can..."

"Son of a *bitch!*" Jamie suddenly clutched his head, dropping to one knee like he was in agonizing pain.

The air froze in Grace's lungs. "Jamie?" She reached out to touch his shoulder, terrified that he was having a seizure. "Jamie, are you alright?" He didn't look alright. Oh God. What could eighteenth-century medicine do to help him if he was really sick? It was all leeches and gangrene. They'd need magic. She'd go get him magic. "What's wrong? Do you want me to...?

Her words ended in a squeak as his palm shot out and caught hold of her wrist. One second her fingers were resting on his sleeve, the next her hand was captured in his. Startled, Grace instinctively tried to pull free, but Jamie wasn't letting go. He held onto her like the world had just tilted on its axis and she was the only thing keeping him steady.

"Fucking hell." His free hand came up to cover his eyes as if he was trying to unsee something horrible. "They hanged me from that fucking tree. They fucking *hanged* me. That's why you're here."

He remembered.

Grace's heart slammed into overdrive. The memory potion had finally worked. This Jamie had caught up with his ghost-self, two hundred years of experiences dumping into his head like a tidal wave. Jesus, no wonder he was freaking out. It must have been like someone setting his brain on fire. She couldn't even imagine how confusing it would be to have another whole existence downloaded into your skull.

"I know." She said softly. "But it's okay. You're safe, now. I'm here. No one will hurt you this time."

Her voice seemed to cut through his overwhelmed haze. His hand dropped from his face and he blinked. "Grace." It was an awed breath. "*Grace*." Blue eyes slashed up to meet hers, wild and hungry, and Grace's throat went dry. Both Jamies were the same person, with all the same memories. ...Which meant this man knew what she looked like totally naked.

And now he could touch her.

She gave her wrist another experimental tug and was perversely turned on when he still didn't release her. Clearly, she had been spending waaaay too much time around a certain pirate, because there was something undeniably erotic about being captured. Still, it would be best for *him* if he took a moment and processed all this.

"Jamie, let's just stop, so you can get your bearings." She tried breathlessly. "This has all got to be messing with your head."

His response to that was to rise to his feet and pull her closer. With her body flattened up against his, she could hear the frantic pounding of his heart and feel the hard length of his growing arousal. He made a sound like a caged animal suddenly let loose on a meal.

"Oh God." Her insides turned to liquid, already wanting more.

Jamie's free hand came up to tangle in her hair. "Can't wait." He got out. "Please, Grace. Can't wait." His mouth sealed over hers, kissing her like it was a religious experience. Like he was starving for her. "Love you so much." Somehow, he managed to pin her arm behind her, ensuring that she was at his mercy while his lips plundered hers.

He needn't have bothered holding her still. She wasn't

exactly trying to escape.

Grace let out a whimper as he backed her up against the brick wall. Other people could come to the armory. She knew that. She also knew that Jamie was about to explode. Nearly two and a half centuries of not being able to touch anything had just come to a head. Grace had never expected anyone to ever need her as much as he did, right then.

"Grace. Grace." He was chanting her name, his body rubbing against hers. "I can't... I need... Oh *fuck*." He couldn't seem to get the words out, his control gone.

Grace knew what he needed to hear. She pulled back to meet his glazed eyes. "Take what you want." She touched his face with her free hand, trying to calm him. "I'm yours, Jamie. You know that. Take whatever you need."

He let out a shuddering breath, already lifting her skirts up. "Need you. Just you."

His fingers grasped the edge of her anachronistic panties, ripping them off of her in his haste. Holy *shit*. Grace's body clenched as he tossed the practical cotton underwear aside and exposed her core. She hadn't expected to be so turned on by the lack of finesse. She'd intended to give Jamie some relief and worry about finding her own pleasure later.

But his primitive need to claim her was amping up her own desire. Jamie wasn't trying to seduce her. Like a stallion let loose on mare, his only goal was to be inside of her. *Now*. This was going to be rough and untamed and world changing. She could already tell and it was really, *really* hot.

He gave a primal snarl of lust, scenting her desire. "*Fuck*. I need you so much."

She could hear other voices on the hill below, getting closer, but there was no way Jamie was going to stop. She didn't even want him to. He lifted her up, supporting her weight, and tugged her neckline down to expose her breasts. Greedy lips latched on, biting down on the soft globe like he wanted to mark her. Grace's head went back with a gasp, as she wrapped her legs around his waist and tried to hold on. He jerked her body forward, so she was completely open to him. It was like being caught in a maelstrom of male passion.

"Now, Grace." He wanted her so badly his hand shook as he opened his breeches. "Please." Throbbing flesh brushed against her, but he didn't go any farther. She realized he was worried. He wanted to make sure she was really going to allow this. He braced a palm beside her head, his desperate eyes meeting hers. "Please, my love."

She smiled and leaned in closer to his ear. "Make me come, Jamie. You're the only one who can."

He gave a hoarse groan and surged inside of her so hard that Grace saw stars. There was no halfway with a pirate. He took every inch she had and a few more she hadn't even known existed. Stretched and full and at his mercy... That was all it took to send her over the edge. God, she really was a pizza-tramp with this guy. Nobody else could bring her to orgasm, at all. Jamie could do it within a matter of seconds. He was *sooooo* her Partner.

Grace's cry of passion was quickly silenced by Jamie's palm. He let go of her wrist so he could seal a hand over her mouth. Jamie didn't slow his thrusts, but he did make sure she couldn't scream out her pleasure. Her body rippled around him, trying to milk his seed, but the iron length of him stayed firm.

God, she wanted him to come inside of her. She needed it. Even in the midst of one climax another one began to build.

Jamie felt her muscles tighten on him and he growled in satisfaction. "Mine." His mouth went back to her breast, lapping at the taunt nipple. "Finally."

As usual, the possessive words were like dumping kerosene on a fire. Grace tilted her head to dislodge his palm and slipped his finger between her lips instead. Jamie let out a hiss of pleasure as she sucked in time with his thrusts, her tongue tracing over the pad of flesh. She wanted more of him inside of her. She wanted everything.

Jamie's eyes gleamed. "I am so in love with you, woman."

Laughter sounded from somewhere nearby.

Grace could see figures moving through the opening in the brick wall. People were only a few hundred feet away now. In another moment, they could stumble upon them. Shit. She automatically tried to squiggle free of the embrace, but Jamie wasn't having it.

"No." He said softly, holding her still. "I'm not finished with you, yet. I'll be making you come again, before you're going *anywhere*."

God, she loved it when he got commanding in bed.

Grace tried to think, but it was impossible with him filling her again and again. Jamie slipped his finger deeper into her mouth, demanding that she resume suckling and she helplessly complied.

He made a low sound of approval, liking her acquiescence. "That's my good lass." He tunneled even deeper and Grace's body clenched. "So hot and wet and tight. Fuck, you're so *tight*." He sounded strained, his free hand moving to squeeze her breast.

Her body arched and she made a choked sound of submission, wanting more. For a woman who'd spent most of her life thinking she was semi-frigid, it was all pretty scandalous. ...And pretty frigging awesome.

This was why all the nice girls of the world secretly wanted to be ravished by a pirate.

"I've changed my mind. I need you to come twice more." He decided. "I'm going to make sure your body knows who you belong to. Twice more, Grace. You hear me?"

She shook her head. No way. Not even he could do that.

Right?

"You donea think I can do it?" He guessed. "Why I'm surprised by your lack of faith, love. Haven't we been working on your positivity? I'm about to claim my second one already. I know you're ready again."

She shook her head again, more vigorously this time. Not with people so close by. Was he crazy?

Jamie gave her a smug look and withdrew his wet finger from her lips. "Your poor starved body can't wait much longer." He commiserated. "No one's been treating it right, all these years, so it's dying for some fun. You're needing some release. What kind of Partner would I be if I denied you?"

Uh oh... Grace held her breath as he slid his hand down between her legs. "Please." She whispered, unsure if she was asking him to stop or begging him not to. "Please, Jamie."

Either way, pleading with a pirate was useless.

The thick weight of his finger pressed into her straining flesh and Grace was lost. His mouth swooped down to cover hers as she sobbed, swallowing her sounds of fulfilment. The other people took another path, away from the armory, and Grace didn't even notice. Her body shivered in his arms, giving him everything she had.

Jamie watched her with a greedy expression, drinking in every small shudder. "My turn." He said gruffly. "Can't hold on much longer." His face was taunt as he pulled back from her.

Her dazed eyes met Jamie's, ready to do whatever he asked.

He stared down at Grace's befuddled face for a beat and let out another groan. "Need you *so fucking much*." He gave her an open-mouthed kiss and then spun her around to face the wall. "Donea want you getting distracted again. It's just you and me." He bent her forward so her hands were braced on the brick and then nudged her legs farther apart. "You and me, lass." He lifted her skirt up, his hand running over her exposed backside. "Now and forever." He slammed into her from behind.

Grace's eyes went wide in shock and pleasure.

No one had ever taken her that way before. It felt wanton and vulnerable. Her body was so wet, and Jamie's angle was so devastating, that the entire massive length of him disappeared inside of her. She let out a keening wail, uncaring if anyone heard. She instinctively tried to move, but Jamie was holding her still, his hand on the back of her neck. The territorial feel of it just enflamed her more.

Jamie gave one more small nudge, proving he was

completely home, and then he held himself still for a moment. Making sure she could feel how thoroughly he claimed her.

"*Jamie!*" She was panting for breath, desperate for relief. "Oh *God*. Oh *please*." He needed to come inside of her, this time. It was the only thing that would satisfy her.

He leaned over her body, his mouth by her temple. "*I* am your Partner, Grace. *I* am the one you need. *I* am your husband material. There is no other for you. Just me. Only *me*."

She would have agreed if there was any oxygen left in her lungs. There hadn't been any doubt in her mind who he was, from the first night she'd met him. Jamie was the one she'd been waiting for her whole life.

He eased out of her and then slid *alllllll* the way back in. "Tell me you're mine." He ordered, his body covering hers like a dominant animal. One large hand flattened next to hers on the wall, giving himself better leverage. "Tell me you belong to me, because I sure as fuck belong to you."

"God, you are so good at this it should be illegal."

"In this century, I'm sure it is." His teeth grazed her ear. "Tell me, Grace. Tell me what I want to hear and I'll give you everything you need. You know I will."

She turned her head to meet his eyes. "I'm yours and you're mine, James Riordan. Now and forever. You're the only man who could ever be my husband or my Partner. I need you so much it scares me."

"God, yes!" His thrusts began again, less measured and more desperate. "You are every good part of me, Grace. Alive or dead, I'll go back to nothingness if I ever lose you." Jamie let loose a roar, finally coming deep inside of her. "*Grace!*"

His release triggered her own. Grace's body spasmed, her mouth opening in a silent scream. The orgasm was stronger than anything she'd ever experienced, wiping every thought from her head. For a timeless moment, all she knew was bliss and Jamie.

Unfortunately, three times in a row was all her system could take. Grace's legs gave out. She would have toppled forward, but Jamie caught her against him, balancing them both. He settled them on the ground, holding her in his lap, while aftershocks trembled through her body. His lips found the side of her throat, kissing her and making soothing noises as she tried to regain her equilibrium.

After a long moment, Grace turned to blink up at him, swallowing hard.

Jamie winced at her distressed expression, seeming to come back into himself. "Shit. What did I just do?" He gave his head a clearing shake. "*Shit.* I'm sorry. Grace, I'm *so* sorry." He smoothed her hair back, his eyes tortured. "I was too rough. I took you in ways you weren't ready for. I know that. I just lost control. I realized I could touch you, and that you really came back here for me, and I had to have you. I didn't stop to think..."

"I'm not upset about *that*." She whispered, cutting him off. "Are you crazy? I was an active participant in every awesome moment of it."

Jamie frowned in relief and confusion. "Then what has you looking worried?"

She chewed her lower lip. "You're kind of loud." She told him as diplomatically as she could. "Somebody probably heard you shouting my name when you came."

"Oh." Jamie smirked, not the least bit repentant. "Well, if they did, I guarantee you, they're nothing but bloody jealous." He touched her bruised cheek, his face becoming more serious. "You're sure you're alright? That wanker Robert didn't hurt you too badly earlier?"

"No. I'm fine. Thanks to you." She leaned against Jamie, her head on his shoulder, loving the simple fact that she could touch him. "Thank you for helping me. For *staying* with me. I know it was hard for you, not being able to just beat him into a sticky, bloody mess."

"You have no idea how much I hate that man." Jamie rested his chin on her hair, holding her tight. "But it's *nothing* compared to the love I have for you, Grace. I would die for you, all over again."

"I'd rather you *didn't*. Hence my time traveling adventures." She moved to kiss him. "Now, I love you, too, but we have to be more quiet. We're probably wanted by the police. Or the Watch or whatever the law enforcement around here is called. We're not going to help anyone if we're locked up in jail."

"I can be quiet, so long as I'm doing something else with my mouth." His lips grazed her neck and then started down her body.

"Stop that!" She laughed and scrambled to her feet, adjusting her skirts before he distracted her. "We're supposed to be looking for Gregory. I'm sure you remember what happens tonight. I'll give you a hint: It involves you, a rope, and me becoming a widow before I even get a wedding."

Jamie glanced up at the vanishing sun. Twilight was upon them. "Aye. One hanging this lifetime was plenty." He glanced at her, smiling as she Velcro-ed her top into place. "You sure you wouldn't rather just go to Jamaica right now? We could be heading for azure blue waters within the hour, leaving this dreary little town behind us for good.

"Your name would never be cleared, if we did that."

"Donea much care."

"You'll care when armed men come to hunt us down." She retorted. "Plus, Clara would still be killed. Crazy nut-job or not, we can't just let that happen. We have to stop this *now*. All we need to do is find Gregory and check his thumbprint."

"And if he's not a match?"

"Then we're onto Plan B and the whole kidnapping thing. Don't worry. I brought knock out powder, just in case we have to drug Clara and carry her out of here."

"I do love the way your mind works, lass." Jamie bounded to his feet, adjusting his clothes. "When *is* our wedding, anyway?"

Grace arched a brow. "Maybe when you actually propose." She teased.

"Miss Rivera, would you do me the great honor of becoming my wife?"

She blinked, surprised by the instantaneous and

completely civilized proposal. "Just like that? No Captain Hookish threats to make me walk the plank if I refuse? I thought pirates didn't take chances on their brides slipping away."

"I donea think I'm taking a chance. Because I donea think my bride is going to refuse. Because I think she's *my* Partner, too."

Grace gave him a slow smile. "I think you're right."

Blue eyes glowed with love. "So say 'yes' then, lass."

"Yes."

He beamed at that simple answer and gave her a smacking kiss. "You are the only Sunday school teacher in all of history abnormal enough to tie herself to a pirate."

"Well, I'm expecting one heck of an engagement ring, considering you have a buried treasure around here some..." Grace stopped short, her eyes going wide. "There he is!"

Jamie turned to look and made a face when he saw Gregory, who was losing a game of ninepins to a group of ten year olds down the hill. Clearly, the Colonial version of bowling was serious business for the "Hero of Yorktown," because he was loudly bitching at the kids as they kicked his ass at it.

"Bloody hell. If that moron truly becomes governor, we're never returning to this state." Jamie gave his head a disgusted shake and headed towards him. "Wait here while I go get his fingerprints."

"While *you* get his fingerprints? *I'm* the one trained to collect evidence, Jamie."

"You're also the one Gregory voted to burn at the stake a few hours back. No one's planning to lynch *me* until tonight." He sounded quite smug about his popularity. "I'm clearly the better choice to get close to the asshole." He paused. "Also, I have a gun."

"Which is unloaded."

"*He* doesn't know that, though. It will be fine." Jamie glanced at her over his shoulder. "All we need is something he touched, right?"

Grace considered his arguments and gave a reluctant

nod. It would take longer to talk Jamie out of doing this than it would to just let him do it in the first place. "Get his beer tankard. There's gotta be usable prints on there. And don't just grab it from him. Try to be *subtle* about it."

"Pirates donea do 'subtle,' love." He winked at her and loped off, no doubt planning to grab the tankard right out of Gregory's hand.

Grace rolled her eyes in exasperated affection. If there was ever a man worth giving up twenty-first century life for, it was that irrepressible jackass. Who needed Netflix and iPads, when she had Jamie around to occupy all her attention? Of course, he was also a little bit high-maintenance. If she wasn't proactive about keeping him out of trouble, God only knew what kind of mess he'd get himself into.

Since it was a lousy idea to let him handle Gregory on his own, she started down the hill after him. They were Partners in this. In everything. There was no way…

"Help!" Eugenia Wentworth came running up, cutting off her thoughts. "Quick! You have to come quickly! I think he's going to kill Clara Vance!"

CHAPTER EIGHTEEN

June 28, 1789- Silly as it seems, I'm quite looking forward to the 4ᵗʰ of July celebration this year.

For once, I feel as if something exciting might actually happen in this dull town!

From the Journal of Miss Lucinda Wentworth

"Huh?" Grace blinked at Eugenia in astonishment. Vaguely she wondered why Lucinda's sister was at the 4ᵗʰ of July celebration. Shouldn't she be in mourning? "Wait, who's doing what? What are you...?"

"Edward Hunnicutt! He has a knife and I think he's going to stab her to death!" Eugenia grabbed Grace's wrist and started pulling her in the opposite direction that Jamie had gone. The last rays of daylight faded, casting her face in shadow. "You have to come now or I'm not sure what he might..."

Grace cut her off, trying to process this new twist. *"Ned Hunnicutt* is attacking Clara? You're sure?"

"Yes! He must have killed my poor sister, too!" Eugenia pulled harder on Grace's arm, trying to urge her along. The girl was stronger than she looked. "I think the man has lost his mind! We have to stop him!"

Grace yanked away from her, shaking her head. What was going on? It didn't make any sense. "Ned isn't the murderer. His fingerprints don't match."

Eugenia gave her a mystified look, her frantic expression fading. "What?"

"His fingerprints! They're different. It couldn't have been him. Someone *else* killed the girls."

Eugenia's eyes narrowed. "What the hell are you talking about?"

"I'm talking about forensic evidence. Science. *Facts*." ...And suddenly a few of the facts from Lucinda's diary were starting to fall into place. Grace stared at Eugenia, her mind whirling.

The Pirate charmed even the unlikeliest of targets with his wicked smile.

No beau will ever seek Eugenia's hand. Although I sometimes get the feeling she's set her eyes on one.

Father likes to say that Eugenia is the brains of our family.

"We don't have time for this!" Eugenia snapped, ignoring the dawning horror on Grace's face. "You have come with me *right now!*"

Grace shook her head harder. "I'm not going anywhere with you." She got out, panic filling her as she realized the truth.

Now it made sense how the killer had evaded capture at the Wentworth mansion the night Lucinda died... Why there had been barefoot prints in the room... Why Eugenia had originally told everyone that she'd heard Lucinda sneak out of the house... Why there hadn't been any evidence of a sexual assault on the body... Why, when Grace had arrived at the scene, it seemed as if Lucinda had been dead for far longer than made sense in Eugenia's accounts of that night...

Standing back from all the individual pieces, Grace could abruptly see the whole picture.

"You killed Lucinda." She whispered. "All this time, it's been *you*."

Eugenia --the plain, pinched-lipped, overlooked sister of the town's most beautiful mean girl-- slowly smiled. "I had a feeling you were a clever one." She said, in an eerily calm voice and her pretense about Clara's peril faded away. "Jamie only fancies girls who are smart or pretty." She extracted a long-bladed knife from the folds of her black skirts. "And really, let's be honest, you're just not that pretty."

Ah crap… It seemed that Jamie had been wrong. Grace *wasn't* the only Sunday school teacher who'd fall for a pirate. Damn it, why did he have to be so frigging appealing?

"Umm…" Grace checked over her shoulder and didn't see anyone headed her way to help. "Let's just stay calm and talk about this, okay?" She tried nervously. "No reason to do anything crazy."

Not that Eugenia seemed to need much of a reason.

"The first time I saw the pirate I knew he was the one for me." Eugenia mused, a far off look in her eye. In a way, it seemed like she was glad to be found out. It gave her a chance to freely talk about her obsession with Jamie. "He was so handsome and strong and free. He was walking with my sister, much to my father's horror… and I knew I had to have him for myself. It was our destiny."

"So, you're some kind of creepy *Fatal Attraction* bunny boiler?"

Eugenia glared at her, annoyed that Grace wasn't listening in reverent awe to her story of true love. "You're not from around here, are you?" She guessed peevishly. "I declare, I don't understand half of the bizarre things you say. Try as I might, I can't quite figure out where you came from or why you're in Harrisonburg."

"I'm here to save Jamie from you."

That was probably not the smartest thing she could've said to the president of his psycho fan club. "Jamie is *mine*." Eugenia bit off, a raw and primitive madness flashing in her eyes. "Not yours. Not Lucinda's. *Mine*. He's finally beginning to realize that, too. When he held me in his arms at the ball, I could tell that he sensed our eternal bond."

"Jamie danced with you. Once. And you think that means you're soulmates?" Grace translated. "He inadvertently showed you some attention and you couldn't bear to give it up. *That's* why you did all this?"

"*I* didn't do anything. It was all *them*. Those other trollops, who wanted to steal him away." Eugenia slapped a palm against her demurely-covered chest. "We have a *connection*. We're *meant* to be together. Everyone knew it, but those bitches distracted him."

"So you decided to get rid of all the competition? All his other dance partners from that night, so it would just be *you*?" Grace edged backwards. "You murdered your own sister!"

"I tried to deal with Lucinda in a reasonable, civil, and ladylike way. *She* was the one who went and made it difficult." Eugenia's tone suggested that committing a gruesome homicide had been nothing but an inconvenience for her. "I went to her room that night and I explained that she needed to give me Jamie. I *know* that she stayed home from church last Sunday to seduce him. I saw him sneaking from the house. You think I could just allow that kind of behavior to continue?"

"I'm not thrilled with the mental picture, either." Grace admitted honestly.

"Lucinda wouldn't listen to reason, though. She laughed when I told her that Jamie belonged to me." Eugenia's pinched lips pinched even tighter. "Laughed!" She shook her head. "She had the gall to tell me that Jamie and I would never be together. That even the two of *them* weren't together, in any significant way. That he was *waiting* for someone." Her voice sneered over the word. "Fool. He was *waiting* for me! *No one else*."

"No." Grace said quietly. "He was waiting for his Partner."

Eugenia didn't even hear her. She was lost in her memories, happy to have a captive audience to admire her brilliance. After years of living in Lucinda's shade, it must have been liberating to finally shoulder her way into the spotlight. "Well, you can imagine, the discussion turned a great deal more unpleasant, after that. I had no choice but to tell Lucinda that she *must* leave my beau alone or I would expose her scandalous behavior to our parents. And do you know how she replied?"

"Um... with a four-letter word, I'm guessing?"

"Worse! With threats of her own. She said she'd go to Jamie and tell him that I'd been spying on them. Watching them *in flagrante delicto*, through a small peephole between our rooms."

"You watched Jamie and Lucinda have sex?" Grace echoed incredulously. "Ew!" Jesus, it was like time traveling into a rerun of *Melrose Place*.

Eugenia gave a prim sniff. "I was merely keeping an eye on him. Making sure my sister didn't do anything *too* vile." She wrinkled her nose in distaste. "In any case, after her threats, I knew then what I had to do with Lucinda. She wasn't going to stop until she had ruined me! So I pretended to go to bed, at the usual time." She smiled at her own cleverness. "But really I was just waiting half an hour, for the rest of the house to fall asleep."

"Waiting *naked*." Grace surmised.

"Well, I wasn't about to get blood on my nightgown. I'm *sure* the servants would have noticed when they did the wash." Eugenia rolled her eyes as if it was only logical. "Anyway, it was all very simple. I got a knife from the kitchen and snuck into Lucinda's room. I'm not sure she had any idea what happened, until after she was dead and roasting in whatever ring of hell is saved for man-stealing whores."

"What about your parents? Did you even think about them?"

"My *parents?!*" Eugenia chortled. "They despised Lucinda. They'll probably thank me for ridding the family of her brashness."

"They'd prefer her dead on the bedroom floor?"

"Well, I was *going* to make sure they never knew she was dead." Eugenia shrugged, as if it was the thought that counted. "I planned to push her body out the window and then hide it in one of the marshes around here. I'd tell everyone that I heard her sneak out and they'd think she ran off with some man." Eugenia paused, still pissed that her plans had been ruined. "...But then *you* interrupted me." She frowned. "How did you even suspect what I was planning?"

"I first read about the murders when I was a kid. My aunt had a book called *Horror in Harrisonburg*." Which she was guessing Eugenia had a hand in writing. She craved attention and the smug sensation of knowing something nobody else did. "I just had no idea Lucinda's killer was going to be her own little sister."

Eugenia seemed confused by that explanation and offended by the phrasing. Both emotions had her temper flaring. "I *told* you, I didn't have a choice! Lucinda wouldn't leave Jamie alone! She didn't love him like I do! *No one* loves him like I do!" Eugenia advanced on Grace, refocused on her mission. "Especially not *you*."

Grace gave a high-pitched laugh. "Well you're right about that! My love for Jamie is *nothing* like your crazy fixation. It's real and so is his love for me."

Eugenia barely heard her. "I thought Clara and Anabel were going to be problems for me. I planned to rid myself of them, once and for all. ...But then *you* showed up and I realized they were *nothing*. Even Lucinda was nothing, compared to you."

Somehow Grace didn't think that was a compliment. "Umm..."

Eugenia made an emphatic gesture with the knife, indicating that she wanted silence. "After all I've been through, my slut of a sister was actually right. She *wasn't* the one he was waiting for." Her eyes narrowed. "*You're* all he can think about now. I see it in his eyes when he looks at you. He wants to marry you. *You're* the one I have to stop."

This was seriously not going well. "You can try to kill me, but it won't do any good. Jamie *still* won't be your Partner." Grace surreptitiously fumbled with her apron. "He belongs to me and he always will."

That was not what Eugenia wanted to hear. "Sooner or later, he'll see that *I'm* the one who loves him! Deep down he *already* knows it, but *you're* keeping him from me!"

"At least I didn't let him hang for crimes that *I* committed. That's how much you loved him. You'd rather see him die than fess up to being a lunatic."

Eugenia had no idea what that meant, but it didn't seem to matter. Her eyes were wild. "I think Clara saw the truth about you from the start. I think you *are* a witch! I think you've put a spell on Jamie to lure him from me!"

Grace's hand curled around the small vial that she had hidden in her pocket. She'd taken it off Loyal's shelf in case Plan B was the only option and they needed to kidnap Clara, but now it was about to save her life.

"I'm not a witch." She told Eugenia very clearly. "I'm a Rivera." She threw the knockout powder, feeling triumph at her easy victory. She scrambled out of range as the green mist exploded all over the other woman and waited for it to do its work.

Except... Why was it green?

Grace's feeling of satisfaction faded into confusion. Knockout powder was supposed to be purple. Even Grace knew that and she hated magic so much she hadn't even watched the stupid *Harry Potter* movies.

There was only one explanation for the green dust settling all over Eugenia: Whatever Grace just used, it was the wrong spell.

Darn it, why did her family have to make everything so complicated? The clay vial had read "tired powder" right on the side of it. "Tired powder" as in "sleeping powder" as in "frigging *knockout powder*," right? She'd checked, before she took it.

At least, she *thought* it said "tired."

Loyal's old-fashion handwriting wasn't exactly Times New Roman. Had she misread the label? If so what had she just doused Eugenia in? Grace actually checked her pockets, as if another vial might somehow have snuck into her apron. All she came up with was the magnifying glass. This wasn't good. As far as Grace knew *no* enchanted powders were green. Well, except the fabled and probably-phony...

Troll powder.

Oh God.

Grace's gaze slashed back up to Eugenia, her lips parting in horror as the other woman began to transform right in front of her. She might have skipped the *Harry Potter* films, but she'd seen *Avengers* and she knew what the Incredible Hulk looked like. Eugenia's body got bigger and greener and hairier as the powder seeped into her system. Her demure black dress ripped along the seams as she grew. Cunning intelligence stayed in Eugenia's eyes, but now she was about six times her normal dimensions.

Grace had just super-sized a serial killer.

Eugenia let out a furious bellow of animalistic hatred.

"Sorry!" Grace blurted out. "Sorry about that. It *totally* wasn't what I was going for."

Eugenia didn't seem appeased. Grace's words to Serenity back at the shop had been one-hundred percent correct: Nobody wanted to become a troll.

Grace winced as Eugenia slammed a wrathful fist against the ground hard enough to shake it. "Umm... Yeah." She considered her options for a heartbeat and then took off running. What else was she supposed to do?

It seemed like a lousy idea to lead a raving lunatic straight into the 4th of July celebration, so she went in the opposite direction. Darting around Eugenia's massive body, she headed for the armory.

Why couldn't the powder make people into those *cute* trolls from *Frozen*? At least then there would be songs and snowman hugs.

Eugenia grabbed at Grace, hotdog-sized fingers barely missing her throat. She caught hold of the tour guide costume instead and Velcro ripped free. The apron came off of her, tripping Grace. She tumbled to the ground, the magnifying glass falling from her pocket and landing next to her.

Crap, crap, *crap!*

If she got out of this alive, she was going to make sure troll powder *stayed* extinct. No *way* were they ever going to sell this stuff on the open market, no matter how much her family wanted to drive Madam Topanga out of business. It would end up in nothing but lawsuits, and flattened cities, and tears.

Eugenia dragged Grace closer, no doubt intent on crushing her bones to make bread.

Without even stopping to think, Grace grabbed the magnifying glass and smashed the lens against one of the rocks lining the walkway. Clutching the largest shard, she stabbed it into Eugenia's hand. The jagged edge sank deep into green flesh. Eugenia let out a roar of pain, loosening her grip enough that Grace was able to squiggle away.

Meanwhile, down below, the gigantic troll was not going unnoticed by the townsfolk. Clara Vance's irritating voice let out an even more irritating screech. "Witch!" It was her favorite word, so of course that was the explanation she went with. "Eugenia Wentworth has been the witch, all this time! I told you! I told you all along! *Look at her!*"

Like Japanese crowds spotting Godzilla, Harrisonburgians pointed, screamed, and ran for their lives. All very unhelpful. But, on the plus side, it was a sure bet no one was planning to lynch Jamie anytime soon. Not with Eugenia charging around like a character from *World of Warcraft*.

"Grace!" Jamie shouted, battling the exodus to reach her. "What the bloody hell is going on!?"

Grace was too winded to answer that. She clambered to her feet and aimed what little magic she knew at Eugenia. The menstrual cramp spell hit like a freight train, but instead of providing soothing, relaxing, drugged-out comfort, it seemed to do the exact opposite. Troll powder apparently reacted badly with other magic. Maybe that was why the recipe was forgotten in her time. Or possibly it was forgotten because it had no practical purpose outside of a demolition derby.

Either way, all the menstrual cramp spell did was give Eugenia's troll-self a raging case of PMS. It slowed her down, but it sure didn't make her happy.

Grace cringed at Eugenia's wrathful bellow. This was *exactly* why spells sucked.

"Grace!" Jamie fought his way up the hill and grabbed her arm. "What happened? Are you alright? What's…?"

"Move!" She yelled and shoved him towards the armory. It was the only place that seemed even halfway safe. The walls were made of solid stone. "I accidently turned

Eugenia into a rampaging monster."

Jamie took the news better than most men would have. "Holy *shit!*" His head whipped around to stare at Eugenia's colossal form, trying to piece together what had happened to the formerly blah-looking Sunday school teacher. "Rivera Doomsday Spell?" He guessed after a beat.

"Troll powder."

He shot Grace an amazed look. "I can't believe you once asked me if I was bored around you, woman." He got the door to the armory opened and ushered her inside. "Okay. So do you have a plan on how we deal with this? Or shall we just leave this accursed town to Shrek?"

"You're hilarious." Grace leaned against the heavy wooden door and looked around.

The armory had circular walls, all of them covered in the town's stockpile of swords, muskets, and pistols. A wooden staircase led to a loft, where the gunpowder was kept in huge barrels. Back in the twenty-first century, it was the only spot in Harrisonburg that bored teenage boys enjoyed visiting. Rewinding two-hundred years into the past, it looked pretty much the same, except the weapons were actually working, sharp, and/or dangerous. Sadly, none of them looked like they would make much of a dent in Eugenia's green hide.

Grace swallowed hard. "Unless there's a bazooka lying around in here, we still have a big problem."

"Why is Eugenia Wentworth trying to kill us?" Jamie demanded, trying to catch up. "I was only gone for ten minutes. What the hell did I miss?"

"She's trying to kill *me*. Not you. She's a lunatic stalker, who thinks you're her soulmate. She's been taking out the competition, one dance partner at a time, and I'm next on the hit list."

Jamie blinked at that CliffsNotes version of the crazy. "*Eugenia* is the killer? You've got to be fucking kidding me."

"Does it *look* like the Jolly Green Giant is kidding around out there?"

"But I never showed even a modicum of interest in that humorless girl!" Jamie's eyebrows compressed, like he was looking for some kind of logic in the horribly, tragically, completely illogical. "Why would she kill her own sister because of *me?*"

"She didn't do anything *because of you*." Grace corrected, not wanting him to somehow blame himself for any of this. "Eugenia killed her own sister because she's a sick, frigging nut-bag. Don't get caught up in her madness, Jamie. My professional diagnosis is she's a narcissistic, sociopathic, bat-shit crazy bitch."

His mouth gave a reluctant quirk. "I'm always strangely comforted when you start cursing."

"You're welcome. Now help me figure out a way to escape the big, huge, troll doll outside." Grace tried to think. How were they going to stop Eugenia from...? Her attention fell on the largest weapon in the armory. Hang on. Maybe there *was* something in 1789 that could cause some real damage. "Jamie? Tell me about the cannons on your ship."

He followed her gaze and made a considering face. "Well, they're a lot like that one, actually." He said in a far more optimistic tone.

"So you can fire it?"

"I'm a pirate, love. What do you think?"

Clearly melting-your-brain sex was just *one* of the many benefits of dating this guy. She arched a brow. "I think we should blast Eugenia back to Middle Earth and set sail for Jamaica."

"I love the way your mind works." Jamie headed over to a stack of cannon balls, which were the size of grapefruit. "We need to get Eugenia in front of the door and then shoot her right through the wood. It'll be far easier to aim, if she's closer."

"Somehow I don't think it's going to take a lot to lure her over here." In fact, Eugenia was already trying to knock through the wall. "Is setting off a canon in here going to light the whole armory on fire?"

Jamie mulled that over for a beat. "Probably not." He finally decided.

"*Probably* not?"

"Well, I doubt anyone's ever tried it before, so I can't say for certain. I've yet to set my ship ablaze, if that makes you feel any better."

"It really doesn't." Grace shook her head, not sure whether to scream or laugh. "For real, this kind of stuff doesn't happen to normal people, right?"

He flashed her a swashbuckling grin. "Nope. Just to odd-ducks like you and me, lass."

"That's what I thought." Grace blew out a long breath and gave up even pretending she was anything but a Rivera. "Okay, then." She pointed towards the door, flinching as Eugenia tried her best to knock the building down around them. "Fire when ready, Captain."

CHAPTER NINETEEN

June 28, 1789- Eugenia and I were just arguing, again. Either the girl is developing a sense of humor or she's lost her mind! You should have heard the nonsense she was spouting!

From the Journal of Miss Lucinda Wentworth

The cannon's detonation was deafening.

Even with her hands plastered over the sides of her head to muffle the noise, Grace still felt like her eardrums ruptured when the blast went off. The cannon rolled backwards on its wheels, as a Newtonian response to the force of the discharge. The iron ball tore through the oak door of the armory, leaving a massive hole in the wood.

Jamie and Grace ducked their heads in unison to peer through it, gauging the success of their plan.

Good news: The cannonball struck Eugenia-the-Troll right on her broadside.

Better news: It sent the lunatic rolling down the hill like a big, green log.

Best News: The cannon firing didn't send the whole armory sky high.

"It worked!" Grace smiled widely. "I take back everything I said about you being a lackluster pirate. That was kind of awesome."

"*Kind of* awesome? I just shot a troll with a cannon, lass. I'm *amazingly* awesome." The force of the blast had bent the hinges of the door and Jamie used his shoulder to force it open. "Now that she's wounded, we might actually have a chance of surviving this damnable night. ...Unless the town

274

tries to execute us again."

"I don't think anyone's going to be in the mood to lynch us." Grace followed him into the gathering darkness. "Especially not you. We can definitely prove that you're not the killer, now. No matter what happens next, we've cleared your name, once and for all."

"Thrilling." Jamie didn't sound thrilled. He sounded like he was ready to instigate some mob justice of his own. "Stay behind me, understand?"

The cannonball hadn't penetrated Eugenia's magically-reinforced, troll-y skin, but it did seem to knock some of the enchantment out of her. However Troll Powder worked, it didn't seem to last long. Especially not in the face of massive projectiles. The spell was already dissipating as they made their way down the hill. The green color was fading from Eugenia's flesh, the normal-sized features returning to her face.

"Witch!" Clara Vance bellowed again, pointing a finger at her. "*You've* been the one plaguing our town, Eugenia Wentworth! *You're* the witch!"

Clara and a few of the braver (possibly stupider) townsfolk hadn't fled at the first sign of a monster attack. Instead, they'd grabbed up shovels, sticks, and anything else they could find in an effort to defend Harrisonburg.

Eugenia staggered to her feet. The black dress was in tatters around her shrunken body, but she'd somehow managed to hang onto the knife. Springing forward, she seized hold of Clara, dragging her around to use her as a human shield.

Clara let out a wail of panic. "Help! *Help!*"

"I'm not the witch!" Eugenia shrieked, all her crazy-fied attention on Jamie. "It's *her!*" She jerked her still-transforming chin at Grace. "She cast a spell on me! She's behind *all* of this. Don't you see? She is just another whore trying to get between us. Just like Lucinda and Anabel and Clara..."

"Me?" Clara scoffed, not knowing when to shut up. "As if I'd ever allow a pirate to court me."

"Clara, zip it before you get yourself dead." Grace warned. "And Jamie, don't get too close to the armed maniac."

He shot her a quick look. "She tried to kill you, Grace. She's not going to just walk away from this."

"She won't. There are plenty of people around who see who she really is. She'll go to jail and we'll go to Jamaica and everything will be fine."

Eugenia clearly wasn't ready to give herself up, though. "You and I are supposed to be together, Jamie. That's why I *had* to do this. Our connection is too deep to deny! I know you feel that, too!"

"All I feel for you is fucking disgust." He stalked towards her, patriot blue eyes burning with fury. "You just tried to murder my fiancée!"

"She turned me into a troll!" Eugenia shouted, moving backwards and dragging Clara with her. "You all saw it! I'm *sure* you're under some kind of a spell. That's why you don't feel our love."

"I donea feel any love for you, because *I donea love you*. I love *Grace*."

Eugenia gave a sob that was part heartbreak and part rage at his refusal to drop to one knee and propose. "She's turned you against me!"

"You did that yourself! Starting with the night you slaughtered poor Lucinda for no goddamn reason, at all!"

"That was probably her doing, too." Eugenia tried, gesturing to Grace again, desperate to win Jamie to her side. "I never would have killed Lucinda if that witch hadn't *made* me do it! It was probably another spell."

"It was you being an evil, heartless lunatic." Jamie retorted. "How could you do that to your own sister?"

"Eugenia killed Lucinda?" Clara squeaked. The blade at her neck still wasn't doing much to curb her hall-monitor tendencies. "Wait until I tell my father! You can forget about teaching Sunday school next week, I can promise you that, Eugenia Wentworth!"

"Clara, *shut up!*" Grace repeated forcefully.

"I knew you'd take Lucinda's side!" Eugenia gave up all pretense of being even kinda sane and screeched at Jamie so loudly that spittle flew from her mouth. "She let you bed her, and had a pretty face, and that's all that men need to fancy a girl! No one even looks at me, unless I *make* them!" She kept moving backwards. "But now *everyone* is looking at me. Now everyone knows who I am. Now *I'm* the Wentworth sister that this whole blasted town will remember. Now I'm the one…"

Her words ended abruptly as the heel of her practical shoe came down on a weird metal framework laid out on the ground. It took Grace a moment to realize it was the launching pad for the fireworks. The rockets poking out of it were cruder than their modern counterparts and way, way bigger than the kind sold at roadside tents during the summertime.

And the long fuse on them was already lit.

Someone must have started it burning before they fled from all the trolls and cannons and hostage situations. Grace knew very little about eighteenth-century fireworks, but she could take an educated guess that flame heading towards them was a bad sign.

"Jamie." Her fingers grabbed his sleeve, dragging him to a halt before he could get any closer. "Wait…"

Wheeeeerrrrrrrr!

The high-pitched ignition of the rockets interrupted her. The Independence Day show was about to start on schedule, even though most of its audience had run for their lives. There was nothing they could do to stop it now. Explosions of brilliant orange began lighting up the sky as the fireworks launched. Far less sophisticated and colorful than the modern Harrisonburg 4th of July spectacular, but no less beautiful. …And no less dangerous, if you got too close.

Too bad for Eugenia that she was standing right on top of them.

She screamed as one of the rockets ignited beneath her, lighting her long dress on fire. The heavy cotton went up like a candle. She went flailing backwards, trying to escape, even as more rockets began to spark to life around her. It was no use. Within seconds, Eugenia was completely engulfed in flames. One rocket after another slammed into her, glowing with white-hot phosphorescence. No one could've survived the onslaught. Within seconds, it was over.

Grace winced, looking away from the ghastly sight of Eugenia's body.

Jamie held up a palm to shield his eyes from the glare of the flames.

Meanwhile, Clara threw herself forward, away from the fire. She landed on the grass, clutching at a wound on her neck. Eugenia had left a shallow cut on her throat when she fell. It wasn't life threatening, but it was seeping blood. Clara wasn't exactly known for her calm demeanor, so of course she reacted like she'd just lost a limb.

"Heeeeelp!" She screamed, crawling along the ground like the overacting victim in a cheap horror film. "*Heeeeeeeeeeeeelp me!*" Her hand reached out to grab at Grace, her fingers grasping her ankle.

Grace tried to dodge out of the way, but it was too late.

Clara's blood touched her skin.

"No!" Grace bellowed, her grip automatically tightening on Jamie's arm. This couldn't happen! She couldn't go back to the twenty-first century! Without Jamie, she would have nothing and she had no idea how she could ever return to 1789 now that Clara was sure to survive. "Jamie!"

She heard him curse and then the world was shifting around her. Harrisonburg's town square faded and Grace was on the floor of the museum basement, again. For a second her heart stopped, panic filling her. "*Jamie!*" She screamed again, frantically looking around for him.

"I'm here." He said and waves of relief washed over her. Jamie was splayed out beside her and that meant everything would be okay. "Are you alright?"

"Yeah." She got out, struggling to get her heartrate under control. For a second, neither of them moved, just processing it all. "I guess we solved the murders." She finally said.

"I guess we did."

"And cleared your name."

"Aye."

She swallowed, heartbroken that she was back in the modern world and far away from the living version of Jamie. They had been so close to their happily ever after in Jamaica. "But the rest of the plan didn't exactly…"

"What just happened? Where did you go?" Robert shrieked, cutting her off. He was standing over them with a baffled expression on his face. "And who the hell is *that?*"

And suddenly Grace realized that he could see Jamie.

She blinked, trying to get her bearings. Her fingers were still wrapped around Jamie's sleeve. She was *touching* him. Her eyes went flashing over to the flesh and blood pirate beside her, joy rushing through her. Just like she'd been able to take the shawl back in time, she been able to pull Jamie forward with her. *Living* Jamie. The Jamie with a three-dimensional body and a heartbeat and all of the Jamies' memories. It didn't matter that she couldn't get back to 1789, because Jamie was now in the twenty-first century.

Triumph lit his beautiful face as he realized what had happened. "I'm alive." He whispered.

"You're alive." She agreed, choking back tears. "Jamie, you're *alive* and you're with me. We really did it!"

"*You* did it." He corrected, his hand cupping her cheek. "It was a hell of a plan, love …Although we seem to have hit a slight bump there at the end. I don't think we're sailing off into the sunset on my ship."

"No kidding." She laughed in delight. "That idiot Clara touched my leg with blood on her hand and screwed up our honeymoon."

"Well, no harm done. We'll just be staying in your century." He gave her a quick kiss. "I'm a bit relieved, actually. I'd have hated to miss *Haunted High's* final season and I quite enjoy the look of you in less layers of clothes."

"You can't be in here, whoever you are!" Robert shouted at him angrily. Until that moment Grace had forgotten that he even existed. "My girlfriend and I are having a private conversation. This is an employees' only area."

Grace blinked, trying to orient herself again. It seemed

like a lifetime ago she'd been battling Robert, but it had only been a few seconds in his time. He was still eager to continue their fight. ...Only now, the odds were slightly better for her team.

Jamie's head swiveled around to look at Robert and his smile was all jagged teeth. "Well that's convenient." He murmured to himself, getting to his feet as gracefully as a shark surfacing from deep water. "I donea even have to go hunting for the bastard."

Uh-oh.

Grace's eyes went wide. "Jamie..."

"So *he's* Jamie?" Robert interrupted scornfully. He smoothed down his hair, as if that would help make the comparison between them less absurd. "The one you've been cheating on me with?"

"I'm Jamie." Jamie told him calmly. "The one who's about to beat you to death."

Grace cringed as her fiancé knocked out three of her ex-boyfriend's capped teeth. Crap. If Jamie was arrested for assault and battery, the police would have a field day at booking. His only form of photo identification was a two-hundred and fifty year old oil painting. "Stop, Jamie! You have no idea what a mess it would be to explain who you are in court."

He didn't seem to care about the legal ramifications. He was too busy ripping Robert apart with his bare hands.

Robert gave a squawk of pain and panic, trying to escape Jamie's fury. Who could blame him? It was like watching a dog fight between a Chihuahua and a rabid timber wolf.

"You think you can hit my goddamn *wife?!*" Jamie bellowed, sending Robert flying backwards with another crushing blow. The smaller man landed on his back, blood pouring from his crushed nose. "You think you can come into her house? Threaten her? Try to rape her? Call her *yours?* *You think I'll just fucking let that happen?*"

Robert scrambled backward like a crab, his penny

loafers slipping on the cement floor. "It wasn't my fault! She started it! She tried to ruin my life!"

Jamie followed him down the aisle like the specter of death. "You're not going to *have* a life, by the time I'm done with you." It was a grim promise. "Nobody touches Grace. *Nobody*." He hauled Robert up to hit him again.

Repeatedly.

Grace realized this was careening towards a murder charge. Jamie had been riding high on emotions for several hours now and he hated Robert with a festering passion even on his good days. Assault and battery was bad enough, but she didn't want her fiancé locked up in jail for the rest of his brand new life. Especially not over a waste of skin like Robert.

"Wait!" She protested, clambering to her feet. "You can't kill him."

"Watch me." Jamie kicked Robert hard enough to break multiple ribs and then planted his booted heel on the smaller man's neck. "Next time you strike a woman, you'd better double-check if she belongs to a pirate, asshole. We tend to be a possessive bunch." He gave a meaningful pause. "Oh wait... There won't *be* a next time for you, will there?"

Robert managed a gurgled response, his face turning purple.

Grace's eyebrows compressed in alarm. This wasn't what she wanted. It was sweet and all, but they had seen enough violence and death today. "Jamie, please. You don't have to do this. We'll call the police..."

"Who did so fucking much the last time!" He interrupted at a roar. "They let him out and he came after you *again!* Do you have any idea what it felt like, standing there and doing *nothing*, while he hurt you?" His voice was anguished. "I couldn't help you, Grace!"

"You *did* help me. You saved me, but *this* won't do me any good, at all. They'll just throw you in prison and then I'll be alone." She gazed up at him. "Don't do that to us. I need you."

His gaze cut over to hers, burning with the intense blue of spacious skies, and shining seas, and every other shimmering American dream. This man was every dream Grace had ever had.

"I need you." She repeated quietly. "You're my Partner, Jamie. Stay with me."

The pressure on Robert's throat eased slightly, as Jamie reluctantly allowed him to gasp in some air. He frowned a bit, but did as she asked. "I do not agree with this decision." He intoned, breathing hard.

"I know." She held out a hand to him. "For me. Just let him go *for me*."

He muttered a Gaelic curse and released Robert. He took his foot off his neck and gave him a disgusted nudge with his boot. "Be grateful my woman is a Sunday school teacher." He muttered with an annoyed scowl.

The other man lay on the floor, sucking in lungfuls of oxygen and sending Jamie a look of total loathing.

Jamie didn't so much as glance at him. "For *you*, Grace." He agreed, still not pleased with letting Robert go. "I would do whatever you ask. You know that. Even when it is a *horrible* idea."

"Thank you." She gave him a misty smile. "I love you too much to lose you."

"I love you too much to be lost." He said softly, moving towards her. "There is nothing that will ever take me from your side..."

Robert let out a sudden bellow, apparently getting his second wind at the sound of their romantic declarations. He leapt to his feet, the broken saber that Grace had lost earlier clutched in his hand. "She was mine first!" He shouted manically and lunged at Jamie, trying to spear him with the blade.

Grace didn't think. Jamie was about to be stabbed and she just reacted. Her palm went up...

And the Rivera Doomsday Spell blasted at full force

Power flowed through Grace. More than she'd ever felt, even during Serenity's séances. The overhead light flickered and then exploded in showers of glass. Papers blew in small cyclones of air. Shelves toppled. Mice skittered away, searching for cover. It was like every cell inside of her had been plugged into an electrical outlet and turned up to full blast.

Jamie gaped at the ceiling as sparks rained down. "Jesus, Mary, and Joseph, I knew you had magic in you." He murmured reverently.

Robert let out a terrified scream as the Doomsday spell engulfed him.

...Then he simply vanished.

All evidence of Robert was gone in a matter of seconds. The box of his office supplies, his knocked out teeth, the blood from his broken nose... It was like he'd never been there, at all.

Grace stood there, her body still vibrating even as the magic faded.

Holy crap! A spell had actually worked!

At least, she *assumed* it worked. Since she had no idea what it was *supposed* to do, it was hard to say if it had actually done it *correctly*, but Jamie was safe and that was all that mattered. She looked up at him, her mind reeling. "Are you okay?"

"I'm fine, which is more than I can say for that wanker Robert." Jamie gazed at her in awe. "Where did you send him, love?"

"I have no idea." The Doomsday spell didn't exactly come with operating instructions. It was strictly a "break glass in case of emergency" kinda deal. Grace let out a long breath. "Given my only powers seem to be of the time travel variety, I'm guessing someplace long ago and possibly far, far away." She wrinkled her nose. "Just so he's far, far away from *us*, I don't even care."

"Well, I'd still liked to have killed him, but that was just as satisfying." Jamie beamed. "I *told* you ya had magic in your blood, lass. More than anyone I've ever met or heard of. Why with your talent, there is no telling the spells you could harness if you tried..."

She cut him off. "I'm *not* harnessing any spells, Jamie. I told you, I don't like them. They never work properly."

Jamie arched an amused brow. "Explain that to

Robert. Oh wait, you can't… You disintegrated him." He chuckled in delight.

"I didn't disintegrate him!" At least, she didn't *think* she did. Grace looked around, trying to spot some sign of her ex, but he was well and truly gone. This one was definitely going to be hard to explain to the museum board.

"In any case, we'll discuss all the fun adventures we can have with your powers later." Jamie assured her in a humoring tone. "We've all the time in the world."

"We're not using my powers for any more 'fun adventures,' Jamie. That was my last spell. I mean it."

Jamie disregarded that. "What's important now is you and I are finally together." He started towards her again, crunching through the antique documents scattered all over the floor. "That's what I was telling you before. There is nothing that could keep me from your side, Grace. I belong to you, just as surely as…" He stopped short.

"Something wrong?" She'd been liking that speech.

"What the bloody hell?" His boot had come down on a piece of yellowed parchment. It was one of the countless documents that Grace had scattered around the basement in her search for the shawl and her tornado of power had stirred it up again. "Holy shit!" He bent down to grab it, an amazed expression on his face. "Grace, you actually found it!"

"I found what?" Grace hurried over to see what he was holding. It was a faded drawing of a coastline, with some trees and a big red X painted on the beach. Her eyebrows soared. There was only one thing in the world it could be. "Oh my God! Is that…?"

"It's mine. *Ours*." He beamed at her, looking every bit the pirate he'd always be, no matter what century they were standing in. "You just found my missing treasure map!"

EPILOGUE

I realized that JMR is the only one of my beaus who never assures me that we'll one day marry, or tells me that he loves me passionately, or swears that I'm the only girl for him. Isn't that refreshing? It's no wonder he's my favorite.

Both of us know we're waiting for other people.

Final Entry from the Journal of Miss Lucinda Wentworth

"Jesus, Mary, and Joseph." Jamie leaned on the shovel and blew out a tired breath. "I donea remember it being this much work to bury the damn thing."

"Well, you were nearly two and a half centuries younger. Also you'd been drinking a lot of rum." Grace arched a brow at him. "I just hope you weren't *completely* drunk when you drew the map."

He made a face at her. "I'm never so drunk that I can't draw a map properly. In fact, we're lucky *I* made it and not some amateur like Ned Hunnicutt. We'd probably be recreating the Panama Canal looking for the treasure chest."

"Just keep digging."

"You're a bit of a taskmaster, love." He picked up the shovel and resumed work. "It can be quite a trying trait. ...Outside of the bedroom, anyway."

"You know what else is trying? You not having a social security number or birth certificate to take downtown and get a wedding license." She retorted. "If we want my greedy techno-nerd of a nephew to make them for you, we're going to have to pay him with something other than magic beans. Trust me. Magic beans are not worth *nearly* what you'd think they'd be worth."

"That Justice lad will use magic to make me the

needed documents and then we can wed?" Jamie stipulated, wanting to be sure of the fine print.

He'd been living in the twenty-first century for two weeks now and Grace was still not his wife. All the rules of the modern world seemed designed to vex him. Serenity had promised to host a lavish reception for them and he was ready to get on with it. Grace's aunt had taken quite a shine to him, if Jamie did say so himself. She said that it was a crime against nature that someone who looked like him had been invisible for so long, which he thought was a grand compliment.

"Justice isn't going to use magic to make your phony documents. He's going to use Photoshop, but basically yeah. That's the plan. We're going to pay him several thousand dollars and he's going to make Jamie Riordan a bona fide citizen of America."

"I'm *already* a bona fide citizen. I was here when the country was founded."

"Trust me, it would be better if we didn't have to explain that part to Homeland Security. Let's go with Justice's fake IDs and save ourselves from a trip to Area 51." She wrinkled her nose. "Although, I *do* think he could've offered us more of a discount, considering I singlehandedly changed the family's fortunes with that financial tip to Loyal. You realize that this is the first time *ever* we haven't been broke?"

Jamie couldn't argue with that. Loyal had eventually figured out that a cotton gin had nothing to do with liquor and invested heavily in the machine. The Riveras weren't nearly so reviled now that they were the richest family in Riveraburg.

Personally, he wasn't at all sorry that Harrisonburg had been renamed after Grace's great-great-great-great-great-great-grandfather. Maybe Loyal had used magic and money to achieve his ends, but at least Gregory Maxwell wasn't governor anymore and Ned Hunnicutt had been booted back to England. The next time Jamie saw Loyal, he planned to thank the man.

In truth, all his zany in-laws were growing on him. Jamie had never had a family before and he appreciated the novelty. Besides, he saw how much the Rivera clan loved Grace and how much she loved them in return. He could tolerate foul-tasting potions and misfiring spells forever to make her happy.

...Although, he had to wonder how long they'd hold onto their new-found respectability, as they were already nagging Grace about troll powder, again.

Grace crouched down next to the hole that Jamie had dug. "How deep did you bury this treasure, anyway?"

"I've no idea. As you delight in reminding me, I'd drank quite a bit of rum that evening."

"Maybe someone else came along and found it." She theorized. "It's been a long time."

"Aye, but the spot is isolated. T'was why I picked it in the first place."

Luckily, the stretch of water and shoreline had become a seabird sanctuary seventy years back, so it had never been filled up with hideous condos and boxy vacation homes. No one came to this spot except gulls and pelicans. ...And maybe an ex-ghost, his lovely fiancée, and their professional-grade metal detector, of course.

His gold was still under the ground, waiting for them. Jamie could feel it.

He glanced up at Grace, who looked adorable in her camisole top and breezy white skirt. A straw hat covered her head and she smelled of ocean and sunscreen. He fully planned to have his way with her on the sand before they left. "If my treasure was stolen, I'll just have to hire some bonny detective lass to track it down for me, again. Any idea where I could find one?"

She grinned, optimism shining from her eyes. "I might have a couple of suggestions."

Like magic, crime-solving was in the girl's blood. She'd never be happy with any other job. Working for the police department might be too much for her, now that she'd discovered her gifts, but there was no reason for her to give up her passion, altogether. Jamie had come up with the idea of Grace becoming a freelance investigator. That way she could pick the cases she wanted to pursue and focus on saving one person at a time, instead of the whole world.

Besides, he quite liked the idea of being married to a private detective. It brought to mind those Film Noir movies he'd watched in the 1940s. God, when motion pictures had been invented, he'd spent *decades* inside theaters, watching them flicker by. He'd thought films were the closest he'd ever get to connecting to someone.

He'd been wrong.

Jamie smiled at his Partner. His bride. The reason his heart beat and his soul was full of love. She was why he had a second chance at life and he intended to live every second of it beside her. He wouldn't have changed one magical hair on her fay little head for all the treasure maps in creation.

Except for the fact that the woman was stubbornly fixated on ignoring her own talents.

"Perhaps our first case should be discovering what happened to poor Robert." He suggested, because it just never got old that the bastard was gone and that Grace's incredible magic had been the thing to send him away.

No one had seen a wanker-y trace of the wanker since the basement, but the police had a warrant out against him for striking Grace. Like the law-abiding girl she was, she'd dutifully reported that he'd attacked her in the museum and she had the bruises to prove it …though her version had Robert escaping out a window and not poofing off to who-knew-where. The police had been quite conciliatory towards a member of Riveraburg's first family and promised to track him down soon. They had men watching his house, just in case he showed up.

Jamie had a feeling they'd have better luck searching the outer rings of Saturn.

Grace might not care for spells, but the lass had a true knack for casting them. The magic inside of her glowed brighter each day. Given a bit of time, he was sure he could convince her to fully embrace her power. It was a part of her, after all. Already he could tell she was more interested in the idea that she was ready to admit.

"Wherever Robert is, I hope he stays there." Grace

said staunchly. "And what is this about *our* first case? I don't need a chaperone, Jamie."

"I know that, love!" He splayed a hand across his bare chest as if he was offended she'd say such a thing. "Why I'd never suggest otherwise. I was merely thinking I could be your glamorous, occasionally sarcastic, sidekick. Someone to bounce your brilliant ideas off of."

...And help to keep her out of trouble. The woman needed him, after all.

"Wearing the crazy clothes you do, you'd frighten away everyone who came to the door."

Jamie looked down at his vividly patterned shorts and shrugged. He'd adapted to modern-style clothing quickly enough, but he still liked a bit of color in his wardrobe. "I'm a fashionable fellow, regardless of the century."

"You're a raving lunatic, regardless of the century. In fact, I don't trust you not to rob all our customers, just for the thrill of it."

Well, he *was* a pirate...

Jamie grinned. "Come now, lass." He cajoled. "Riordan and Riordan Investigations has such a lovely ring to it."

"Riordan and *Rivera* Investigations." She corrected.

Jamie pretended to ponder that for a beat and shook his head. "Doesn't trip nearly so easy off the tongue." He didn't care what modern customs allowed, he wanted her to have his last name. The woman was his and everyone should know it.

"If you don't like the company's name, you could always get your *own* job. But I'd better warn you, pirates in this century just bootleg DVDs."

Jamie snorted. They'd see about that. "Riordan and Rivera-*Riordan*." He offered, focusing on one battle at a time. "Triple R Investigations."

"What are we? A dude ranch? There's no way..."

The shovel clanged against metal, cutting her off. Jamie and Grace's eyes met for a beat and then he was hurrying to clear away the sand covering the treasure chest.

She leaned over the side of the hole, trying to get a

better look. "Do you see it? Is it there?"

"I see it! It's here!" Jamie beamed at her. "I told you it would be!" He leaned up to give her a smacking kiss.

"You know we're going to have to give some of this to the government." Grace warned, one hand on her hat so the force of his kiss didn't knock it right off her head.

"Bullshit! I stole most of it before Virginia was even a state."

"And you buried it on public land. They're going to want a cut of everything we find."

That was preposterous. "It wasn't public when I buried it. I think it belonged to the Indians."

"It's '*Native Americans*,' now. And none of that is going to matter to the nice IRS auditors."

"No one else even knows it exists, Grace."

"That's not the point. Honest people report financial windfalls."

Jamie snorted at that idea. "Fuck it. We're pirates and pirates donea share our treasure. Everyone knows that."

"I'm not a pirate, Jamie."

"Of course you are! Pirating is in your blood, lass, same as magic and investigating. No sense in pretending to be normal, at this late date." He winked at her. "Besides, I fought against taxation in the War. I'd be a hypocrite to start paying them now." He pried the lid open with the shovel, laughing with glee at the sight of his gold.

"That is absolutely *not* why the Revolution..."

She trailed off as her eyes took in the mountain of golden coins, emerald necklaces, ruby brooches, silver chalices, diamond pendants, and sapphire rings shining up at her from the box.

Freed from their wooden tomb, the treasure glistened in the summer sun with a magic all its own. It was a large enough haul to see them set up for the rest of their lives. Large enough that even Jamie was impressed and he was the one who'd stolen it all.

Jamie smiled as Grace's lips parted in astonishment at

the fortune he'd just uncovered. "*There's* your engagement ring, love."

"Oh my *God*."

"I thought you'd like it." This treasure had belonged to Grace long before she was even born. He'd always meant for it to provide security for his wife and family. Every cent had been gathered for this very moment.

"It's really ours?" She got out, still gazing down at the pile of gold and jewels.

"Aye. No more need for peaceful green cornfields to feel safe." He climbed out of the hole to cradle her face between his palms. "It's azure blue waters, now. You and me and a pile of money, doing whatever we wish. Now and forever."

She tore her eyes away from the treasure to meet his gaze. "*You* make me feel safe, Jamie. I don't need peaceful green cornfields *or* azure blue waters for that. And I don't need a treasure chest full of gems as an engagement ring. I'd marry you if we had to spend the rest of our lives giving Ghost Walks every night."

Jamie adopted a considering expression. "Those dreadful tours you hosted *would* be a great deal livelier with me lending a hand. I could help you get the stories straight." He kissed the top of her head. "Or at least I'd help you concoct better lies."

She gave him a playful swat. "You really are a scoundrel."

"That I am." He slung an arm around her shoulders. "And so are you, at heart. Now, do you really want to pretend we're some dreary *normal* folks? Hand over our scads of riches to people who had no part in winning them?" He arched a brow. "Or do you want to take our loot, set sail for Jamaica, and spend our days looking for mermaids and solving crimes?"

A huge grin spread across Grace's face. Just as he knew she would, his uptight Sunday school teacher of a bride threw her lot in with the odd-ducks and scoundrels of the world. The lass would never be normal, thank the Good Lord.

"Fuck it." She said happily and his heart filled with joy.

"Let's be pirates!"

AUTHOR'S NOTE

I've been on ghost walks all over the US. New Orleans, San Francisco, Arlington, Cape May... It seems like every city I visit has some "haunted" tour that promises to tell you all kinds of scary tales and I always end up buying a ticket. Few live up to the spine-tingling hype, but I would always recommend visitors give these kinds of tours a try. Even the bad ones usually have something fun about them.

This book was inspired by a particularly unmemorable ghost walk I took in Williamsburg Virginia. My mom and I were there one summer and bought tickets for a nighttime tour. Our guide tried hard, but the tour was not particularly scary and the temperature was about 100 degrees, so no one had much fun. As I stood there, watching fireflies dance like fairies and waiting for it to end, I got the idea for this story.

The fictional town of Harrisonburg is directly based on Williamsburg, which is a fully restored Colonial town. There are indeed shops that show you how paper, wheels, and guns were made, which is actually more interesting than Jamie would have you believe. I found the wig maker's shop especially fascinating. (As a side note, a great many people in the eighteenth century wore wigs. By the 1790s, younger, more fashionable men were going without them, though, and Jamie is thankfully a fashionable guy.) Williamsburg also has houses to tour, lovely museums, a hedge maze behind the governor's mansion, an armory full of muskets on display, and, on July 4th, a spectacular fireworks show. Although this book might suggest otherwise at times, I truly have nothing but positive things to say about the place.

For various reasons, I took creative license with some of the historical details used in this story. I never intended for it to be a textbook. It is not a completely accurate account of the social mores, technological capabilities, and/or vocabulary used by post-Revolutionary Americans. If you're interested in the reality of the 1700s, though, Williamsburg is definitely a place you'll want to visit.

To my knowledge, there have never been any serial killings on Williamsburg's picturesque cobblestone streets. The murders in this book are entirely a work of fiction. America's first documented serial killer was actually H.H. Holmes in 1893 Chicago. He built a hotel that was really a house of horrors and killed his unsuspecting guests in sadistic ways. (I briefly mention Holmes in *Not Another Vampire* book, for those interested. And if you'd like more detailed information about him, I recommend reading *The Devil in the White City: Murder, Magic, and Madness at the Fair that Changed America* by Erik Larson.) Holmes came just a few years after Jack the Ripper terrorized Whitechapel in England. That said, I am of the opinion that there were almost certainly serial killers before the late nineteenth century. Urbanization just made their grisly work simpler, with strangers living in close proximity, and the growing media made it easier to document.

In response to men like Jack the Ripper and H.H. Holmes, the early twentieth century saw police forces become more professionalized. In fact, I would argue that modern forensic investigation owes something to those early sensationalized murders. The public wanted something done to stop madmen and the police responded by developing new techniques for solving crimes. For instance, Jack the Ripper was the first case to have a criminal profile drawn up and, by 1901, England had developed a system for classifying fingerprints. It's sad to think how many old crimes will remain unsolved forever because they did not have the technology we have today. But, on the other hand, it is partly because of those crimes that there was a push to develop more scientific investigations.

In case you're wondering, Luminal can indeed detect very old blood. When sprayed at Lizzie Borden's house, for instance, the floor joists below the murder scene still glow over a hundred years after her parents were killed. Also, it is possible to use an infrared lens to photograph blood spatter that's been painted over. As far as I know, no Revolutionary era crime scenes have ever been Luminaled or UV photographed, but I'm taking an educated guess that it would work.

DNA testing has been performed on blood evidence from historic cases like Jack the Ripper and even the Lincoln assassination, usually with mixed results. DNA degrades over time. In this book, it is likewise assumed that old DNA evidence would be of little investigative value for Grace, but that there would still be traces of blood soaked into things like wood and fabric. Lifting fingerprints with Mothwort would not be possible in real life, though, as the herb is entirely a product of my imagination. For the record, so is troll powder, regardless of what the Riveras might believe.

I took a Crime Scene Investigation course in college. (I took a lot of eclectic courses in college, including classes on tennis, horror films, Baroque art, and the "philosophies of animals." It's part of my nature to be skipping from subject to subject depending on what interests me and how many credits I needed that semester.) I would have to say that the idea of making Grace a crime scene technician comes straight from that class. I think it would be a fascinating job, but also incredibly difficult to come face-to-face with the worst humanity has to offer every day. Like Grace, I'm not sure I could handle it.

On the other hand, I have no background at all with pirating, yet I feel like I'd be awesome at it. In my head, it's all *Pirates of the Caribbean* and Errol Flynn. I did very little research into that profession other than Netflixing DVDs, because --let's be honest-- I doubt Jamie knows a lot about his job, either. He's not Blackbeard. He's just a guy who liked to steal gold and scandalize all the nice girls in town. Both of us are far more interested in the romance of legend than the scurvy-filled reality of Colonial seafaring. If anyone asked him what it was *really* like, he'd just lie about it anyway. Jamie is a guy who enjoys a good tale better than dull "reality." It's one of the things I like best about the scoundrel.

Jamie and Grace's relationship took very little effort to write. They understood each other, right from the beginning. Nearly every scene of this book has the two of them interacting, because they seemed to always want to be together. The plot of this book took far longer to figure out. (Trust me, it isn't easy to draft love scenes where one partner isn't corporeal.) In the end, it came together as I envisioned it, but it took some work to get there. ...Well, *I* had to work at it. Jamie and Grace were honestly more interested in bickering than in figuring out the logistics of time travel. So feel free to blame any sketchy quantum mechanics on them.

If you have any questions about ghost tours, Luminal, or the philosophy of chimpanzees, drop me a line at **starturtlepublishing@gmail.com**. We love to hear from you!

Don't Miss the first book in Cassandra Gannon's
A Kinda Fairytale series:
Wicked Ugly Bad
Available Now!

Once Upon a Time ...

Scarlett Riding is NOT an ugly stepsister. Cinderella is the evil one in the family and Letty is determined to prove it. Unfortunately, that's kinda hard to do from behind bars. After the debacle at the ball, Letty and her sister Dru were dragged off to the Wicked, Ugly and Bad Mental Health Treatment Center and Maximum Security Prison. While Cindy's planning her dream wedding, her two stepsisters are being forced to endure life in the dreariest dungeon in the land.

Luckily, Letty has a plan to change that unhappy ending. If she can just get to Prince Charming and prove the glass slipper doesn't fit Cinderella's foot, she can reclaim her life. In order to do that, though, she needs to convince The Big Bad Wolf to lend a hand in organizing a jailbreak.

Marrok Wolf isn't sure what to make of the idealistic redhead in his group therapy sessions. With fifty counts of Badness on his criminal record, Marrok's used to being surrounded by crooks and scumbags. Scarlett wants to lecture him about equal rights for trolls! When the little do-gooder comes up with an elaborate plan to break their entire "share circle" out of prison, though, Marrok is certainly willing to go along with the plot. And not just because he wants to see her naked. The woman may not be wicked, ugly, or Bad, but she's definitely the only one who can save him.

Together with a wicked witch, a timid bridge ogre, an evil prince, and other villains straight out of a storybook, Scarlett and Marrok are about to make sure that Baddies finally have a happily ever after.

Printed in Great Britain
by Amazon